Barbara Butcher has previously published two poetry collections. She has written prize winning short stories, articles and co-written a play. She has also written and acted in an acclaimed film for a talking heads monologue. In addition to her writing she is an award winning hypnotherapist, stress management consultant and relationship counsellor.

Dear Harry,

Love & best wishes
from

Barbara.

THE OTHER CANAL

Barbara Butcher

Matador
5 Weir Road
Kibworth Beauchamp
Leicester LE8 0LQ, UK
Tel: (+44) 116 279 2299
Email: books@troubador.co.uk
Web: www.troubador.co.uk/matador

ISBN 978 1848767 140

British Library Cataloguing in Publication Data.
A catalogue record for this book is available from the British Library.

Printed and bound in the UK by TJI Digital, Padstow, Cornwall

FSC
MIX
Paper from
responsible sources
FSC® C013056

Typeset in 10pt Palatino by Troubador Publishing Ltd, Leicester, UK

Matador is an imprint of Troubador Publishing Ltd

*In memory of my dear parents who encouraged me
every step of the way.*

Acknowledgments

With thanks to Sonja and Elizabeth for their help and support, to my dear friends who encouraged me to keep going and to Spike for his artistic expertise. Thanks also to those who read the first draft and made all the right noises.

CHAPTER 1

Laura smiled to herself as she settled back on her bunk. Friends had thought she was mad to embark on a trip to Thailand alone and her family had tried to talk her out of it. They probably thought that now she was a pensioner she should slow down a little, but here she was, on the last leg of her journey and feeling wonderful.

She had sat for a long time watching the sun sink behind the broad leafed trees as the train rumbled along the track on its long journey to Bangkok. How strange, she had thought, it isn't really the sun sinking, it's us moving backwards. Or is it forwards? Her sense of direction was never her strong point. Once it was dark, a smiling Thai steward brought her dinner. It was surprisingly good and afterwards she had dunked a teabag from her holdall into the cup of hot water she had ordered and drank whilst she tried to read. The fluorescent light made everything look cold and a little sinister. She made sure the door was locked and soon took off her sundress and relaxed under the thin sheet on the bottom bunk bed. This was the last leg of her holiday and she had loved every minute of it. She was glad she had plucked up the courage to come to Thailand on her own. She knew that many pensioners did far more adventurous things than this, but on the other hand many of her contemporaries had looked at her as if she were crazy and, as no-one had been willing to come with her, she had decided to go it alone.

It was too early to sleep, so she propped herself up on the pillow and began to read again. Out of the corner of her eye she thought she saw a movement on the far wall. She felt the hair on the back of her neck and on her arms stand up. She shut the book and held it tightly in her hand, subconsciously ready to attack. After a couple of seconds she saw a cockroach emerge from the bottom of the bed and scurry up the wall to the top bunk. She scrambled out of bed and picked up one of her flip-flops from the floor and when another followed the first, she swatted it against the wall. It splattered and stuck to the flip-flop. Laura got out the insect repellent spray from her holdall and sprayed the bottom of the bunk. Back in bed, she sat with her knees drawn up under her chin, warily watching the end of the bed. She wondered if the train had been fumigated in Chiang Mai. There had been no problem on the outward journey, so she had been lulled into a false sense of security. Well, there was nothing to be done about it. She had never heard of someone dying from cockroach bites and she decided she was not about to die of fright. Since her divorce she had gradually become more adventurous and had enjoyed a couple of holidays on her own in Europe. She had survived finding a scorpion in the bathroom in Tuscany and been amazed at the rows of severed heads in a Monolithic Church in France. A couple of cockroaches were not going to spoil things now.

She still felt a little uneasy and realised that her hands were shaking as she picked up her book. She found that she could not concentrate and so decided to write in her journal. That would hopefully distract her and she could bring it up to date. She had kept the journal for many years, in fact before she had left Trevor. She found it comforting sometimes to re-read her entries from those far off days and to be reminded of just how unhappy she had been, as this reinforced the reason why she had left. She had married at nineteen and Trevor had been in his mid twenties. Her mother had approved, saying that the Civil Service was a nice steady job and that he would go far. She had not noticed at first just how controlling he was. He had even cancelled her driving lessons, saying the roads were too dangerous. Later she realised it was his way of keeping her at home. She had left school at sixteen and met Trevor a few months later, so had not had any opportunity to learn and grow, but as the years went by and the children were born, she had begun to realise her potential. Whilst Trevor spent the evenings in his research books, she became interested in art, music and philosophy and generally found life fascinating. She loved being a mother and was always the one who took the children to museums, fishing, camping and concerts as Trevor was too busy. As she matured and found her own voice the marriage became increasingly volatile, but she decided to stay until the children had finished their education. At least she had spared the children all the details of the death throes of their marriage and she had tried to keep things calm after the divorce. After all, Trevor was their father. Sometimes as she re-read her journal from those days she felt like a different person. As she took up her pen she found herself humming, "I will survive, I will survive."

'After the hustle and bustle of Bangkok, Chiang Mai seemed a world away – particularly up in the hills. I went by bicycle rickshaw, called a saam lor, to the foot of the hills and then in a jeep up to the hill tribes. The women sit outside their huts doing the most amazing embroidery. Their clothes are so colourful. I had hoped to see the long necked women but had to be contented with photos of them in the Hill Tribe Museum. The women I saw were carrying large bunches of twigs and green leaves on their backs. I don't know if it is cannabis as I don't really know what that looks like! My guidebook in England suggested taking little toys for the village children and they loved them. They also liked English coins. They are adorable.

I chose the Suriwongse Hotel because I knew it was near the Night Bazaar and that meant I would not have to negotiate streets at night on my own. As it was I kept my money under my shirt and didn't go into any bars. There was so much to see, so many interesting things to buy. I did get some real silk shawls, although if it really is silk is anyone's guess! I have decided to wait until I get back to Bangkok to get the rest of my presents.

The Thais really are the most charming, smiling people. I did remember being told that they never lose their temper, but if you really annoy them they will have you shot! I am very wary about the possibility of someone dumping drugs in my bag.

I am writing this curled up in a ball on my bunk on the train back to Bangkok, being attacked by cockroaches. Ah well, if that's the worst that can happen "I will survive, I will survive..." I am now looking forward to getting back to the hotel in Bangkok and having a bath and a glass of chilled wine. Lovely. I wonder if I will have time to look at the Grand Palace again. It is so spectacular. I also want to see the floating market before I leave on Thursday. Goodnight Little Book. I will try to s l e e p.'

Laura put the book and the pen back in her holdall and carefully scraped the cockroach body off her flip-flop, shuddering with revulsion as she did so. There seemed to be no more coming so she thought it would be a good time to venture out to the toilet which was situated a short way along the corridor. Not a very savoury place, but needs must. She put on her flip-flops and stuffing her bum bag into her handbag took it with her and unlocked the door. The corridor was deserted, just the thin fluorescent light and the rumble of the train. The toilet door was slightly open and she went in and closed it behind her. The floor was wet so she hung her bag on a hook behind the door and suspended herself above the toilet, being careful not to sit on it. As she stood up again she noticed a bundle lying under the sink, something wrapped in a towel. She rinsed her hands and then bent to take a closer look. As she looked she could have sworn it moved. For the second time that night the hairs on the back of her neck prickled and her heart started to pound. The bundle moved again and she heard a faint mewing, like the sound of a kitten. Very carefully she pulled back the edge of the towel to reveal a tiny baby. Its face was puckered and crowned by a mop of black silky hair. Its eyes were closed and she wasn't sure if it was asleep, but it was certainly alive. Instinctively she picked it up and held it against her chest. The towel at least was dry. Her first thought was to get it out of the lavatory, away from the smell of latrines. She opened the door and went out into the silent corridor, looking up and down in either direction. There was some sort of safety or connecting door a short way along the corridor and she made for that, hoping to find a guard or a steward. Holding the baby in one arm she tried the door, but it was either stiff or locked. She called out, "Is there anyone there?", her voice sounding slightly hysterical. Silence.

Feeling very shaken Laura went back into her cabin, locked the door and sat on the bed, rocking the baby and wondering what on earth to do. Her hands were shaking as she rolled the towel back a little further and looked carefully at the baby. It had a small amount of white liquid around its mouth and she wondered if it had recently been fed. She reached for her handbag to get a tissue and her heart lurched with the first hint of the true fear that was to come. She had left her bag in the toilet. She carefully laid the baby on the bottom bunk, securing it with the pillow and her holdall so that it would not roll off and ran back to the toilet. The bag was gone. She stood for a moment, frozen to the spot. She looked along the corridor; all was silent, but now it felt menacing. In perhaps less than five minutes someone had taken her bag. There had been no sound, no doors opening or closing. She went back into the toilet and looked again with the disbelief of one who doubts what they see. The bag was definitely gone. And with it her passport, money, credit cards, telephone numbers and mobile phone.

Laura walked back to her cabin in a daze. The baby was sleeping. Her mouth was dry so she reached into her holdall for the water bottle, but by now she was shaking so uncontrollably that she had difficulty in opening it. Hot tears sprang to her eyes, but the main emotion she realised was fear – a terrible, paralysing fear. "Think," she told herself. "Think." She would sit it out until morning and then leave the train at Bangkok and get to her hotel, get some food for the baby, explain what had happened and get hold of the British Consulate, or Embassy, or whatever it was called. No good trying to explain to the train guard. She felt inexplicably protective about this small scrap of humanity on her bed and was not about to hand it over to a train guard. It? When the baby awoke she must find out at least if it was a boy or a girl. Supposing its nappy needed changing? Was it wearing a nappy? The best thing was to try to get some rest, stop panicking and wait until dawn when the train would finally arrive in Bangkok. She checked the door again, then propped her holdall against it. She was still terrified but settled down beside the baby and tried to relax, taking deep breaths and counting slowly from one to ten in an attempt to slow down the beating of her heart. At least she had her train ticket. She had checked it when she got into bed and had put it on the little bedside locker. She carefully put it into the pocket of her holdall.

Laura must have dozed because she woke up having dreamed about kittens. For a couple of seconds she wondered where the kittens were until she remembered the baby, which was now crying beside her. It was daylight and she guessed it would not be long before they arrived in Bangkok. She unwrapped the baby gently from the towel and found it was dressed in a cotton romper suit. She could tell by the smell that it needed changing. There was no way she was going back to the toilet, so she took a pack of tissues from her holdall, undid the romper suit and removed a rather dirty nappy. She wiped the baby as best she could and then put a rolled up pair of her own pants inside the romper suit. Luckily she had some antiseptic wipes in her holdall. The baby was a girl. A noisy, angry, beautiful little girl. The train was slowing down, so Laura hastily rewrapped the baby in the towel and, with her holdall over her shoulder and the baby in her arms, warily made her way out of her cabin. The baby stopped crying, trying to nuzzle against Laura's breast.

Once again, the corridor was deserted, although as the train stopped she could hear doors slamming further along. She pushed open the door and descended onto the platform, looking up and down, trying to take in details of the other passengers. The platform was suddenly crowded. Thai business men in suits, monks, elderly Thai women, tourists, back packers. Everyone looked as if they were on a mission and knew exactly where they were going. She couldn't see anyone who looked remotely as if they would have dumped a baby on the train. Laura trailed along behind, carefully adjusting her holdall and the baby, who was now screaming loudly, against her chest.

She handed in her ticket and then made her way out into the busy street. Taxis and tuk-tuks jostled for attention. The noise after the relative quiet of the train was overwhelming. She felt utterly bewildered and even at this early hour she was already soaking wet from the heat and humidity. She had never realised before the security and comfort of money, credit cards and her passport. She was totally exhausted and the screams of the baby made her head spin until she thought she would faint. She had no idea how far it was to the hotel. Hotel? Laura could not even remember the name of the hotel. Her head hurt and the screaming baby was making her fraught. She would walk. That's what she decided – to walk until she came to a hotel and would go in and tell them what had happened. She would ask for some milk for the baby, try to describe her hotel and hopefully someone would understand and at least let her use the telephone and help her find the number of the Embassy. She began to walk, the holdall dragging on her shoulder and the baby wriggling in her arms. She looked down at her and could see she was red and very distressed, her little face puckered and her gums pink and angry. The noise coming from that small mouth was unbelievable.

Laura was now sweating profusely. The heat, coupled with her fatigue and anxiety, were making her legs feel as if they would give way. She could feel her dress sticking to her wet body, which was beginning to flag from the weight of the holdall and the baby. After what seemed miles she saw a hotel which seemed familiar. On some level she knew that all the hotels looked the same, just like the Thai people, but she was desperate for it to be her hotel, although in her heart she knew it could not be as she had taken a cab to the station when she had set out, and it had seemed a long way. Yes, revolving glass doors, marble foyer, fountain, flowers. She walked up to the Reception desk and waited whilst the receptionist dealt with a Thai business man. She wished there were some Europeans there so that she could explain properly. She was beginning to feel fainter and the screams of the baby were now interspersed with bouts of holding her breath, her lips becoming blue.

At last it was Laura's turn.

"Please, will you help me. I need to find my hotel. The baby needs some milk. My name is Laura Jones. Someone has stolen my bag and in it was my passport and money. I have found this baby and she is starving. Could you find someone to help me please?"

Her voice had risen to a wail, louder than the cries of the baby. Her hair was stuck to her head with sweat and the holdall had pulled her dress off one shoulder. The receptionist smiled serenely and said she would call for the manager. She made a telephone call and almost before she had finished speaking the manager arrived and took charge of the situation. He took Laura into a side office and smiled at her benevolently. They sat on large sofas and she could feel her hot, damp legs sticking to the leather. Laura burst into tears. Long sobs of fear, distress and pent up emotions shook her body. The manager offered her some water. Taking deep breaths she explained again, asking for some milk for the baby. He stood up, smiled and bowed and said he would be back in a moment. The baby was screaming loudly and Laura jiggled her up and down to try to placate her. After an interminable time the door opened and the manager reappeared with a maid and a policeman. The policeman smiled and, raising his voice so that he could be heard over the noise, told Laura to hand the baby to the maid. Laura suddenly felt very protective of the little girl. She turned to the maid and asked her to bring some milk. The maid did not understand, so the policeman translated in that strange sing-song voice she would come to distrust and then told Laura again to hand over the child.

"Madam," he said. "You are not registered at this hotel and it would be better for us all if our staff looked after this baby so that we can listen to what is going on here."

He smiled again and Laura handed over the baby just before she fainted.

When she recovered there was a tray of tea and biscuits on the little table in front of her. The baby and the maid had gone, but the policeman and the manager were standing near her. The manager handed her a damp cloth with which she wiped her face and then she drank the tea before carefully explaining what had happened. She still felt dizzy and spoke very slowly and clearly, as if she were explaining things to a child. When she had finished she asked if they would kindly ring round the other large hotels to find out which had the booking for Laura Jones.

"I think it must be the shock. I just can't remember the name of my hotel. The rest of my luggage is there. I need to make some telephone calls and also change my clothes. Where is the baby?"

The policeman waited until she had finished her tea and then stood up.

"Please, come with me."

"I need the toilet." The policeman escorted her to the ladies' room and waited for her outside. At least the toilet was clean and after she had relieved herself she washed her hands and face. The woman looking back at her from the mirror was unrecognisable. Her hair was stuck to her head and she was as white as a sheet with black circles under her eyes. She gripped the edge of the sink for support feeling sick and faint again.

The policeman led her out of the hotel and into a waiting police car. He sat in the front next to the driver, but there was no sign of the maid or the baby. Laura felt her anxiety levels rising.

"Where's my baby?" As soon as the words were out of her mouth she felt uneasy.

"I mean, where's the baby?" She thought that if the policeman turned and smiled at her again she would wipe the smile off his face.

"Don't worry, Madam, we will sort this out."

Laura tried to smile back. "Kop koon kah," she said. They crawled through the madness of Bangkok traffic until they reached a police station where she was taken into a rather sparse waiting area. The policeman carried her holdall. There was, she noticed, a guard at the door.

By now Laura's head was thumping and she realised she was starving hungry. Apart from a cup of tea and a biscuit, she had had nothing since the previous evening and now it was midday. She waited for what seemed hours and finally a different policeman came in and ushered her into an office. It smelled of stale smoke and she noticed that the ashtray was full of cigarette butts. Her throat was burning and she desperately wanted some water, but was too afraid to ask. She sat facing him whilst he shuffled papers at his desk. He then looked at her and asked if she had anything to say about the charges. Laura was stunned.

"What charges do you mean?"

"The charge is that you bought a baby on the train from Chiang Mai to Bangkok believing that you could keep the child without having to go through any adoption formalities. Of course it could be that you intended to sell the child on for other purposes."

Laura was totally shocked. "But if that was so, why would I inform the hotel about what had happened? And what other purposes do you mean?" Her voice came out as a hoarse whisper.

The policeman smiled. "You have no money, no identification, no passport and yet we are supposed to believe you. Where are your credentials?"

Laura felt as if she were in a film. "I need a lawyer. Please contact the High Commission or British Embassy or whatever it is called. I am a British Citizen and I have done nothing wrong."

Laura was aware that her voice was now becoming louder and faster but she could not stop. The policeman thrust a document across to her.

"Please sign."

She looked at it, but it was all in Thai, so she refused.

"It is not in your interests to refuse. This is just a copy of what you told the policeman who arrested you."

"Arrested me?" Laura was nearly hysterical. "I did not know I was arrested. Please get me some representation. And I will not sign anything I do not understand. I want to phone my son in England. And please can I have some food."

The policeman handed Laura a pen. "Sign please. We can then take you to your room and get you some food."

He leaned back in his chair and waited. Laura picked up the pen and signed her name, writing below: "Under duress."

The policeman took a cursory glance at the document and then, taking it with him, abruptly left the room. Laura was left alone and realised he had taken her holdall with him. She could smell her own body odour and needed the toilet again, but did not dare try to leave the room. After about twenty minutes the guard returned and she was led through a door at the back into a narrow corridor lit with flickering fluorescent lights and with what looked like cages on either side. They turned a corner and came to an area with a cell on each side. They reminded Laura of the cages animals are kept in at a zoo with bars from floor to ceiling. She was pushed inside one of the cages and the door locked behind her. She could hear the clang of the lock on the outer door and the guard's footsteps retreating down the corridor. Panic took over as she screamed after him. "Come back. There's been a mistake. Don't leave me here. Help!" She sank to her knees, looked around and saw a wooden partition at the end of the room. The smell was enough to tell her it was some sort of toilet, and having seen the state of the holes in the floor in Chiang Mai her stomach heaved. She stood up and went to investigate. Sure enough there was an evil smelling hole in the floor and some wet newspaper by the side. She had no choice but to relieve herself, retching as she did so. There was a bucket of foul water by the hole. A rusted tap on the wall did not work, the end of the pipe disappearing into a mouldy hole in the floor. There were no chairs or bed in the room, so she crouched back down on the floor and wept.

Around three in the afternoon a bowl of grey rice was thrust through the bars together with some cold smelly water. She was so hungry that she scooped up some of the rice and water and with a mouth full began to shout through the bars. No-one came. At 6.00 p.m. a guard arrived at the cell.

"Someone will come to see you in the morning." He unlocked the door and threw in her holdall and a filthy mattress. Her holdall had been searched and her toilet items and hairbrush removed. Her underwear and some clothes were still there so she changed and using the holdall as a pillow laid down on the smelly mattress and fell into a fitful sleep. She awoke to the sound of screaming, doors banging and rattling of bars. Someone was being thrown into the opposite cell. She tried to get back to sleep but thought she could hear a scrabbling sound at the toilet end of the cell. She went to investigate and in the flickering fluorescent light saw a large rat sniffing round the hole in the floor. At her approach, it scuttled across the area and down the hole round the end of the water pipe. Horrified, she sat back down on the mattress, and, pulling her dress up over her nose and mouth, watched a cockroach run across the cell. At dawn, she was handed a cup of watered down tea by a surly guard who spoke no English. There was a man crouched on the floor in the opposite cell but Laura had neither the energy nor the will to call out to him. He probably didn't speak English anyway.

At 11.00 a.m., three people arrived outside her cell and she was almost hysterical with relief to see two of them were Westerners – one male and one female. They were carrying some sort of equipment in black bags, but Laura was so relieved to see them that she did not take much notice. The third person was a Thai guard.

"Laura Jones?"

"Yes, thank God you are here. Are you from the British Embassy?

11

What is going on? Can you get me out of here? Can I speak to my son? This is all a misunderstanding." Her voice was getting higher although she tried to keep the panic down. "Please, get me a lawyer and please get hold of my son Nigel. Let me give you his number."

The man introduced himself as Alan. "This is my assistant, Tessa. We will use all our powers to get you publicity to help get you out of here." They were from the British press and Laura felt a surge of hope – they knew about this at home and soon she would be released.

"Did the Embassy send you? Have the Thai authorities alerted them?"

"We'll make sure the British authorities and your son are informed as soon as we leave."

Alan handed her some chocolate and then began to ask her about her life. What was she doing in Thailand on her own anyway? He understood she was divorced and lived alone. He seemed well informed, knew she had two children but wanted to know whether she felt lonely and whether she missed having grandchildren. Laura was so grateful for someone to talk to, a friend who would get her out of this hell, someone who would listen.

"A few photos would help your case. Is that OK?"

By the time Laura said again that she needed a lawyer, they were busy taking photos of her through the bars. They promised to contact Nigel and ask him to get a solicitor for her. Tessa looked at her pityingly.

"Don't worry – we'll do all we can." Then they left.

Hope. That was what they had left her with. Nigel would sort it out. She just had to be patient.

CHAPTER 2

Nigel Jones had had a hard day at the office. He'd had a grilling from his boss about the way he had handled a video conference, he had 42 emails to deal with and the telephone had not stopped ringing. His PA was off sick with stress and he had to attend a meeting with his boss, Frank, and the accountant at the end of the day which he knew would last for hours and achieve nothing. He finally got away at 8.00 p.m. only to find that the next train had been cancelled and there was an hour to wait. He slammed his briefcase onto a seat and phoned Felicity from his mobile to explain. She was not amused.

"Honestly, Nigel, this is the third time this week I have put your dinner in the bin. By the time you get home we will have no evening – again."

"Sorry, Fliss, but there's nothing I can do about it. See you asap"

Another frosty reception he thought and, picking up a copy of Metro from the platform floor, tried to distract himself during the wait for the train.

Nigel would have loved to change his job, but the kudos of landing this one had gone to his head and on the strength of it they had bought a large Victorian house in Clapham. Fliss taught at Roehampton College and their joint incomes just about covered the huge mortgage. To leave now would be crazy. Once he had hit forty, Nigel began to realise that he was pretty much stuck. He was on the books of several agencies but as he had never quite made it to the top, no-one ever head-hunted him. Fliss was thirty-eight now and had become increasingly broody, but Nigel insisted that they could not afford a family yet.

"My bloody clock is running out! When the hell do you think will be the right time?"

It was one of the few areas they argued about and just recently Fliss had become more moody about it.

Deep down Nigel knew she was right, but he was also not sure he wanted their lives turned upside down by a screaming child, especially if Fliss enjoyed being a Mum so much that she did not want to return to work. He did not want that sort of responsibility. He certainly did not want to downsize and he was not happy with the idea of a situation where they had a child, Fliss went back to work and they had a nanny. He knew that everyone thought he was so successful and that his mother was particularly proud of him. "My son works in the City," she would say. She knew he was not actually in the City as such, but it sounded more important than saying London. Nigel was not so sure about his father. Since his parents divorced he didn't see much of him. Come to that, he had never really known what his father thought about anything anyway. If his father had ever said he was proud of him, no-one would have been more shocked than Nigel.

He finally arrived home at 9.15 p.m. to an icy reception from Fliss.

"Make yourself an omelette. I'm going to have a bath and an early night with a book."

Nigel's stomach was rumbling with hunger, but he felt too exhausted to cook. He made himself a cheese sandwich which he washed down with copious amounts of red wine, finishing with a small brandy and then watched TV until midnight, by which time he felt faintly queasy. Fliss was either asleep, or pretending to be when he finally fell into bed, unwashed and smelling of booze. He was dreaming about climbing some rocks and being cut off by the tide when the telephone interrupted his panic. His heart was still thumping as he reached for the light and then the phone.

"Yes, this is Nigel Jones. Who? Who did you say? Where? Thailand?"

He was immediately wide awake. He knew his mother was in Thailand and he felt a sudden sense of doom.

"Mrs Laura Jones? Yes, I am her son. What has happened? Is she alright? What? Please say that again. That's ridiculous. Certainly. I

14

will do that first thing in the morning. Please give me a contact telephone number – just wait while I get a pen."

He took down the number, carefully writing it on the sleeve of Fliss's book and then put the phone down. His head was spinning with shock and brandy. Fliss was sitting up, blinking in the lamplight, her dark hair sticking up as if she too had had a fright.

"For God's sake Nigel, what's going on? It's 5 in the morning. Surely it's not your bloody office."

Nigel had his elbows on his knees, his head in his hands. He looked at her as if just realising she was there.

"It's my mother. She's been arrested in Bangkok. We need to phone the High Commission in the morning and we have to get legal advice."

"On what charge, for God's sake Nigel. She's not into drugs or anything – has someone put something in her bag? You read about it all the time."

"No, you don't read about it all the time!" Nigel shouted. Then, calming down, he said very slowly and quietly, "She's been arrested for buying a baby."

There was a stunned silence, neither of them able to grasp the situation. Fliss was the first to speak.

"It must be a spoof," she said. "Someone is playing a joke on you."

"I wish," he said "but it certainly sounded authentic. We can't do anything until the morning. I think I need a coffee to clear my head."

Fliss was out of bed immediately, wrapping her housecoat round her and taking charge. She was always good in an emergency and the previous tensions between them were forgotten. Nigel put on his slippers and dressing gown and they went down into the kitchen. She put the kettle on and Nigel got the telephone directory out of the cupboard and banged it down on the counter. He perched on one of the stools and looked up the dialling code for Thailand.

"It's an authentic code they gave me." He knew he was clutching at straws, vaguely hoping it was a hoax call. "What the hell is going on? Stealing a baby, for God's sake. How on earth did she get herself into such a situation?"

Fliss poured the coffee.

"Well, they'll soon find out it's all a mistake. What would an elderly woman be doing stealing a baby? It would be impossible to get it out of the country for a start! Why would any European do it?"

Nigel sipped the steaming coffee.

"Money," he said at last.

Fliss stared at him uncomprehendingly.

"But they said she had bought the baby, so presumably they think she paid. How would they think she could make money?"

Nigel put his head in his hands. "They could think of lots of ways. Selling on for child abuse – after all this is Thailand we're talking about. Or perhaps body parts."

Fliss shuddered. "Stop it Nigel. It's Laura we are talking about! The only way she would ever buy a baby would be to rescue it from such a fate. You know what she's like – wouldn't harm a fly. And even then she would try to alert the authorities. There's no way she would part with her money for such a transaction. She hates anything dodgy."

"Yes. We know that," Nigel replied, "but Thailand is a different world. We know she would never do anything like that, but we're talking about a totally different culture."

He looked at his watch. It was 5.30 a.m. It must be mid-day in Thailand. "You get an hour's sleep if you can. I'm going to look up phone numbers of the High Commission and solicitors so I can get cracking at 9.30."

Fliss gave Nigel a hug. "If you're sure."

In spite of the coffee, she dropped off to sleep for an hour until the alarm woke her at 6.30 as usual. But there was to be nothing usual about this day. Grabbing her housecoat she ran down the stairs. The kitchen was empty, the kettle hot and a coffee pot was on the stove. She poured herself a coffee and went across to Nigel's study. He was sitting at the computer, jotting down telephone numbers in a small notebook. He looked up at her and attempted a wan smile.

"I've got the number of the British High Commission and also the name of a barrister who seems to deal with this sort of thing. No

16

good going to our old solicitor from Rivers and Rivers. We really have to have some sort of armoury in case we are going to need it, although I suspect it is all a misunderstanding. But we do we need a tip top lawyer. I'll get straight on the phone at 9.30. Hopefully the High Commission will be up and running by then."

Fliss put down her cup. "What about Ellie? She will have to be told of course."

Nigel thought for a moment. "I rather thought I ought to wait until we have some news."

"But that may take all morning. Don't forget the time difference. If I had a brother and he didn't call me about something as serious as this I would be very upset."

"You're right," Nigel replied. "I'll call her around 8.00, before she sets off for work. Talking of which, I'll leave a message on Frank's answer phone to tell him I won't be in today. I really don't want to talk to him and have to explain. I'll do that now. What about you? Can you get the day off? You must be exhausted."

"No can do. We have exams coming up and I can't possibly not be there. I'll manage. Thanks anyway. Could you make me a couple of slices of toast while I have a shower?"

After Fliss had left for work, Nigel had a shower, some toast and more coffee and then telephoned his sister. He was rather afraid she would have the answerphone on, but she answered almost immediately.

"Hi Ellie, it's Nigel."

"What's up? You never phone at this time of the morning. Problem?"

"Mum's got herself into a spot of bother in Thailand. I had a call in the early hours. No, she's not had an accident or anything like that, but I thought you should know that, um, well…" He hesitated.

"WHAT? For God's sake Nigel, what is it?"

"She's apparently been arrested and is in custody in Bangkok. Now try not to worry. I'm contacting the High Commission later on this morning and I am sure they will sort it out. It must be some sort of misunderstanding."

Ellie's voice was trembling now.

"What charges? Is it drugs – for God's sake tell me it's not drugs.

17

I read about a woman who had drugs planted on her and she was banged up over there for years."

"No, Ellie, it's not drugs." He hesitated again. "She's been accused of buying a baby."

There was a long silence.

"Nigel, please say that again?"

"A baby, Ellie. She was in possession of a baby and they say she bought it. That's all I know. I just have a contact number and I am sure it will all be sorted out this morning."

He could hear the hysteria in her voice, could imagine her hand shaking as she held the phone.

"Nigel, I'll drive straight over to you. I'm almost ready to go out of the door, so I'll phone the office and leave now."

"Don't do that, Ellie. You'll only get caught in the rush hour and it's a difficult journey at this time of day. I'll call you just as soon as I have news. I don't think you should be on your own. Can you get a friend to sit with you? Take your mind off it a bit?"

"Take my mind off it? Are you JOKING? It's our mother you are talking about. I just don't believe any of this! Yes, OK. I'll phone Steph. I'm sure she'll come round. Please, phone me THE MINUTE you have any news of any sort from anyone. Do you promise?"

By 9.00 Nigel had managed to eat another piece of toast and had more coffee. He showered and shaved. The face looking back at him from the mirror looked old and drawn. He was sure the few grey hairs that peppered his temples had multiplied overnight. He ran his fingers through his dark curly hair and then put on a suit, shirt and tie. He usually dressed more casually and was not sure why he decided on formal clothes, but it made him feel more efficient. Perhaps subconsciously he would be mentally more prepared to explain things at the High Commissioner's Office. After watching the second hand on his watch for a while he forced himself to look at the television until 9.30, and then picked up the telephone.

By 10.15 Nigel's jacket was slung on the back of his chair and his tie loosened. He had tried calling the Thai number he had been given in the early hours, but could not make himself understood. He was perspiring profusely and was sure his blood pressure was through the roof. He then went through his list of numbers. No, he could not see the High Commissioner, no he could not have an appointment for that day and yes, it would be a good idea to get legal representation. He made his fifth cup of coffee and in desperation rang his solicitor. He was less than polite to the receptionist who said Mr Rivers was in court all day.

"No need to shout, Mr. Jones. I really can't do anything about it, but you could come in and see Miss Beresford at 3.00 p.m."

"This is an emergency. I need to see someone this morning." Before she could reply he had hung up. He then tried the barrister's number he had found on the internet and was told that the barrister was in court all day but they could give him an appointment for the following week. "I'll call you back," Nigel said through gritted teeth.

He was just about to call work when Ellie phoned.

"No, no news Ellie. I can't get hold of a solicitor so am going to phone work to see if the company's solicitor can see me this morning. Have you got someone with you? Good. Now for Pete's sake stop crying, I can't hear a word you are saying. Look, I'll phone you back as soon as I know something. Just sit tight and have a cup of tea."

He replaced the receiver and, in spite of his assurance to Ellie, felt he was out of control of a situation he didn't understand. Since Ellie had returned from working abroad, she had become increasingly neurotic and would be of absolutely no help.

He finally decided to go into the office. At least he would be in town and he could go straight to the solicitor if it could be arranged. He could also just turn up at the High Commission. He splashed cold water on his face, did up his tie, grabbed his jacket and briefcase and headed for the station. On the train he texted Fliss to update her, left a message telling her not to worry and that everything was under control.

Frank, after an initial jaw drop, was straight on the phone to the company solicitor and miraculously an appointment was arranged for midday. Dobson and Jenkins's Chambers were rather more luxurious than Rivers and Rivers. Nigel arrived just before midday and sank down into a black leather sofa. He began to feel light headed, probably all the coffee. He stood up and wandered to the window, looking out over the busy street and feeling as if he were in a film.

Sebastian Dobson was immaculately dressed, tall and with grey neatly cut hair. Nigel was ushered into the office and he began the tale, starting from the dawn telephone call. Dobson listened with the fingers of both hands under his chin, like a pyramid. Every now and then he would jot something down with a silver fountain pen. Nigel felt as if he were functioning on two levels – the Nigel who should be in the office, and the Nigel who had been dropped into a nightmare. He gave Dobson the number he had been given from Thailand and, finally exhausted, stopped talking.

After a brief silence, Dobson said "Well, Nigel, we need to contact the High Commission again and then we need to get you out to Thailand as soon as possible and I believe it would be advantageous if one of our team went with you. We really do not want to rely on Thai representation. It will cost you, of course, but I am sure you realise that we are dealing with a different system out there. It is not uncommon for people to be held without trial for a very long time."

"I'm sure I can raise the money. Perhaps we will get compensation once it is all sorted out?"

Dobson did not need to speak – his expression said it all and Nigel's heart sank.

"How soon can we go?"

"I'll make a few calls and get back to you this afternoon. Will you be in the office?"

Nigel gave him his mobile number and took a taxi to the office, where he left another message for Fliss and tried to phone Ellie, whose phone was engaged. Frank took him out for a sandwich and a pint and told him to go home. He left Ellie a message saying he was on his way to pick up his car and would then drive across to see her. He was at Ellie's by 4.00 and phoned home to leave a message for Fliss.

Ellie was calmer but very pale. Apparently Steph had stayed for a while and made sure she had some lunch before making her promise to let her know when she had some news. Nigel told her what had happened so far.

20

"How much will it cost? Where on earth will we find the money? Can I come?"

"No, you hold the fort here and we'll stay in touch by phone. Now, what about Dad? He's rolling in it now he has his big pension. We've never asked him to help before, but this is an emergency."

Ellie spluttered into her tea, splashing it everywhere. "Ha ha," she said. "The reason why we never tell him anything is that he is only interested in his new life and his wretched writing. Last time I tried to talk to him he told me he could not be interrupted as he was writing his memoirs. We know that if we ask him for help he will say, "Well, quite honestly my investments are tied up and I have a new kitchen to pay for."

"I know, but this is a bit different and after all Mum is his ex wife and the mother of his kids, even if they are divorced. She's had a much harder deal than he has."

By now Ellie was puce with rage. "Shut up, Nigel. You don't know the half of it. Mum never told you the whole story. Since the divorce, she has scrimped and saved to pay for this break and when she gets back will still have to work. It's a blessing she took that counselling course, but getting clients is not easy at her age. Why should she have to worry about marketing herself because she lost out through raising us? If she hadn't done that, he wouldn't have his big fat pension. And all their married life she used to do part time work."

"Steady on, old girl. You'll have to fill me in when all this is over, but in the meantime I think you should give him a bell. Harder to refuse a girl…."

A slug of brandy later, and Ellie dialled her father's number.

"Ellie. What a surprise. To what do I owe this pleasure?"

Ellie took a deep breath. "Dad, Mum took a short break to Thailand and seems to have got herself into a spot of bother."

"Really?" The tone already said, "What has it got to do with me?"

"Yes, she's been arrested…"

Before she could finish her father interrupted. "Well, trust her to get into trouble. I suppose someone put dope in her case?"

His lack of concern should not have surprised Ellie, but it did. She soldiered on. "It is pretty serious and obviously a case of mistaken identity. She has been accused of buying a baby and Nigel has to go out with a solicitor to see what can be done. He needs to go as soon as possible and obviously funds are short. We were wondering if...."

"Quite honestly Ellie, I really cannot get involved. My investments are all tied up and I'm just having a new bathroom. Besides which, of course, your mother is no longer any concern of mine."

"Thanks," Ellie said through gritted teeth and hung up with that 'I told you so' look on her face. "Nigel. I'm good at PR. Let's get some publicity and get Mum out. This is something I can do!"

"Ellie. That is the last thing we need, believe me. Just be patient and promise me you won't do anything hasty. I know what you are like when you are emotional like this. You don't think straight! Promise me you will leave it to me for the time being."

Ellie looked at him blandly. "OK," she said, a little too readily.

Just as he was about to make her swear to keep out of it, his mobile rang. It was Dobson. "We've got you on a flight in the morning at 7.55 a.m. from Heathrow. Our Jeff Clarkson will accompany you. He's had some explaining to do to his wife, but as it's so urgent he's coming. He's a very experienced lawyer. He'll pick you up at 5.00 a.m. In the meantime he will liaise with the High Commission so at least they will know what is happening"

Nigel explained the gist of the call to Ellie and promised to keep her up to date and then drove back to Clapham.

Fliss looked exhausted when she came in so they opted to have a takeaway for supper. They sat on the sofa with their meals on trays.

"How was Ellie? Any news from Thailand?" Nigel decided to wait until they had eaten before he told her about his trip to Thailand. During their meal he told her that Ellie was OK and that she had called Trevor. Fliss was not surprised at the outcome. Fliss had hardly any family of her own. Her father had died when she was young and her mother had remarried and emigrated to Australia. Tragically she had died of cancer just before Fliss met Nigel. She had little to do with her stepfather and had been an only child. Before his parents' divorce she had envied Nigel his family, but afterwards it was Laura who had been the rock. Poor Nigel. It must be hard not to be close to your father, and especially so for Ellie who, as far as Fliss could gather, had always suffered from a lack of confidence. When Nigel finally updated her and she was over the shock of the expediency of his trip, she seemed relieved that he was going out to Thailand.

"I'm sure you'll sort it out Nigel. It is just a big mix up and I expect you will come back with her, safe and sound."

Nigel tried to smile reassuringly, although in his heart, he felt they were in for a long haul and he guessed that Fliss knew that too.

Nigel packed a small case with a couple of lightweight shirts, a pair of light trousers and some sandals, whilst Fliss found his passport and dug out his worldwide annual travel insurance policy. That night, for the first time for months, they fell asleep in each other's arms. The alarm went off at 4.00 a.m.

Jeff Clarkson arrived soon after 5.00 a.m. He introduced himself and shook hands with them. Nigel liked him immediately. He was probably in his early fifties, thinning light brown hair and built a bit like a rugby player. Nigel asked him about financing the flight, hotel and his fees.

"Sebastian said we'll sort it out later. You just concentrate on us sorting this mess out and getting your mother home."

CHAPTER 3

In Richmond, once Nigel had left, Ellie had picked up the phone and got through to Directory Enquiries. In spite of what Nigel said she could sort this out. "National Morning Mail, please." It was late afternoon and she hoped they would not be closed or, worse still, a maddening selection of numbers to press. She dialled the number and was relieved there was a live person answering. She asked to be put through to the News Desk. She had read about National Morning Mail's campaigns for justice and seemed to remember headlines like "National Morning Mail thanks its readers for raising £500,000 towards the campaign to bring justice for...." She couldn't quite recall exactly what it was for, but she was sure freeing her mother was just as important.

She was put through to Colin on the news team who listened whilst she told him the few details she had. He didn't sound as excited as she thought he would until he realised that Laura was the ex wife of a retired top Civil Servant.

"I have asked my Dad to help, but he is too busy writing his memoirs and putting in a new bathroom." She knew she sounded bitter but her anger and disappointment coupled with shock and fear gave her a runaway tongue.

"I think this may be of great interest to our readers, Ellie." His tone was suddenly reassuring. "Would it be possible to send someone to see you straight away? We may just catch a slot for tomorrow's edition. Also, we actually have a couple of journalists in Thailand at the moment who are covering a drugs arrest. I think we could link up nicely."

Ellie then phoned Steph as promised to update her on the latest. They had always been there for each other in times of trouble and

Ellie had been very supportive when Steph's marriage had broken down. She told Steph that she had contacted the newspaper who were interested and were sending someone round.

"I'd be careful, Ellie. The papers can be pretty devious and I think you should leave it to Nigel and the lawyer."

"I can't just sit here Steph. Anyway, it's too late. Someone should DO something."

An hour later Ellie was making tea for two reporters, Craig and Darren. Her hand was shaking as she handed them steaming mugs. She blurted out the whole story as far as she knew whilst Craig took copious notes.

"Tell me something about your mother, Ellie. Why was she in Thailand on her own? Has she travelled alone before?"

Ellie sipped her tea, noticing the tremor in her hand.

"After she and my Dad split up she found it really hard. Although she was able to buy a house, she got no maintenance or pension. Whilst she was married she devoted all her time to bringing us up and so had no career and therefore no entitlement of her own. I think the law changed recently, but too late for Mum, so she works part time and managed to save for this holiday. She knew she wouldn't be able to afford it again. She wanted to do it while she still could. She is a home lover really. She'd be happiest with enough to live on and a couple of grandchildren to spoil. I think my brother and I are a disappointment really."

She paused for a sip of tea and now she had a captive audience plunged on again.

"No kids for me at the moment and who knows about Nigel and his wife. I know Fliss gets broody, but Nigel likes the good things in life and they both have great jobs. Mum only lives two streets away in Granville Drive so it would be ideal for babysitting if I ever have kids, but there you are. Do you think you can help us raise some money? Nigel has a flight to Thailand in the morning with a solicitor. It will all cost a fortune." She paused for breath, knowing she had been gabbling on, but nerves had got the better of her.

At this point Darren said he needed something from the car and excused himself.

Craig continued to ask a few more questions and also for a photo of Laura. Ellie found one of her mother sitting in the garden under a cherry tree which was full of blossom. She handed it over, tears filling her eyes.

"Please help us," she said. She made Craig some more tea. When the door bell rang she rushed to answer it, half hoping it would be someone with good news, but it was only Darren. He was holding his notepad and Ellie noticed screeds of notes.

"No more tea thanks Ellie. We'll be in touch."

Ellie thanked them for coming so quickly. "Please start a campaign to free Mum as soon as possible!"

They gave her their cards and left. Ellie poured herself a glass of wine and was just wondering if she could eat anything when the phone rang. It was Jane, Laura's next door neighbour.

"Sorry to bother you, Ellie, but is everything alright? As you know Laura gave me a key so I could water the plants and keep an eye on things. Well, I've just had a journalist call on me to ask some questions about your mother. I don't know how he found me, but he had an official card from the National Morning Mail. I told him I didn't know anything about her except that she is a good neighbour and very helpful with baby-sitting for me. I also said she was on holiday. He asked a lot of questions and when I asked him why he just said they were writing about her travels. I hope that is alright?"

"Don't worry, Jane. There's been a bit of a mix-up. I'm sure Mum will explain when she's back." Something kept Ellie from blurting everything out. People would know soon enough, when the National Morning Mail ran their campaign.

After she had eaten, Ellie phoned Steph again to update her on the latest developments. "Sorry I didn't ring sooner, but the reporters have only just left."

"Oh God, Ellie. I hope you were careful in what you told them. I just have a gut feeling you could make things worse. You really should leave it to Nigel and the lawyers."

"It's fine, Steph. They were very helpful. It can't do any harm and at least I feel I have done something!"

"Don't bank on it. From what you have told me I very much doubt it."

Ellie could tell that Steph was holding back an angry retort. After they had finished speaking, she drank some more wine and phoned Fliss. She decided not to tell her about the newspaper, feeling somewhat apprehensive after Steph's reaction.

Fliss sounded calm. "We're just going to have something to eat and then Nigel will pack a few things and we will get an early night. He's off really early. We'll keep you informed and I'm sure it will all be sorted out. Try not to worry. It's obviously some hideous mistake. It's not as if she was carrying drugs or gems. There's no evidence."

"No." said Ellie, somewhat dryly. "Just a baby."

Ellie then phoned the agency and told them she would have to take a few days off. The great thing about temping was that there would always be someone else to fill the gap. There was no way she would be able to work until things were resolved. She ran herself a warm bath and put in a few drops of lavender oil. She nearly dozed off in the fragrant, soothing water and after she had dried herself she put on some lavender moisture cream, wrapped herself in a fluffy bathrobe and warmed up some milk.

She slept fitfully. The sound of the newspaper thudding on the mat startled her. She looked at her watch. It was 7.00 a.m. Obviously the paper boy was awake early, wanting to finish his round before school no doubt. Ellie put on her housecoat and made her way to the kitchen, picking up the paper as she went. Her head was muzzy and her mouth tasted foul. She put on the kettle and spread out the paper on the counter. In a wide column down one side of the front page she read:

STOP PRESS Exclusive. Ex-wife of retired top Civil Servant Trevor Jones arrested in Thailand on charges of allegedly trafficking a baby. Her daughter told us that the family is in shock. One neighbour said how much Jones enjoyed baby-sitting for her and had said how she would love grandchildren.

Jones is currently being held in custody in Bangkok. Her son is believed to be flying out with his solicitor. Two of our reporters, currently in Thailand to cover a drugs case, have interviewed her and she seemed shocked and disorientated. Cont'd P.5

Ellie turned quickly to page 5. There was no mention of a Save Laura Jones campaign, just details of her Dad's career, the fact that he had two children and was currently writing his memoirs. There was a small picture of her mother sitting under the tree in the garden.

Ellie dropped the paper, rushed upstairs and threw on some clothes. She must speak to her Dad before he was contacted by the press. After his reaction to her call asking for his help she knew that this sort of publicity was the last thing they needed. Perhaps now he would offer some financial help, but she needed to warn him before he found out through the press. She was also worried that he may have had a paper delivered already. She remembered Steph's words about involving the press and had a sick feeling she had done something awful, but she must focus on talking to her father. She doubted he would be up. She grabbed a coat, bag and keys and drove like a lunatic the five miles to her father's house. She pulled up in the drive and parked. There was no car on the drive, but his BMW was usually parked in the garage. It was rather early, so she rang the doorbell a couple of times, assuming her father was still in bed. The house was silent. Perhaps he was away. Even though she had only spoken to him the day before, it had hardly been conversational and there would have been no reason for him to tell her if he was going anywhere. The wrought iron gate at the side of the house was not locked, so she went round the back. Her heart skipped a beat as she saw that the back door was open and the kitchen window smashed. She gingerly stepped inside. There had obviously been an intruder. There was mud and glass on the draining board and a wine glass and cups were smashed on the floor. She heard the glass crunch under her feet as she went into the hall. She stood, listening, but there was no sound. Her heart was thumping as she tiptoed into the sitting room and then the dining room. The drawers of the sideboard had been upended on the floor but everything else was intact.

Feeling sick with fear she tiptoed upstairs and into the master bedroom. The bed had not been slept in. She felt somewhat relieved. It seemed as if he were indeed away and that intruders had broken in and perhaps been disturbed by something – passing traffic perhaps. Certainly the TV and HiFi equipment downstairs had not been touched. She crept across to her father's study. The door was ajar and as she went in she saw to her relief that he was sitting at his desk. The room was in chaos, the computer was missing and there were papers all over the floor. She called him from the doorway "Dad" and then stepped over and touched his arm. He slumped sideways on to the floor. His skull had been smashed and the blood had dried black on his face, his mouth frozen in a grimace showing his gums and teeth.

Ellie was aware of the sound of screaming, but it took a few moments to realise that it was in fact her own voice. She was shaking so badly that her legs barely functioned as she ran from the room. Downstairs she tried to dial 999, but the phone was dead. She pulled out her mobile and called the police and then sat on the stairs in total shock.

CHAPTER 4

Nigel was tempted to have a stiff G & T on the plane, but resisted, knowing how much worse he would feel after the long flight. Whilst waiting for the plane, he and Jeff struck up an easy conversation. Apparently Jeff used to be a private detective, running his own business. He had been working for Dobson for 10 years and from what Nigel could gather was used to legal tangles within the corporate world, although this was the first time he had come across something of this magnitude. He tried however to be reassuring, but without giving a false sense of security. He had gone over some legal points which although were probably meant to make Nigel feel easier had left him feeling very apprehensive. It seemed that the Thai legal system was a law unto itself and that prisoners, even before trial, were not well treated. He would not allow himself even to think about the possibility of his mother being tried and found guilty. What he already knew about the notorious "Bangkok Hilton" chilled his blood. There was a two hour stopover in Abu Dhabi and whilst Nigel tried to relax he felt agitated and restless. He just wanted to get to Bangkok and see his mother.

On the last leg of the journey the plane was not full and he and Jeff were able to stretch across two seats each in the middle wide row. The meal had not been too bad and he drank lots of water. He envied the club class comfort of which he had glimpses up the stairs and through a curtain. Champagne seemed to be flowing. Never mind, at least the company had arranged a flight at short notice and he had legal representation with him. He hoped that Ellie would not get too hysterical and that Fliss would cope. At least tonight his dinner would not be in the bin, he thought wryly. From time to time he and Jeff chatted in between watching a film and reading. It seemed strange that as the hours went by the sky changed and for a while they could just see a golden orb reflecting on the plane and then fantastic pink and gold clouds before it was dark. Odd to think it was still afternoon back home. In spite of everything, or perhaps because of it, Nigel slept as the plane bore them to whatever was in store.

He was awoken by the cabin staff dispensing hot flannels prior to some food. He and Jeff ate their meal in silence and then Nigel made for the toilet where he had a wash and shave, feeling much more awake. He wondered how Fliss and Ellie were coping. The time change and the long flight were quite disorientating. The last hour seemed interminable. As the plane began its descent, he and Jeff moved across to peer out of the window at the paddy fields and little spirit houses. In other circumstances, this would have been the start of a holiday, somewhere Fliss had always wanted to visit.

After they had landed, they switched on their mobile phones and both had messages to phone home, but due to the time difference they decided to wait. Once through immigration, they took a taxi to their hotel, and on checking in, were given more messages from home to call immediately. There were messages from Fliss, the office and Dobson. It would still be the middle of the night at home so Nigel decided to send a text and wait until later to call.

Nigel and Jeff's rooms were opposite each other on the third floor. Nigel dumped his bag and put the service kettle on for some coffee. He had a quick shower and changed into light trousers and a short sleeved cotton shirt. Once he had finished his coffee he went across to Jeff's room where he found him looking at a map of Bangkok, getting his bearings on the location of the police station and the British Embassy. They agreed the best course of action would be to go to the Embassy first and find out what they had to do to be able to visit Laura. Jeff had the number of the Embassy and managed to get through without much difficulty. An appointment was made for 12 noon and he scribbled down directions. The BTS Skytrain would take them to Phloen Chit and the Embassy was situated 200 yards down Wireless Road. The humidity and heat hit them as they stepped out of the hotel.

They found the Embassy without difficulty. At least it was cool inside and they were ushered into a smart office where a woman introduced herself as Anna Pickering. She was British and to Nigel's surprise already had a file with Laura's name on it.

"The Royal Thai Police alerted us when she was arrested. We have already had conversations with the police department. The usual format is that a suspect is taken to court within three to seven days of being arrested, but unfortunately in practice the system here works rather differently and the time could be up to twelve days or more. We are going through the formalities but cannot promise anything at this stage. Our job is also to make sure your mother is treated well. As you will see, the holding cells are, to put it mildly, not very sanitary. We can have a clean mattress and some basics sent to her, but you will have to pay for them. She will be allocated a Case Worker who will liaise with you, with Mrs Jones's permission. It will be up to the Public Prosecutor to decide whether there is enough evidence to proceed."

Nigel felt sick. "How serious is this? Have people been arrested for this sort of thing before? Surely they must know an old age pensioner would not buy a baby." He knew his voice was sounding angry but could not stop himself.

Jeff took over, taking some Baht notes out of his wallet. "No idea of exchange rate, sorry. How much should we give you for supplies?"

"We can take sterling as well. £50 will get her a mattress and some basics." She reached across for a duplicate receipt pad, signed it and handed a copy to Jeff.

"What should we do next?"

Anna Pickering looked at Nigel sympathetically and then addressed Jeff. "The best thing you can both do is get to see Laura and try to put her mind at rest. The police know you are coming and we have faxed them authorisation. Here's a copy. Be as calm as possible. She has had a bad shock and the calmer she is the better it will be for her. Give me your mobile number and we will liaise as closely as possible and let you know how our negotiations are going. Our job is not to interfere with the Thai justice system, but to give advice and information." She turned to Nigel. "You do have your lawyer with you Mr Jones, which is good. We can supply a list of Thai lawyers, but many of them do not speak English." She stood up, signalling that the interview was over, and shook hands with them.

Once outside in the humidity, tiredness took hold of Nigel. Coupled with the reality of the situation and his anxiety he suddenly felt quite weak. "Let's get back into the centre and have a snack or something Jeff, and then it will be a more respectable time to phone home."

The city was heaving with people and the heat and the smells were overwhelming. The traffic and fumes were unbelievable and in spite of the situation, Nigel gazed in amazement at the tuk-tuks and the motorbikes with three or four people hanging on for dear life. They walked past stalls selling fried locusts on sticks, unappetising chicken pieces and fruit until they found a place for a drink and a snack. Nigel felt somewhat dispirited after their meeting with Anna Pickering. "It doesn't sound good Jeff."

"Don't worry Nigel. They have to be devil's advocate. They'll get her out soon. At least they were already on the case."

"It's 6.30a.m. at home. I'm going to take a chance and phone Fliss." He put in the code but there was no signal. "What time does Sebastian surface?"

Jeff automatically looked at his watch, still on UK time, and then raised his eyes as if to say, "What an idiot."

"He is an early bird. I'll try his mobile now. Perhaps my phone will have a signal."

Sebastian answered almost immediately, sounding wide awake, almost as if he had been expecting their call.

"Hi. Jeff here, calling you from sunny Thailand. We've just been to the Embassy and are about to go to where they are holding Laura."

There was a moment's silence, then Dobson's voice, sounding awkward and strained. "Jeff. I take it that Nigel has not had any news from home?"

It was a statement more than a question. Jeff felt his heart rate go up and a tension in his jaw. "No. Just messages to call, but of course the time was not good. It was in the early hours your time when we finally got through customs. Nigel did try to phone Fliss, but he had no signal. What's up?"

"There's no easy way to tell you this and you will have to do your best with him. His father is dead."

Jeff went white. "What?"

"Look Jeff, is Nigel with you? Let me have a word. I think he ought to be the first to know what has happened."

Jeff handed the phone across to Nigel. "Be prepared for bad news Nigel."

As Nigel took the phone, a feeling of dread made him light headed. In that brief moment he thought that perhaps Fliss or Ellie had had an accident. "What on earth has happened?"

"I am so sorry Nigel. Your father is dead. He was murdered, apparently by an intruder. Your sister Ellie found him yesterday morning. UK time of course. By then you were airborne. Apparently she had gone to try to get him to help with finance for a campaign to free Laura. She was at the police station most of yesterday with your wife. I'll get them to call you again as soon as possible, but in the meantime, if you can cope with it, get to see your mother as soon as possible, do what you can and then get back here, hopefully with her, but if not you've got a good bloke in Jeff and he can stay on until it's sorted. I am so sorry."

Afterwards Nigel could not remember what he said to Dobson. It was as if another part of him took over whilst inside he was crumbling. He handed the phone back to Jeff, his face ashen. He sat for a while, his head in his hands, hunched over the table.

"Nigel, I am so sorry. I just don't know what to say. Do you know what happened? Sebastian said Trevor is dead."

"I just can't get my head round this," Nigel replied. "Apparently there was a break in and Dad was murdered."

Jeff stood up. "I can't imagine what you are going through." He got a brandy from the bar. "Here, drink this." Nigel felt the fiery liquid burn his throat.

They walked out into the heat and Nigel tried the phone again. This time there was a signal. There were two text messages from

Fliss. "Please ring me urgently Nigel." "Nigel, as soon as you get this, please call me." There was also a voice message. It sounded garbled and he thought he could hear Ellie crying in the background. There was also a message from Dobson asking him to call him back.

He called Fliss immediately, but there was no answer, so he left a voice message "Fliss, I have heard the news. So sorry you couldn't get hold of me. Please call me again. I have tried before, but there was no signal and now no reply." He then tried Ellie's phone which was apparently switched off, so he left her a similar message.

He turned to Jeff. "Let's go to my mother. I doubt she will have heard. I don't know what time visiting hours are but in the circumstances it had better be now."

Jeff pulled the address of the police holding cell out of his pocket and they called for a taxi.

They were dropped off at an ugly building with few windows. There was a desk inside with a counter on which was a telephone, an untidy array of documents and a couple of overflowing ashtrays. There was an armed guard standing at a door at the rear of the building. No-one came to the desk and Nigel bit back his frustration and asked the guard whether someone could help them. He knew enough about Thailand to not show anger, but he could not summon up a smile. Everything seemed unreal. The guard nodded and spoke into what appeared to be a radio telephone. After a few minutes a man in uniform came through the door. Nigel assumed he was a policeman and hoped he spoke English.

"I am Nigel Jones. I believe you are holding my mother here and we would like to see her please. This is my solicitor Mr Jeff Clarkson."

"May I see your papers please?"

They showed him their passports and Jeff handed over a copy of the fax from Anna Pickering. After about five minutes of perusing the fax and their passports and writing things down in a large book he stood up. "Follow me please."

They were led to a small room where they were searched. Their keys and belts were put in a plastic tray on a desk and more paperwork was produced.

"Sign please. For the belongings."

There seemed to be no option but to sign. He then led the way past another armed guard and along a dark corridor. The policeman carried a gun at his hip. He produced a bunch of keys from his pocket and unlocked another door to the right of them. As they went through Nigel could already smell the unmistakeable odour of dirty latrines. They passed several cells which had large metal doors with barred viewing windows. Eventually they turned a corner and he nodded towards a larger cell which had bars on one wall through which he could see his mother crouched on the floor, her back to the door. At the sound of their footsteps she raised her head and, on seeing Nigel, rose to her feet and ran to the bars. Her hair was dirty and dishevelled and she looked pale and haggard.

"Nigel. Thank God." The tears came now as she stretched a hand to him through the bars.

Jeff averted his eyes whilst emotions overcame Nigel too. After a few moments Nigel spoke. "We'll get you out of here, Mum. It's all a dreadful mix-up. Jeff here is a solicitor and we'll soon get to the bottom of all this."

Laura wiped her eyes on her sleeve. "I know you will," she said. "I was so confused, I couldn't remember even remember the name of my hotel. I think it was something like the Erawan, but in all that muddle I just could not think straight. The National Morning Mail were here yesterday and were very helpful. Apparently Ellie had phoned them and told them all about it and they are going to start a campaign to get me out."

Jeff turned to Nigel with a look of alarm.

Nigel spoke to his mother more sharply than he intended. "How the hell did they get involved so quickly? Did they tell you anything else?" He doubted that the news had filtered through to her as the time difference would have meant that details of the murder would not have reached her yet.

Nigel turned to Jeff. "Jeff, can you see if you can explain to the heavies why I need to speak to my mother somewhere else? We really do need an office or somewhere other than this hell hole."

The policeman had gone and the guard was gazing inscrutably ahead. Jeff went over to him and asked if he would take him back to the reception desk to ask for a private place where Nigel could be with Laura. The guard did not move. Obviously he had no intention of leaving Nigel alone with his mother. Nigel decided to continue talking to his mother until the policeman came back to tell them they had to go, then he would sort something out.

Laura gradually regained her composure. She recounted to Nigel the whole story, right from boarding the train in Chiang Mai. Nigel got more and more angry as he realised the total injustice of what had happened. "How on earth did the press get here so quickly?"

"Apparently they were already here to follow the case of a young woman arrested for supposedly carrying drugs. They said Ellie was trying to get them to support my cause through the paper. They kept asking me all kinds of questions about family life, about not being a grandmother yet and about Trevor. I suppose they know what they are doing."

Nigel wanted to bang his head on the wall with anger and frustration, but needed to stay calm and convincing. Ellie meant well, but she was always rather hysterical and from what Laura had said, could easily have made things worse.

Jeff asked Laura if she had been interrogated, what the sanitary arrangements were, although the smell told him that they were not good, what the food was like, if she had seen anyone vaguely official. She told him she had asked for the British Consulate but did not really know if she should have asked for an Embassy. She didn't know the terms. She had also asked for a lawyer, but nothing had happened. She had asked if she could use the telephone and, although this was refused, she had given permission for them to phone home.

"Nigel, what do you think happened to the baby?"

"I really don't know Mum, but I would advise you not to ask. It may make things worse."

Eventually the policeman returned and told them their time was up. Jeff went over to him and whispered in his ear while Nigel distracted Laura. He wished Fliss was there to help break the news. He was really out of his depth. The policeman left the area and Jeff whispered to Nigel that he was going to seek official confirmation of what they had told him. They were in for a long haul. Nigel sat on the floor and Jeff leaned against the bars.

"How are things at home? What about Ellie? She must have been worried sick. I am going to get out of here soon, aren't I Nigel?"

Another guard came in with a dish of grey rice and some meat which could have been goat or snake or anything else that may once have lived. There was a pitcher of water.

"I can't eat much. The toilet is disgusting and there is no washing facility. If this is the police cell, what on earth is the prison like?" Her voice was rising in panic.

"Don't even go there, Mum. We'll get you out."

Laura toyed with the meal, eating very little, but drinking some of the water.

"We'll be back with some food and supplies and the Embassy are going to bring round a clean mattress." Nigel spoke as naturally as he could but realised he was shaking and had a blinding headache.

Eventually the policeman returned and spoke quietly to the guard who then walked over and unlocked the cell door. Laura's face lit up. "Are they letting me go?"

"No Mum, not yet. I have asked if we can go somewhere more private."

Nigel was outraged when the policeman put handcuffs on Laura, but in spite of his protestations she was led out with her wrists handcuffed. She looked so drawn and had aged about ten years. They were led to a spartan office with two chairs and a small barred window. The policeman left but once again there was a guard by the door.

"I am so sorry, Nigel. It seems that by trying to do a good deed I have caused all this havoc. I am sure you are doing your best, but please get me out of here!"

Nigel waited a moment to gather his thoughts and to control his emotions. He had not been close to his father, but the fact that he was dead was a huge shock. He was also dreadfully tired. He took a deep breath.

"Mum. There's no easy way to say this and I am so sorry to add to your distress. Dad has…..died."

It was as much as he could do to say the word. To say "Dad has been murdered" was too brutal, and yet she would have to be told. Laura's eyes widened and her hand went up to her mouth.

"Trevor? Dead? How? Did he have a heart attack? He hated publicity and I am sure this must have angered him."

Nigel waited a moment and then said as gently as he could, "I'm so sorry Mum. Apparently there was an intruder and he was attacked. He was found dead in his study."

Laura said nothing. She was staring at Nigel, her mouth slack and her body immobile. For a moment Nigel thought she would faint. He turned to the guard.

"Please get my mother some water."

The guard did not move or answer him.

"For God's sake have some pity. My mother may pass out any moment. We have had some bad news."

There was no response. Nigel went to move round the table to put his arm round Laura, but the guard signalled to him to sit down. Laura was still in shock when the policeman came back in.

"Please, get her some water. Bad news has made her ill." He spoke slowly, glad that he was still sitting so that he did not tower above the policeman. He remembered it was insulting to a Thai for anyone to look down on his head.

After a brief hesitation the policeman left and returned with a cup of water. It was not a good colour, but the action of handing it to her snapped Laura out of her catatonic state. With trembling hands she took the cup and drank thirstily. Eventually she spoke.

"Nigel. I feel I am in a nightmare. I just can't take this in. I just want to lie down and sleep and wake up and be back home. Poor Trevor. What a dreadful way to die. Why Trevor? Why kill him? What on earth is going on? Please get me out of here. I should be with Ellie."

She began to sob as she was led back into her cell. Nigel followed, feeling utterly helpless. Jeff was nowhere to be seen – probably back in the reception area. The handcuffs were removed and Laura was again locked into the disgusting holding cell. The guard took up his place by the door. She held on to the bars for support and looked at

Nigel with such weariness that he just wanted to stretch out and hold her. How could this have happened to his mother in such a short space of time? She seemed so much smaller. So old. Her eyes were red rimmed with crying, her skin yellow and lined. He stretched out his hand and clasped hers against the iron bar and for a moment they just stood, no words being adequate. Nigel broke the silence.

"Mum, the Embassy staff are being really good. They'll help us sort this out. It's been a hideous mistake. Hang on in there and try to stay strong. We'll get you out of here. We'll get some food to you and in the meantime the Embassy will also let you have clean bedding and clothes plus more supplies of food, water etc. I'll have to go back to sort things out at home but Jeff is going to stay on. He's a good lawyer and won't rest until we have a result. You will come home soon. I promise."

Laura nodded, pursing her lips in an effort to control her rising panic. Nigel turned and walked away, fighting back his own tears. She heard his footsteps retreating into the distance and stood for a long time hoping he would return.

The belief that Nigel would sort it out, the mantra that had held her together, had slipped away. She sat on the filthy mattress, knees pulled up under her chin and let the grief and fear wash over her. She felt like a piece of flotsam in a churning sea. She forced her mind away from the fear of permanent incarceration in a living hell and focused on the news about Trevor. Although their marriage had been unhappy she felt incredibly sad that he had been murdered. She lay down on the mattress in the foetal position, rocking her body like a child.

Pictures and images floated across her mind. Meeting Trevor just after she had left school she remembered walking hand in hand into a coffee bar, into a cinema, into the church where they got married, into their first flat. They had had some good times but even in those days she realised he was emotionally repressed, but in her innocence thought he would change. When the children were born, he expected the house to be perfect when he came home from work, with the children in bed and no evidence of toys or washing anywhere. He had never really courted her. Never brought her flowers or taken her out for a meal. Even at her young age she had been aware that his fractured childhood had an influence on him, and made excuses. Now she realised she had tried to make up for the loss of his parents. He had been raised by his grandparents in what seemed to her to be a warring household. Putting her down seemed to give him a sense of authority.

It took a lot of courage finally to take the steps to divorce him. She had worked part time throughout the marriage, hours to suit so she could be home for the children. Trevor had bullied her during the financial settlement, telling her that if she tried to get any of "his" pension he would drag her through court. She was petrified and because she had signed an agreement "In Full and Final Settlement" she was now unable to redress the situation, even though the law had changed since her divorce. It was so unfair, but now that he was dead, she felt grief and sadness for the lost years. Regret that they had met when she was so young and that after the first flush of love, they had lost each other.

Laura drifted off to sleep with the memories becoming fainter as the churning seas in her mind began to become calmer. She woke with a feeling of emptiness. So much loss. The young man she married had met with a violent end and here, in a disgusting Bangkok cell, she mourned.

Gradually the reality of the here and now become only too apparent and she realised that the numbing fear had gone. It had been such a relief to see Nigel. He would sort it out. He had to. The alternative was just too awful to think about.

CHAPTER 5

Fliss had been getting ready for school when she got the call from Ellie. At first she could not understand a word she was saying and thought she had cracked up with all the strain about Laura and with Nigel being away. Finally, between sobs, she heard the words, "Dad's been murdered. I'm waiting for the police at his house. Can you come?"

For a moment Fliss was speechless.

"Fliss. Are you there?"

Fliss realised that Ellie was in no fit state to explain anything. "I'm on my way."

She put the phone back and then felt a rush of adrenalin as her whole body began to shake uncontrollably. She poured herself a glass of water and then phoned school to leave a message for the Head, saying that there had been another family emergency and she could not come to work and would call in as soon as she had some news. She grabbed her coat and a few minutes later was in her car and on her way. The rush hour traffic was building up and she was frustrated with the necessity to keep slowing down. Her mind was in turmoil and she had to concentrate to be able to drive safely. Once at Trevor's, she had to park some distance away as there were two police cars and an ambulance, as well as Ellie's car, which was parked in the drive. There was white tape blocking off the gate and a policeman standing there.

"I have heard the news. I am Mr Jones's daughter-in-law and I understand his daughter Ellie is here. Please, I must see her."

Just as she was explaining to the policeman, Ellie came out of the house with a policewoman. She looked dreadful and was shaking so badly Fliss thought she would fall over. She saw Fliss and staggered down the drive to her.

"Thank God you have come. There had been a break in. I found him in his study, just sitting there, but when I touched his shoulder he tipped over and……" her voice rose hysterically, "…..half his face was missing."

The policeman had stepped to one side and Fliss put her arms around Ellie. "Deep breaths, Ellie. You are in shock. Don't try to explain now."

A policewoman had joined them. Fliss turned to her.

"Can I get her some coffee or water or something?"

"Sorry, nothing must be touched. I am just taking her to the police station to make a statement about what she has told us. You can come too. Follow us down if you wish. Sorry, I can't take you in the police car. We have to question her first."

Fliss sat in the police station whilst Ellie was taken to an interview room. A policeman made her a cup of tea and she found she, too, was shaking with shock. She took out her mobile, but a policeman asked her to use it outside. She went out and called Nigel, but his phone was switched off. He was obviously already airborne, so she sent a text asking him to call her urgently, then switched off her phone and went back into the police station. She tried to work out what time it would be in Thailand and what time in UK when he had landed, but her head was spinning. Poor Nigel. She really wanted to tell him herself before he heard the news from anyone else. Ellie had said there had been a break in and that Trevor was sitting at his desk. She couldn't understand why intruders would kill him. And if something else was going on, what on earth was so important that Trevor was killed? From the scant information she had it seemed as if he had not put up much of a fight. She drank the tea and began to feel a bit better. Even in the aftermath of shock she found herself thinking that she must be the strong one. She had not known Trevor well, but for Nigel and Ellie it must be unbearable. Not only had their mother been arrested in Thailand, but now they had also lost their father.

After what seemed an eternity Ellie emerged from the interview room. She was very pale but more in control.

"Let's go home. The police will let us know how things progress. I must phone Nigel."

Fliss put an arm round her. "I've left him a message. He's already taken off, Ellie. I'm sure he will call back when he can and then we will have to break the news to him."

They stepped outside and she switched her phone back on and rang the school telling the head that she was in for the long haul and they had better get a deputy for the time being. Fliss drove straight to Ellie's. She didn't trust her to drive her own car, even if the police would have let her back through the cordon to collect it. After coffee and perhaps something to eat they would call the police to ask when they would be allowed to collect it.

"Now. Do you feel up to telling me what happened? Why were you there? Did you have a premonition or something?"

"No. That's what the police wanted to know. Why I was there."

Through fresh tears Ellie explained how she had tried to help by talking to the National Morning Mail, how their reporters had interviewed neighbours without her knowledge, how they had reported that Laura was in prison in Thailand, identifying her as the ex wife of Trevor Jones, retired top Civil Servant, how they had said that Laura had wanted grandchildren and how she herself was now worried that this would impact badly on the story of stealing the baby. She realised she had talked too much and the paper had reported that she said Trevor was writing his memoirs. She knew that in spite of his high profile he was a rather private man, and she had been afraid that he would see the paper and get upset, and had wanted to get there first. She confessed that secretly she had also hoped she could get him to change his mind to help financially in getting justice for her mother.

Fliss fought back the desire to shake Ellie. Why on earth she had felt she could take matters into her own hands, without consulting Nigel, Fliss would never know, but then Ellie always was the emotional one of the family.

Ellie talked non stop for a couple of hours, obviously still in shock, describing the scene she had found and berating herself for being so stupid about the way the press reported things.

"But it wasn't your fault, Ellie. There is no way Trevor could have known about the press and anyway the burglars would have had no interest in it all. Don't confuse the issues. Yes, it was probably a daft thing to talk to the press, but none of this is your fault." Fliss, ever the pragmatist, managed to calm Ellie down a little although she was still shaking badly.

After coffee and toast they telephoned the police and asked if it was OK to collect the car. The police said they could collect it after 2.00 p.m. that afternoon as they wanted to fingerprint it.

"Why on earth would they want to do that?" Ellie was highly anxious again.

"Just routine. Don't let's just sit here. Let's walk to the park to get some air and pop back for a sandwich before going to get the car."

They put on their coats and opened the front door. Outside the gate there were at least six photographers – paparazzi style, Fliss thought. They hurried back inside the flat and Fliss called the police station to tell them.

"Sorry madam. Nothing we can do about that. They are not breaking the law. That's the press for you."

"How on earth did the press get involved so quickly?" Ellie's voice was shrill.

"I expect neighbours reported it, or sometimes the police tell the press about serious crimes."

Fliss had never felt quite so helpless and alone. She felt in some way responsible for looking after Ellie but inside she wanted to shout "What about ME?" She kept herself busy making some lunch, encouraging Ellie to eat something and drink some herbal tea. "Too much caffeine will only make things worse," she said. "Drink this. It's calming."

The girls sat in silence for a while, each in her own private chaos. At 2 they put their coats back on and faced the shouts and flashes of the crowd of reporters. They took Fliss's car and drove to the park, just to get some air and exercise before collecting Ellie's car. She was obviously in no fit state to be on her own. Hopefully things would quieten down when the press realised they were not going to talk to them. Ellie had done enough of that already. They walked down to the pond and stood looking at the ducks.

"It all looks so bloody normal. Stupid ducks, what do they know?"

Ellie's voice had risen to the verge of hysteria and then she started crying again, great sobs shaking her whole body. She didn't take much persuading to agree to go home, pack a few things and go back with Fliss. She was obviously in no fit state to drive, so Fliss rang the police and arranged to pick up the car the following day. They ran the gauntlet of reporters again and once safely indoors Ellie started to pack a small case, but could not even think what to put in it.

"Just a few essentials, Ellie. Nightwear, underwear, toiletries, your makeup bag and a change of clothes."

Eventually they were ready. The reporters had not given up.

"When did you find your father?"

"What are your plans now?"

"Have the police any idea who did this?"

Tight-lipped, they got into the car and drove away. Ellie talked incessantly about going to Trevor's and finding the body, shuddering violently as she described the graphic details of his injuries. With an effort Fliss kept her voice calm.

"That's enough now, Ellie. No need to keep going over it. Let's talk about how we can help Laura when she gets out. Once Nigel gets the news, he will have to break it to her. She will be in shock too and will need our support."

What she really wanted to do was yell at Ellie to shut up. She so wanted to get home and find Nigel there, taking control of everything.

Traffic through Richmond was unbelievably slow – schools were coming out and the journey took a lot longer than expected.

"Nearly there," she said as brightly as she could, her knuckles white on the steering wheel.

There was no respite when they got home. There was a stack of messages on the phone and it continued to ring incessantly. Friends, colleagues, people she had not spoken to in ages came out of the woodwork to hear the gossip. She eventually left a new message on her answer phone saying she would only take urgent calls and those would be on her mobile. That way the "hangers on" would not be able to get hold of her as they would not have her mobile number.

She called Nigel's mobile and left another message. He would still be flying whilst back home his world had fallen apart yet again. Her nerves were at breaking point but she insisted on cooking a meal, basically to take her mind of things. The freezer was well stocked and they could sit out a siege if necessary. They restricted themselves to one glass of wine, knowing they needed to keep clear heads, although they would have welcomed the oblivion of getting stoned. The police called Ellie on her mobile, asking where she was. They reminded her that they had asked her to let them know her movements. She could not remember that, and the implied rebuke reduced her to tears again. She handed the phone to Fliss who confirmed the arrangement to pick up Ellie's car the following day.

Fliss insisted they went to bed at a reasonable time. She had a herbal sleeping remedy which they both took. Fliss was utterly exhausted and surprisingly slept quite well. She woke with a start at dawn knowing she would soon speak to Nigel and presumably break the news to him. She doubted he would already know. The thought of that made her feel sick.

Ellie on the other hand could not sleep. She kept seeing her father's bloodied face and spent most of the night sitting up in bed, rocking with such grief and despair that, at one point, she did not think she could survive. She just wanted oblivion and could understand people taking their own lives.

They were up very early and Fliss tried Nigel's mobile again. Ellie was sobbing as Fliss left him another message to call home urgently. A few minutes later a voice message came through on the mobile, sent a few hours earlier. At the sound of Nigel's voice, Fliss felt weak with relief. He had apparently already heard the news and had been trying to get hold of her. He was now on his way to see Laura.

They both jumped when a few hours later the home phone rang. It was Nigel. For a moment Fliss could not speak.

"Fliss. You OK? I couldn't get hold of you before. I have heard the news and have had to tell Mum. I just can't get my head round all this. I've also had a call from the National Morning Mail. What on earth possessed Ellie to talk to them?"

"She was trying to help raise some money by starting a petition or something. I can't see how it would have been linked to a break in."

"I don't know many of the details, but gather he was found pretty early in the morning, presumably Wednesday your time. Must have been just as I was taking off. Where is Ellie now? Is she OK?"

"Ellie is with me here. I'll hand you over in a minute. But tell me about Laura. How is she? Are they going to release her?"

There was a slight pause before Nigel replied in what seemed to Fliss a very restrained and considered voice. "She's holding up OK. Naturally she is very distressed by the whole business, and then hearing about Dad was very upsetting. The Embassy staff are being very good and we have let them know what has happened. Jeff is going to stay out here to liaise and I am going to get back as soon as I can. I am sure there is a lot to sort out and I just want to be there for you. How is Ellie?"

"She is pretty shocked so I won't go into too much detail, Nigel. Have a word with her and then tell me more about Laura and the conditions there. How soon do you think you can get back?" Fliss hated herself for the pathetic tremor in her voice as she asked the question.

Fliss handed the phone to Ellie, whispering to her not to tell Nigel about the paparazzi. There was nothing he could do from so far away. Ellie took the phone and started to sob again. Nigel took control and managed to calm her down.

"Don't talk about it now, Ellie. I'll be back as soon as I can get a flight. Hang on in there. I'll call as soon as I have flight details."

Ellie took a deep breath. "How's Mum?"

"Bearing up. Jeff is being brilliant and will stay on and get things sorted out. Try not to worry. I'm so sorry you had this to deal with on top of everything else. Hang on in there. I'll be back as soon as I can."

The police rang at 9.00 a.m. and asked them to remain at home for the time being. A police officer would be with them by 11.00 a.m.

and they would also deliver Ellie's car. Fliss was grateful for that as she still doubted that Ellie was fit to drive.

"I can't tell them anything else," Ellie said. "I can't bear going over it all again."

"Do you want me to phone your doctor for a sedative?" Fliss noticed Ellie was shaking badly and obviously still in shock.

"I've got some valium from when I was in Paris. I'll take one of those. I just can't believe all this has happened." She was crying again and it was as much as Fliss could do to hold on. She was near to tears herself.

Ellie was calmer by the time the police arrived. They had brought her car back and given her the keys. They then went over her statement from the day before and asked her if there was anything else she could remember, anything that may be relevant. Had her father any enemies that she knew of? How old were she and Nigel when their parents divorced and were they aware of his high profile job? They asked Fliss to let them know when Nigel arrived, as they would want to interview him too. Then they left, ignoring the photographers who were camped outside the house. After lunch, they both rested and managed to sleep for a couple of hours. Hopefully Nigel would get a flight easily. Fliss longed to see him. She was totally exhausted with it all and could only imagine how Nigel must feel after two long flights, seeing his mother and now the news of his father's death.

He arrived late the following afternoon. They heard the slamming of the taxi door and the photographers shouting questions at him. Fliss ran and opened the door, carefully concealing herself behind it so as not to be photographed and quickly let him in. He looked dreadful. His eyes were red rimmed and he had not shaved. He dropped his bag on the floor and they hugged for a long time. Fliss clung to him, grateful to feel his strong arms round her and ashamed of her lack of control as she cried onto his shoulder. They were suddenly aware of Ellie standing stock still in the middle of the hall, her ashen face half covered by her hands. Nigel let go of Fliss and hugged Ellie whose knees buckled under her. He half carried her into the sitting room and she collapsed onto the sofa. Nigel stood awkwardly as Fliss knelt by Ellie and put a blanket round her. "Talk to her Nigel. I'll get some tea."

"I'm so sorry Nigel. I talked to the papers as I thought I could raise some money to help. I don't know whether that made the burglars aware that he was on his own and maybe thought there was money in the house. His face was..."

"Don't go over it now, Ellie. It won't bring him back. The police will get to the bottom of it."

"And how's Mum? When is she coming home? Have they sorted it all out yet?"

Nigel told them the bare facts, but did not go into details about the appalling conditions or Laura's despair. Yes, he had told her about Trevor and she had been shocked but was OK and Jeff was still there sorting things out with the Embassy. He realised that Ellie could not take much more and also realised that Fliss had been holding things together but was herself near the edge.

Later, while Fliss and Ellie made a simple pasta meal, Nigel went into his study to check the messages on his office phone. There were half a dozen calls about work and he listened while he unpacked his briefcase. The last message was such a shock that his heart literally missed a beat and he felt dizzy. It was definitely his father's voice, but as he had never heard it before. It was rapid, breathless and strained. "Nigel. I'll expect you at the other canal......" Then the phone went dead.

CHAPTER 6

Jeff showered, had breakfast and went out. He intended to get a taxi to the railway station but walked for a while, just to soak up some of the atmosphere of Bangkok. It had all been so manic that he had not had time to take in any of it. Within minutes his shirt was stuck to his body, his hair was soaked and his mood worsening. No wonder Laura had been in such a state when she staggered into a hotel carrying a baby. She was right. All the hotels looked much the same.

The Embassy were being as helpful as possible, but as they pointed out, Thailand had its own legal system and although there was no actual evidence to implicate Laura in any crime, there was also no evidence to explain what she was doing with the baby in the first place, or to support her story of how she lost her passport and money. The fact that she had also seemed to lose her memory about where she had been staying had not given her much credibility either. On the other hand, unless there was evidence to charge her, in which case things would get incredibly worse, they would have to eventually let her go. According to Thai law the maximum holding time in a police cell without charge was seven days although the Embassy staff had told him that it could be much longer. Apparently there were many breaches of the law and Amnesty International was working to get things changed, but nothing could be taken for granted.

Nigel had called and updated Jeff on the situation at home. The press were being a pest and the newspapers were having a field day.

Jeff realised he was too hot and tired to take any interest in the frenetic, colourful scene around him, so called a taxi and went to the railway station. He wanted to check out as much of Laura's story as possible. The station was pretty chaotic, just as she had described it.

He wanted to take a look at the scene Laura would have been confronted with when she got off the train with the baby. He felt she needed reassurance that someone upheld her story. The more he understood what had happened to her the more he admired how she had held up under the strain. She was an old aged pensioner and yet she had struggled on with the baby out of a sense of pity.

He was beginning to get some idea of how confusing it must have been for Laura. If she had indeed been staying at the Erawan Hotel she must have got transport to the Station when she set off for Chiang Mai, but had obviously been too distraught to make sense of anything when she arrived back in Bangkok. He had a coffee near the station and then took the skytrain to the Erawan. Apparently it was the right hotel and the staff told Jeff that the police had collected Laura's luggage but had obviously been told not to talk to anyone about it. They just smiled politely and knew nothing.

Jeff had told Nigel he would make one more visit to the Embassy and then go back to see Laura. After that there was little he could do and he would return home. His work was piling up in London and he could not afford more time away. Apart from that he wanted to be back at home with his family. The humidity and heat were unbearable and he had had enough. He bought himself a beer and then went to the Embassy. Reception told him that Laura had been allocated a Case Worker called Jennifer Lazenby, but she was not available to talk to him. No amount of pleading that he had to return to UK made any difference. Jeff went back to his hotel, changed and had some lunch, then set off for the police station. On the way he bought Laura some bottled water, some tissues, some bread and some fruit. The police station looked grimmer than ever. He would have to wait, he was told. Laura had visitors. After half an hour two young Western men emerged, obviously reporters judging by their equipment. Jeff was incensed.

"Who gave you permission to see her?"

"It's a free world, mate, and business is business."

Jeff stuffed down the desire to hit out at them and said that if he had any more information he would let them know. That way he got their cards. Sunday World Digest. That was all they needed.

Laura had a little more colour, although the heat was unbearable and the smell made Jeff want to heave. The reporters had seemed more helpful than the previous ones, she said, and would do their best to get funding for a campaign. They had wanted to know more about Trevor than about her, but that was understandable given his high profile.

"It may be best not to talk to anyone, Laura. It's not just about getting you out. There's a murder enquiry and anything you say may well make it more difficult for the police in London to do their job."

Laura looked chastened, so Jeff changed the subject and told her about his visit to the railway station.

"I have to hand it to you, Laura. How you walked to a hotel in this humidity I will never know. At least the police have got your luggage back from your own hotel. It was the Erawan."

"How is Nigel? How are the girls? What is going on in London? Have they caught anyone?"

The questions came thick and fast and Jeff answered as best he could. He had to be very diplomatic in telling her he had to go back. She would of course be completely alone in this hell.

"I think the best way I can help you is from London," he said in as comforting a voice as he could. "I can get the High Commission to liaise with Thailand easier from there, and also of course give Nigel the legal support he needs to get you out."

Laura was silent for a moment. Then she said in almost a whisper "Jeff. Do you know what happened to the baby?"

"Sorry Laura. I've no idea. The priority is to get you out and, with respect, it's best if you keep a low profile about anything to do with the baby. I'm sure you remember why that's important."

She nodded, biting back a reply. She looked dreadful but was wearing a clean shift style dress. She said that a lady called Jennifer Lazenby from the Embassy had come with some clothes, a mattress and clean towels.

He stayed with Laura for about an hour, giving her the clean water and supplies he had brought with him, warning her not to talk to anyone except representatives from the Embassy. She was near to tears as he left but managed a smile.

"Thanks Jeff."

Back at his hotel Jeff phoned the Embassy to tell them he was returning to the UK and that from then on Laura had no support from home. He was told that they would now liaise through the High Commission in London. He then organised a flight home and called Nigel to update him. Nigel's voice was completely flat. He sounded exhausted and after listening to Jeff, he seemed to find it a great effort to talk about Trevor and all that was happening. Jeff gathered that the press were being a pain, Ellie was on the verge of collapse and Fliss was trying to hold everything together. The police had sealed off Trevor's house and were coming back to Nigel's for a further interview later in the day. Jeff gave Nigel his flight details and rang off. He took a shower, packed his bag, booked a taxi, set his alarm for two hours and crashed out on the bed.

He made himself read a paperback at the airport, aware that being left with his thoughts for a couple of hours was not a good thing. He was irritated that there were no through flights. He just wanted to sleep forever. After supper on board he put on his eyeshades and slept. The flights seemed interminable. He read and dozed, wondering why he had got involved in the first place. After finally landing at Heathrow, he switched on his mobile and checked his messages whilst walking towards passport control. There was a message from Nigel.

"Hi Jeff. Sorry I was so zonked when we spoke. Look out for your name on a board outside. I've ordered you a car. Go home and get some rest and call me when you can. Hope you get this message."

Back in Clapham, Nigel was exhausted. It had been bliss to soak in the bath Fliss had run for him and to get into bed. He was asleep as soon as his head hit the pillow. Fliss lay awake for ages, everything going round in her mind. She could hear Ellie snoring in one of the spare rooms, sleeping heavily from her sedation. They managed to eat breakfast together, their minds swinging from Laura to Trevor and to all the arrangements that had to be made for a funeral, and then thinking about Thailand and getting Laura out. Nigel felt dreadful. His head was thumping and he could hardly stay awake

The police arrived mid-morning. Ellie was dreading it, but the

54

police had no more questions for her at that time, so Fliss kept her occupied in the kitchen preparing vegetables for lunch which she knew no-one would want, but at least it kept their minds off things. There were the inevitable reporters with cameras at the ready whenever they had to open the front door.

The police spent about an hour with Nigel asking a lot of questions about Trevor's career. They seemed to be well informed already. Nigel had a few questions of his own.

"What have you found out? Was anything taken? I can't believe he was killed by random burglars."

"It's early days, Mr Jones. We will keep you informed of course."

They said they would call him to formally identify his father's body the following day. For some reason Nigel did not tell them about the telephone message his father had left. He realised later that even then he had a gut feeling that something was seriously flawed in the assumption that this was a break-in that went wrong.

According to the police, the only significant item that was missing was his father's computer. Apparently there was also an empty CD ROM rack on the floor, suggesting files were missing. The bedroom had not been touched, which was unusual in a break-in, as it was there that burglars usually looked for jewellery. He was surprised at the details they wanted to know about his father's career. When they were growing up, he and Ellie had seen very little of him. He worked long hours and spent most of the evenings in his study. From time to time he would be away on an overseas trip and Laura held the fort admirably, but seemed to know little about his work. Nigel remembered when he was quite young that his mother had grumbled about something called P.V. and later, after the marriage had ended, had said that she often felt her privacy was under threat. Nigel now realised that his father was obviously under the Official Secrets Act and the Positive Vetting meant that every detail of their lives may have been under scrutiny.

When the police had gone, he and the girls sat in the sitting room and, with the excuse of a pre-lunch drink, opened a bottle of wine, trying to make sense of it all. Ellie had half a glass, worrying about the valium she had taken. Speaking very slowly she went over yet

55

again how she had thought she was helping, how she had been taken in by the friendliness of the reporters, the sense of betrayal when she saw the papers and the subsequent horror of finding Trevor.

"Once I realised there had been a break-in, I went to see if he was OK. He was just sitting at the desk. There were a few papers on the floor and the CD rack, but nothing else looked strange. I was just so relieved to see him. Then....Oh God! His poor face…"

"Don't Ellie. Going over it is not going to bring him back. Come and help me dish up some lunch."

The girls decided they would all have lunch on trays as Nigel was sitting on the sofa in front of the TV. As they walked into the room they stopped in their tracks. There were shots of them coming out of the house, pictures of Trevor's house and pictures of Nigel getting out of the cab. The newsreader went into detail about the murder and then there were photos of Laura and a report about her still being imprisoned for alleged baby trafficking. Nigel switched it off when he saw Ellie's face. She sat in horrified silence, her tray untouched on her lap.

They didn't venture out that day. They could see from the window that reporters were lurking outside and decided to keep their heads down. There would be plenty to do the following day. Nigel did some work on his computer, answering his emails and calling the office. Fliss rang the school to update them on the situation and Ellie sat most of the afternoon staring into space. Fliss made a quick pasta for supper and after she had cleared up found Ellie asleep on the sofa. She made her a warm drink, sorted out her pills and gently aroused her and got her into bed with a hot water bottle.

When she got back downstairs Nigel was asleep in the armchair, snoring gently. She thought about waking him and getting him up to bed but decided to leave him there. At least for a while he was out of the agonising thoughts that must be churning round in his mind. She went up to bed and was vaguely aware of him coming up at some time in the night. He was still asleep when she woke at 7.00 a.m. so she went down and made some tea for them both and took it back to bed. He awoke as she got back into bed and they sat up and drank their tea. Then he put his arms round her and they lay together silently, relaxing into the comfort and warmth of each other.

"I can't talk about it yet, Fliss. I need to focus on getting Mum out and if I talk about Dad's death I know I will not be able to cope."

"When you're ready, Nigel. I am so sorry."

Ellie came down to breakfast just as Fliss was making scrambled eggs and toast. Nigel was drinking black coffee.

"What time do you have to get to the ..." Fliss could not make herself say "morgue" but it was implicit.

"Eleven. You know I just can't get my head round all this. Mum gets arrested for, of all things, stealing a baby. Or, let's face it, abduction. The newspapers get hold of it and mention that she is the ex-wife of Trevor Jones, 'top civil servant'. The next thing is that Dad is murdered. I feel we have a jigsaw puzzle here and that there are crucial missing pieces." He had not told either Fliss or Ellie about the phone message. He still could not understand why alarm bells were ringing in his head but something just did not make sense. Maybe it was a defence mechanism – something to get his teeth into rather than just accept the horror of a random burglary.

"Nigel, do you want me to come with you?" Fliss glanced across at Ellie as she spoke, did not want to upstage her, she was after all the daughter, but knew she was just not up to it.

"No thanks, darling. I'd rather be on my own. I'll go into the office afterwards to see how things are going there. I'll call you to let you know when I'll be back. Ellie, try not to worry. I am sure there will be good news about Mum's release soon."

Nigel had seen morgues on TV, but nothing had prepared him for the stark reality of his father's body under a sheet. Even before the sheet was pulled back he could feel tears pricking the back of his eyes. Although he had never been close to Trevor there were still memories of some good times. He knew that Trevor had not had an easy childhood himself and Laura had always made excuses for his remoteness.

"Your Dad never had a Dad himself. He provides for us in the best way he can."

Nigel grieved for himself, for the Dad he had never really

known – the little boy who had grown up during the war with no Dad of his own. Unbidden, the feelings threatened to overwhelm him. The morticians had done their best and half of Trevor's face, although badly bruised, was recognisable. As for the rest....For a moment Nigel thought he was going to be sick. His heart was pounding and nothing seemed real. He touched his father's shoulder. "Goodbye Dad. I'm so sorry."

Later he sat for a while in the stark waiting area until he felt more composed. He then had to sign some documents identifying the body so that it could be released. He guessed there would have to be more forensic tests and an inquest, but would not allow himself to think about it.

Afterwards he caught the train into town, stopping for a coffee at Starbucks to gather his thoughts before going into the office. He was amazed that the world was going on as usual around him. Girls and women chatting over coffees, business men with the Financial Times, shoppers, tourists. And Nigel, who had just identified a man with his face half missing who also happened to be his father. At forty two years old he suddenly wanted his mother. He wanted to hear her reassuring voice, as he had done during his growing up years. He didn't want her to be in a disgusting cell half way round the world. He wanted her here, in Starbucks, shopping and chatting and smiling. He wanted this nightmare to end. Nature stepped in and replaced overwhelming grief with anger. This was better. He could do something with this.

As he walked into his office, Frank stood up and put an arm on his shoulder. "You shouldn't have come in Nigel. I am so sorry..."

"It's OK. I need to do something or I'll go mad. Thanks so much for organising Jeff for me. He's been a Godsend. I thought I would pop in and see if everything is under control here. I won't be able to do much until we get the funeral over and get my mother back. I guess there are a few clients I should ring and a few loose ends to tie up."

He moved over to his desk and began sorting things out. His PA brought him the English panacea – a cup of tea, and together they drew up a list of prioritised items. Francesca had worked for him for a couple of years and was not only efficient but discreet. She made all the right noises of sympathy and then got on with it. He made a few calls including one to the High Commission. He obviously had a higher profile now because they could see him at 12.30 p.m. He sent a text to Fliss telling her of his plans and took a cab to the High Commission

The woman who saw him was both conciliatory about the loss of his father and efficient about the situation in hand. She had done her homework and was up to speed with current events and had obviously liaised closely with the Embassy in Thailand. It seemed that they could not hold Laura for more than a few more days without charge, and as there seemed to be little solid evidence, it looked as if she may be freed in the foreseeable future. Once that happened the Embassy would put her in a hotel while they sorted out some papers for her. The passport may take longer, but certainly they could arrange finance, flights etc. and, in the meantime, the Thai authorities were still investigating Laura's story. She would let Nigel know as soon as there were further developments.

Nigel left with the first glimmer of hope that Laura would be home in the not too distant future. He bought a sandwich and ate it on a bench in a park, once again amazed at the normality of life going on around him. He then took a cab to Dobson and Jenkins for his meeting with Jeff. Nigel went first into Sebastian Dobson's office to thank him for letting Jeff help him.

"I'm so sorry to hear about your father, Nigel. As if you didn't have enough problems at the moment."

Nigel then turned and went across to Jeff's office, knocking on the door before going in. Jeff was drinking black coffee and looked terrible.

After pouring Nigel a coffee and making a few pleasantries about the journey, he got down to basics.

"Have they any clues as to who did it?"

Nigel filled him in with as much as he knew and then they got down to talking about Laura, the situation in Thailand, and the fairly optimistic visit to the High Commission. Jeff nodded encouragingly.

"It's not all doom and gloom. They can't hold her indefinitely without charge and, as you say, they don't have any evidence to prove she actually paid for the baby. There are negotiations going on as we speak and I got a call today to say that the Home Office has become involved. This could be because of the high profile of the case now that Trevor has been murdered. I'm not sure what is going on, but am in close touch. Your mother is holding up and the Embassy is making sure she has food. It's my guess there will be an announcement soon."

"Jeff, I can't tell you how grateful I am for your input. I am sure it is over and above the call of duty. I hope your wife was not too upset by your absence."

Jeff grinned at him. "It's a long time since I've had to dash off like that. When I was a private eye she got used to it. Not sure how much I'd get away with these days. I'm just sorry it got so messy and that Laura is still there."

Nigel thanked him again, walked to the station and caught a train home. Walking back from the station in the fresh air seemed to clear his head. As he turned the corner into his road he saw the reporters and cameramen lined up outside the house. There were from both BBC and ITV as well as the usual journalists and he realised it was no longer just a newspaper scoop, but that the radio and TV wanted a piece of them too. He longed to lash out, but kept his composure.

"Nothing to say right now."

Fliss and Ellie were baking. One part of him relished the wonderful smell of fresh baking, but the other part was furious. How the hell could life be so normal when his father was lying a few miles away with half his face missing and his mother holed up in a Thai cell? He kissed Fliss and gave Ellie a hug. They sat round the kitchen table and he brought them up to date with what he had learned from Jeff. They didn't ask about the ordeal of identifying the body but after a while he announced that he would have to spend some time in his study organising the funeral. He had to check with the police first as to when they could release the body and then get busy. He had no idea as to when an Inquest took place and made a

60

mental note to ask about that too. In the meantime he had to go out again to collect the death certificate and register the death.

Presumably he would also need a coroner's report. After a few phone calls he set off to begin the complicated process of dealing not only with his father's death, but the complications arising from death by murder.

When Nigel got back the girls were watching the evening news. There were pictures of Fliss in the doorway as she tried to shoo photographers away and another picture of Trevor's house. Then there was a picture of the police station in Thailand. The two events were obviously inextricably linked in the minds of the press and now the public at large. Why on earth they had to link the two he couldn't imagine. After all, the divorce had taken place years ago. He hated the way the media called it a "story" anyway. Why couldn't they show some respect and call it a "report". It was almost, "Once upon a time there was a family called Jones who lived in London and were happy and successful. Then the storm clouds came and cast a spell on the family. There was death and imprisonment, murder and intrigue. No-one lived happily ever after…."

CHAPTER 7

The plane landed at Schipol on schedule. Her hands were unsteady as she handed over her passport for checking. Laura Jones. The official took a cursory glance at the unflattering photo of her taken in a booth some years before. She only had hand luggage so she didn't need to go to the carousel. Instead she went to the ladies' room and took the first cubicle, dumped her bag on the floor and turned to lock the door. Before she had a chance, it was pushed forcibly from the outside. She didn't have a chance to scream before she was hit with a tremendous blow to the head.

The alarm was raised when someone saw a thin trickle of blood coming from the closed toilet door .The door was not locked and she was crouched in the corner on her knees, the blow to the head had smashed half her face. She must have died instantly.

That same afternoon two plain clothes policemen arrived unannounced soon after Nigel returned home after obtaining the death certificate. He showed them into his study telling, Fliss and Ellie that the police were back. The two men stood somewhat uncomfortably and one of them, speaking very quietly, came straight to the point.

"Mr Jones. I am sorry to tell you that we have had a report that Laura Jones has been found murdered at Schipol airport in Amsterdam."

Nigel could hear Fliss and Ellie washing up in the kitchen. He could hear what the police were saying. He could hear the pounding of his heart. He was speechless. He sat down heavily and put his head in his hands. He had been in denial before, but this was real denial! Jeff had said the wheels were in motion to get a release for his mother. They would have to get the paperwork, passport etc. It would take days, even if there was a release date.

"I am so sorry, Mr Jones." The largest of the policemen was the spokesman and was showing genuine sympathy. "We will need you to go out to Amsterdam to make a formal identification."

To their surprise Nigel started to laugh. "Haven't you read the papers? Seen the news? Do you not know that my mother is in prison in Thailand? Is it rocket science to assume the person found in Amsterdam was travelling on my mother's stolen passport. Am I in the wrong profession or what?"

He was now shouting and laughing at the same time. Fliss and Ellie ran in when they heard him.

"Why don't you just leave us alone?" Ellie was white faced and shaking.

"Don't get hysterical Ellie. It's a mistake. A woman has been murdered in Amsterdam and she was carrying mother's passport. They want me to go to identify the body! No way."

He walked across into the sitting room with the police and the girls following, picked up the phone and dialled Jeff's number.

"Jeff. There are police here telling me that my mother has been murdered in Amsterdam. They've found a body with her passport. Will you make a quick call to confirm Laura is still in custody... Well, forget about the time zone and phone the High Commission here. They must know if she's been released. This is just ludicrous. Call me back as soon as you can."

Nigel made Ellie and Fliss sit down and poured them all a small brandy. The police declined.

"Here's a toast. To Laura's release."

His voice was high pitched, not like Nigel at all. The girls looked at him as if he had totally lost it, but sipped the brandy anyway. Nigel drank his in one gulp and collapsed onto the sofa. The police stood awkwardly as they waited for the phone to ring. When it finally did they, all jumped and Nigel snatched up the phone. Everyone held their breath, trying to make sense of Nigel's replies to the voice they could only just discern on the other end of the line.

"Yes. When will they be sure? Why would they want to do that? OK. Can you get on to it first thing and let me know? Thanks Jeff. Cheers."

Nigel spoke to the girls first. "The High Commission say they do not believe it could be my mother. They also say that when she does come back, she will have an escort. They could give no further information." He then turned to the two policemen. "I know you are only doing your job, but heads should roll over this. Please go."

The phone rang incessantly throughout dinner and although each ring made them jump they resisted the temptation to answer it. Nigel would play the messages back later and weed out the press and those purporting to be wellwishers who only wanted to know what was going on. When Nigel eventually played the calls back, one of them was from Jeff. Nigel rang him immediately and filled him in on the police visit. He had calmed down a bit but was still fuming.

Jeff was solicitous. "Tough Nigel, but they're only doing their job."

Ellie went to bed early and Fliss went up to have a bath. Nigel poured himself another brandy, put on some music and the next thing he knew it was 3.00 a.m. Fliss did not move as he finally climbed in beside her, too tired to be aroused by the faint smell of ylang ylang which she used to use in the bath when she felt sexy. He was asleep before he could put his arm round her.

Next morning Nigel was up first and made tea for the girls. They were all in their dressing gowns watching Breakfast and eating toast when the News came on.

"There has been a dramatic twist in the case of the imprisonment of Laura Jones, ex wife of the murdered retired Civil Servant, Trevor Jones. A body carrying Mrs Jones's passport has been discovered at Schipol Airport. Initially it was thought it could be that of Mrs Jones, but the BBC has had confirmation that Laura Jones is still in custody in Thailand. First reports suggest the woman had been murdered. Dutch police are carrying out forensic tests. We will have more on that story for you later."

"And they all lived happily ever after." Nigel was firing on all cylinders and at his sarcastic best.

Jeff rang shortly after 9.00 a.m. to confirm that Laura was indeed still in custody in Thailand. He said he was going to contact the Embassy to find out what was going on and would call Nigel later. It was midday when he phoned again.

"Nigel, I think it best if I come to see you. You are probably more help there with the girls and making funeral arrangements than coming to the office. I'll be with you by 1.00 p.m. Perhaps we could have a pie and a pint somewhere."

"Nice thought, Jeff, but those days are gone for the moment. Press are everywhere. You'll have to fight your way through, I'm afraid. God knows how these so called stars cope with it all. It's a bloody nightmare!"

They all jumped when the doorbell rang. Nigel went to the door, shielding himself as he opened it. He thought it was Jeff, but it was the grocery order. Fliss had been her usual efficient self and as well as basics there were pizzas, crisps and loads more beer. The pizzas were in the oven when Jeff arrived, somewhat rattled by the paparazzi. They all ate round the kitchen table debating the latest. The news on the TV was a repeat of the morning. The woman had not been identified and the Dutch were not commenting.

Fliss was glad she had ordered pizzas, something she rarely did. Rubbish food, she usually called it, but somehow it was perfect for the mood they were all in. Even Ellie ate a large piece, tempted by the smell of the hot pastry, tomatoes, cheese and pepperoni. She even managed a small beer, ignoring the warning about keeping off alcohol when on tranquillisers. She certainly had more colour and Jeff tried to lighten the mood by regaling them with a story about a case he had dealt with when he was a private detective. Apparently a man who, about to be confronted by an irate husband, had climbed out of the window and fallen straight into a bed of stinging nettles. As he had no trousers on he had suffered rather badly. Jeff was a tonic and Nigel realised that he himself had been somewhat swamped by all the emotions from Fliss, Ellie and Laura in the past few days. It was good to finally have a laugh.

After lunch Jeff and Nigel went into his study to talk. Jeff sat down and spoke quietly, obviously wondering if the girls could hear him.

"Apparently the Home Office is involved and there is tight security around getting Laura back."

Nigel was quiet for a moment before replying.

"Jeff, I want you to treat what I am about to tell you in strict confidence." His tone was serious and he waited for Jeff to give him that assurance.

He knew that hearing his father's voice again would be unnerving and Trevor's ghastly face in death flashed into his mind. He got himself under control and rewound the message.

"Listen to this, Jeff. It's my Dad's voice, sent the night of the murder."

Jeff listened, mesmerized. "Good God. Have you told the police?"

"No. For some reason I haven't told a soul, not even the girls. Something just doesn't make sense. Maybe I've been reading too many thrillers, but since this latest incident in Amsterdam, I can't help thinking all of it is somehow linked. Mum being arrested and then Dad being murdered. And now the murder of someone carrying Mum's passport. This message is so odd. It's been going round and round in my mind. It sounded as if Dad sent it either expecting intruders, or having heard them. He rarely called me and none of the message makes sense. Canals for example. He didn't have a boat, he didn't fish. Just supposing, and this really is fiction thriller stuff, he had something to hide and was trying to tell me where it was."

"What makes you even think that Nigel? There could be a logical explanation."

"Well, the attack came after Ellie had told the press he was writing his memoirs. His computer, CD Roms and his mobile were missing, but nothing else of any value. So, if we take this blockbuster further, we could say that once it was realised that Dad was writing his memoirs he needed to be silenced and the evidence destroyed."

Jeff thought for a moment before he asked, "And how does this link in to a murder in Amsterdam? And how does it link in to the wretched baby?"

"Perhaps the baby thing was not linked, but started the whole cascade effect. It must have been difficult for Mum during the height of Dad's career, what with all the secrecy of his job. She had to go to various functions with him but I don't think she ever really knew what he did. I know he never talked about the work. Looking back it seemed pretty hush hush. Supposing whoever is responsible for this thought that Dad may have told Mum more than he should. If so, perhaps it would be a good idea to silence her too. Perhaps this poor woman in Amsterdam was a case of mistaken identity. After all she was carrying Mum's passport and if it is in fact to do with State secrets, no wonder the Home Office is involved. I really don't want to alert the police to this. Unfortunately Mum has already talked to the British press in Thailand, although seemingly about nothing significant, but who knows? At some level I feel there is a deeper threat here than a random couple of murders. There is also some comfort in the fact that there would really be questions asked if, after this Dutch murder, mother was silenced too! If I'm right she is probably safer now than she was twenty four hours ago. On the other hand, perhaps I am just paranoid and the poor Amsterdam woman was into drugs and the rest is coincidence."

Nigel played the tape again. Jeff looked puzzled. "How far is the nearest canal?"

"Well, there is a canal where Ellie and I used to fish for tiddlers when we were kids, but it's miles away. We used to live in Wembley for a while, near the Grand Union. Dad did come fishing with us once or twice although it was usually Mum who took us. There is a particular spot where we sat and fished and ate our sandwiches."

"Come on. Let's go."

Nigel stared at him in amazement. "Look Jeff, you've got things to do. Apart from which it's quite a way away and why would he want to hide something there? It's probably got nothing to do with it. I just wanted someone to run this by as it's been driving me nuts."

"Sorry it's all so awful for you, Nigel, but I really want to be in on the action! It could be that your father needed somewhere to hide whatever it is away from the house. Somewhere you both knew. I am sure you are right and it is a red herring, but unless we have a look you will never know."

Telling the girls they were going to Jeff's office, they made their way past a couple of hopeful hacks and got in Jeff's car. Neither of them noticed the blue Astra that pulled out after them. The traffic wasn't bad and it took them under an hour. They parked on the road near the bridge in Alperton which Nigel recognised. The towpath was deserted. As they walked along the muddy bank Nigel was transported back to boyhood by the smell of the water and the lapping sound against the bank. There was a factory opposite. When he was a kid it must have been a saw mill because he could remember the sound of sawing and the sight of stacked planks opposite.

"This is the spot." Nigel stopped on the towpath in front of a large tree. "I am pretty sure that this is where we sat to have our picnics all those years ago."

They crouched down, not knowing what they were looking for, but already Nigel felt the anxiety lifting. At least they were doing something.

"I wish I had a penknife." Nigel scraped around the bottom of the tree with his fingers, but the ground was hard. "Let's walk along for a bit. Maybe it will jog my memory. Then we can go back to the car and see if there's something to dig with in the boot. If not, we can try to buy a gardening fork or spade in Alperton and if push comes to shove you can drop me off at home and I'll come back with some stuff from the garage."

They got up and walked for a while along the bank. A woman with a dog walked past and nodded at them. There were no boys fishing. Nigel remembered several boys fishing in the old days. They used to have drag nets which their mothers made from hoops and canvas. Perhaps that was in the school holidays and this was still term time. They walked back and Nigel stopped again at the tree. It was bigger than he remembered, but obviously it must have grown quite a bit in thirty years. He found a plastic biro in his pocket and began poking around the roots. A man passed by and both he and Jeff felt somewhat uncomfortable to be seen digging around a tree with a biro. They made their way back to the car empty handed and Nigel felt a bit foolish but also happy that he was being proactive.

"Sorry, Jeff, I just have to do this."

Jeff nodded. He was a good bloke, Nigel thought. Whatever he privately thought of this stunt he was going along with it. They got back in the car and drove along the Bridgewater Road, past Alperton Station, but could see no suitable shops. It seemed easier to just keep going.

"Plan B then," Nigel said. When they eventually got back the press had mercifully given up. Jeff parked his car in the road and Nigel put his in the garage.

Fliss and Ellie were watching afternoon TV. Jeff sat with them for a while drinking tea and making small talk.

"Where's Nigel?" Fliss asked.

"He's just gathering a few papers to take to the office."

He distracted them for a while, hoping they would not wonder why Nigel had garaged the car, something he had not done for ages. Nigel put a spade in the boot, grateful for the space in the garage and away from the prying eyes of any reporters who may have returned.

Jeff insisted on coming along for the ride. They set off again in Nigel's car, both aware that this was probably a waste of time, but doing it anyway, like two small boys off on an expedition. The traffic was heavier, but they made good time. After they had parked the car Nigel took the spade from the boot. He had brought a fold-up camping chair with him and rolled this round the spade so that it was not obvious what they were carrying. Feeling like criminals they made their way down the steps on to the tow path and along to the tree. Once there they stood stock still.

Jeff was the first to speak. "God Almighty, Nigel!" There was a sizeable hole dug out right round the tree. The earth was piled up to one side. There were also knife marks at the junction of the lower branches and the tree.

"What the hell..?" Nigel felt the hairs on the back of his neck prickle and looked around anxiously.

Their return to the car was somewhat rapid and once inside Jeff locked the doors and turned to Nigel. "Seems you were right, old boy. I think this has gone far enough and as your legal representative I insist that you now tell the police."

They were silent for a while. Nigel noticed Jeff kept checking the wing mirror and glancing over his shoulder. It seemed to Nigel that they were in a film and on one level he wished it was true. On another level the horror of the past days was all too real and now it seemed this was just the beginning of something that he did not understand but knew was dangerous.

Nigel shook his head. "Let's give it another day Jeff. There's just something telling me not to involve the police. I can't say why but it's a strong feeling I can't ignore. Sorry if it's making you feel uncomfortable. I know you are doing your job, but please..."

"I do feel uncomfortable, Nigel. The police should be told and if you want me to continue helping you, then we need to be up front about this. The police need all the leads they can get."

Nigel knew Jeff was right. Perhaps being so exhausted and in shock was making him paranoid." Nigel shrugged his shoulders. "OK."

They caught the rush hour going back, but Fliss didn't seem to notice the time and there were no questions asked. Nigel backed the car up to the garage and, quickly unloaded the spade and chair.

Fliss insisted that Jeff stay for supper and as it was his wife's book club night, he agreed. Ellie had made a chicken casserole and for the first time since the whole business had started Nigel felt hungry. Afterwards they had coffee and watched the News.

"Well, let's see what jolly stories they have tonight."

"The Dutch police are carrying out forensic tests on the body of a woman which was found in a toilet at Schipol airport yesterday. She was carrying the passport of Laura Jones, the ex wife of murdered, retired Civil Servant Trevor Jones. Laura Jones is still in custody in Bangkok, accused of baby trafficking. Mr Nigel Jones, their son, is seen on the left going into their house earlier today with his lawyer. None of the family was available for comment but it is understood that Mr Jones is liaising with the Thai authorities and the High Commission in London."

"Well, if we are being followed it would be difficult to tell which are reporters and which are spies."

As soon as the words were out of his mouth Nigel realised what an idiot he was.

"What do you mean about being followed? And what's this about spies?"

Ellie was sitting bolt upright in her chair, her eyes wide with fear. With sudden clarity Nigel remembered that it was Ellie who had found their father. He still had ghastly images of Trevor in the morgue and of course that was after he had been cleaned up. What Ellie saw must have been horrific.

"Sorry, Ellie, a stupid thing to say. All these events, coupled with jet lag, seem to have addled my brain."

Fliss said nothing, but from the look she gave Nigel he knew there would be a bed time grilling. Jeff stood up, thanked them for their hospitality and told Nigel he would be in touch in the morning. Nigel saw him to the door.

"I know I'm being paranoid, Jeff, but I don't trust the phone. Let's arrange to meet up and talk out of the house rather than on the telephone."

Jeff grinned at him. "OK. Look after the girls, Nigel."

Nigel double bolted the door and put the chain on once Jeff had driven off.

Fliss made Ellie some hot milk and made sure she had taken a sedative, then went to bed and waited for Nigel. He took a shower, hoping that she would be asleep when he got to bed, but she was reading a magazine, obviously waiting for him.

"What's going on, Nigel?"

He sat on the edge of the bed and told her about the phone message, that he had decided not to tell the police, but had listened to it again with Jeff. He then told her how they had gone to the canal where he used to go with Trevor when he was a boy.

"Oh Nigel, what a shock to hear his voice! Why on earth didn't you tell me? I'd like to hear it tomorrow. But it does sound as if you are playing cops and robbers! Why didn't you tell the police? I bet you didn't find anything!"

"No, we didn't. And presumably the person who dug round the tree after us didn't either."

"What do you mean?"

Nigel told her the rest of it.

"Tell the police, Nigel. I don't feel safe."

"I will Fliss. Jeff persuaded me it is the right thing to do. I'm just so confused by the whole thing. Anyway, I'm going to do it tomorrow."

They talked for a couple of hours. Nigel went over everything again ad nauseum: Laura was arrested in Thailand on a charge of baby trafficking. Ellie alerted the press and told them that she wanted to raise money to fund a campaign to get Laura home. She had told the press that she could not ask for help from her father because he was not actually generous with money and besides, he was too busy writing his memoirs to get involved, the inference being that Laura had got herself into a scrape that was none of his business. The newspapers had printed most of this and then Trevor was murdered.

At some point he had managed to leave a cryptic message for Nigel. Then there was the murder of a woman carrying Laura's passport. This did not of course prove that Laura did not actually hand over the passport, which was what the Thai authorities suspected, but it did prove that someone purporting to be Laura had also been killed.

"Suppose, just suppose that Dad was privy to some information which someone would not want to be made public. Just supposing that "they", whoever "they" are thought that Dad had confided certain secrets to Mum when they were married. It would be embarrassing if secrets came out in Dad's memoirs and if Dad were silenced then Mum would have to be silenced too. I remember Mum saying that Dad was PV. I was quite young at the time and only later realised what Positive Vetting meant. I know it sounds far fetched Fliss, but I am just trying to make sense of it all. And that would explain the gut feeling I have about the police. They are pawns when it comes to the Secret Service or MI5 or MI6 or whoever it was Dad was working for. Or, of course, if I'm on the right track, there could be foreign powers that would find Dad's memoirs pretty interesting."

Fliss was silent for a moment. Then she looked at Nigel and said quietly, "Perhaps a Thai cell is the safest place for Laura."

They turned the light out at around 3.00 a.m. and woke exhausted when the alarm went at 7.30. They let Ellie sleep while they had tea and toast in the kitchen, keeping the TV turned down.

"There has been some development in the case of the murdered woman found in the toilet at Schipol Airport. She has been identified as Gabriella De Jong, a Dutch woman in her forties. She had travelled from Thailand and a post mortem showed that she had two bags of heroin secreted in her body. She had apparently made an arrangement to meet a friend at Central Station and when she did not show up and the news broke about a murder, the friend went to the Police and identified her. It is thought that she worked as a prostitute in Amsterdam and was acting as a drugs courier so that she could start a new life. The friend is continuing to help Dutch police with their enquiries. The victim was carrying the passport of Laura Jones, the ex wife of murdered civil servant Trevor Jones. Laura Jones is still in custody in Bangkok accused of baby trafficking."

There were pictures of the toilet at Schipol and then a picture of Laura. It must have been taken in the cell. She looked old and distraught – not like the Laura who had set off on the holiday of a lifetime. Nigel's fists were clenched and Fliss could see the whites of his knuckles. She walked over and turned the TV off and then put her arm round his shoulders.

"There has to be a link. What was it Dad was trying to tell me? It must be something big to have us followed like that. I know this sounds like a spy movie, Fliss, but just suppose Dad's work took him into the realms of MI5 or MI6. When it was reported he was writing his memoirs, it could be that someone wanted to stop him blowing the whistle. After the Shayler affair and then Stella Rimmington's book it does make me think. Then of course there is the possibility of foreign spies. I do need to go to the police, I know, but I also need to do some brainstorming about Dad's message. And then there's Mum. I hate to even think that "they" wanted to silence Mum too, in case Dad had ever confided in her. It just seems bizarre that this woman had Mum's passport, and then she was murdered. How come they hadn't already got a trace on the passport as it had been reported as stolen. Also, the poor woman was in her forties. How could they have let her go through on Mum's passport, although

I do seem to remember Mum had had her passport for a long time so obviously looked younger than she is now. Sorry to go over it all again but it helps me see it more clearly when I talk about it."

"Oh God, Nigel. This gets worse. I don't know whether to think you are seriously deluded or to think there may be some truth in what you say."

"I'm going to see Jeff and get him to stir things up with the High Commission and the Embassy. And also try to find out why the Home Office is involved. This just can't go on. The Thai Authorities must be nearly out of the time they can hold her without charge. Let's just hope it's actually safe to get her out!"

"What's going on?" They had not noticed Ellie standing in the doorway. She looked even more fragile than she had the day before. Her hair was sticking up, her face pallid and in her striped nightshirt with a teddy on the front she looked more like a child than a grown woman.

"I think it's my turn to do something. I think I ought to go out to give Mum some support." She sat down and Fliss gave her some coffee.

"That's a noble thought, Ellie, but you have been through a lot yourself and I think you need to get well. We don't want you collapsing in Thailand!"

"I just feel so helpless." She burst into tears. "I want my Mum. I want to get back to normal."

Fliss put some bread in the toaster. "We all do, Ellie, but this will come to an end."

After breakfast Nigel sat with Ellie and told her about the phone message. It seemed easier than trying to hide things.

"No talking to the press."

Ellie was near to tears again. "I've learned my lesson. I will never trust reporters after all this. I just hope it was not all my fault. Can I listen to it please?"

Nigel took her into the study and Fliss followed them. At the sound of Trevor's voice, Ellie began to cry again and both Fliss and Nigel felt very emotional. They went back into the kitchen, but Fliss excused herself and went upstairs. If she heard Ellie going on any more about the way she had found her Dad and whether it was all her fault Fliss thought she would lose patience with her.

When Ellie had recovered her composure Nigel phoned the office.

"Don't even think about coming in, Nigel. Everything is covered for the moment. Just do what you have to do. So sorry."

Then he used his mobile to phone Jeff. "Do you fancy a fishing trip, Jeff?"

Jeff hesitated and Nigel thought he heard him sigh. "I suppose you'll go even if I say no, so I may as well join in the fun. Let me know when you want to go."

CHAPTER 8

With both Nigel and Jeff gone, Laura felt that Jennifer Lazenby from the Embassy was her only friend and contact with the outside world. Jennifer had worked in Thailand for four years, spoke reasonable Thai and had become used to the heat. She would probably return to the UK in a couple of years, but in the meantime enjoyed her job and the ex-pat life in Thailand. At thirty-four she needed to take stock of the future, but her career path had been exciting and no-one had come along to make her opt for settling down and having a family.

Jennifer knew that the authorities could not hold Laura indefinitely without charge and, as there was no hard evidence to incriminate her, it seemed unlikely that they could charge her. She had told Laura about the murder in Amsterdam, wanting to let her know before any reporters came in and made things worse. As she left, she told Laura in no uncertain terms not to talk to the press. "Leave it to me Laura."

The time difference made things very frustrating, but Jennifer managed to have fruitful conversations with Jeff and with the High Commission in London. The Thai authorities would not want to lose face by keeping a British old aged pensioner in custody if she were innocent. Jennifer had lived and worked in Thailand long enough to know how important face was to the Thais. If things were handled diplomatically in London, she knew the press could be used to Laura's advantage, but there had to be a fine line between persuasion and causing offence. The last thing they needed was the more salacious papers making slurs against the Thais. It was time the powers that be used their contacts with the more reputable papers. As she ate her lunch she realised she was like a terrier with a bone. She could not stop thinking about the murdered woman in

Amsterdam. It could either be a coincidence and a genuine drugs problem or, and this was the thought she was finding challenging, a case of mistaken identity, and if so, who would want to kill Laura? There was no hard evidence to prove Laura was lying about the baby and Jennifer thought it would not be too long before Laura would be freed. But how safe would she be? Jennifer needed to make quite sure that Laura, if and when the time came, would leave Thailand with an armed police escort.

Jennifer had told Laura not to mention the baby to anyone. She did not want it to look as if Laura were unduly concerned about a baby she had just happened to come across in a lavatory. She knew, however, that Laura had felt desperately sorry for the child and before she visited her again she wanted to give Laura some news.

It took her most of the afternoon to track down the orphanage the baby had been taken to and after a couple of phone calls was on her way. It was on the outskirts of Bangkok and the traffic was appalling, but eventually Jennifer arrived at the orphanage and parked outside on scrubland. It was a rundown area with a few mangy dogs sniffing around. There was a reception area of sorts and Jennifer introduced herself, saying she had called earlier and got permission to visit the baby, who had been named Nitnoy and was being looked after by carers and some volunteers. One of the volunteers was an English girl called Emma. She was in her gap year and had an interest in children. She offered to show Jennifer round and to take her to see Nitnoy.

Jennifer had seen a lot of things in her time in Thailand and had been aware of the custom of putting disabled children into institutions outside the city, but nothing prepared her for what was to come. Some of the children with disabilities such as cerebral palsy were in their cots all day, their legs tied to the cot bars with rags to stop them kicking. In some cases their hands were tied too. Emma told her that when she had arrived these children were in bed nearly all the time, but she had managed to get them up and in some cases to borrow wheelchairs and take them out. She had painted murals on the walls and made sure those who were able could have their meals at a table. She had taught them a few words in English and also some songs. Her energy was amazing.

Nitnoy was in a cot in a room with at least 10 other babies. She looked a good weight but was very listless. The basic needs of feeding and changing were taken care of, but cuddles and stimulation were not part of the routine. Emma did what she could but would soon have to return to University. She picked the baby up and handed her to Jennifer. The little girl opened her eyes and looked at Jennifer. No wonder Laura had felt bonded to her. She was beautiful.

"Would you mind holding her so I can take a picture for a friend of mine?"

Emma held the baby and made cooing noises to her. Nitnoy seemed to smile for the camera like a pro, although it could have been wind. Jennifer asked Emma for her contact details in the UK and said she would be in touch. As she left she felt profoundly disturbed by what she had seen and determined not to tell Laura about the conditions.

Back in her office she printed out a picture to give to Laura once she was out of custody. She did not want to give it to her before. Laura was tired and overwrought and Jennifer did not want to do anything which would set her off talking about the baby again, particularly to the press.

Jennifer worked long into the night, talking on the phone to the High Commission in London and to both the Home Office and the Foreign Office. Although Laura's passport had been recovered, someone had tried to use her credit card in South Africa. The liaison between the Embassy and the British High Commission had been productive in getting Laura's cards blocked after her arrest. Jennifer's job was to get Laura home. Privately she was intrigued about the latest developments, but it was beyond her remit to speculate on the murder of the young woman in Amsterdam. She guessed that Laura's son, Nigel, would want to come over again, but of course there would be the funeral of his father to take into consideration. If they could get Laura released soon, it would save the son having to make another trip. After sending several emails, Jennifer finally closed the office, keying in the security number on her door and setting the security code on the outside door.

She lived in a large house in the Sukhumvit district. Too big for her really, but the house, an occasional driver and a maid were some of the perks of the job. Once home she poured herself a large brandy and sat down to watch some late night TV before having something to eat. It was 1.00 a.m. when she finally got into bed only to be awakened by her mobile phone ringing around 3.00 a.m. She answered it immediately, "Hello". There was silence at the other end. "Hello. Who is it?" Silence. She rang off and switched the mobile off. She fell asleep quite quickly but was awakened again by her home phone ringing at 5.00 a.m. If this was another silent caller she would not be amused. She picked up the phone and, made it quite clear she was not happy. "Yes?"

It was Dave Ellis, her superior officer. "Sorry Jennifer. I've just had a call from Security. There's been a break-in at the office. I think we need to be there. I'll pick you up in twenty minutes."

Dave looked as tired as she felt.

"How did they get in?" As the last one out, Jennifer felt somehow responsible, although she knew she had set the security properly.

"No idea. Somehow they got through the main security door, and then to the offices. Your computer was intact, but security have taken it away to see if any of the files, emails etc. have been copied or deleted. They will have to send someone in to check if they have managed to hack into the server. The office is also being fingerprinted. They would have got away with it, but they triggered one of the alarms by not resetting the system on your door before opening the main door. They escaped before security arrived."

Dave parked outside the office, next to a police car and a security van. There was a guard on the door. They showed their passes and were handed cotton gloves. Fingerprinting was already being done throughout the building.

Jennifer looked at Dave. "Why are we here Dave? It seems as if everything is being taken care of." She looked exhausted.

"They just need you to check the drawers and any papers you keep. They need to make quite sure nothing is missing."

Jennifer looked carefully round the room, then went through the

79

drawers while Dave checked his own office. He went back to see how Jennifer was doing.

"Everything seems in order. Can I go home now?"

Dave dropped her off around 7.30 a.m.

"I may be a bit late, Dave. I don't feel much use to anyone right now."

She was back in bed and asleep before Dave was at the end of her road.

Back in London Jeff and Nigel were returning from a fishing trip. They had been to the local sports and camping shop and bought fishing rods, bait and two stools. They had taken a bucket from the garage and made their way to the Grand Union canal. By now, Jeff was not only intrigued, but wanted to keep an eye on Nigel to make sure he went to the police when they got back. Jeff had insisted before they set off that Nigel rang the police to make an appointment to see the Chief Inspector of the CID. An appointment was made for 4.00 p.m. that afternoon which gave them plenty of time for fishing. Nigel had made it clear that he did not expect to find anything, or even catch fish, although he was secretly happy to be back at his childhood haunt. He just wanted to see if they were being followed. The journey was uneventful but Nigel continually checked the rear view mirror.

It was quiet by the water and the smell of the canal once again took Nigel back to his boyhood. There were a couple of cyclists and a jogger, but apart from that they didn't see a soul. The tree was in the same state as the day before. They stayed for about an hour and Nigel was surprised to find that actually fishing was very relaxing, although he didn't enjoy putting the wriggling maggots on the hooks. It had been a lot easier when he was a kid because they just threw drag nets into the water. Nigel didn't ask Jeff what he thought of the exercise. He was just grateful he had gone along with it and although Jeff refused to handle the maggots he seemed to enjoy casting the line and for a while they actually forgot why they were there. They were pretty sure they had not been followed. Neither of them took any notice of the cars parked outside the site of the old sawmill on the opposite bank. It was now an engineering company and everyone was working inside. Even if they had thought about the cars in the factory car park, they were too far away to see that the single occupant of a blue car was watching them through binoculars.

They had a pub lunch on the way back, making small talk about anything but the situation. Nigel had been so unnerved by the previous events at the canal that he found himself suspecting anyone and everyone near them in the pub. Jeff was right. He needed to go to the police. He knew he should have told them before. Jeff dropped him off at home around 3.00 p.m. Nigel was grateful that the press had lost interest for the moment and that he was able to walk up the front path without a barrage of flash lights and questions.

Fliss had just made tea. Ellie was lying down with a headache. She was still not sleeping well.

"She really wants to go out to see Laura. It must be so hard for her having found Trevor like that and not to be able to see her Mum. Don't you think it would do her good, Nigel? And Laura too for that matter."

"Let's see what news there is from the High Commission. I'm sure they can't hold her for much longer. She may be home sooner than we think".

Nigel's optimistic tone reassured Fliss.

"How did the meeting with Jeff go?"

"Oh, fine. I've decided to tell the police everything. I expect to get it in the neck for not reporting the phone message before. Wish me luck darling."

"Do you want me to come with you?"

"No thanks. I'll be fine. You stay and look after Ellie. I'll come straight home. I'll just give them a ring as I want to speak to the CID and not a Mr Plod."

When he finally telephoned he said he had some information about the murder of his father and wanted to talk to someone from the CID. He was told to come straight down to the station. He finished his tea, kissed Fliss on the cheek and left.

After he had gone, Fliss poured herself another cup of tea, enjoying a rare moment of solitude. In a strange way the dreadful events of the past week had brought them closer together. There was terrible stress of course, but it was different from the remorseless hours and pressure Nigel experienced when he was at work. As for herself, she could now do the cooking and chores without the endless marking of papers and form filling she had to do when she was working. She would have to go back soon, but found it oddly satisfying to look after Ellie and to try to keep the home fires burning. Perhaps in a way it did fulfil some of the maternal longing that was never far from her mind. She was adamant she wanted a baby. As this entered her mind her thoughts turned to the baby in Thailand. From what had been reported, and from what Laura had told Nigel, she thought she would have done just the same. Certainly she would have taken the baby back to her carriage and from what she had heard about Thailand, she could understand why Laura would have thought it safer to try to get to a hotel to get help rather than approach anyone at the station. From that one gesture of human kindness their whole world had been turned upside down. It was a disaster that Laura's bag had been stolen. Nigel was right. It seemed too much of a coincidence that Trevor should have been murdered after Ellie had talked to the press. And now the poor woman in Amsterdam. Fliss gave a shiver and, putting her mug down on the counter, went to the front door and put the chain across. Nigel would have to ring the bell, but she felt decidedly spooked as she went over things in her mind. He was a good man and she was lucky to have him. The way he had coped since it all happened had shown her just how strong he was.

They had been introduced at a friend's twenty-first birthday party. She had seen him as soon as she had arrived. He was standing talking with a group of young men and something had amused them. He was laughing and she thought what a good looking man he was.

"Who is that tall, dark haired guy in the group?"

Her friend Amy looked at her quizzically.

"That's Nigel Jones. Come over and I'll introduce you."

They wandered over and Amy said, "Sorry to barge in on the joke guys. Can I introduce you to my friend Felicity – Fliss for short?"

And that was how it began. They all chatted for a while, but it became apparent that Nigel wanted to know Fliss better and later in the evening they danced together for several CD tracks. He took her out for dinner the following week and it was obvious to everyone that they had fallen in love. They got engaged six months later and were married the following year.

Fliss had always got on well with Laura. She was the best sort of mother-in-law, always there if needed, but never prying. In the early days, she and Laura had gone on shopping trips together, enjoying coffee and Danish pastries as part of the ritual. In those days, before Laura left, Trevor was rarely at home, and when he was he seemed to live in his office. Nigel and Fliss were invited there for Sunday lunch from time to time, and Trevor would make a big deal of carving. He would sharpen the knife and then thinly slice the meat whilst Laura dished up the potatoes and veg. Fliss would stir the gravy and Nigel uncork the wine. It became clear early on that there were certain things Laura was not allowed to do. Like carve the joint. Trevor would also check the al dente consistency of the vegetables and tell Laura that in future they should have another three minutes. He always checked that Laura had warmed the plates. If Nigel had been like that, Fliss thought she would have retaliated, but Laura seemed to let it go over her head, although sometimes Fliss would notice the tightening of her mouth. Apparently when Laura and Trevor had first married, he did not want her to drive and had even cancelled her driving lessons. As the children grew up it had been Laura who took them camping and fishing. It was also Laura who went to the parents' evenings, Sports Day and Speech Day, Trevor being too important at the office to take a day off.

Conversation at these Sunday occasions was not particularly easy and Fliss remarked once to Nigel that Trevor always seemed to put him down.

"Just the way he is," Nigel replied.

It was a shock to Nigel when Laura finally said she had asked Trevor for a divorce, but Fliss was not totally surprised. How sad that now Laura had finally broken free from the cage of her marriage, she had finished up in another prison.

Nigel felt rather apprehensive as he sat in the waiting room at the Police station. He was glad that he had insisted on seeing the Chief Inspector of CID, although the case was now of such high profile this would in all probability have happened anyway. After ten minutes he was shown into a small office. At a guess Nigel would have put Chief Inspector Moulton in his fifties. He shook hands with Nigel.

"Sorry to hear about the death of your father. Great shock no doubt."

He opened a thick file in front of him.

"I understand that you wanted to talk to me because you may have some information that could help with the case."

Nigel took a deep breath. "I was in quite a state of shock as you can imagine. I was in Thailand at the prison with my mother when I got the news about Dad. I came straight back and what with all the upset and the jetlag, I am afraid I did not mention a couple of things when the police interviewed me."

He went on to tell the Inspector about the strange message on his answer phone and how he had tried to interpret it. The Inspector nodded from time to time, but made no comment. Nigel went on to tell him about the trips to the canal and what had happened there.

"I have talked it over with Jeff, my legal advisor, and he convinced me that I couldn't deal with this on my own. Apart from which, I now feel alarmed for the safety of my wife and my sister. Jeff and I must have been followed on that first trip to the canal, and who knows about the second, although we did not see anything. And this murder in Amsterdam of the poor woman carrying my mother's passport did not help."

Inspector Moulton's silence had the effect of making Nigel talk faster and as he finished he realised he had almost been gabbling. It was such a relief to get it all out and hand it over to someone else.

"Could I have a glass of water please?"

Water and coffee calmed him down.

"Thank you, Mr Jones. It would of course have been helpful for us to have had this information before. After you have finished your coffee, I would like you to make a statement about what you have

84

told me. This will be in the interview room and it is routine to tape the interview. There will be another officer present."

Nigel found his palms were wet with sweat. He remembered feeling like this as a boy when he had tried to explain something to his father who would not listen, but just kept shouting at him. "OK," he said.

It was all surreal. So like television that Nigel almost expected John Nettles to walk in the door.

Nigel sat at a table with a tape recorder on it, and Inspector Moulton and a policeman sat opposite. After announcing the date, time and names of those present the Inspector asked Nigel to tell him again what had happened. When he had finished he proceeded to question Nigel. Had he been aware of being followed? How long was it before they had returned to the canal? Did Trevor often leave Nigel telephone messages? Had they been to the canal together since Nigel was a child? What, according to Nigel, had Trevor's job entailed? How long since Laura and Trevor had divorced? Did Trevor ever discuss his work at home? What did Nigel think about his sister having talked to the press? How had his mother taken the news of her ex-husband's murder? Was Nigel thinking about returning to Thailand to see his mother? The questions seemed endless. Eventually the tape recorder was switched off and Nigel and the Inspector returned to the office.

"Thank you Mr Jones. Please don't make any travel arrangements without checking with us first."

"What do you think it's all about, Inspector? Do you think all these events are linked? Is there anything else we can do to get my mother home?"

The Inspector did not actually say, "We ask the questions now, Mr Jones," but the bland expression on his face as he dismissed Nigel with, "We'll be in touch," said it all.

Nigel looked at his watch on the way back to the car. It was nearly 7.00 p.m. He phoned Fliss on the mobile.

"Nigel. I was getting worried. How did it go?"

"I'll tell you later. I'm on my way now."

CHAPTER 9

Jennifer was back at her desk by lunchtime. Dave had called her at home and told her not to mention the break-in to anyone. Everything was as usual when she arrived in her office, with no sign of any disturbance or of the fingerprinting exercise. She was not sure if her computer had been checked in situ, but nothing seemed to have been touched. Dave seemed somewhat edgy, which was not surprising considering the lack of sleep. He called her into his office and handed her a cup of coffee, being on his third already.

"I don't want to talk here. Let's have a chat over lunch."

They walked to a nearby bar and Jennifer realised she was hungry. She ordered some noodles and a beer. Dave just had beer.

"They have checked your computer and it seems some of the files have indeed been copied – and in the middle of the night. What did you have on there about the Jones' case?"

"Just records of my conversations with London and with Nigel Jones, plus a profile of Laura Jones's ex – sorry, late husband. I couldn't find much about Laura. She is listed as a Counsellor with the BAC in London, but apart from that nothing of any distinction."

"What about him?"

"Senior Civil Servant. Apparently he worked for a few months in the Middle East in the 70s, around Black September time, and then a couple of other overseas jaunts, but his last years were in Whitehall. Retired three years ago. Can't remember offhand when he got divorced, but some time ago. Lives on his own. His daughter is reported by the press as saying he was writing his memoirs. I have all the press cuttings since Laura Jones was arrested. You can have a look when we get back."

Dave was in his last year in Thailand. The perks were good but his wife didn't like the heat and humidity, or the long hours. He would be glad to get back to UK. He drank his beer and began to feel better. He enjoyed working with Jennifer. She was very efficient. She was also very attractive, but Dave knew better than to stray. Apart from anything else, he did love his wife and kids and had seen too many ex-pat marriages go down the tubes for a bit of frivolity. When he had first come to Thailand, before the family came out, he had ventured to a couple of clubs in Patpong but found them too sleazy for words. The little girls waiting to go out the back with whoever paid for them were not much older than his daughters and he had found the spectacle of the Live Sex Show quite degrading. He was not a prude by any means, but the novelty of having dried peas fired at him from the stage by tubes pointing at him from tight fannies was hardly titillating. He had sometimes felt ashamed to be British, and watching the tattooed, pierced, sweaty young men on their stag nights having sex on stage with such young girls turned his stomach. One of them, no older than twelve, had pulled a long string covered in razor blades from her vagina and it was at that point he had left. Apparently the very little money the girls were paid by their pimps was sent home to the north for the education of their brothers. No, he would not be sorry to take his girls home.

The case of Laura Jones worried him. In the beginning it seemed little more than a drugs bust, only this time a child trafficking offence. But the more he studied it, and especially after the murder of Trevor Jones, and then the murder of the Dutch woman who was carrying Laura's passport, the more uneasy he felt. Then there was the question of the break-in. He decided that when they got back to the office he would call the forensics back and have the place swept for bugs, after the staff had gone home. Another late night, he thought ruefully.

Dave finished his beer and ordered a couple of coffees. He could do with another beer but needed a clear head.

"We need to get her out. From what you say her morale is quite low and since the murders, the press have really got their talons into her. When is the next meeting with the Thai authorities?"

"Today at 4.30 p.m. There are officially only two more days before they either charge her or let her go. I think we can put some pressure on. There is no evidence and they really don't like all this press coverage."

Jennifer had not told Dave about her visit to the orphanage. It was not in her remit and it had been in working hours, so she had thought better of it. Apart from anything else, she really wanted Laura to have the photo when she got out. Not if, she thought, but when. And with her increasingly fragile state and the press coverage, Laura could quite conceivably tell someone when Jennifer gave her the photo. Not that she, Jennifer, had done anything wrong, but now things had got so complicated she really felt she should tell Dave about it. She finished her coffee and then launched into what now felt like a confession.

"You did what?"

"Laura was so distressed about the baby she needed some reassurance, so I promised her I would make sure the baby was OK."

She then went on to tell Dave about the orphanage and about the delightful Emma who had held Nitnoy so that she could take a photo for Laura when she got out.

Dave sighed. "Another time, please ask. But I guess it hasn't done any harm. I see from the inventory that you have taken Laura a mattress and blanket. Presumably some food too? It's tough in there at any age, but for an old lady...."

"Yes, the past few days have taken their toll. She seems to have good family support. She is convinced the son, Nigel, will get her out. Let's see what this afternoon brings."

"I think I'll come with you. Not that I don't trust you, Jennifer, but two of us may just turn the tide. With luck we will be able to wake London up before we go."

Dave was used to treading a middle road with the Thais. When it was palpably obvious someone was guilty of drug smuggling, it was fruitless to plead their innocence and the only way forward was an ingratiating apology using such phrases as: 'This does indeed seem to be the case and we can only plead mitigating circumstances.'

In Laura's case there was absolutely no evidence and Dave could not see how the Thais could possibly press charges, especially now the world was witness to the whole thing. If they could get the Thais to realise that they may lose face by keeping Laura holed up, there was a fighting chance that she would be out sooner than later. It was a matter of diplomacy. Dave knew that Jennifer was good at negotiation, but at the same time he felt his presence would add weight to the argument.

Back at the office he managed to get hold of the High Commission in London before they set off for the interview. Considering the gravity of the situation, including two murders, their contact with the Commission seemed pretty low key. The inference was that it was unfortunate that Trevor Jones had been the victim of a break-in, but that there was no reason to connect it with the case of his ex wife having been found in possession of a baby. They also said that due to the hostile press it would be better for diplomatic relations to get Laura back as soon as possible. The matter of the Dutch woman was unfortunate, but that was a domestic issue in the Netherlands. Dave bit back a sharp retort. He drank a glass of water after the conversation. He had a rather nasty taste in his mouth. He tapped on Jennifer's office door. "Let's go!"

Laura sat on the edge of the mattress writing in her journal. The only way she could cope was to lose herself in her writing or by making up conversations in her head. She slept badly and the stench of the cell still disgusted her. Jennifer had brought some wet wipes and a new cotton shift which made her feel a little cleaner. A room deodorant spray or a scented candle had been denied. She found herself fantasising about food, remembering the Sunday lunches at Nigel's, the smell of fresh coffee and, although her stomach was upset, she knew that she would never take food for granted again. As pictures and images came into her mind, she was reminded of an incident when Nigel was about seven years old. He had nearly drowned in an accident at the swimming pool and that night she had heard him crying in bed. He told her that as he was going down for the third time, his life flashed before him and he could see the mountains in Austria where they had been on holiday. He also remembered his first day at school. She suddenly wondered if she herself felt that she would die in this stinking cell because of all the memories that were surfacing. She so wanted it all to be a dream, to wake up at home in her own bed with its clean sweet smelling sheets and the sun streaming in the window.

Writing whilst sitting cramped up on the mattress was making her neck hurt. She put down the pen and began to invent an imaginary scene. This was one of the ways she got through the interminable days. This time, she imagined that the hard mattress was a couch and that she was describing her life to a counsellor, who sat in a chair on the other side of the room asking about her early years, listening without interruption and taking notes, and it also helped her make sense of the conflicting emotions she was feeling.

"I suppose it was a lonely childhood really, but as I didn't know any difference it seemed normal. We rarely had visitors to the house. Mum was very shy and lacking in confidence. Actually she was an accomplished seamstress and had worked at one of the top London fashion houses of the day. She made all my clothes and I remember the dresses she made me when I started going to dances just before I met Trevor. Like her, I also had no confidence, but when I look at photos of myself from those days I see a blonde haired, blue eyed teenager with the world at her feet. At fifteen I went to ballroom dancing classes on a Saturday morning with my friend Pat and then to dances at the Town Hall. That was where I met Trevor. I so loved being held and swept along by the music of Ted Heath. Pat and I usually got the late bus home. Not many boys had cars in those days. Sometimes we used to wear full circle skirts with masses of stiff tulle frills on the petticoats. We used to soak them in sugar water to make them dry stiffly so that the skirts swirled out as we did the heel turns. Quite often our nylons would be snagged and we would take them to the invisible menders at the top of the road.

In hindsight it was quite a lonely childhood. I didn't like being an only child and I guess that didn't help when Trevor began to be controlling after we were married. I had no experience of the banter between family members and took everything to heart. I think he took advantage of that. I guess I just tried too hard and really wore myself out. As well as working, I still did all the cleaning and homebaking and gardening. I remember making two dozen cakes, an apple pie, quiches and biscuits every Friday night while Trevor was at Badminton. Well, euphemistically at Badminton. While the cakes were cooking, I cleaned the house so that over the weekend I was free to take the children out. Trevor was always so rude to me and eventually Nigel began to copy him. I do regret being a doormat. I should have stood up to him instead of trying to hide my tears from the kids."

Laura shook her head, letting the image fade, and stood up to stretch her legs. A couple of cockroaches scuttled away as she walked round the cell. That night she dozed fitfully. Jennifer had brought her a few books but she couldn't concentrate. Nigel was her rock and she had to have the belief that he would get her out of this nightmare. The fluorescent light was still a problem and she tried sleeping face down but found it too uncomfortable. There was no outside window so she could not judge when it was daylight. Laura had discovered that by leaning on the tap whilst twisting it round she could get enough water to wash after a fashion. She still gagged at the sanitary arrangements. She was awakened by the sound of footsteps and the jangle of keys presaging the warm liquid that could have been tea and the grey matter that could have been porridge. She now had a very upset stomach which made the sanitary arrangements even worse.

Jennifer arrived soon after Laura had eaten as much of the food as she could face. On previous occasions she had brought fruit, wipes and a newspaper, as well as the mattress. This time she was carrying a document case. She was smiling and as she took a document out of the case, she held it up for Laura to see.

"Good news, Laura. The Thais are releasing you with no charge."

For a moment Laura felt numb and then she burst into tears. Shortly afterwards a guard arrived and unlocked the cell door. Jennifer gave Laura a moment to compose herself and then led the way to the office where Laura had handed over her belongings in what seemed like a lifetime ago.

"Just a few formalities. You need to check your belongings and then sign this form."

As if in slow motion, Laura checked the contents of the box. As far as she could remember, everything was there. After the formalities, Jennifer led her outside to a waiting taxi and they set off through the chaos of Bangkok to the Erawan Hotel. Laura was literally speechless and Jennifer let her be. She sat in the cab in a stupor, looking out at the traffic and street traders in a sort of trance.

Her legs felt like jelly as Jennifer led her into the foyer. In spite of her ordeal and the fact that all the hotels were so similar, Laura thought she recognised this as the one she had left her luggage in whilst she went on her "adventure" to Chiang Mai. Jennifer checked her in and then they took the lift to a room on the second floor.

"Jennifer, thank you so much. What happens next?"

"Don't think about anything yet, Laura. Those are your cases over there. This wasn't your original room, but we have brought you back to this hotel so that you can have some sort of familiarity. The police have gone through your luggage so you will need to check everything is in order. Then just take a nice hot bath and I'll have some food sent up to you in an hour. Then have a sleep. I'll be back later and we'll go through the things that have to happen next. We will sort out money, passport etc as soon as possible and get you home. You will have an escort so don't worry about anything. I expect you are anxious to phone home, but the time difference makes that a bit difficult. I am sure your family will be made aware of what is happening as soon as possible, but when I get back you can certainly make a few calls. I'll see you later."

Laura didn't know whether to stay stretched out on the wonderful double bed, run a bath or run round the room. She was so tired and yet elated. While the bath was running she opened her suitcase and, looking at her clothes, realised how filthy she was and what a joy it would be to put on clean things after what seemed a lifetime. Her underwear was neatly folded and what should have been familiar seemed to come from another planet. She made herself some coffee and opened a packet of sweet biscuits. She felt she would never take anything for granted again. The delight of the fragrance of coffee, the sound of running water, the steam on the mirrors were wonderful. She wiped some of the steam off and peered at herself. She looked dreadful. Old, thin and haggard. She undressed and sank into the warm, scented water. What bliss. She drank the cup of coffee whilst in the bath and began to feel better. Once she was clean and had washed and dried her hair she put on some makeup. Not that she needed to as she wanted to sleep, but, yes, she needed to for herself. Once she had put on some lipstick and a bit of colour on her cheeks, she felt more like her old self.

"Welcome back Laura Jones," she said into the mirror.

She slept until the waiter arrived with lunch. Chicken and sticky rice and fresh fruits to follow. Jennifer would be back soon and then she could phone home. Thank God there had been no reporters outside the police station. After her meal she lay down on the bed again and leafed through an in house magazine whilst waiting for Jennifer, her guardian angel.

In the meantime, Jennifer made her way back to the office with a great feeling of relief. The meeting with the Thai authorities the day before had been a total surprise. Ready to do battle, albeit a tactical battle, Dave and Jennifer had been ushered into an office they had not been to before. There was the inevitable picture of King Bumiphol on the wall and the Thai official seated at the desk stood and shook hands with them before inviting them to sit. He had a sheaf of papers in front of him which he shuffled through in silence before looking up and addressing Dave.

"We believe the best way forward in this case is to hand Mrs Jones over to the British police for questioning. We have nothing further to add and of course have done our best to look after her interests during her stay whilst we made investigations. You will be aware that there were circumstances which led us to believe warranted further investigation, but we now understand that the British are willing to take over."

There was a silence and it became apparent some sort of reply was expected.

"Thank you very much. I am sure the British authorities will do all that is necessary to establish what actually happened and, in the meantime, thank you for clarifying the matter. I am also sure that when Mrs Jones has returned to England, she will be grateful for the hospitality she found in your beautiful country."

Dave stood up and Jennifer, trying to hide a smile, followed him out, back into the heat and humidity of the city.

"What was all that about?"

"No idea. Hopefully there will be clarification from London later in the day. We can't say anything to Laura until it has been confirmed. I suggest we sort things out with London and, if indeed, all is as we hope, you could go to her tomorrow and break the good news. Let's keep our fingers crossed."

Finally breaking the news to Laura had been one of the most gratifying things Jennifer had had to do. Once she had left Laura in the hotel she went back to the office to work through the formalities of making the final arrangements for Laura's flight back to London. The powers that be in London had insisted on an escort for her and although Jennifer was curious about the catalogue of events – the woman at Schipol, Trevor's murder and even the break in at her own office – she couldn't help being relieved to see the back of it all. It took her a couple of hours to make most of the arrangements. One of the aides was due to return to London for a vacation and it was agreed that he would accompany Laura. She would have to ask Dave about an armed guard. An emergency passport was being prepared and one of the secretaries was organising a flight. The earliest would be the following morning which would give Laura a little time to adjust and to make those important telephone calls. Jennifer finally telephoned Laura at the hotel.

"Feeling a bit better?"

"Much, thanks. Is it OK if I run up a phone bill?"

"Sure. And then get yourself dressed up and we'll go and get some dinner. I'll pick you up at 7.00 p.m. And tomorrow you fly!"

Jennifer took the photo of Nitnoy out of the drawer, put it in an envelope and then into her bag. At least Laura would have something she could look at when she remembered that little bundle from the train. Jennifer decided not to tell her about the bleakness of the orphanage. A line had to be drawn now.

Laura felt better once she had eaten some lunch and dozed until mid afternoon. The smell of the food was wonderful but she found she could not eat it all as she had stomach cramps. What she did eat was delicious. Then she phoned Nigel. He picked up the phone immediately and when he heard her voice, she could hear his emotion as he realised she had been released. She spent a few minutes bringing him up to date and then spoke to both Fliss and Ellie. As expected, Ellie was crying too much to be understood, but her joy was obvious.

When Jennifer arrived she was pleased to see Laura looking so much better. She was wearing a summer dress which looked too big for her. Jennifer guessed that even in less than a week Laura had lost quite a lot of weight. They went to a fish restaurant and the food was excellent. Laura ate slowly and had one glass of wine which she did not finish.

"I don't want to be too wiped out tomorrow and my stomach is giving me problems. I still can't believe all this. I can't thank you enough Jennifer."

During the meal she told Jennifer about her call home.

"I got in first with the news. They had no idea and are just over the moon. I spoke to Nigel first and then my daughter Ellie and Nigel's wife, Fliss. As soon as Ellie heard my voice she burst into tears and I couldn't get much sense out of her! They will all be at the airport. Can you let them know details when you have them?"

"Yes, of course. Great news Laura. I am sure you will take it easy when you get back as you have had quite an ordeal. I'm afraid the family won't be able to pick you up. You've become quite high profile at home and it has been decided that you will have an escort and a car will meet the plane. Don't worry, we'll let your son know the arrangements. As I said, you have been through quite a lot and sometime you will need to have a doctor check you over. It's not surprising you have a bad stomach after the food you had to eat, not to mention the water. You will have to get a doctor to check you out when you get back."

"I was only trying to do a good turn. Poor little baby. I wonder what became of her."

Jennifer handed the envelope to Laura. "A little keepsake for you."

Laura slid the photo out and gazed at the picture of the baby in Emma's arms.

"Is this…?"

"Yes. I tracked her down to an orphanage and, as you can see, she looks well. You did a good deed after all. I am sure if you had not picked her up, she would probably have died, and now she has the chance of being adopted."

Jennifer felt that bending the truth a little was the best thing to do in the circumstances. Laura's eyes welled up.

"Thanks a million. If there is any way you could keep me posted on her progress I would be grateful, but I have learned a lesson and don't want to get involved more than that!"

Whilst they finished their meal, Jennifer filled Laura in on the arrangements for collecting her the next day. They walked back to the hotel and Laura was overwhelmed by the noise and the traffic. Jennifer settled Laura into her room and gave her a hug.

"Good luck. Have a good flight and enjoy being back with your family."

"Thanks again Jennifer."

Laura packed quickly and was in bed delighting in the feel of smooth sheets and darkness as she drifted off into dreamless sleep.

Jennifer had booked an early call for her and she had breakfast in her room. The aide called for her just after 9.30 a.m., introducing himself as Dennis Whitby. He showed her his identity papers before handing her a sheaf of documents and a new passport to sign. Her luggage was taken down to a chauffeur driven limousine and they set off to the airport. Laura looked out at the bustling Bangkok streets with its motor bikes, tuk tuks, fumes, noise and street vendors. Every time they stopped at lights someone tapped on the windscreen and tried to sell them orchids. A week ago she had found everything a delight. Now, as she settled back, she shivered, with shock and exhaustion as much as with the cold air conditioning in the car.

Laura assumed that Dennis had organised some sort of VIP status, because they were whisked through customs and relaxed in an opulent lounge with soft music, coffees and little coconut sweets. There was champagne on offer, but neither of them had a drink. Dennis knew all about her, so it was a relief not to have to go over the whole thing again. He was going to spend a month with his parents in Surrey. Yes, he told her, he liked the job in Thailand but it would be good to see the English fields again and to catch up with family.

Jennifer had thought of everything and, once they had boarded, Dennis handed Laura a couple of magazines and paperbacks for the journey.

"I suggest you sleep as much as you can although there will be some films of course. There is a two hour stopover in Abu Dhabi, and although it is a nuisance it does break the tedium!"

The food was quite good and Laura watched a film before she put on her eye shades and slept. Dennis was an ideal companion and talked to her when appropriate, leaving her in peace when she wanted to sleep or read. The last leg of the flight seemed interminable. As they were flying over Europe, Laura began to feel nervous. She had to remember that, as well as the relief of seeing her back safe and sound, Ellie and Nigel were still dealing with the murder of their father. Nothing could compare to the hell of her stay in Bangkok, but she couldn't help feeling that the life she knew before would be gone for a long time, if not forever. This was brought home forcefully to her when they landed. One of the flight attendants came up to them and asked them to remain seated until everyone else was off the plane.

"What's that about, Dennis?"

"Security. I think you're a high profile case, Laura. There's been a lot of media attention. Don't worry. It's not every day you're a VIP."

He smiled at her, but she felt he was not telling her everything. At last everyone else had disembarked and Laura and Dennis walked off the plane to the top of the steps. At the bottom there was an armed guard in military uniform.

"Mrs Jones? I am here to escort you safely into the Terminal."

They were escorted to an office where they had to wait whilst their luggage was security cleared.

"How do they know which is mine anyway?"

"Don't worry, Laura" Dennis was reassuring. "Everything had a special security tag. I told you that you're VIP at the moment."

If Laura had imagined coming through customs into the arms of her family, she was to be disappointed. After what seemed an eternity and many forms to sign, the guard escorted her and Dennis through the terminal building and into a waiting car. To her surprise the guard got in as well. Dennis must have realised she looked a little worried.

"We are taking you to your son's. The family are waiting for you there. There has been quite a bit of media interest in your case, especially since the death of your ex-husband, so for security reasons we are making sure you have as smooth a passage as possible."

It seemed that the media were not aware that Laura had flown into London as there were no reporters or photographers, although no doubt they would soon catch up on the news.

Laura's head hurt. Not only did she have a splitting headache, but she was disorientated and very confused. Something was terribly wrong. She couldn't quite put a finger on it, but she could not believe that all this red tape was because of the wretched misunderstanding about a baby. And surely Trevor's death should not impact on the arrival of his ex-wife back to the UK. Nigel would sort it out.

The media had indeed caught up. As the car drew up outside Nigel's, Laura could see a barrage of photographers and reporters. With Dennis on one side, the security guard on the other and the driver bringing up the rear with the luggage, they escorted Laura through the throng to the front door.

"How are you Mrs Jones?"

"What is it like to be back Mrs Jones?"

"Can you tell us how you feel Mrs Jones?"

The door opened and they quickly went inside and Laura collapsed sobbing into Nigel's arms. Ellie, white faced and shaking, put her arms round them both and they stood in a huddle, Fliss watching anxiously from the kitchen doorway. After a few moments they all went into the sitting room and Fliss offered to make tea for Dennis and the guard, but they declined and thanked them, shook hands with Laura and left.

"I can't believe I am actually here."

"We can't either Mum! You gave us a bit of a scare!"

"There seems to be a lot to catch up on. I am truly sorry to hear about your Dad. Have they caught anyone? Was much taken?"

She was drinking her tea so missed the knowing glance between Fliss and Nigel.

Ellie carefully put down her cup and excused herself. Nigel stood up.

"You get some rest, Mum. There's plenty of time to catch up when you are feeling stronger. We've made up the spare room for you, so if you would like to rest, we will call you when supper is ready."

Laura got into bed fully clothed and was asleep immediately. She didn't hear the doorbell or Nigel letting Jeff in, who had run the gauntlet of photographers.

"They will soon get fed up. I told them there was nothing to report. So, your Mum got back safely. That must be a relief. Is she resting?"

Nigel took Jeff into the sitting room whilst the girls busied themselves in the kitchen making coffee and planning what to have for supper later. Ellie was looking better already.

"Thank goodness you thought of getting a grocery order online Fliss. What about a casserole?"

"Good idea. We'll have a cup of coffee and see what's what with Jeff and then get cracking."

Nigel sat down opposite Jeff. "What's new, Jeff?"

"The police want to interview Laura. I understand it will be the Special Branch. Whatever is going on Nigel, this confirms you were right all along. I assume they will want to interview you some more after your little contretemps with them. It will be interesting to know their line of questioning. I can't help thinking there is involvement at a pretty high level. This press intrusion must be driving them nuts."

"Us too!" Nigel remarked wryly. "By the way, there will be a delay in making funeral arrangements. Apparently there have to be more forensic tests before they release the body. I'm still not sure when there will be an inquest. I'm really fed up with all this red tape. I know I should have told them about the phone call, but this reaction seems a bit extreme."

Fliss came in with a tray of coffee and Ellie brought in some biscuits. Jeff settled back in the chair and looked at the girls thoughtfully. Fliss sipped her coffee.

"What's going on Jeff?"

"Well, the police want to interview Laura tomorrow. I don't expect for one moment they will bring charges of baby trafficking! They will probably want a full report from Laura on what happened and they will no doubt ask lots of questions about Trevor. If they permit it, I think it a good idea for you to have a legal presence when they do, and I will be happy assist if you wish."

"Yes please. We certainly don't want anyone else! Apart from going through it all again, you did a sterling job in Thailand."

Nigel looked across at Fliss who nodded her head in agreement. Ellie, still looking puzzled, asked, "Why would they want to talk about Dad? After all Mum had not seen him for years?"

"Just routine," Jeff said.

Fliss distracted them with handing round the biscuits. At some point, Fliss thought, she would have to have a chat with Ellie. In fact, at some point, Ellie would have to go back to her flat and return to work, but she obviously needed a little more time. She was still very fragile and her eyes welled up at the mention of her Dad.

Fliss and Ellie left the men to talk whilst they cleared up and then began to prepare supper. Ellie peeled and chopped the vegetables, whilst Fliss browned some chicken pieces. When they had put the casserole in the oven they rejoined the men. They put the news on at 6.00 p.m. and, after some reports from Afghanistan and a reported stabbing in the East End of London, there came the inevitable shot of their house with a view of the backs of Laura and the escorts.

"It is understood that Laura Jones, ex-wife of the murdered top Civil Servant Trevor Jones, landed back in London today after her release from prison in Thailand. She was driven under armed escort to her son's home in Clapham. The case against her for baby trafficking in Thailand has been dropped. No-one is available for comment but here we see Mrs Jones entering the house this afternoon with an escort. Trevor Jones's funeral has yet to be arranged. It is not known if Mrs Laura Jones will attend. The Dutch police in Amsterdam do not seem to think there is a link between the murder of the Dutch prostitute and the case of Mrs Jones's arrest in Thailand. The Dutch woman was carrying Mrs Jones's passport, which had reportedly been stolen in Thailand."

The news was obviously upsetting Ellie again. She picked up her cup and headed for the kitchen.

Fliss turned to Nigel. "Oh my God! Does Laura know about the murder in Amsterdam? If not, then we should say something before she sees it on TV."

"Leave it until tomorrow, Fliss. I'm not sure if she knows and we don't have to have the telly on again tonight. Tomorrow she may be less tired and able to cope with more bad news."

Laura woke up to the smell of chicken casserole and realised she was very hungry. She still had a splitting headache. She freshened herself up, once again revelling in the luxury of hot water. She went downstairs and into the sitting room, surprised to see Jeff.

"Laura. How are you?"

Jeff stood up and Laura extended her hand.

"Jeff, thank you so much for all you did for me in Thailand. I am sure I would still be in that hellhole if it wasn't for you!"

"It was a team effort Laura. The team in Thailand pulled out all the stops too you know. They managed to get you out without loss of face to the Thais. Most important!"

Laura went out to the kitchen for a glass of water to take a couple of pain killers for her thumping head.

"She looks remarkably fit." Jeff said.

Privately Nigel thought his mother looked gaunt and had aged considerably.

"She's lost a bit of weight, but apart from obvious fatigue seems to be OK. It will be a relief when tomorrow is over."

Laura came back into the sitting room and Nigel told her gently that the police wanted to interview her the following day. He didn't tell her it was Special Branch, and if she thought it unusual that the police were coming to them rather than them going to the station, she didn't say.

Supper was a convivial affair with no-one talking about the

impending police interview, or the funeral arrangements. Jeff had stayed for supper and Laura actually managed to talk about her time in Chiang Mai, before the drama.

"I wish I'd bought more things in the Night Market. I had decided to do my present shopping in Bangkok, rather than have to carry too much on the train. I had always wanted to go to Thailand, but don't ever want to go back."

"Mum! How like you to be thinking about presents after the ordeal you have been through!" Nigel was amazed at her resilience.

Ellie looked better and was more animated. Seeing her mother sitting round the table with them was such a wonderful relief. Looking across at her made Ellie realise for perhaps the first time that their mother was elderly and was not going to go on for ever. She blinked back the tears and joined in the conversation.

After supper Nigel and Jeff went into Nigel's study for a talk.

"I don't know how much you want me to get involved with all this, Nigel, but I must say I am still intrigued by your Dad's telephone call and it looks like the police are too. Let's get tomorrow over and hopefully the funeral and then, when things have died down a bit, perhaps you will have a clear head and something else about the cryptic message will click into place. He obviously thought you would understand it."

Nigel stood stock still. "Thanks Jeff. I think it already has. You're a star. I need time to mull this over but…."

"What? What did I say?"

"Let me think it through. Promise to tell you soon."

Jeff left around 10.00 p.m. "Thanks for supper."

"It's the least we could do. Goodnight Jeff."

They were all in bed by 11.00 p.m. Nigel noticed that Fliss had put on her sexy black nightdress. It had been so long since she had worn it that he was quite surprised. On the other hand, he didn't want to get too excited, there had been so many rebuffs in past months, that he had almost given up hope. Fliss got into bed and for once did not pick up her book. Instead she turned to him and kissed him in the way he remembered they had kissed in the first flush of passion years ago. He was immediately aroused and she made it apparent that too much foreplay was not necessary. As he slipped into the viscous warmth of her, she moaned with pleasure and they both exploded together.

"Sorry. Too soon" he said, once he got his breath back.

"Not at all. It was fantastic. And we can take our time in the morning."

CHAPTER 10

Laura was up first. In addition to an upset stomach, jetlag had played havoc with her body clock and her mind was still reeling with recent events. She made some tea and took two cups up to Ellie's room. In spite of her own problems she was worried about Ellie. Although everyone was saying she was looking better now that Laura was back, she actually thought that Ellie looked dreadful and they hadn't had an opportunity to talk together. Carefully balancing the little tray in one hand, she quietly opened Ellie's door. She could just see the top of her daughter's head poking out of the top of the duvet. She put the tray on the dressing table and, moving the pile of clothes onto the end of the bed, sat on the bedside chair and drank her tea. After a while Laura opened the curtain slightly so that she could see the garden. After the darkness and stench of the cell, it was so wonderful to look out onto a blue sky and green grass. Ellie turned over after a moment or two, opened her eyes and looked at her mother with sudden recognition and surprise.

"Good morning darling. There's a cup of tea for you when you are ready."

Laura sat on the side of the bed and Ellie threw her arms around her.

"Oh Mum. We were all so worried about you. I can't believe you are here!"

Laura held her close and could feel her daughter shaking with sobs.

"Finding Dad was so dreadful. I thought he was just sitting at his desk and then when I touched his shoulder he keeled over and half his face was missing."

Laura caught her breath in shock. She knew Trevor had been

104

killed by an intruder but had no idea that Ellie had found him. No wonder she had looked so awful. Her mother was thousands of miles away in prison and then this. Laura fetched Ellie a box of tissues and her tea. After a while she calmed down.

"Do you feel up to telling me what happened? Why were you there?"

Ellie took a deep breath and told Laura everything.

"I know it had nothing to do with it, but I wish I hadn't talked to the press. Everything seemed to go wrong after that."

"Don't think like that, Ellie. The press would have got hold of the story eventually and at least I knew that someone on the outside was rooting for me when reporters arrived."

For more than an hour Ellie and Laura talked about what had happened.

Then Ellie said, "Nigel is saying some pretty strange things. I heard him and Jeff talking about being watched. I don't know Mum, but I feel there is more to all this than meets the eye. You heard about the woman murdered in Amsterdam? She was carrying your passport. It all goes over and over in my mind."

"Yes, Jennifer told me about that poor woman. I don't know many details though."

Ellie told her as much as she knew. Laura thought about it all for a moment.

"I'm sure the police are doing all they can."

Laura tried to sound reassuring but there was a niggle at the back of her mind that she would think about later. She felt uneasy about Ellie telling the press about Trevor writing his memoirs. Trevor had always been very guarded about his work and Laura had never really known what he did. She knew he had made trips to GCHQ and that he was Positive Vetted. She remembered years ago that someone had interviewed the neighbours about Trevor and for a long time she had wondered if their telephone was bugged, but had put it down to reading too many spy stories.

"Let me run you a nice warm bubble bath and then you can come down to breakfast when you're ready."

"Mum, it should be me looking after you."

"I am feeling much better and it seems to me that what you witnessed was far worse than a shitty cell in Thailand."

They both laughed at her mother's uncommon use of language. Thailand seemed to have had quite an effect on her.

They all met up for late breakfast and Nigel informed them that the police would be arriving at midday to talk to Laura.

"You are honoured, Mother. Not only are they coming here, but it will be the Special Branch."

Laura was not amused. "I know enough to realise that Special Branch are for keeping the country safe from terrorists and for protecting vulnerable people. I didn't think I was that important. Perhaps they think the baby was booby trapped or something."

She rummaged around in her bag and brought out the envelope Jennifer had given her. She had looked at the photo many times on the plane, and again last night before falling asleep.

"This is my baby." she said archly. "This is Nitnoy."

"Mum, wherever did you get this?" Nigel's voice was loud and strained.

"Jennifer Lazenby from the Embassy went to the orphanage for me and took this picture. Don't worry, Nigel. I haven't shown anyone and only looked at it on the plane when my minder was sleeping. Forewarned is forearmed, so to speak, although I guess I shouldn't talk about being bloody well armed."

There was a stunned silence as they all digested Laura's new found descriptive powers.

"Sorry," she said "but to be imprisoned for trying to help a baby seems so bloody unfair. You can see how beautiful she is. Jennifer says she may be adopted at some point. She didn't say much about the orphanage, but at least she is safe. How anyone can dump a baby in a toilet is beyond me."

She finished a piece of toast whilst the others made desultory conversation to cover their confusion.

"Now," she continued, "tell me what is happening about the funeral? I assume there was an autopsy. Have they finished examining the house? And, Ellie, after the dreadful shock you have had I want to know if you have been to the doctor for any help.

Perhaps after the funeral we will all be able to get back to normal. I hope the police will let me go home once they have found out about my terrorist activities and, Ellie, you can always stay with me for a while. You need to give yourself time before you try to get back to work. And how long will it be before those bloody photographers leave us alone?"

Fliss and Nigel exchanged glances that said, "Who needs the doctor around here?"

Ellie rummaged in her bag. "I have been to the doctor Mum. Would you like a valium?"

"No, I bloody well don't. Apparently I do need to go to the doctor for a check-up. It's routine after being held in that sort of a place and I do still have an upset stomach, but I don't need valium. A visit to the hairdresser would be more helpful. I'll make an appointment later for both."

Jeff arrived at 11.30 a.m. and the police arrived at exactly midday. There were two of them, in plain clothes. They introduced themselves as Inspector Williams and Inspector Sweeney from Special Branch. The press seemed to have bigger fish to fry because there was no sign of them outside the house. The men shook hands politely with Laura and asked if they could go somewhere quiet. Nigel showed them into his study and asked if it would be all right if his solicitor was present.

"That will be acceptable Mr Jones. We will also want to spend some private time with you, and of course your solicitor, after we have finished talking to Mrs Jones."

Laura sat herself down on the chaise, Inspector Williams sat on Nigel's swivel chair and Inspector Sweeney sat opposite Laura on a wicker chair. Jeff was perched on the desk until Nigel moved to sit next to his mother. Laura wished she had sat on the wicker chair. She was low down on the chaise and, in spite of herself, felt nervous and intimidated, but the policemen did their best to put her at her ease.

"Well, Mrs Jones, it seems as if you have had quite an adventure."

"You could say that Inspector, although it was not what I expected from a holiday."

"We have had a report from the Foreign Office and we

understand that the Thai authorities have dropped all charges. Your solicitor, Mr Jeff Clarkson, has given us full details and the British authorities see no reason to pursue the matter. You were just in the wrong place at the wrong time."

Laura smiled at him. "Yes, you could say that, Inspector and, although I paid a price, you could say that I was in the right place at the right time to save that baby!"

"Yes, that's another way of looking at it. Now, I hope this will not be too difficult for you, but we really need to talk to you about your ex-husband, Mr. Trevor Jones. I know you had been divorced for some time, but if condolences are in order please take them as read."

Laura's nervousness disappeared and was replaced by a sense of extreme irritation.

"Trevor? Why do you need to talk to me about Trevor? I heard whilst I was in Thailand that he had been murdered, but it was my daughter who bore the brunt of what happened. Nigel and I were both in Thailand at the time so I don't think I can be of any help with your investigations."

"Just a few formalities. Perhaps you would be more comfortable about things if we asked our questions in private. That is, if your son was not present."

Laura looked at him astounded. "I am sure there is nothing I want to keep from my son," she said sharply.

"We haven't found the culprit, so any light that can be shed on Mr. Jones's background would be of great help. We know that he had lived at Holly Croft for seven years. He was of course quite a well known figure. We understand that in 1970 he spent nearly a year in the Middle East. Can you remember, Mrs Jones, what his remit was?"

"Not really, Inspector. It was such a long time ago?"

Laura could not keep the incredulity out of her voice. She'd spent days in a hellhole in Thailand, her children had lost their father in the most dreadful circumstances, her daughter was on the verge of a nervous breakdown, the press and media were having a field day and here was this supposedly high ranking Special Branch officer asking her about her ex-husband's work 30 odd years ago. She surreptitiously pinched her palm, digging her nails in until it hurt, to remind herself not to swear at him. Release, relief and exhaustion seemed to be having a strange effect on her.

"Did he discuss his work with you?"

"No. Never. I knew he was sworn to the Official Secrets Act and he never talked about work and I never asked him. I learned more from the press after he had published papers on various issues. May I ask where all this is leading, Inspector?"

Inspector Sweeney ignored the question.

"I am afraid I need to ask you a few personal questions, Mrs Jones. Are you sure you would not like your son to give us some privacy?"

"My son can stay here. I have nothing to hide."

"Very well. If you are sure. Obviously you and your ex-husband had your differences as you subsequently divorced. Were there ever any third parties involved in your problems?"

Laura glared at him. "I raised two children in a home where my husband was mostly absent, either physically or emotionally. I was virtually a single parent but always there to go to the necessary functions as a loyal wife, sipping champagne at Air Vice Marshalls' dos between days of nappies and keeping the wheels turning at home so he could pursue his eminently important career and ensure he had his eminently large pension all to himself once the marriage folded. I also worked part time. No, Inspector, I had no time or energy for a life outside my children. Whether he had mistresses is now academic."

Before Inspector Sweeney could draw breath Laura continued, "I have read my fair share of spy stories and I do know the function of Special Branch. I may look like a dotty old lady but I have had contact with the real world and, before you get too hot under the collar, I can think of no reason that my ex-husband would be murdered and no, he was not a closet homosexual and he did not wear my underclothes and there was no evidence of blackmail during our unfortunate marriage."

With this, she smiled at him as she carefully crossed one leg over the other. She still had slender ankles and was wearing fur trimmed mules. The two officers glanced at each other, both trying to keep a straight face. Nigel was examining the rug and seemed to have developed a slight tic in one eye. Fortunately there was a knock on the door.

"Tea, anyone?"

Fliss glanced at Laura who looked red faced but quite composed. She had been worried that Laura would break down and there would be a lack of tissues, but tea seemed more the order of the day.

"It's nearly 1.00 p.m. Can I make you a sandwich?"

"We are nearly finished with Mrs. Jones. Give us another 10 minutes and then we will have a short break before speaking to Mr. Jones. Thanks anyway." He turned back to Laura.

"Mrs Jones. Sorry to be pedantic, but Mr Jones was abroad for nearly a year. Were you aware of any liaisons he may have had during that time?"

There was something in his tone that caught Laura off guard. She felt her cheeks flush and she pinched her hand harder, this time to stem the flow of tears.

"I didn't learn about it for years" she said. "I found a few letters when I was clearing out the house before we moved. They were from a woman he met when he was abroad. They were a bit of a shock. She was writing to say she was upset not to have heard from him after he got back to England, especially, she said, as he had promised to marry her. I was of course deeply upset and challenged him about it, even though it was years later. I told him I could have found someone too but stayed for the children. I remember he said that it was something men did and was acceptable, but that I was a wife and a mother, therefore it was unacceptable! It was all so long ago that I can't see it would have any bearing on the matter in hand. He's dead and there's no point in raking the past now. I always believed that the children should keep their memories of him, although he wasn't there much."

Inspector Sweeney waited a few moments for Laura to compose herself. Nigel's face was a picture and Jeff was looking out of the window as if he had not heard it all.

"When did you last see Mr Jones?"

"My daughter Ellie had suspected appendicitis three years ago and we passed each other in the corridor at the hospital. He barely nodded at me. We had been on fairly amicable terms until I tried to get him to redress the unfairness of the divorce settlement. Money to Trevor was like a red rag to a bull. I think he would have preferred to see me starve than admit the settlement was inequitable. It's always been me that has helped out the kids. I still have to work Inspector. Yes, before you ask, I am angry, but I am sure I am not a suspect in murdering him, especially as I was in Thailand at the time. Although I suppose I could have had a contract taken out. But seriously, I do feel sorry that he should have met such dreadful end. No-one deserves that."

Inspector Sweeney noticed that Laura's eyes were beginning to well up. People defended their emotions in many ways when they had been through what Laura had been through and although she was quite personable, she was not a young woman. The tension of the past week plus this intense questioning must be a great strain on her. Perhaps now was a good time for that lunch break.

"Thank you for your frankness Mrs Jones. Let's have a break now and then I will speak to your son. We will call you if we need to speak to you again."

Lunch was a stilted affair. Jeff had to get back to the office so left before lunch and the two officers just had a cup of tea, remaining in the study writing up their notes.

They refused a sandwich or a piece of cake. The family sat round the kitchen table eating ham sandwiches and drinking tea. Ellie had made a sponge cake. She found that comforting as it reminded her of the good times at home with Laura and Nigel when they were growing up. Their mother always baked cakes for them to have a treat when they came home from school. It all seemed so long ago. Nigel was particularly quiet, no doubt digesting the revelations from his mother and also wondering about the interrogation to come. When they had finished Nigel wandered back into the study. The two men were standing looking out of the window.

"Ah, Mr. Jones. We just need to ask you a few more questions."

"Sorry, Jeff had to get back. Hope that is not a problem."

Nigel sat on his black swivel chair, Inspector Sweeney sat on the wicker chair whilst Inspector Williams perched himself on the edge of the desk.

"First of all, commiserations again about the death of your father. It must have been a great shock, especially as you were so far away from home."

"Thanks." Nigel waited. He guessed they were going to give him a hard time about Trevor's message.

"Obviously we know about your father's message from the statement you made. Can you tell us why you did not tell the police about this sooner?"

"I just wasn't thinking clearly. Hearing his voice like that when he was dead was just – well, bizarre. I guess I needed to process it and to try to work out what the message meant."

"And have you, Mr Jones?"

"No, I'm afraid not. It just doesn't make any sense."

"We would like to listen to the message if we may. Sorry if you find it upsetting, but of course we need to do everything we can to bring your father's killer, or killers, to justice."

Nigel walked over and rewound the answering machine. There had been several new messages, but eventually he pressed the Play button and was once again shocked to hear his father's voice. He was struck again by the urgency in the voice and the abrupt ending.

"You have already told us about your little foray to the canal, which was not productive. Have had you any further ideas as to which canal he is talking about?"

"No idea."

"With your permission Mr Jones we would like to take the answer phone tape away with us. If it is an integral part of the machine, then we will take it all. We will of course replace it once we have had the message analysed."

Nigel didn't know if they meant put back the existing machine once they had finished with it, or actually replace it with a new one. He didn't feel it was appropriate to ask, so kept quiet.

"How often did you see your father, Mr Jones?"

"Rarely. We had never been close. He never asked us over and for our part we occasionally invited him here for a drink at Christmas or on his birthday, but he never came. I think he was worried he would bump into Mum. Once I phoned him to ask if he could help Ellie out financially as she was in a spot of trouble, but he was having a new kitchen put in and said he didn't have any spare cash. He always seemed to be busy. I think he went to the odd reunion, but I don't really know much about his private life. Now, of course, I wish things had been different. He was always too busy with his career when we were growing up. It was usually Mum that took us out. We did go on holiday sometimes, but he was pretty stern. I don't think he ever really let his hair down. They were both at our wedding. He bought us a carriage clock."

"When did you last see him?"

"Last week, in the morgue." Nigel's voice broke as he replied.

"Take your time, Mr Jones."

"I suppose it was about eighteen months ago. He had been clearing out his garage and for some reason had my old bike. He rang up and asked me to pick it up. I went round there the following weekend. It was a sunny day and he made some coffee which we drank sitting under the apple tree in his garden. He gave me a bag of apples to take back to Fliss. I'm glad I have that memory."

"What do you know about his career?"

"Not much. I think he wrote a paper once when he got back from his stint abroad, but most of his work seemed very hush hush. I don't think Mum knew much either."

"Any enemies that you know of? Anyone with a grudge against him?"

"Not that I know of. And anyway, I thought it was supposed to be a robbery that got out of hand?"

Nigel knew he was pushing it, but wanted to know just where this line of questioning was going – or coming from.

"The answer phone message changed all that, Mr Jones."

After another quarter of an hour the interview came to an end.

"Will you want to question Ellie, my sister?"

"Not right now. She had a pretty intensive interview after she discovered the body and I believe she was, quite understandably, in a state of shock. We will have this message analysed and get back to you as soon as possible. Our engineers will be calling on you, with official ID of course. Thank you for your time. If you think of anything else you can ring the station that is dealing with the robbery and they will get a message to us. You have their number don't you?"

Nigel nodded and then led the way out of the study into the sitting room where they shook hands with Laura and then called out goodbye to Fliss and Ellie who were in the kitchen. Once they had left, everyone breathed a sigh of relief. Fliss opened the windows and put the kettle on.

"Not more tea, Fliss. What about a brandy?"

Later on in the afternoon a couple of engineers with police identification came in and removed the answerphone machine. Nigel called Jeff from his mobile to inform him and to update him on the interview.

"If the phone wasn't tapped before, Jeff, I bet it will be when it comes back!"

CHAPTER 11

The following morning Nigel had a call from Frank.

"How are things, Nigel?"

"A bit chaotic, Frank. The police came round yesterday. Mum seems to be settling down. Jeff has been a Godsend. I expect you want to know when I will be back!"

"No rush, Nigel, but if it is not imminent then perhaps you could come in to tie up a few ends. If you want to work shorter hours while you get straight that will be fine."

"Thanks Frank. I am hoping to get clearance for the funeral soon. Once that is over I think things may gradually settle down. I'll make a few calls this morning and try to come in for a couple of hours this afternoon."

"No need to do that Nigel."

"Actually I think it will do me good."

Before leaving for the office Nigel called the police station and asked to be put through to the Chief Inspector.

"Nigel Jones here, Chief Inspector. We would like to make funeral arrangements as soon as possible. Can you give me any idea of what is going on? I would like to know what happens about an inquest and was also wondering if forensics have finished and whether you can release the body."

He hated saying 'the body.' He found it difficult to equate that mangled face with his father and found that the image of him in the garden with the apples came into his mind. He choked back his emotion and waited.

"Let me get through to forensics and I will call you back shortly."

Nigel then rang Jeff to tell him he was going into the office that afternoon.

"My job is done really, Nigel. The remit was to get Laura out and we have done that. Let's have a chat later about billing etc. Give me a bell and tell me when we can have a meeting."

"No problem."

Nigel, in spy mode, read between the lines. "Let's talk about the canal, but let's not trust the phone." He felt a tingle of excitement up his neck. What an ally Jeff had turned out to be. As he put the phone down it rang again. It was the Chief Inspector at the police station.

"Good news Nigel. You can go ahead with the funeral arrangements. And by the way, we have warned off the press so you shouldn't be bothered by such blatant intrusions. Hopefully the funeral will be as low key as possible in the circumstances although your father was well known. Also, we have gone through your father's papers and apparently you and his solicitors are executors. If you want to call them they are Blasey and Blaskett and you need to talk to Philip Blasey." He gave Nigel the telephone number and then rang off.

Nigel now knew he bore the title of executor but didn't really know what that entailed. At least the solicitor would keep an eye on things and Nigel realised there would have to be Probate, but was not sure what that meant either. He guessed that for a start he would be in charge of the funeral arrangements and then possibly have to sort out finances and personal details. He wondered if his father had wanted to be buried or cremated. Neither so soon, he thought dryly. Perhaps he should contact Philip Blasey to see if his father had made a choice before he rang the undertakers.

Philip Blasey's secretary said he should have been in Court, but there had been an adjournment and so could see Nigel at 11.00 a.m. He went back into the sitting room and Fliss gave him a reassuring smile. She knew how difficult things were and wanted to cheer him up.

"The photographers seem to have given up so we thought we would take Mum out for lunch after she has had her hair done. Do you want to come?"

Everything looked so normal: his wife, sister and mother sitting on the pale cream three piece, a vase of freesia scenting the room, talking about hairdressers and lunch. Nigel realised he was clenching his fists and made an effort to smile at them all.

Elllie looked much better and Laura seemed happy with the idea. Nigel told them about his increasingly full day and, picking up his briefcase, made his way out to his car. First of all he went to register the death and collect Death Certificates before heading off to his father's solicitor. He suddenly felt very old and could feel the tension in his shoulders and neck threatening to turn into a vicious headache.

Philip Blasey was a kindly looking man in his early sixties. He shook hands with Nigel and said how sorry he had been to hear the news.

"I thought I would see you in due course," he said. Nigel filled him in on the details so far. No, no-one had been caught, yes, a terrible business. Philip opened a thick file and spent a few moments leafing through the documents and then opened the Will.

"Your father's instructions are that he is to be buried in the family plot. Apparently he booked a place some years ago, next to his parents in St. Hilda's, Church Road, Rislington. Not too far. He also stipulated that he wanted the Will to be read after the funeral. I'll leave it to you to make the arrangements and then perhaps after the funeral you and the immediate family will come to my office for the reading at a mutually convenient time. Again, I am so sorry."

Nigel left Blasey and Blaskett's office and walked to an undertaker's he had often passed on his way to the station. The office was closed. Business was obviously not brisk. He took a note of the telephone number and went across the road into a pub for some lunch. He was not particularly hungry, but thought that if he ate something he would begin to feel better. He ordered sausage and mash, but only ate half. He drank a half pint of beer and went back to the car, then drove to the station to catch the train to his office.

He was glad to be at work and went straight to Frank's office. Frank immediately stood up and came round his desk to put a reassuring hand on Nigel's shoulder.

"Bad do, Nigel. What's the latest?"

117

Nigel sat down and for an hour filled him in on what had been happening. He didn't mention the phone message or the concerns he had shared with Jeff – or the fishing trip. No point in Frank thinking the strain of the past week had pushed him over the edge.

"I need to arrange the funeral now that forensics have finished. The sooner the better really. Ellie is feeling the strain most I think – she found Dad of course. I'm not sure about Mum. I guess she will come to the funeral, but it really is up to her. She's been through a lot and of course they were divorced. On the other hand I have never heard her say a bad word about Dad, although he was less than courteous about her sometimes!"

"Take your time Nigel. Come back when you are ready. No pressure, but if you can spare an hour now, there are a few urgent things in your in tray that perhaps you could take a look at?"

Nigel spent the best part of two hours tying up loose ends and answering some of the hundred or so emails before making his way home. Francesca had done a good job of filtering out the spam emails. She told him how sorry she was to have heard the news and for a moment looked as if she would cry. Nigel shuffled some papers and then gave her a list of things that needed attention urgently. He called Fliss just before he left to say he was on his way.

There were no reporters surrounding the house and he was glad for everyone's sake, but particularly for Ellie who was still worrying about having contacted them in the first place. Nigel made his way into the kitchen and took a couple of paracetamol for his blinding headache before going across to his study. The answerphone had been returned, but apart from a call from the police checking the line, there were no new messages. He rewound it until he found his Dad's message. He was glad the police had not erased it although it still gave him the shivers. Laura had gone up for a nap after their lunch out, whilst Fliss and Ellie had decided to take a drive over to Ellie's to check on the mail, telephone calls etc. Fliss also wanted to gauge Ellie's reaction to being in her own flat – she certainly couldn't stay with them forever and apart from that Fliss needed to get back to work. Once the funeral was over, perhaps things would gradually get back to normal – whatever that meant.

Nigel phoned the undertaker who had the kind of voice that vicars use at funerals – a sort of sing-song, as if he should start the conversation with "dearly beloved". Nigel gave his name and said he needed to make arrangements for the funeral of his father, Trevor Jones. If the undertaker was aware of the high profile case, he gave no sign. He told Nigel he would like him to make an appointment to call in to make arrangements.

"Will you be using the Chapel of Rest, Mr. Jones?"

Nigel was not sure what this meant, so the undertaker explained that many people liked to see their loved ones in the coffin, once they had been made to look as good as possible. Nigel wondered how they could make his father look good with half his face missing, but on the other hand he didn't like the thought of him being sealed into his coffin in the morgue.

"Yes. Perhaps that would be the right thing to do. Let me ask the police about that. I'm not sure of their procedure. My father wanted a burial at St. Hilda's in Rislington. Yes, a burial."

"And how would you like Mr Jones senior to be dressed?"

"What do you mean? Don't they wear a shroud?"

"Not these days, Mr Jones. They usually wear their best suit."

An appointment was made for the following afternoon at 2.00 to discuss matters. Nigel then rang the police and was put through to the team handling the forensics. No problem, they would release the body to the undertaker if Nigel would call in and sign the appropriate forms. Nigel put the phone down and poured himself a brandy. He would call in and sign the forms in the morning and then present them to the undertaker. He would also have to see if he could get into Trevor's house to take a shirt, tie, socks and suit out of the wardrobe. He wondered if he should find some shoes too. Probably. Trevor would look a bit odd in his best suit and just socks on his feet. In spite of himself Nigel grinned at that irreverent thought. He called the police again, this time to tell them he needed to get some of Trevor's clothes for the funeral. It was arranged that he could go, but with a police escort.

Meanwhile Fliss and Ellie had arrived at Ellie's flat. She rummaged around in her bag for her key. It seemed a lifetime ago since Fliss had helped her pack a bag and she was glad she was there with her. After being in Fliss and Nigel's house for a while the flat seemed small and had an air of neglect. There was the usual collection of junk mail and papers on the mat which she sorted through whilst Fliss made coffee.

"I am sick of all this rubbish. It all goes straight in the bin."

There was nothing pressing in the mail, although there were a few sympathy cards from friends and neighbours. Ellie then checked the answer phone. There were a few calls from friends and well wishers as well as several calls from reporters asking her to call them back.

"Not a chance in hell."

She made a note of the friends that she would call back at some point and then went to her computer to look at emails. She could have checked them at Fliss's but she had not had any inclination to log on given the state she had been in. There were thirty messages and she immediately deleted the sales pitches and those with attachments promising good luck if you sent it to eleven friends within twelve hours, or you got bad luck. Perhaps she had deleted too many in the past she thought bitterly before deleting them all. There were several messages of condolences which she kept ready to reply to when she felt stronger.

After coffee, Fliss insisted that Ellie put away the clothes that were lying around the bedroom floor. She plumped up the pillows and threw away some dead flowers.

Whilst Ellie was sorting out her clothes and putting some in the laundry basket, Fliss went through the fridge, putting out of date stuff and some rotting vegetables into a carrier bag to take back and dispose of at home.

"How do you feel about us doing a shop tomorrow and stocking the fridge with a view to you coming back?"

"Fine."

Fliss knew from her tone that Ellie was not at all sure, but was thinking that she was in the way and had been relying on Nigel and Fliss for long enough. She ignored Ellie's tone and together they locked up and left.

On the drive back she suddenly felt guilty. Ellie was still looking decidedly off colour and was understandably still shocked. "Look, Ellie. If you want to leave it until after the funeral it's fine. I hope you don't mind, but I've packed your black dress and coat just in case you're not up to returning just yet."

"No, I need to do it soon I know. Thanks for everything Fliss. It's OK."

There was a slight quaver in her voice which made Fliss feel even worse.

"Let's play it by ear, Ellie. See how you feel in the morning. I expect Mum will want to get back to her own place soon too."

Nigel's meeting with the undertaker went well. Eddie Groves looked as if he were near retiring age. He was obviously very experienced and put Nigel at his ease with the right blend of sympathy and businesslike efficiency. Nigel said he would let him know if any of the family wanted to visit the Chapel of Rest. Eddie looked in his appointment book.

"We could possibly have the funeral on Thursday next week. If that would be convenient, I will call the vicar to see if that would be suitable for him. Would you like me to do that now?"

Nigel nodded. After a short call everything was arranged.

"The vicar will call you to arrange an appointment to go over hymns, music and eulogy. Would you like the funeral to go from your house?"

Nigel hesitated. He was worried that if the funeral went from the house and the press got to know about it there would be another scrum for pictures.

"I think it would be better if it goes from here, if that is possible. Press and all that."

"I understand. Do call when you have sorted things out with the vicar and we will make the necessary arrangements."

During supper Nigel told them about the funeral arrangements. Afterwards they watched TV for a while, although Laura soon fell asleep on the sofa. Jetlag and lack of sleep were still taking their toll. Fliss made them all hot chocolate and everyone was in bed by 11.00 p.m. Nigel was exhausted, but Fliss was still being amorous and Nigel was not going to turn her down. He had waited too long to have the old Fliss back and now he was able to take his time. At least something good had come out of all the pain. Afterwards they fell asleep, curled together like spoons and slept soundly. Even Ellie had stopped her nocturnal tea and toast picnics in the middle of the night.

Ellie could not face seeing her father in the Chapel of Rest. The image of him in the study would be with her forever. In unguarded moments she would get flashbacks and she knew she was too traumatised to look at his face again, even if they had made a good job of patching him up. She felt guilty because she knew she should support Nigel, but there was no way she could go. Fliss and Laura also decided they did not want to, but Nigel was adamant that he would go as a mark of respect.

The undertaker had done a good job and the coffin was lined with purple silk and lit by subdued lighting and candles at each end. There were fresh flowers on a small table. Trevor was wearing the suit, shirt and tie that Nigel had taken from Trevor's bedroom. He had felt very uncomfortable going through Trevor's things, especially as the policeman stood silently watching him as he rummaged through the sock drawer. He had found a pair of shoes in the bottom of the wardrobe.

Trevor was lying with the missing part of his face turned to one side so that the damage was minimised as much as possible. The half of his mouth that was visible was set in a hard line. Nigel touched his hand. It was rigid and cold. It was not his father – it was a body. Some soft music was playing in the background. He stood quietly for a moment and then felt a tear trickle down his cheek.

"Good bye Dad. Sorry we never got to have that chat. You did your best. Thanks."

A secretary was typing away in Eddie's office and Nigel waved in salute as he left. Strange how normal everything was outside. He had never given a thought to undertakers before, but now wondered how often there were bodies lying at the back of undertakers' offices. He took a deep breath and strode off down the street.

There was still a lot to do. The family had chosen hymns and music and then there were flowers to be ordered. For obvious reasons they decided against an announcement in the paper. Nigel spent a couple of hours writing about his father's life and work. He was confident he could hold it together for the service.

Laura decided that she did want to go to the funeral. As Trevor had not remarried she would not be treading on anyone else's toes. She still felt pretty fragile herself and although she did not want Ellie and Nigel to have to worry about her as well, she felt she wanted to pay her last respects.

On the Thursday she and the girls seemed to spend forever getting dressed in their mourning clothes. Nigel had arranged for a black limousine to pick them up from the house, but the coffin would arrive at the Church from the undertakers. The police had managed to keep the press away from the house, but when they arrived at the Church, there were at least ten photographers crowding round the gate and a police presence was preventing them from getting into the churchyard. They all hurried inside, ignoring the calls from the press. Even though Nigel had kept low key about the funeral, the Church was packed. Some of Fliss and Ellie's friends were there and there were ex-colleagues of Trevor's. Nigel noticed that two men in sombre suits and ties were sitting on their own near the back. He wondered if they were ex-colleagues but something about them made him feel uneasy.

The service went smoothly. Nigel did a reading from Corinthians and after the vicar had said a few words he stood at the front by the coffin and, abandoning his notes, talked about his memories of his father when he and Ellie were growing up and then about his father's devotion to his work and his achievements. As he stepped down he noticed to his surprise that Laura was crying.

The vicar had done his homework and said some nice things about Trevor. During one of the hymns Nigel found himself wondering if the two men at the back were policemen. After the funeral service the vicar walked in front of the coffin as the pall bearers left the Church, Nigel and the family following behind. Friends and colleague queued up to shake hands with Nigel, but the two men had disappeared and were not in the line-up. Nigel made a mental note to find out if there had been a police presence.

The sun came out as the family followed the procession to a newly dug grave some distance from the Church. The vicar said another prayer and the coffin was eased into the ground. Ellie was shaking as she threw the rose she had been clutching on to the coffin. The sound of the earth falling on the wooden lid and the smell of earth was too much for her and she burst into tears. Nigel put an arm round her, but was too choked himself to speak. "The final nail in the coffin." The phrase came to him unbidden. They stood for a short while then turned and walked back towards the Church. Nigel thanked the vicar and then they got back into the waiting car which managed to weave its way past the photographers who were pointing their lenses at the windows of the car. As they arrived home Nigel was relieved to see there were no photographers outside the house.

They had not invited anyone back, but Fliss had bought some canapés and Nigel opened a bottle of champagne. Laura raised her glass.

"May he rest in peace and may those who did this be brought to justice."

Fliss was glad she had suggested Ellie stay until after the funeral. She was very pale and her hand was shaking as she raised her glass.

"What the hell are the police up to? Why haven't they arrested anyone?"

"Who knows?" Nigel replied dryly.

Later, Nigel went into his study and, closing the door, played his father's message again. Hearing the voice after the funeral was surreal. Now that it was over he would wait for the dust to settle and then work on his hunch. He needed to talk to Jeff sometime soon. As he dropped off to sleep that night he was picturing the faces of the two strangers at the funeral. Something told him he must be very careful.

124

CHAPTER 12

Laura decided to go back home a couple of days after the funeral. No amount of pleas from Fliss and Nigel for her to stay for longer made any difference.

"I have to get back to normal otherwise I will turn into a helpless old lady."

They laughed at her as she said this. The thought of Laura giving up was absurd. They all insisted on taking her back and settling her in. Her neighbour, Jane, had stacked the mail neatly on the counter in the kitchen and had watered the plants. Fliss had made up a box of groceries which she unpacked into the cupboards and fridge while Nigel carried the luggage up to the bedroom.

Laura felt as if she had been away for years. Everything looked odd. Even though it was early afternoon she went round switching on lamps, making it look more welcoming.

"You go. I'll be fine."

Her voice sounded strong which made it easier for them to leave her on her own. On the way home Fliss reassured the others. "She'll be fine. She's tough. Let's hope she doesn't go off on another adventure for a long time!"

Once they had gone Laura went upstairs and unpacked. Fliss had done all the laundry when Laura had first arrived home, so all she had to do was put things away and stack the case in the cupboard in the small room. Then she went back downstairs and played back her answer phone messages. There were lots of concerned messages from friends, from the ladies she played bridge with and from the clinic where she worked part time as a counsellor. There was also a message from Jane.

"Hi Laura. Welcome home. Give me a ring when you can and I'll pop round."

Ellie had told Laura that the press had interviewed Jane and she guessed Jane wanted to explain what had happened. She decided to call her once she had gone through the post. Apart from bills and a couple of welcome home cards, most of it was junk mail. She sorted it all out and put the junk paper in the recycling bag she kept in the shed in the garden. The garden was not looking too bad. Someone had cut the lawn – she guessed Jane had been busy or that she had sent her husband round. She put the kettle on and phoned her.

"Laura! Are you home? How wonderful. Can I pop round?"

Jane arrived fifteen minutes later with a homemade lemon drizzle cake. They sat together having tea and cake whilst Laura filled Jane in on what had happened in Thailand. She didn't go into too much detail about Trevor and Jane realised that she didn't want to talk about him. Privately she thought Laura had aged, but that was to be expected. She had lost weight which made her face look drawn.

"Have some more cake, Laura."

After tea and some chat, Laura had more colour.

"Did Ellie tell you about the press calling on me?"

"Yes. She did mention what had happened. I am sorry you had to get involved Jane."

"I hope I didn't speak out of turn. I just told them what a good neighbour and friend you are. They mostly wanted to talk about family issues. Of course that was before ..."

Laura smiled reassuringly. "Don't worry Jane. Things will soon get back to normal and it is great to be home. Thank you so much for keeping an eye on the house."

"It was my pleasure. Did you find out what happened to the baby?"

"She's being taken care of in an orphanage and at some point will probably be adopted. I know I did the right thing."

When she had gone Laura put on the oven and transferred the contents of one of the frozen meals Fliss had left for her into a glass dish. She refused to have a microwave and also never cooked in the plastic containers. She knew the family thought she was being fussy but through her counselling work she had got to know other complementary medicine practitioners and received many alternative journals. The information she had read about food being heated in plastic seemed to make sense. Better safe than sorry, she thought.

A couple of days after Laura had left, Ellie felt she too was ready to go home. It seemed very quiet in her flat after having been with the family for so long. The first evening home she put on some music, switched the heating system on as the flat felt a bit damp, and made some hot chocolate. Then she settled down on the sofa to sort out the new batch of mail that had accumulated since she and Fliss had been there. There was more junk mail, a few bills and several sympathy cards from friends. She then dealt with answerphone messages. It was lovely to hear the supportive voices of a couple of close girl friends, asking about Laura and then saying how sorry they were to hear about Trevor. There were several from Steph and also from Liz and Izzy who she had known since college days. They usually all met up for a meal about once a month. Liz's bubbly voice brought a personal touch to the room and she felt better.

"Hi Ellie. Are you there? How about we meet at the wine bar on the first Friday you are back, at 8.00 p.m.? Just let us know when and we'll make sure we are free whatever! See ya."

After a long scented soak in the bath Ellie put on her soft bath robe and made herself a sandwich from the bag of provisions she and Fliss had bought that morning. She put on a CD and curled up on the sofa with a book, but couldn't concentrate to read. Her mind was in overdrive. She still felt bad about involving the press during Laura's imprisonment and, although Nigel had told her that the break-in would have happened anyway, she knew from the way he was unusually edgy that there were things he was keeping quiet about. Although she suspected there was a link between Laura's dreadful experience and Trevor's murder she could not put her finger on it. And then of course there was the unfortunate woman in Amsterdam. Ellie wondered why she had not been stopped at passport control or customs, as Laura was high profile and she would have thought her name would flag up on their computer system. It was all academic now anyway.

Ellie liked her flat. She had been a nervous wreck when she had first moved in. After leaving University she had moved to Paris to work for a property developer who was setting up a Paris branch of his rapidly expanding relocation side of the business. She spoke quite good French and her Business Studies degree had helped land her a good first job. She had met Louis at a night club. With his dark good looks and sexy French voice she had soon fallen for his charm. Although she had been out with a few guys at University there had been no-one special. This was the first time she had ever realised what that heady feeling of "in love" was about. She was totally out of control of her emotions for the first time in her life and when Louis asked her to his apartment on their second date she did not hesitate. Looking back she realised she knew nothing about him, but at that time nothing seemed to matter. She had never been on the pill. Not having fancied anyone at Uni. she had decided not to mess about with her hormones until she met the right person. She knew a lot of the girls were sleeping with guys they hardly knew and one or two had caught chlamydia. Once she met Louis however, she seemed to take leave of her senses. When she went back to his apartment he insisted they drink brandy with their coffee and after two or three it was so fabulous to have him lift her off the settee and gently carry her to his bed. The room was spinning and she remembered saying, "No, Louis. I don't want to do this. Please let me go. I am not on the pill. I have never done this before."

He covered her mouth with his, kissing and biting and then slid his hands under her blouse, caressing her hardened nipples. She did not want this and yet the brandy was confusing her. Physically she wanted him but she did not want to lose her virginity to someone she hardly knew. She tried to get off the bed but he had his hands up her skirt and removed her panties. She was powerless to stop him. The sharp pain took her breath and then his rhythm built up until she felt an explosion inside her which left her shuddering and breathless.

"You really were a virgin," he said. "Most girls tell you that to get you turned on and the 'no' usually means 'yes' anyway."

Even in her befuddled state Ellie knew that 'no' meant 'no' to her. She was shaking and upset.

He left her to get herself sorted out and by the time she went back into the lounge he had his jacket on.

"I'll run you back to your place."

A cold glass of water in the face would not have sobered her up more quickly. Ellie was furious.

"Is that it? Am I dismissed now?"

"Don't be like that cherie. I have an early start tomorrow."

Ellie did not want him to know where she lived.

"Just call me a cab please. I'll wait downstairs."

He phoned for a cab and then took her down to the security doors and waited with her until the cab arrived. With a wave he was back indoors. Before they set off she asked the cab driver to let her know the name of the street they were in, having already noted the name on the apartment block and the number of his flat. At least she had his first name and his address. Next morning she went to work in a daze. She didn't know enough about French law with regard to rape and also could not face going to the police station and having to have examinations. She realised that if she wanted to do that she should have done it straight away, not the next day, after she had showered. She immersed herself in work for the next couple of weeks, making herself push it from her mind.

She knew immediately her period was late that she was pregnant, although prayed it was just the shock of the experience that had messed up her hormones. Morning sickness kicked in quite soon and a pregnancy test confirmed the worst. She was out of her mind with fear. She couldn't countenance abortion. She had read too much about the foetus feeling pain. She would go and tell Louis. She could go back to England, have the baby and live on any maintenance he could be persuaded to pay and surely she would be entitled to benefits. She also knew that although her mother would be shocked she would be there for emotional support.

It was a rainy Tuesday evening when she took a cab to his apartment block. She waited until a couple came along and after they had keyed in the security code she slipped in with them. She took the stairs to the third floor and, with her heart in her mouth, rang the bell. He was wearing a track suit, his hair wet as if he had just had a shower. It seemed to take him a minute to realise who she was.

"Louis, can I come in? I need to talk to you."

He stepped aside and she walked into the room. The table was strewn with papers – he had obviously been working. He went into the kitchen and came back with the bottle of brandy and two glasses.

"Well. This is nice," he said. "Have you come back for more?"

He gave her a look which told her immediately he was not talking about the brandy.

"No, no. I need to tell you that you got me pregnant that night. I have to talk to you about it. I will go back to England, but I will need some financial support from you." She tried to keep her voice strong although she had to dig her finger nails into her palm to keep from crying.

"That is a very old trick," he said. "You were easy. You have probably done it every couple of days since then. You can't prove that it is mine."

"But you know I was a virgin. I'm not like that. You know I asked you not to. No means no." She took a deep breath, and then said, "What you did was actually rape."

He glared at her and poured himself a brandy.

"You were no virgin," he said "and in France you would be laughed out of court." He drank the brandy and then poured himself another which he drank equally quickly. Then he stood up and walked over to her, grabbed her by the hair and forced her onto the floor. This time he raped her brutally, biting her neck and punching her face when she tried to struggle. Then he stood up, pulled his track suit trousers back on and hauled her to her feet, frogmarching her to the door and throwing her out with her bag after her.

Ellie staggered down the stairs and into the street. She walked in a daze for what seemed miles, her legs feeling as if they did not belong to her. Eventually she got a cab back to her apartment and with trembling hands locked herself in. She went into the bathroom took off her clothes and showered for what seemed hours, until her body was bright red. Then she wrapped herself in a bath sheet and lay on the bed and sobbed.

The bleeding started around 3.00 a.m. She packed towels between her legs but the blood soaked through them and through the mattress. She tried elevating her legs up the wall, but still the blood flowed. She went to the bathroom to get more towels and sheets, but her legs buckled under her and she passed out. When she came round she called for the emergency services and was in hospital having a blood transfusion by 8.00 a.m. A doctor came to see her mid morning.

"I am sure you know you have had a miscarriage. What about your partner? Can he look after you for a few days?"

Ellie needed to sort her thoughts out. If she reported Louis, what evidence did she have? She had no idea of the legal system in France, about DNA testing and what it would do to her work credibility if she were involved in a rape case. She began to sob again and the doctor said he would come back when she was feeling better. She had never felt so alone. She also felt unutterably stupid. How could she have been so naïve? They gave her a sedative and by the afternoon she was able to eat something.

When the doctor came back he asked her about the bruising on her face and thighs. The sedative had made her calmer. She told the doctor she was fine and did not want to talk about it. The last thing she wanted was to have to explain and to have the police involved. In England she would certainly have done so, but in France she felt totally out of her depth. She asked to use the telephone and then rang work to tell them she was sick. She was discharged next morning, the doctor having given up on getting her to talk.

She desperately wanted to talk to her mother, but knew how shocked, concerned and worried she would be. She didn't want to talk to Nigel. For one thing she was too embarrassed and for another she didn't want him coming over to France to sort out Louis. She didn't want to talk to Fliss either as it would be very unfair to expect her to keep the secret. She had to take responsibility for her own actions. She had learned a valuable lesson. She had also said goodbye to trust and hello to panic attacks and nightmares. She tried to go back to work but kept having bouts of depression, so after a few months she returned to London and began temping. That way she could leave whenever things got too much for her. The family knew that she had been ill in France, but she had never told them what had happened. They knew how fragile she had become and thought that finding her Dad had been the last straw.

The music had stopped and she realised she had been lying on the sofa for over an hour. She had just got into bed and turned the light off when the phone rang. It was Laura.

"I just thought I would ring to say goodnight. Hope all is well."

"Thanks Mum. I'm OK. How are you?"

"Fine. It's nice to be back in my own home. What a time we have all had. Once the Will reading is over perhaps we can all get on with our lives." Privately they both knew that life would never be the same again.

CHAPTER 13

The Will reading was surprisingly simple. Trevor's assets were to be divided equally between Ellie and Nigel. As Nigel and the solicitor were joint Executors and Nigel didn't really understand what Probate meant, he was very relieved that the solicitor would take over that side of things. Whatever it cost it would be worth it. What Nigel was not prepared for was the huge amount of work involved in sorting things out. The Will and the house deeds were lodged with the solicitor but the rest of the paperwork – insurances, bank statements, investments, etc., would be in Trevor's office, which of course had been ransacked and then searched. The house had been off limits, apart from Nigel getting permission to collect Trevor's suit and shoes albeit with an escort.

Once the Will was read, the situation changed and soon afterwards he was given permission to enter the house, now technically half his. Nigel was not mercenary, but was somewhat relieved that money would be coming in to cover the bill from Sebastian Dobson. He did not yet know how much it would be, but guessed that it would be very high, taking into account Jeff's time, flights, hotel, etc. He was not sure who would pick up the tab for Laura's flight home, but rather hoped it would be the British Government. Whether they could liaise with the Thais over wrongful arrest was anybody's guess.

Nigel took a morning off to start going through Trevor's study. It felt very strange to be sifting through his late father's things. The chair he had been sitting in when he was murdered had been put back in its place in front of the desk. Nigel couldn't help looking to see if there were any blood stains. There had certainly been plenty on the carpet and someone had covered them up with newspaper, which was still in place. In a way he wished that Ellie or Fliss was with him, although he had wanted to go on his own the first time. He opened the window in an attempt to bring some fresh air into what he still thought of as the crime scene.

The police, or forensics, or whoever had been involved in the search had done a pretty good job at the house and all the paperwork that had been thrown on the floor had been placed into neat piles on the desk and the files they had come from stacked next to them. There was no order to them and it took Nigel the best part of the morning to arrange them back into the correct files in date order. Trevor had been pretty meticulous, so although it was a tedious task it could have been worse.

Nigel went into work for a few hours every day, then went to Trevor's. He made a mental note to call it his and Ellie's house now. He took loads of files home and then spent most evenings trying to make sense of the various documents and making notes of who should be contacted with regard to investments, insurances, etc. He had been prudent enough to get several original Death Certificates which made life a bit easier.

Ellie had sat white faced throughout the process at the solicitors. She still seemed to be very fragile and Nigel was worried about her. She had not been herself since she had returned from France, but that was ages ago, at least eighteen months or maybe even two years, he thought. As far as he knew, she went out occasionally with a couple of girl friends, but never seemed to have a boyfriend. Perhaps when things had settled down he would get Fliss to have a heart to heart with her. He doubted she would open up to Laura. Everyone was trying to help Laura get back to normal after her ordeal and Nigel didn't want to add to her problems and possibly Ellie felt the same. What she had witnessed at their father's home that fateful morning was enough to send anyone into a state, but Ellie had been very nervous and highly strung before that had happened. Nigel knew she was worrying that her part in alerting the media to Laura's arrest and saying that Trevor was writing his memoirs had in some way contributed to what followed. Deep down Nigel thought the same, but admitting as much to Ellie would in all probability tip her over the edge.

It took Nigel a couple of weeks to make all the phone calls, write letters and liaise with Philip Blasey. He was totally exhausted and was grateful that they were being so understanding at work. Fliss was very tired too. She had tried to hold everything together, but the media attention had been a shock. Two or three evenings a week after work she would go round to Laura's to make sure she was OK. Laura seemed to be doing remarkably well, most of her anxieties were focussed on Ellie who had still not returned to work. Apparently the Agency had called a few times with temporary work, but she said she was still off sick. Once a week she and Laura would go out for lunch and do some shopping together. They both went round to Nigel and Fliss each week for Sunday lunch, but Nigel would go off soon after to sort more things out at the house. One Sunday after lunch, Nigel suggested that Ellie went with him.

"It's half your house now, Ellie. I know it will be a trial to begin with, but everything is back in place and you will have to go there sometime."

"I don't want to go. I want it sold. I never want to go there again." Her voice had risen to near hysteria.

Fliss uncharacteristically banged her coffee cup into the saucer.

"Look here Ellie, we've all been through hell – especially you and Nigel, not to mention Laura. It's time we pulled together to get back to normal. Get over yourself."

Ellie's usually white face went scarlet. She seemed too shocked even for tears. Equivalent to a slapped face, Nigel thought, remembering films where the heroine was hysterical.

Ellie looked at Nigel for support, but he just said quietly, "Come on Ellie. You've got to start somewhere or you'll finish up a fruit cake. Get your coat on. We'll all go."

Ellie looked venomously at Fliss, who walked over to her and gave her a brief hug, but not for long enough to encourage a bout of crying.

"Come on. Get your coat. We'll clear up afterwards."

Laura had been in the kitchen topping up the coffee pot and came back in when she heard raised voices. Ellie looked at her pleadingly, but Laura, aware of the atmosphere, put down the coffee pot and asked where everyone was going.

"Back to Trevor's. Do you want to come?"

Nigel's words hung in the air as the enormity of the suggestion sunk in. It would obviously be a trial for Ellie, but the thought of Laura going into Trevor's domain, his private world which she had not been privy to for so long, seemed at that moment even more difficult. There was a momentary silence, all eyes on Laura. She took a deep breath, looked at her highly distressed daughter and said, "Yes, of course. I'll get my coat too, but I am coming to support all of you. I don't want to nose around at any of his things or personal effects. But as it is your house now, I don't see any reason not to come." Fliss, as practical as ever, put some milk and sugar into a bag for the inevitable tea.

Nigel had the key and let them in the front door. He guessed he would have to have one cut for Ellie at some point. Although she was shaking, Nigel realised it would have been worse if they had gone round the back. The kitchen window had been repaired and everything was tidy although the house had an air of neglect. Laura went out into the back garden and came back with some roses which she put in a vase she had noticed on the window sill. She then started to make tea and somehow the sound of the kettle breathing and the brightness of the flowers changed the atmosphere. Ellie stayed near her mother. There was no way she was going upstairs.

Whilst the others were up in the study, Laura made herself useful with the vacuum cleaner. There were white powder footprints on the carpets together with twigs and leaves that had been trodden in from the garden. After an hour she called them down for a cup of tea. They each had an armful of files which Nigel said they could sort through at home. She had not realised just how much there was to be done.

"Do you want to get a gardener in to at least cut the grass? It's pretty bad and you do have such a lot to do."

Nigel wandered out into the back garden and sat on the bench whilst he drank his tea. His mother was right. The garden was a mess, but there was still this little niggle in his head that he had not had time to think about and at that moment his subconscious was telling him not to have any strangers at the property. He glanced round the garden, at the apple tree and the shrubs that were in need of attention, at the holly threatening to choke the clematis and at the dandelions, a strange riot of colour between the old dried daffodil heads and leaves. He noticed that the terracotta pots had been emptied. Some of them were upside down. He took his tea down to the garden shed, checking that everything there was in order. He needed to talk to Jeff soon.

They left around 6.00 p.m. Ellie was much brighter and helped make sandwiches back at Nigel and Fliss's and then they all watched television for a couple of hours. Ellie drove Laura back and stayed with her for a while.

"You OK now?" Laura's voice was concerned.

"Sorry Mum. I don't know what comes over me. After all you went through and here am I making a fool of myself."

Laura looked at her shrewdly. "You weren't right before all this business. Perhaps some day you will tell me about France. I found it very difficult to talk about Thailand, but once you get through the pain barrier it is a huge relief. Think about it." Ellie was surprised at her mother's perceptiveness.

"Thanks Mum. We'll all get through this. I'll give you a ring in the morning. Good night."

When she was gone, Laura got ready for bed but found she could not sleep. She wrote in her journal for a while and then turned the light out again, but still sleep would not come. Everything seemed to be in a state of chaos. Nigel having to deal with all Trevor's affairs, Fliss trying to keep the peace and Ellie obviously hanging on by a thread. As for herself, she realised she was going to have to get back to her old routine. There would be questions from friends and strange looks from others, particularly at the bridge club and probably the W.I., but at least the media frenzy had died down and she really needed to get herself back to some normality. She hadn't felt up to resuming her counselling and had been referring clients to a colleague. Her mind often went back to the baby. She kept the photograph of her in her bedside drawer and looked at it every night, saying a prayer for the little girl's happiness in the future. She was so grateful that Jennifer had gone to the orphanage and taken the photo for her. Perhaps she would try to get in touch with her at the office although she doubted she would have any news. Perhaps Jennifer would be allowed to give her the name of the orphanage and she could telephone to see how the baby was. On the other hand, having convinced the Thai authorities that she had not been abducting a baby, perhaps she ought to do nothing. She was eternally grateful to have her freedom and still woke up some nights with the memory of the dreadful smell in that cell. Even now she was still having stomach problems. Perhaps after a few more weeks she could talk to the family about her feelings. Nigel would sort it out. Poor Nigel. With that thought she finally drifted off to sleep.

Nigel couldn't sleep either so he got up, poured himself a brandy and sat on the sofa thinking things through. Fliss was back to being too tired for sex and after such a passionate interlude, Nigel felt disappointed. On the other hand he too was quite exhausted and realised that the upheaval of sorting out all Trevor's things plus dealing with Ellie, not to mention keeping an eye on Laura, had drained Fliss. She was back at work and most evenings had a lot of marking to do. Nigel would be patient. Eventually, when Ellie and Laura were back to some semblance of normality, perhaps they could have a holiday, just the two of them. He didn't say as much to Fliss but found himself thinking how right he had been not to give in to her broodiness. The last thing they needed in the middle of all this was a screaming baby. She hadn't mentioned it lately so perhaps she too had gone off the idea. They had good incomes between them and now some money from Trevor's estate, so they could really let their hair down and have some great holidays. Perhaps when Trevor's house was sold, they could even think about moving up market again.

Trevor's last cryptic message went round and round in Nigel's mind and he now had a hunch as to what it meant. He also knew that something sinister was going on and needed to talk to Jeff about it. He decided to ring Jeff in the morning, but from the office. He guessed he was being paranoid, but since the telephone had been removed and then replaced he couldn't help thinking it was bugged. Too many spy novels he told himself somewhat unconvincingly. The brandy kicked in and ideas floated round in a slightly incoherent way. He gradually became drowsy and took himself back to bed around 2.00 a.m. Fliss was sound asleep making the gentle snoring sound she always did but vehemently denied. Nigel went to sleep immediately.

In the morning he was up first and made the coffee. Soon he could hear Fliss in the shower, so he put some toast on for her. She came down dressed for work in her smart grey suit. She looked tired but still very pretty and he felt a rush of love for her. He gave her a hug and she gave him a disconcerted look.

"What was that for?"

"Just because."

"Thanks for the toast Nigel, but I need to get to school very early with all these papers. See you later." She gave him a kiss and was gone.

Nigel ate the toast which was cold and drank some more coffee before having his shower and getting ready for the office. The train was on time and he managed to get a seat and read the paper on the way to town. As it was Monday, there was not too much mail or too many emails. Frank seemed relieved he was back more or less full time again and Nigel would be eternally grateful for the support he had received from his boss. He dealt with some urgent paperwork in his in tray, gave his PA a stack of correspondence to deal with and then phoned Jeff. It seemed ages since they had talked, although it must have been just before the Will reading.

"Hi Jeff. It's me, Nigel. Any chance we could meet for lunch today?"

"Let me take a look at my agenda. Yep, no problem. Where do you want to go?"

"I need somewhere we can talk privately Jeff. What about the Italian near your office? My shout."

Jeff watched Nigel as he scanned the menu.

"You've lost weight Nigel. Need feeding up a bit!"

"Well, in that case I'll have a large pizza and a large glass of red."

They sipped the wine whilst waiting for their meal.

"What's up? Any further developments?"

"All seems quiet on the Western Front. Have you seen the Mafia since the funeral?"

Nigel was glad he had chosen somewhere quiet. He realised he would have been paranoid to be having this conversation with Jeff in a busy pub. He told Jeff about the Will, about the family going round to Trevor's house and the fact they had not turned up anything that shed light on Trevor's message. The pizzas arrived and they ate in silence for a while. Nigel ordered another glass of wine. Jeff declined as he was driving later.

"I think the house phone is tapped."

Jeff stared at him, a piece of pizza poised between the plate and his mouth.

"What?"

Nigel told him about his study telephone having been taken away and then returned.

"But, if that was by the police for the forensics, there isn't a cat's chance in hell it was tampered with. And how did they get to the house phone? Nigel, you've been watching too much television."

Nigel looked at him gravely.

"We'll see." he said. "Remember the tree when we went on that trip to the canal? And those guys I told you about at the funeral, the Mafia as you call them? I did ask the police, and they denied any presence at the funeral. Dad would never have left that message if there had not been something very big afoot. Don't forget, I rarely heard from him. You went over the top helping me with that fishing episode and I am grateful. I want you to take a deep breath and do something else for me. Say no if you really don't want to get involved. I have a hunch about Trevor's message and if I am correct this whole business is out of our league, but I want to get to the bottom of it."

Jeff changed his mind and ordered another glass of red. For a while he did not speak and then said "OK. What do I have to do? I'm not equipped for sweeping your house for bugs or checking the soles of your shoes, but anything else and I'm your man."

He was laughing as he said this, but Nigel, with his newly

polished paranoia had already removed his shoes and was inspecting them carefully at the dinner table. He then realised that if they were being watched it would look as if he was suspicious so he said in a loud voice, "I think I have a stone in my shoe."

The wine kicked in and they both began to laugh. After a few minutes Jeff looked at him seriously and said again, "What?"

Nigel leaned across the table and began whispering to Jeff, "I think I know the answer to Dad's riddle and I think I know where he hid whatever it is he wanted me to find, but I don't think it is safe to retrieve it. To make sure I am going to make a call from home to the bank and tell them I want to set up a safe deposit box for some of my father's valuable items, to be redeemed once we have sold the house. If I am right, something will happen and we will know the phone is tapped."

Nigel paused for breath, looking expectantly at Jeff who was looking back at him in stunned silence. Nigel continued, "I'm going to do it tomorrow. Don't phone me of course. I'll call you when I get back to the office. If anything happens to me don't do anything for a while, just let the dust settle. I'll be OK of course, but just in case …."

Nigel leaned over the table and whispered, "The answer may be under the holly bush at Dad's, but if anything happens to me then it won't be safe for you to look there."

Jeff looked at Nigel, his glass paused half way to his mouth. If Nigel was in any doubt that he had gone too far, this moment would have been the moment of truth. Jeff took a mouthful of his wine before speaking.

"You are serious aren't you! I know what happened at the canal, but this is getting out of hand. I can't believe you just said all that. When I said I would help you, I didn't envisage all this cops and robbers stuff! And if for one moment you are right, which I doubt, they – whoever they are – are obviously not to be underestimated. I don't think you should do this bank trip Nigel. I think you need to go home and go to bed with a couple of aspirin."

"I can't see any other way round it. If I make the call to the bank and there is some intervention, then it will never be safe to check the holly tree. I know what you are thinking – how can they check the back garden all the time! Believe me Jeff, if my phone is bugged then Dad's garden is probably not safe either."

"But why the bloody holly tree for God's sake? Like I said Nigel, get some rest and we'll talk again."

Nigel was quiet for a moment. Then he leaned over and continued to whisper. "It's down to you really Jeff. When you said it was a cryptic message it reminded me that Dad was a cryptic crossword buff. Before they split up we used to try to do some of the clues as a family. Dad seemed to have what Mum said was a warped mind! He was so good at them. I remember thinking when I first heard the phone message that it was a pretty cryptic message. That was the clue of course. I thought about it for a long time before coming up with the answer. 'I'll expect you at the other canal.' Ilex is holly. I got that far but couldn't work out the rest. Then it dawned on me! The other canal! What is another canal, Jeff?"

Jeff looked at him blankly. "Grand Union? We've been down that route. Kennet and Avon? I dunno."

"Other canal." Nigel whispered. "What about 'root canal'? 'I'll expect you at the other canal' would be a great crossword clue for holly root!"

"Sounds more like Hollywood to me!" Jeff laughed at his own witticism.

"I'm serious Jeff! It just feels right. I need to do the experiment with the safety deposit box, just to prove, or disprove a point. If nothing happens, I can do some gardening. If not, then we will need a Plan B and if, God forbid, anything happens to me, I want you to take over."

"Right, Chief Inspector Barnaby." Jeff raised his glass and added, "Be careful! Not that I believe a word of it!"

They finished their pizzas in silence. Nigel drank his wine feeling disappointed and rather stupid. Like a schoolboy caught on a prank.

Jeff finally broke the silence. "Think about this for a moment. Why not have a Sunday lunch party in your old man's garden. Sorry, your garden now! Ask the family of course, and close friends, a sort of goodbye to Trevor and hello to a new life. Tell them it's a garden party with a difference. Everyone who is invited will be asked to

142

weed a small patch of garden and put in the bulbs or seeds or plants that you will ask them to bring as a living tribute to your Dad. You make sure you do the holly bit. At least it will put your mind at rest. If you want me to come, I will and then I can make sure everyone is distracted when you are in that direction. I will bring my wife too. It's about time she met you! After all the time I have spent with you it would be no wonder if she thought I had a bit on the side! If anyone is watching, they will have a job to make sense out of anything we are doing." If Jeff was being ironic about anyone watching he managed to keep a straight face, although the idea of anyone hidden in a tree with secret cameras was not, in his opinion, a remote possibility. If Nigel needed humouring, then he would go along with it. Particularly if there was a party involved.

Nigel knew this was the most sensible suggestion. He had been caught up in his own private spy story. Yet he was still determined to make that call to the bank. He had a safety deposit box at home and also an old collection of Trevor's cigarette cards. Cops and robbers indeed.

"Thanks Jeff. Quite understand. I'll think about it, but in the meantime I want to get a security box to the bank. I'll call you."

"Look Nigel. I'll go along with what you say but let's have the garden party first. As I said, no-one will make any sense of what we are doing, even the guy sitting on the roof with binoculars!"

Nigel glared at him. "That's not funny!" When Jeff did not reply he continued, "OK. You win. But as soon as the party is over we'll test the water so to speak, and whether I find anything or not I really want to do this."

Nigel paid the bill and they parted outside the restaurant, Jeff walking back to his office and Nigel back to his to explain why he was so late. Both of them looked over their shoulders as they walked along the street. There were no strangers in dark suits. Just a guy in an open-necked shirt and grey trousers mingling with shoppers and sauntering behind Nigel and a dark haired bespectacled man with a Waterstone's bag tagging along behind Jeff.

CHAPTER 14

Nigel explained to the family that a proper garden party would help tidy up the mess in the garden and make the house more saleable. After a couple of ifs and buts from Ellie it was deemed a good idea. They all agreed on having it the following Sunday. The weather promised to be good and once they were enthusiastic it seemed as if the sooner the better. Fliss rang a couple of friends who agreed to come to 'The Gardening Party' having had the chores part of it explained to them. They appeared glad to hear that things seemed to be getting back to normal. Ellie asked Steph along with Liz and Izzy, who were equally delighted, having been worried about Ellie for a long time. Laura said she would ask one of the ladies she played bridge with and her neighbour, Jane. Jeff's wife, Ann, agreed to come. There would be quite crowd and there was much planning of shopping, menus etc.

"It doesn't have to be a full blown meal." Nigel knew he sounded churlish, but his mind was consumed by his cops and robbers theories.

"I thought paella and Sangria with extra beer and wine. Then strawberries and cream. Easy." Fliss was always good at these sorts of events and in spite of working long hours, Nigel knew she would cope. It would also give Laura and Ellie things to do.

The week seemed to pass quickly. Nigel was making more headway with the paperwork and finally some cheques were arriving. There were a few old insurances plus a life cover and other bits and pieces coming in. There were also free issue shares from a building society, not that they amounted to much, but they all had to be dealt with.

Nigel was sent on last minute shopping duties early on the

Saturday morning. Fresh fruit for the Sangria, the booze, nibbles, etc. Laura and Ellie had bought chicken and prawns the day before. None of them was keen on squid but Ellie had developed a fondness for mussels in France, so Nigel bought them on the Saturday so they would be as fresh as possible. They took everything over to Trevor's – they still called it "Dad's" – late on the Sunday morning and, whilst Ellie and Fliss made the paella, Laura cut up French sticks and made pretty butter curls. Nigel had checked there was ice and Fliss had found a large yellow tablecloth which looked lovely spread out on Trevor's big garden table.

The guests began to arrive around 2.00 p.m. carrying an assortment of plants, pots, bulbs, shrubs and bottles of wine. Jeff brought a bottle of brandy. His wife, Ann, was a pretty blonde woman, probably in her late forties. They all liked her immediately. Nigel trusted Jeff and knew that he would not have divulged anything of their fears to his wife, although she was of course au fait with the Thai situation and the subsequent media frenzy. She made a point of talking to Laura and Nigel heard her saying, "So, at last we meet. As you can imagine I have heard so much about you from Jeff. I must say you look very well. Let's hope today is a new start for all of you."

Nigel thought her very diplomatic. There was no hint of commiserations, just a practical 'Let's move on' attitude. A bit like Jeff he thought uncharitably.

The lunch was a huge success and fired up with Sangria and wine they all decided to wait for the strawberries and cream until later on in the afternoon. Ann was the first to start on the garden. She had brought a couple of pairs of gardening gloves with her, so she gave Laura a pair and together they began to clear weeds from the flower beds. Fliss's friends had brought their partners, who made short work of cutting the lawn, whilst some of the women filled the pots with compost and others dug holes for planting. Jeff organised everyone, making out he had a plan for tall shrubs at the back and smaller plants in front. Nigel had no idea if he knew what he was doing, but was grateful he was keeping people away from the bed near the holly.

Nigel knelt down at the base of the bush, trying to control his excitement and the tremor in his hand. There was no doubt Jeff thought he was mad and it was all Nigel could do at that moment to believe in himself, now that it was crunch time. He forked round the front of the bush and then when the hilarity round him seemed louder than ever he prodded round the back. He guessed that if he was right, Trevor would have hidden whatever it was in some sort of haste. After a short while he unearthed a tiny package wrapped in a small piece of polythene. His hands were trembling as he palmed it and then pretended to be weeding a bit further along, putting it in his pocket whilst pulling out a tissue, to make it look as if he needed to wipe his nose. He knew he was being paranoid but was being extra careful. His heart was pounding wildly as he straightened up and walked over to the table and poured himself a small shot of brandy. As he turned, Jeff glanced at him and he gave him the thumbs up sign. Jeff grinned broadly.

Everyone continued working, and as they fortified themselves at regular intervals the conversation and laughter became louder as the afternoon progressed. At length people began to sit back around the table to admire their handiwork.

"Well done Nigel and everyone. Look, we have an instant garden." Fliss held up a glass of orange juice and proposed a toast.

And indeed they had an instant garden. The beds were full of leaf and flower and colour, the lawn neatly trimmed and the mad idea was vindicated. Fliss put on some music and made some more Sangria. Those who were not driving got very merry and the others were caught up in the happy atmosphere. The strawberries and cream were much appreciated and then people began gradually to drift away.

"Lovely afternoon. Thanks so much for asking us." Ann gave Laura a hug and kissed Fliss and Ellie.

Fliss was flushed and happy although she had only been drinking fruit juice. "Need to keep a clear head. Nothing worse than a drunken hostess," she said. "And anyway, one of us has to drive."

Ellie and Laura were already doing the washing up when Nigel folded away the last of the chairs and came in to wash his hands.

"Won't be a minute" he said, disappearing into the toilet.

"Trust a man to be caught short when there's drying up to be done," Laura laughed.

Nigel locked the door and sat on the closed seat of the toilet. He pulled the little packet out of his pocket, feeling like a junkie about to shoot up. He unrolled it carefully. It was a memory stick. He looked again in the wrapper but there was nothing else. He sat there for a moment, thinking that presumably only a few short weeks ago his father had wrapped it up and taken it to the holly bush. When had he done it? Did he back up regularly and keep hiding it, or had he realised he was in danger? Nigel was aware of a banging on the door.

"Come on Nigel. Laura is in the upstairs loo and I am bursting."

He put the memory stick back in the wrapper and put it in his pocket.

"Coming. Sorry Ellie. Be my guest."

For a moment he thought the safest thing was to hide it in the shed, but somehow he did not want to part with it. He would find somewhere secure at home and wait until he had time and privacy to look at it on his computer. The Sangria and brandy were making him elated. He needed to be very careful. He even had the ridiculous thought that his father was playing a trick on him from the grave and that all he would find would be a Mickey Mouse movie. The thought made him smile as he came out of the toilet.

"What are you laughing at?" Fliss was eyeing him from the corner of the kitchen.

"Nothing. Just happy. What a great success. Welcome to our half of the house."

He kissed her just as Laura came back into the kitchen. "That's a nice sight," she said.

They all had coffee in their new garden, the last rays of the sun lighting up the flowers, some of which were already closing their petals for the night. Before they left Nigel popped up to the study and found Trevor's collection of old cigarette cards. He remembered his Dad showing them to him when he was little, but they had obviously not been touched for a long time. He had no idea if they were valuable, but they would serve his purpose. Ellie drove Laura back, Nigel locked up and Fliss drove home. He scanned the street as they left, but there were no parked cars with occupants. Once again he wondered if he was being paranoid. How on earth would "they" have been able to monitor the garden anyway? But he had already realised that he was playing with forces he did not understand.

Whilst Fliss was preparing for bed, Nigel held the memory stick in his palm and wondered where the hell he was going to hide it. It needed to be away from the computer, just in case, although God forbid that they had intruders like Trevor. He didn't want to carry it on him, but could not think of anywhere to hide it where Fliss, or anyone else would find it. He half wished he had left it behind the holly. On a whim he put it at the bottom of the leather bag containing his binoculars. Fliss never used them and they were stacked away on a shelf in the spare room with his old school reports His curiosity as to the content of the stick was overwhelming, but he not only needed to be patient, he needed to be sober.

His head was spinning slightly from the Sangria and brandy so in spite of the excitement he was asleep the minute he put his head on the pillow. He vaguely heard the alarm and Fliss get out of bed, but the next thing he knew was Fliss shaking him and telling him there was strong coffee in the kitchen and he had better get a move on. She kissed him on the cheek and he could smell the fragrance of her, fresh from the shower. "Bye," she said. "See you later".

As soon as she had gone Nigel thought about fetching the memory stick and seeing what was on it, but he wanted to phone the bank first to make the appointment to take in the safe deposit box. He drank his coffee and ate some toast, willing the hands of the clock to get to 9.00 a.m. He had a rather frustrating time trying to get through to the bank whilst listening to appalling music. Eventually, having listened to the blurb about the call possibly being recorded for security purposes and, having run the gauntlet of pressing various numbers, he got through.

"Nigel Jones here. I need to bring in a safe deposit box with some of my late father's things. Sentimental value really. Do you need to know what is in it? I'd like to call in around 11.00 tomorrow morning."

The assistant manager he spoke to sounded about sixteen. Nigel was beginning to feel middle aged. After having gone through some more hoops, giving them his account number, confirming that he was the sole account holder, his password, postcode and house number he was finally told that the bank definitely did not want to know what was in the box.

He then rang Jeff, praying he would have got to work early. Jeff answered immediately, sounding slightly hung over.

"Hi Jeff. Nigel here. Thanks for coming yesterday. It was good to meet Ann. Hope you both enjoyed it."

"Great party Nigel, thanks."

"Jeff, I need to run by you a couple of things that have emerged about Mum. I need to have the contact details in Thailand just to tie up a couple of legal points. I also have to go to the bank at 11.00 tomorrow morning with a safety deposit box which has some items of Trevor's in for safe storage. Better safe than sorry after that break in! Is it OK to pop in afterwards? I'll try to be with you before lunch. Just 10 minutes if you have time."

"Fine Nigel. See you tomorrow."

Nigel hung up and then, in spite of his anxiety about what was on the memory stick, went to work. He needed to know what he was up against, if anything, but at the moment was too anxious to spend the morning looking at it when he should be at work.

The day went by uneventfully and he and Fliss spent a pleasant evening talking about the success of the party. He was up early the following morning and, after Fliss had gone, he showered and dressed. When they had moved into the house they had stored a few pieces of jewellery and some mementoes in a safe deposit box and a friend had looked after it until they got straight. He went and fetched it down from the wardrobe in the spare room, resisting the temptation to get the memory stick from the binocular box. He put Trevor's cigarette card collection in the box, locked it and put the key in his pocket. He made sure the front door was securely fastened behind him as he went out to the car and put the box in the boot. He tried to look nonchalant as he checked the road for strange cars whilst backing out of the drive, but all looked normal. He decided that he would park in the station car park, which was almost opposite the bank, and carry the box across the road. He was half prepared in his mind for a smash and grab robbery, but at least he would know. The other half of him thought that perhaps nothing would happen, that Jeff would have a laugh and that Mickey Mouse would indeed be on the memory stick.

He had only gone a short way when he realised there was a problem with the car. He was finding it difficult to hold the steering and there was a rumble from one of the wheels. He managed to pull over and stop. He got out and walked round the car, looking at the tyres which were all intact. He was furious. If his hunch was right 'they' would be waiting for him at the bank. He had visualised a car screeching to a halt in the car park and men in dark glasses would leap out and snatch the box as he was unloading it from the boot. A delay like this would mess it up entirely. He got out his mobile phone and rang recovery. Whilst he was waiting he went round again to the back of the car and bent down to prod the tyres. That was the last thing he remembered before waking up in hospital.

Apparently by the time the recovery service had arrived Nigel was unconscious on the pavement, Two passersby had already called for an ambulance, which arrived shortly afterwards. Fliss was the main ICE number on his mobile and she arrived at the hospital about an hour later, having driven from work in a state of shock and panic. Nigel was being examined when she arrived, so she had to wait in the waiting area and no-one seemed to know anything about what had happened or how he was. Eventually a young doctor came over to her and said Nigel had sustained a blow to the back of his head which had knocked him out. They were going to run some tests on him to ascertain whether he had concussion and also whether he needed a scan. Fliss could see him briefly before they began more investigations. It was not a life threatening injury, but as Nigel appeared to have no memory of the event, the police had been informed, as it seemed that he had been attacked from behind. Someone had already called the police to tow the car away. The doctor was sorry that he had no information as to its whereabouts.

When Fliss finally got to his bedside Nigel was propped up in the bed looking pale but with no obvious sign of injury. She went over and kissed him on the cheek.

"Nigel. What on earth happened?"

"I have no idea. I remember leaving home to go to the bank to take Dad's cigarette cards for safe keeping and then there was a problem with the car. I called the recovery services and I think I went round to check the tyres but that is all very vague. I don't remember anything else until I woke up in here. I have a blinding headache and they are going to run some tests."

"Oh Nigel. What a dreadful thing to happen on top of everything else."

"Fliss, I really need to know what happened to the car and whether the safety deposit box is still there?"

"Don't worry about that now Nigel. When I leave here I'll contact the police and find out what has happened. I imagine they will come to see you."

"Fliss. This is very important. Please call Jeff and tell him what has happened. He was expecting me this afternoon. I need to speak to him urgently. Just trust me on this and don't give him any details over the phone. Just the bare facts."

The young doctor appeared round the screen. "Sorry Mrs Jones. I must ask you to leave now as we need to run a few tests on your husband. You can call us later and we will tell you when you can come in again."

Fliss kissed Nigel. "Don't worry about a thing Nigel. I'll get on to that as soon as I get back."

CHAPTER 15

Fliss went straight home and, although she wanted to phone Laura and Ellie immediately for some moral support, she kept her promise to Nigel to phone Jeff. Luckily she found Jeff's work number on his card which they kept in the little ashtray along with cards from taxi firms and tradesmen. Her voice was shaky when she got through. She wondered, uncharitably, when it would all end.

"Jeff, this is Laura. Nigel has had an accident and is in hospital. It is not too serious but he may have concussion so they are keeping him in for a while to run a few tests. Apparently he was on his way to the bank when it happened. The car has been towed away by the police and Nigel is anxious to check that nothing has been stolen. Can you possibly make a few calls to see if you can track it down?"

Jeff took charge immediately. "Good God, Laura. This on top of everything else. Yes, of course I will. What is the registration number?"

"Hold on Jeff. Sorry, I don't know it by heart." She went over to the key cupboard and took down the spare set of Nigel's keys which had a tag with the number on.

"Do you want me to call you when I have some news Fliss? Presumably Nigel won't have his mobile switched on in the hospital."

"Thanks Jeff. I'll just phone Laura and Ellie and then will keep the line free. If by any chance I am not here I will probably have had a call to pick up Nigel." She gave Jeff her mobile number and rang off.

Neither Laura nor Ellie was at home and Fliss did not want to alarm them by calling their mobiles, so she left messages for them to call her back. She sat for a long time just thinking. Deep down she did not think this was a random robbery, just as she did not believe

152

Trevor's break in was a random robbery. She needed to hold things together for the others, but felt decidedly spooked. All she could do was wait for the phone to ring. She got up and put the chain on the front door, then sat down again and made herself do a Suduko in the paper. Laura always made her laugh by calling them "Sodding Uko's" as she found them difficult. She was more into words and loved crossword puzzles. Apparently when they were married, she and Trevor had that in common. Fliss smiled to herself, grateful that she and Nigel had more in common than a crossword puzzle. They both loved entertaining, had taken a wine buff's course and also loved walking together, especially by the sea. She felt guilty that she had been a bit hard on Nigel in the months before all the trouble, but she had been deeply upset by his refusal to have a family. She jumped when the telephone rang to interrupt her reverie. It was Jeff. The car was being held securely by police whilst it was fingerprinted. The CD player and radio were intact. There was nothing in the boot other than a spade and a tin of gentles.

"What are gentles?"

"Er, well Fliss, they are maggots."

"Maggots? What on earth were they doing in the boot?"

"Er, well, Nigel and I had talked about going fishing, so perhaps he was preparing for it."

"Fishing?"

Jeff changed the subject hurriedly. "Let me know when the old boy is home and I'll pop over."

Fliss was able to pick Nigel up early in the evening. He still had little recollection of what had happened, but there was no brain damage and his skull was intact. This could not be said of his mood. He was furious with himself. He had just not envisaged his car being tampered with. He also had a splitting headache which pain killers did not seem to have touched. He desperately wanted to lie down and pretend none of it had ever happened. He even resented Laura for having gone to Thailand in the first place. Fliss listened to him rant, told him he could not have an alcoholic drink and was making him a cup of tea when there was a ring at the door.

"If that's a visit from Mr Plod, I'm not at home!"

Even if she had wanted to, Fliss could not have made Mr Plod believe that, as he could obviously hear Nigel shouting as she opened the door.

"So sorry to disturb you, Mrs Jones. I guess you are used to us by now. I'm afraid I do need to ask your husband some questions about what happened today and to inform him of the whereabouts of his car."

Apparently there was no damage to the body of the car and nothing was taken apart from the security box. There were two wheel nuts missing on one of the wheels and the car would be released once it had been fingerprinted. Nigel was less than polite when he was asked how much he remembered and made it obvious that he was not going to be very helpful.

"Before you start, I don't remember anything. OK?"

"Of course, Mr Jones. Just a few questions if you don't mind. Can you remember when you first noticed the car had a problem?"

"Not really. I just remember pulling over and getting out to inspect the tyres. That's the last memory I have. The hospital said it looks like I was hit from behind. Perhaps someone saw me put the security box in the boot and was following me. Who knows? Another random burglary and another knock on the head. Have you arrested anyone for my father's murder yet? You've had long enough."

"Do you think you may have been followed, Mr Jones? Can you remember looking in your mirror when you pulled the car over?"

"What part of 'I don't remember anything' do you not understand?"

When Fliss finally showed the policeman out she whispered an apology. "He's had a shock and has a splitting headache. Sorry about that."

"No worries. Understandable after all that has happened. No doubt we will be in touch soon."

Fliss sat down on the sofa next to Nigel. "See? That wasn't so bad was it?"

"That" said Nigel forcefully "is just the beginning. I give it twenty-four hours and we'll have Special Branch back."

154

Fliss desperately wanted to question Nigel about the attack, about the security box and about maggots, but wisely decided she would sleep on it. Jeff phoned Nigel on the mobile and, although Nigel would rather have been sleeping off the headache, he told Jeff he could call in around 8.00 p.m. If he had thought they would have finished supper by then, he was mistaken as first Ellie called and then Laura, responding to Fliss's earlier call. Ellie predictably went into a state and suggested that Nigel should consider buying a German Shepherd and having wrought iron security gates. Laura went into Mum mode and said she would make them an apple pie. They were still finishing supper when Jeff arrived.

"Sorry Jeff. You'll have to have tea. Nigel can't drink whilst he is on these painkillers and I think the sight of you or me with a glass of something would just about finish him off."

After loading the dishwasher Fliss excused herself and went to have a bath. Jeff sat down and looked at Nigel.

"So, you were right, Nigel. Sorry I pulled your leg about cops and robbers stuff. I suppose you were dicing with death – almost literally. Have you looked at the thing yet?"

Nigel noticed Jeff didn't say 'memory stick' and even with his headache wondered if Jeff had caught the cops and robbers bug and thought the house, as well as the phone, might be bugged. "Presumably you mean the print out from the insurance. No, not yet." They looked at each other conspiratorially and chinked their tea cups. Fliss insisted on cups and saucers in the sitting room. Mugs were for the kitchen.

"It's good of you to come over, Jeff. Sorry about the tea. If anyone makes me any more tea I will throw it over them. Tea for this, tea for that – I'm awash with the bloody stuff. I could do with a stiff brandy, but my head feels as if I have had six already. Sorry I'm so edgy. I'm sure I will feel better in the morning and perhaps I can pop in to your office for a chat?"

After Jeff had left Nigel was sorely tempted to look at the memory stick, but he was not sure if Fliss was going to bed after her bath or would interrupt him and in addition the headache was still vicious. He decided to do it as soon as Fliss had left for work in the morning. Fliss had phoned Frank who sounded resigned to yet another fiasco in the Jones' household. Nigel knew the office would not expect him in so soon after the incident, so he could finally find out what all the fuss was about and then report back to Jeff later, from the secure environment of his office. The pain killers had dulled the pain a little but he felt very disorientated. The enormity of what had happened was beginning to sink in. Whoever wanted access to Trevor's memoirs had actually tampered with the car and attacked him. He could have been killed. He felt highly anxious about the family being involved too, but was impotent to do anything about it. If his theories were correct, then asking for police protection would fall on deaf ears. These people, whoever they may be, were obviously above the law. He wondered if there was some sort of hierarchy. The invisible big boys at the top, controlling and filtering down through heaven knew what agencies –perhaps even Interpol, judging by the murder in Amsterdam – right through to Mr Plod, so no-one actually questioned orders because it would all seem to be going through the right channels.

The following morning Nigel woke up with a muzzy head, but the extreme pain had gone. Fliss however was unwell. She had been sick and seemed to be going down with a bug. Whilst feeling sorry for her, Nigel really wanted her out of the house. He made her black coffee and encouraged her to drink some water. After a while she began to feel better.

"There is a bug going round and one or two of the others were off at the beginning of the week. As I left early yesterday, I really ought to try to go in. If I can't cope I'll just have to come home."

Normally Nigel would make sure she was back in bed with a hot water bottle if she was poorly, but he found himself almost encouraging her to go.

Once she had gone he finished his coffee and then went up and retrieved the memory stick from its hiding place. He found that he was shaking as he inserted it into his computer.

It seemed to be an untitled copy of Trevor's memoirs. Nigel felt a mix of emotions including disappointment that there was no note for him. He had half hoped for a 'Dear Son, If anything happens to

156

me I want you to have this copy of my memoirs and for you to know what a great son you are.' He felt angry that his father's life had ended so violently and sadness that they had never been able to talk. But the most overwhelming feelings were curiosity mixed with fear as to what he would find after all the cloak and dagger stuff of the previous weeks.

Nigel was in for the long haul. It was a lengthy document, starting with Trevor's early days in the Civil Service and his rise to recognition during his times in the Far East and in the Middle East. Nigel remembered his father coming home from one of the trips. He had brought home a carved bear for Nigel, a doll for Ellie and a long pipe which bubbled through water. It had stood above the fireplace for years.

There was no mention of the long separation from home, just information about the telecommunication systems over there. That was in 1972 and afterwards there were details of other foreign trips and a factual report of "Black September" and the situation at that time in Jordan.

Nigel skimmed through page after page of how Trevor had worked his way up and what he had thought about various personalities that he had seen as difficult characters during his career. There was a lot of information about the politics of the time and about foreign policy. At no time did Trevor mention home life or family.

After about an hour Nigel's headache threatened to return so he went and made himself coffee and a piece of toast and brought it back to eat at the computer. As he resumed his reading Nigel thought there was nothing that had been worth hiding. Perhaps his father had a grandiose idea of his own importance. Nigel plodded on until he reached the early nineties and realised that the tenor of the writing had changed. By then, Trevor was working in Whitehall, with odd trips to GCHQ. He wrote about being instructed to attend a meeting at a house in Catford. His superior would not give him any details, but told him that it was of a highly confidential nature. Nigel felt a tingle of apprehension as he continued reading.

I found the house and was let in by a middle aged man, quite smartly dressed, who did not introduce himself, but showed me into a large dining room. There were two others present who identified themselves as John Sharpe and Peter Hills. They showed me their passes from GCHQ and as the meeting progressed I realised their true roles were in procurement and management of the SAS and other secret agents. They had apparently been watching my performance and, as they said, 'dedication' over the years and needed a 'front' to co-ordinate operations between MI5, MI6 and the SAS. I was to be the link and the less each member of the Secret Service knew about the others, the better. Each member had an appointed task which they undertook with no questions asked.

Nigel was dismayed that this was the last mention of the 1990's and that Trevor's narrative jumped forward to 2007. The style had again changed. It was as if what had transpired was either so traumatic or dangerous that even as he wrote his memoirs, Trevor was afraid of stating his role during those years. Or, Nigel later thought bitterly, ashamed. He read on.

I am now retired from all that and am getting old. I have never betrayed the Official Secrets Act, but as time goes by there are many things I was party to which weigh heavily on my conscience.

Nigel felt his heart begin to pound. Trevor talking about feelings and opening up about his work was so out of character. He continued reading in a state of high anxiety.

These things cost me my marriage, closeness to my children and, unless I unburden myself, may cost me my sanity. Of course, unburdening myself may now cost me my life, but I am prepared to take that risk. We were so brainwashed that it almost became a game and I truly believed then that she had to go, but now I can't believe I was party to such evil. The red herring of the Fiat Uno seemed brilliant at the time and was so easy to organise.

Nigel's mouth dropped open and his heart was hammering so hard in his chest he thought he would have a heart attack. He read the paragraph again and found himself talking out loud. He just kept saying, "No. No. Not that, Dad. Not that!" With a growing sense of dread he continued to read.

The power of the International spy network was unstoppable – right down to the details of the lighting in the tunnel and the delays. Now my own children are grown, the depth of my shame for those boys is unbelievable. Now I am out of it, I wonder how I could have been party to any of it, but we were so brainwashed about the security of the state and long term consequences and also so far along the chain that it all seemed normal. I have wondered if that is how the Gestapo and SS came to commit such atrocities.

Mohamed Al Fayed will eventually have his day in court, although when is anybody's guess. Nothing will come to light. There has been so much hype and media reporting over the years, and of course the extreme expression of grief at the time, which sent reverberations around the paparazzi and press, totally masking the truth. The other thing that will probably happen is that by the time the grieving father has his say, he will be so incensed that he will make outrageous claims and any grain of truth will be obliterated and he will lose any vestige of credibility.

The case of the journalist was different. It was complicity by silence. She had made a BBC appeal in early April 1999 and then on April 23rd there was the bombing of the Radio-Television Serbian building by British and US planes in which 16 employees were killed. There had to be reprisal, but if we had been seen to protect her it would have been obvious that we had infiltrated Serbian intelligence, although we actually could have intercepted. They moved quickly and she was killed soon after. At the time it seemed to make more sense to allow it to happen than not. I remember it reminded me of the parachute drop in Crete during the Second World War – another case of lambs to the slaughter and complicity by silence for the same reason.

We knew earlier that month that plans were being made and so it was easy to set up a fall guy. Although it was inevitable that at some time he would be released, there have still been no links made to the real perpetrators, and if at some point there are links then there will never be an unbiased enquiry. In hindsight it is now hard to understand how we – the collective 'we' in the employ of our masters – could countenance such things, which is why I have to unburden myself.

The final turning point for me was the 'suicide.' Once again all the cogs move towards the same goal. The Hutton enquiry was rigorous about David Kelly's distress concerning his involvement in the weapons of mass destruction and the forty-five minutes remark. It did also cover the fact that Bahai's do not condone suicide and that David was in fact a Baha'i and had been for some years. Little regard was given to the email he sent shortly before he went on his last fateful walk in which he issued a warning of 'many dark actors playing games.'

It was unfortunate for him that by discussing intelligence matters with Gilligan, he had in fact breached the Civil Service code. At that moment he became a smoking bomb. His years at Porton Down and subsequent work in Iraq had given him the expertise to have an expert opinion on the weapons of mass destruction.

In time it will be realised that the release of medical records and the results of the post mortem have never been made public. Some of those who know the truth wield power and I prophecy that this information will never be published during the lifetime of all of us.

Dock Green moves slowly at the best of times. And of course over the years I have learned so much about moles. Press moles; Government moles; Police moles – all with their little pink noses underground, silently digging the dirt until they come up blinded by their own cleverness at having caused such destruction.

I realise of course that all this must not be published in my lifetime, apart from which, no reputable publisher would touch it. And as for the press – would they dare? Even now I fear for my life, but in a strange way I feel more at peace having set it down. And I am truly sorry to have been complicit. I am not really Secret Service material at all.

Nigel sat staring blindly at the last page for a long time. Every now and then a word here, a sentence there, would leap out at him, but the overall realisation of what it meant was just too awful to think about. And yet he had to. Here, in black and white, was verification of what many had whispered about for years. In black and white. In

160

his father's memoirs. Trevor Jones. Father of Nigel and Ellie Jones. Trevor Jones, deceased.

Suddenly Nigel found himself crying. First of all a few tears and then great sobs. The shock was profound. What he had just read defied belief. He felt that all he had believed in had crumbled in front of him. His father, the government, the country, the judicial system, honesty, values. After a while he pulled himself together and made himself re-read the final pages, almost wishing he had made a mistake, that the words would somehow unscramble themselves and make some sort of sense, some sort of dignity about his father and his career. It also registered with him that, apart from David Kelly, his father had not actually named names. It was as if the secrecy that he was sworn to spilled over into the document. Or it could be that naming would make the reality too much for Trevor to bear. No-one would ever know now.

Nigel then became angry. What a legacy. His father had made sure that Nigel would be the first person to know the truth and he did not want this burden. He sat for a long time staring blankly at the screen, trying to compose himself. He then removed the memory stick and switched off the computer. He found he was shaking badly as he put the memory stick back in its hiding place. At that moment he had no idea what to do next. No wonder his father had been a target once poor naïve, gullible Ellie had told the press that her father was writing his memoirs.

Nigel went into the kitchen and sat at the counter with his head in his hands for a long time, thoughts churning round in his mind. He was totally dumbfounded. Was this how the Secret Service worked? Recruiting seemingly ordinary Civil Servants who would never be suspected? Then presumably came the grooming process, the stepping up of the PV process and who knew what else. Ellie, of course, must never know. Even as he thought this he realised that to protect Ellie, nobody could ever know. Then there was his mother. How on earth would Laura feel if she realised the man she had been married to for all those years had been party to such evil. And what about Fliss? She already knew something was up. They had never had secrets from each other, but this was not just a secret. This was a ticking bomb. And then there was Jeff. Good old Jeff who had held his hand all through this mess. Did he owe it to Jeff to come clean? And would that be fair? And how much more of a ticking time bomb would it be if Jeff knew too? The more people who knew, the more likely it was that someone would tell someone else and eventually the news would break. First as rumours and then with explosive reports. And what about the nation? The great British Justice System. The inherent good nature of the British nation. The whole constitution in jeopardy for the greater good. And would it be for the good? Wasn't it the Queen herself who said something like 'There are forces at work...' She would never have suspected just how powerful those forces were. Yes, some people would get satisfaction if the news broke, but the price would be such a political, even global, seismic shock that the country might never recover. And what about France? And what about reverberations in the Islamic world? The enormity of it was all too much and Nigel felt totally overwhelmed. After all the whispers, the conspiracy theories, the so-called revelations, here, in an ordinary house in Clapham, Nigel Jones had been handed information he wished he had never seen. And all because an elderly woman had found a baby. How many were involved? The faceless, nameless men who were party to such evil. Nigel could see in his mind a stack of dominoes which reached up into the sky come crashing down on him in an unstoppable cascade. He didn't want any of this. For a moment he wanted to smash the computer, smash the study, burn and destroy any knowledge of Trevor Jones. On one level he realised his thoughts were out of control, not making any sense. On another level the Observer Self watched him and waited to see what he would do next.

He took the memory stick out of the computer and put it in his pocket. He then went upstairs and washed his face in cold water. The face reflected back at him from the mirror was colourless. Thank God, he thought, that he could see no resemblance to Trevor. All these revelations had to be buried with his father. All this knowledge had to be put somewhere else in his head. He went downstairs, had another coffee and phoned Jeff.

"Sorry, a bit later than planned. Fliss was not well this morning and got off to work a bit late. OK if I come over now?"

Before he left he had the presence of mind to go back to his computer and clear the cache. He was not sure why, but a voice in his head prompted him. "Better safe than sorry." As he did so he suddenly had another thought. What if none of it was true? What if Trevor, having written about the boring stuff, suddenly decided to write a fictional novel ending to his memoirs? There was no proof. Yes, that was it, another conspiracy theory. He managed a wry smile to himself and, double locking the front door, set off to meet Jeff.

By the time he got to Jeff's office it was nearly lunchtime, so they decided to go to the Italian.

"How's the head, Nigel? Able to stomach a glass of red and a pasta? You still look a bit under the weather. Not surprising really."

The restaurant was busy with young women on their lunch breaks, a few men in suits and some 'ladies who lunch.' They managed to get a table for two in a corner. The restaurant was noisy and the smell of Italian food suddenly made Nigel feel hungry.

After they had ordered Jeff leaned across and talked in a quiet voice to Nigel, who was decidedly and understandably very twitchy.

"Now, tell me what happened? Presumably they tapped the phone or they wouldn't have known about the security box. And presumably they tampered with the car? Whilst it was on the drive? Bit risky. In the night I suppose?"

The wine arrived and Nigel took a mouthful before replying.

"Can't remember much I'm afraid, Jeff. Guess you are right. Of course there were only cigarette cards in the box. Not worth a great deal. They, whoever 'they' are, must have been disappointed, but it served the purpose of knowing they are still after the information."

"Have you had a chance to look at it yet?"

Nigel made an effort at eye contact and told Jeff that he had not had a chance yet.

"Aren't you curious old boy?"

"Of course I am, but I need time when I will not be interrupted. I promise to tell you as soon as I know what it's all about."

The lie hung between them for a moment. Nigel took a large mouthful of wine.

They finished lunch and chatted for a while about whether they thought the police would find any evidence about who had hit Nigel and taken the box, but both knew they would come up with a blank. Apparently there were no witnesses, although the local press were putting in a piece asking for witnesses to come forward to help the police. Nigel hoped that would not alert the press again. He didn't want a repetition of the last fiasco, and although he was sure it would not be necessary, he would call Ellie and Laura and tell them not to talk to the press just in case they called. Nigel said he thought Ellie and Laura were spooked by the latest turn of events but he hoped to see them later.

"Well, I'd best get back to work. Some of us don't have the excuse of a knock on the head to take a sickie!" Jeff stood up and turned to leave.

Nigel followed him. "I think I may go in for a couple of hours." He still had a headache, but knew he did not want to be in the house on his own until Fliss came home. He needed distraction. He just couldn't think straight about what had happened and work suddenly seemed an attractive alternative.

He tapped on Frank's door on his way into his own office.

"What the hell are you doing here? I thought you were supposed to be a zombie, not walking wounded!"

Nigel grinned at him. "With our luck lately, seems this is the safest place to be."

As soon as the words were out of his mouth Nigel regretted them, but Frank, blissfully unaware of the sinister undertones, laughed as he took a phone call.

Nigel worked through the afternoon. He had more or less caught up on the backlog of work and was almost up to date. He sent Fliss a text, saying he was at work but would get an early train and hoped she was feeling better. Should they have a takeaway? She sent a text back an hour later, obviously in the staff break, and asked him to bring in a Chinese. She was obviously feeling better. Nigel got to the Chinese restaurant around 7.00 p.m. The staff remembered him from many previous visits, but also because of the publicity. They greeted him warmly and asked how he was. For a moment he felt quite a celebrity. Their small stature and dark straight hair took Nigel back to Thailand and although there was a difference in appearance, the obvious similarities made his heart beat faster. As he sat and waited for his order he allowed his mind to return to Trevor and the memory stick. All afternoon he had resolutely pushed it from his mind, mentally putting it in a trunk with a padlock every time it threatened to invade him. Now it was as if the very magnitude of it had forced the lock and it was there with an overpowering force. He had no idea what to do or where to turn. There was no-one he could trust to tell and to put the burden on family was not only unfair, but dangerous. With the best will in the world, women gossip! He trusted Fliss implicitly, but how unjust to hand her a smoking bomb! And even if none of it was true, once the lid was off Pandora's box there would be no going back.

"Missa Jones?" The voice interrupted his reverie and he stood up and keyed in his credit card number and walked home, carrying a brown bag smelling fragrantly of fried rice, chicken and black bean sauce, cashews and sweet and sour prawns. In spite of his anxieties he suddenly felt hungry again. Once home he put the food on the kitchen counter and went upstairs to wash his hands and take the opportunity to put the memory stick back in its hiding place.

Fliss had opened a bottle of chilled white wine and set the table with candles and the decent cutlery.

"What's this in honour of?"

"Just because! I'm sorry I've been a bit off colour. It's you who need spoiling! I couldn't believe you had actually gone in to work! How's the head?"

"Fine, thanks. I met up with Jeff for lunch. He's equally puzzled by the attack. They must have had a disappointment to find just cigarette cards!"

Nigel began to feel a bit more human.

"I don't understand what you mean, Nigel. If you mean what I think you mean, then you are inferring 'they' whoever 'they' are, knew there was a safety deposit box in the boot. Unless the house was watched while you loaded up, why target you? Do you mean it was not random? Just like Trevor?"

Nigel forked up some chicken and rice and chewed slowly, giving himself time to think. There were no flies on Fliss. This was one of the things he loved about her. She was so shrewd and he felt bad for not confiding in her.

"I don't know what I mean," he lied. "I'm obviously not thinking clearly. Don't take any notice darling."

Fliss ate in silence, an ominous sign in itself. He guessed there would be a grilling at some time. She was looking much better, but drank only water. After they finished their meal they settled down on the sofa to watch some TV, their evening interrupted twice as both Laura and Ellie rang to see how Nigel was feeling. Fliss went up to bed around 10.00 not having broached the attack again. Nigel was relieved and, pouring himself a small brandy, sat down to watch some more TV, but couldn't concentrate. His mind would not shut down no matter how hard he tried to control it and none of the strategies worked. He was desperately tired which made things worse. At one point he felt that the wretched memory stick was boring a hole through the binocular box, through the wardrobe and floorboards and physically entering his head. He got up and washed down two paracetamols with a glass of water, turned off the TV and went to bed. Fliss was asleep, her dark hair just peeping above the duvet. He had a shower, brushed his teeth and quietly slipped into bed beside her.

He thought he would be in for a restless night, but the next thing he knew was the alarm going off at 6.30 a.m. Fliss was already up. He put on his slippers and dressing gown and went downstairs. The kettle was hot, but there was no coffee made. He thought he could hear Fliss in the downstairs loo. He walked down the hallway and tapped on the toilet door.

"Fliss. You OK?"

"Yes thanks. Just a bit queasy. Think something in the Chinese has set me off again. I'll be OK in a minute."

Nigel went back to the kitchen and made the coffee. He felt strangely guilty, as if his accident had given Fliss yet something else to worry about. He realised, not for the first time, that it was all his family that were having the problems. Poor Fliss. She really had no family support of her own, just Nigel and all this chaos.

She came out of the loo looking rather pale, had a sip of coffee and flew upstairs, late for work. She came down a short time later looking as immaculate as ever. Nigel privately thought it very clever that whatever she did to her face in ten minutes from her magic make-up bag worked such miracles. She smiled at him brightly.

"Don't worry. I'll make a slice of toast in the staff room. I'm fine."

After she had gone Nigel could smell the lingering fragrance of her perfume.

The paper arrived and he made himself some toast and read the headlines before setting off for work, somewhat late, but he had a good excuse with his head injury. As he was shaving he had noticed he was sporting a slightly black eye. A badge of honour, he thought. Even as he thought it, the word "honour" stuck in his throat. What honour. The son of…Just as he was going into one of his distressing reveries, the telephone rang. He toyed with the idea of leaving it and just getting off to work, but decided to answer it. Mr. Plod himself.

"What time would it be convenient to call in for a chat, Mr Jones?"

It was on the tip of Nigel's tongue to say it would have to be in the evening after work, but the last thing he wanted was for Fliss to be more alarmed.

"How long will it take? If it's quick, you can come now and I will ring my office and tell them I am working from home for a while."

He made the call to Frank and then set to work on his laptop, answering some emails and generally keeping his mind off the memory stick which seemed to be consuming most of his waking hours.

Mr Plod arrived around 9.45 a.m. Nigel was polite but distant. He didn't offer tea and it was as much as he could do to offer a seat.

"We have finished examining the car, Mr Jones. There are no fingerprints. The boot lock was forced, probably with some sort of screwdriver. It would not have taken a practised thief a second or

167

two, although it was rather risky with passersby, but it seems no one noticed anything. However, it is clear that the wheel had been tampered with and that someone had wanted to force you off the road."

Nigel's mind said, "I know," but his voice said, "Really? Surely not?"

"Did anyone know you were taking a safety deposit box to the bank?"

"Only the bank and my wife. And my lawyer."

"Thank you, Mr Jones. We will of course need to interview the bank staff, but at some time I would like to speak to Mrs Jones and your lawyer."

"Is that really necessary, Inspector?"

Nigel hated himself for promoting Mr Plod, but wanted some leeway in getting off the hook. "My wife has had a lot to contend with lately and is most unwell. I really don't want her upset anymore."

"Sorry, Mr Jones. Just doing our job. We'll be in touch once we have spoken to the bank, and do you have a number for your lawyer?"

When he had left, Nigel headed off for the office. He should not have been surprised that the police had found the car had been tampered with, but even so he felt shocked. These guys seemed to be an invisible force – like fighting smoke. As he left the house to walk to the station, he found himself looking over his shoulder, crossing the road twice, quite unnecessarily and felt the now familiar throb in his head. He was very glad by the end of the week to have his car back and the insurance claim in place.

CHAPTER 16

Laura settled in quickly considering what she had been through. She had received several calls and letters offering her money to sell her story to the press.

"I am not interested, thank you," and she would ring off without getting into conversation.

She resumed bridge, which she used to enjoy. Most of the ladies were either married or widowed. Sometimes if someone new joined the group she would hear the others wondering if the newcomer was divorced or widowed. She sometimes felt like wearing a badge round her neck with the sign "divorced", but basically they were nice people with kind hearts and widow's pensions, or wives of retired business men, which allowed them to do things and talk about things that were out of Laura's league. She also played regularly with three of the ladies from the club, privately in each others' homes. She realised when she first resumed playing that she had obviously been the subject of much speculation. Not surprisingly, of course. So she told them the bare bones of what had happened without going into any of the awful details of the cell. She also glossed over Trevor's murder and once it was all out in the open they got on with the serious business of calling No Trumps. After a few weeks she started to see clients again. She was never very busy, but enjoyed helping people and the little money she earned helped with the bills.

Laura had known one of her friends, Clare, since they had their first jobs after school and it was when she met up with her that she could let her guard down and really open up about all of it. Clare lived in North London and was happily married and had a busy life, so they didn't meet often, but when they did it was very therapeutic for Laura and they always managed to get a fit of the giggles, like they had done all those years ago.

Her neighbour Jane was very supportive and would sometimes pop round for tea and a chat. What with all that and visits to or from Ellie and Sunday lunch in Clapham, life was full. She was a bit concerned about Nigel. He was sporting a few grey hairs round the temple and was very dark under the eyes. She knew that if she asked him anything she would be accused of fussing. She loved Nigel dearly but sometimes he could have a caustic turn of phrase. Laura suspected that there were undercurrents about the whole catalogue of disaster that he was keeping to himself. She was pleased he and Fliss were happy together and just wished Ellie would find someone. Since their conversation about Paris, Laura had not broached the subject again. Ellie knew her mother was there if she wished to confide and Laura decided not to pry. Gradually Laura put on a bit of weight and began to put the horrors of her so-called holiday behind her.

As for Ellie herself, she had resumed part-time temping and seemed to be having some good evenings out with her friends. She thought that at some point she might enrol in an interior design course. She couldn't afford to have anyone in to spruce up the flat which was getting a bit shabby and some ideas of what she could do herself would be good. Nothing expensive. She browsed through some magazines, cutting out ads for correspondence courses and devouring the sections on make-overs. Yes, in general life was good and she was grateful to be in her own home, but she found that she was getting restless.

Back in Clapham, probate was taking longer than Nigel thought, but gradually he was getting through the paperwork. He had a chat with Ellie and they decided to put Trevor's house on the market as soon as everything was signed and settled. Nigel had received the invoice from Dobson and although there could be no price on getting his mother home, the magnitude of the bill stunned him. He kept it from Fliss until one evening she asked him about it. He went to his study and came back with it for her to see and as he handed it over he told her not to worry. Once the money and the house were sorted out it would not be a problem. In the meantime their joint salaries were quite good and the bank would lend them some money until everything was resolved. Fliss handed it back silently, looking a bit pale.

"Don't worry, Fliss. It's all under control."

That night Fliss slept fitfully and in the morning was queasy again. The schools were off now for the holidays so she went back to bed. Nigel had some emails that he could do from home so hung around for a bit to make sure she was OK. She got up around 11.00 a.m. just as he was thinking he should go in to the office. She had put on a pair of black trousers and as Nigel turned to look at her he thought she had put on a bit of weight.

"You're looking more like your old self Fliss, in spite of being under the weather. You had lost a bit too much weight."

He knew enough about women not to comment on her having put weight on, and thought he was being very tactful. Not tactful enough, he thought, when she burst into tears. He put his arms round her and made reassuring noises. She pulled away from him and perched herself on a kitchen stool by the counter, dabbing her eyes with a tissue and making gulping noises as she tried to stop crying. Nigel felt as helpless as most men do when women cry. He poured her a glass of water and waited.

"Fliss, what is it? Is it the strain of everything? You have been strong for everyone and I am so proud of you."

Fliss took a deep breath and then, in a strange, shaky voice said, "Nigel. I'm pregnant."

Nigel's jaw dropped. "You can't be, Fliss. You've been on the pill for years. It's just the strain of the last weeks."

Fliss made a big effort to pull herself together. "Sorry, Nigel. The whole business of Laura and the baby and all the talk of her not having grandchildren just made it worse. I had been telling you for a long time how badly I wanted a baby but you took no notice." She stopped talking and kept her eyes averted.

Nigel felt his heart rate go up and found he was clenching his fists. "So, you didn't take the pill?"

"No."

"Without asking me?" His voice was clipped and didn't sound like Nigel at all.

"Nigel, I had asked you a hundred times and you had refused."

"But we had never discussed actually trying for a baby, had we? Had we?" he repeated, shouting at her now. "How dare you do this to us Fliss."

He began to pace the kitchen floor and then stopped dead in his tracks, a new realisation dawning on him. "And so those passionate nights when I thought I had got my wife back were when you were using me as a sperm donor."

Fliss's face shuddered as if she had been struck. "Don't you dare speak to me like that. You are my husband and I love you. I just wanted your baby. When this has sunk in you will be pleased. And think about Laura…"

"Don't use my mother as a pawn in your little game."

Fliss got down from the stool and went across to put her arms around Nigel, but he span round on his heel, grabbed his coat and bag from the hall and slammed out of the door. Fliss knew that it would be bad but had not expected anything like this. She took herself back up to bed and curling up into the foetal position cried herself to sleep.

She woke up with a splitting headache just after midday, went downstairs and looked out onto the drive. The car was gone so she assumed Nigel had stormed off to work in the car instead of getting the train, but just as she was about to go back upstairs to splash cold water over her face the telephone rang. It was Frank.

"Sorry to disturb you Fliss. I was after Nigel. Is he coming in to work or is he working from home all day? It's just that there are a couple of things I need to run by him and I he's not answering his mobile."

"He's not here at the moment, Frank. Sorry I can't be more helpful. I'll get him to call you if he comes in before he gets back to you."

Fliss went upstairs and washed her face. She felt a bit queasy but made herself have some soup. The row with Nigel had upset her dreadfully. She put her hands flat on her tummy. "Hello little one. Take no notice. It will be all right."

She had read scare stories about stress being bad for the foetus and this added to her distress. She desperately wanted to talk to someone but did not want to confide in anyone until she had made up with Nigel. She had never seen him so angry and by 3.00 p.m. when she had no news she began to worry. She had tried his mobile several times but it was switched off.

After Nigel had slammed out of the house, he was so furious that he wasn't sure what he was doing or where he was going. He just got in the car and drove. There was no way he could go to work in such a state. He had somehow managed to compartmentalise the shocking revelations on the memory stick whilst he decided what to do about it, but Fliss's news was the last straw. He felt betrayed and trapped. He drove for a little over half an hour without noticing where he was going and then saw a sign to Leatherhead. From there he joined the M24 and was able to put his foot down in the fast lane and let off some steam. His chaotic thoughts were distracted finally when he found himself in Worthing. He parked the car at a hotel on the front and realising he should eat something went in and ordered a beer and a sandwich. He sat near the window and watched the sea for a while. Afterwards he went for a walk along the stony beach. It was quite windy and he began to calm down. He didn't know why he was there, but knew he did not want to go home.

He stopped and picked up a handful of pebbles, walked down to the sea edge and began skimming the stones along the water. There were quite a few kids playing in the water and some families had made themselves comfortable on the stony beach with windbreaks, sun loungers and bivouacs. Out on the horizon he could see a cruise liner. There would be hundreds, perhaps a thousand people on board, sunning themselves, swimming, drinking, playing cards and yet from the shore the ship looked like a matchbox toy. From the deck those who looked landwards might see a faint strip of coastline. Nigel would be invisible. That, he decided, was how he felt. He had never felt so adrift.

He walked back to the promenade and into the town where he bought a toothbrush and some toothpaste before sitting at a pavement café and having a coffee. He wished he had bought a newspaper to hide behind and to distract him from his thoughts, but had to just be a people watcher for a while. Being holiday time, the town was heaving with holiday makers – toddlers, kids in buggies, young children with ice creams. Kids everywhere. To Nigel they seemed an irritating and noisy distraction. He fiddled with the plastic bag containing the toothbrush and paste and wondered what the hell he was doing. He knew he ought to phone Frank. His boss had been more than understanding with the Laura affair, the death of his father and then the attack on him and subsequent hospitalisation, but this unscheduled absence would in all probability be pushing it too far. He pulled out his mobile phone and switched it on. He could see a message from Fliss and one from work. He didn't want to read them but sent Frank a text. "Sorry Frank. Something has come up that I have to deal with urgently. I can work the weekend. Nigel". The weekend seemed another planet, but he owed it to Frank to toe the line once he had his head together. If ever, he thought. He then switched off the phone.

Nigel paid for the coffee and walked round the town and into the memorial gardens. Even in there, children were running around, their parents ignoring the 'Please Keep Off The Grass' signs. He found himself thinking that a holiday with kids was his idea of hell. He went back to the hotel and although a part of him wondered what on earth he was doing, another part of him went through the motions of booking a room for the night. They had no single rooms. The hotel was nearly full but they could offer him a double for one night only. Would he want dinner? The thought of mooching round the town on his own looking for a decent Italian restaurant was not appealing, so he said yes. He also thought that the restaurant would be better than sharing space with casual trade in the bar.

He signed for the room and was surprised that he had to think hard to even remember the car registration number. He took the key swipe card and then the lift to his room. If the receptionist noticed he had no luggage, she made no comment. Before he opened the door he knew what the room would be like. Double bed with heavy cover, thick curtains, windows that did not open, TV, tea and coffee making facilities and a cupboard for a toilet and shower room. It would suffice. The last thing he could face was a confrontation with Fliss, but at some point he knew he would have to make contact.

He lay on the bed and allowed the thoughts to come in. How dare she trick him in this way? Not only had she broken his trust but he felt mortified that he had been fooled into thinking he had his passionate, sexy wife back. Gradually realisations dawned on him. The slightly thickened waist, the early morning sickness. What an idiot he had been. He just could not get his head around Fliss of all people being so devious. Yes, his throwaway remark about being a sperm donor had been cruel, but true. He bunched up his fists and punched the bed.

It was nearly 6.00 p.m. He wondered if Frank had phoned home, if Fliss already knew that he had not gone to work. Good. She could worry. He could picture her making herself busy whilst waiting for news, like she had when they were waiting for news of Laura. On the other hand he could still picture her stricken face with tears brimming in her eyes as he had stormed out. He knew she had been a rock for him through all the troubles. Problems with his mother, his sister cracking up, his father's murder. She probably would have liked the support of her blood family in all this. Certainly she had made friends at the school, but they were really just colleagues that she socialised with from time to time. She had no close friends that she could confide in. Her life had been her work and Nigel.

He propped himself up on the bed and let the thoughts tumble round in his mind. Yes, she had told him on many occasions that she badly wanted a baby, that her clock was running out and he had always told her he wanted to wait until their finances were more stable. Now, with Trevor's legacy, they would be much better off. Why had she not felt she could talk about it to him? His mind went back to the memory stick. He now thought of it as an incubus – evil permeating from its hiding place into his very soul. He had walled himself off from it, finding it too horrific to deal with and not knowing how to handle it. When he had returned from Thailand he had been exhausted and then with his father's death he had been pushed to the limit of his stamina, plus the fact that since the attack on him he did not feel particularly safe in his own home. He vaguely wondered if he had been followed to Worthing. 'They' would be pretty confused if he had. No, if he were honest he would have to admit that he had been pretty unapproachable and the strain on Fliss had probably been more than she could cope with. Even so, what she had done was unforgivable. The anger welled up again and he got up, went into the bathroom and had a quick wash. Fliss could stew for a bit longer and then he would phone. He picked up the key card and went down to dinner.

He ordered steak, fries and a bottle of red wine. He felt that ordering the wine was putting the seal on his not returning that night. He wondered if he was having a nervous breakdown. He put his hands out in front of him, but they were as steady as a rock. As he lowered them he realised the waiter was hovering with the wine.

"Sorry," he said, feeling foolish. There was only one other lone diner, an elderly man who had immersed himself in a crossword whilst eating. Other than that, the other diners were either couples or families. Nigel drank the first glass of wine quickly, before the food arrived. The steak was perfect and it was a long time since he had had chips. Fliss made sure they ate healthy foods and she had banned chips. He had more wine with the meal and then ordered coffee which he drank before finishing off the bottle. He felt decidedly tipsy as he walked to the lift. He knew he was walking stiffly, trying not to look as if he had drunk too much. Back in his room he sat on the bed and put the TV on. There was nothing that interested him and he knew he was just putting off the moment when he would have to contact Fliss, so he switched it off again.

He wondered if Fliss had contacted Ellie or Laura and if so whether she had confided in them. He really didn't want either of them worried. They had had too much anxiety lately and his having had a serious row with Fliss would not go down well. Then he wondered suddenly, what if she told them about the baby, and about his behaviour. Baby? "Baby." He found himself saying it out loud and the very word stuck in his throat. He couldn't countenance that a child, his child, was growing in Fliss. His analogy of an incubus came unbidden into his mind. This was not a baby. It was a minute piece of living tissue that had nothing to do with him. It was Fliss's doing and she could get on with it. As these thoughts swam round in his fuddled mind he realised he was drunk and that he was in no fit state to call Fliss. He had already said something pretty awful and he needed to simmer down, sleep it off. He took the coward's way out and sent Fliss a text, refusing to read the three that had now come in from her.

"Not taking messages. Need to calm down. Am safe, don't worry. Will call you in the morning. Lock up."

He couldn't bring himself to put AML as they always did on messages. He didn't know where or what All My Love meant for him at this moment. He cleaned his teeth, stripped to his underpants and got into bed.

The room was pitch dark because of the heavy drapes and Nigel slept deeply until a nightmare awoke him at 5.00 a.m. He dreamed he was on a rock, cut off by the tide. The waves against the rocks threatened to suck him into the teeming ocean and he was having difficulty keeping his balance on the slippery rocks. He sat up in bed, his heart racing, and put on the bedside light. He had a splitting headache, so made himself a cup of tea and took a couple of the painkillers the doctor had given him when he had been knocked out. He then had a shower and cleaned his teeth. He wiped away the steam on the mirror and stared at the unrecognisable man looking back at him. His eyes had black bags under them and the dark stubble round his chin made him look macabre. He got dressed and sat on the edge of the bed, thinking. Whatever else was going on he realised he needed his job. Somehow things would get sorted out at home although he was still seething. The incubus upstairs needed to be dealt with, either physically or in his mind, but his job was of paramount importance. Frank's patience must be wearing thin. He opened the drawer in the apology for a dressing table and took out a sheet of headed paper.

"Had to leave early. You have my credit card details. Call me on my mobile if you need confirmation of security code. You can bill me at the following address." He carefully printed his name and address and his mobile phone number, signed it and then took the lift down to reception. No-one was about so he put the note on the desk together with his key card and left. He knew he should have eaten something and hoped the bottle of wine was through his system. The last thing he wanted was to lose his licence.

CHAPTER 17

Whilst Nigel had been walking along the beach Fliss had been beside herself at home. She knew she had behaved very badly in what she had done, but had been unprepared for such a violent reaction. She sat for ages on the sofa thinking things through. She knew Nigel had been under unprecedented pressure and since the funeral he had been extremely tetchy. Maybe she had chosen the wrong time to tell him, but when would have been the right time? She felt she had done her bit, supporting him through the whole Laura drama, looking after Ellie after she had found Trevor, the whole nightmare had been totally about Nigel's family and whilst she had willingly held the fort, it seemed that her needs had fallen on deaf ears. She too was angry. Nigel's words about just being a sperm donor had hurt her to the core, perhaps partly because she knew she had tricked him. She had not taken the pill and had deliberately seduced him when she knew she was ovulating. What sort of a wife did that? Maybe it was impossible for a man to understand the deep longing a woman has for a baby and once she hit thirty-eight she had become increasingly desperate for a child. Even her breasts ached when she saw women with their babies. Every time she had tried to talk to him he had refused to countenance having a child, so she had taken unilateral action. As she sat thinking she realised that it would indeed turn their world upside down. Things would certainly be easier with some extra money from Trevor's estate, but she would have to stop work, at least for a while. The whole balance of their marriage would change. And did she really want to go back to work and leave a child with a nanny or au pair? Fliss knew that Laura would be thrilled to be a grandma, but it wasn't about Laura. It was about conception by deceit.

She got up from the sofa and made herself a cup of tea and then started cooking. She always found that therapeutic and it also made her believe that Nigel would be back for supper. She made a large pan of chilli con carne and it had just started simmering when the phone rang. She dashed over to answer it, but it was just one of her colleagues from school trying to organise a girls' night out. Mechanically Fliss wrote down the date and venue, hoping she sounded enthusiastic. Then she got out the telephone book and rang the hospital. As soon as they answered she hung up. It was far too soon to phone police and hospitals. It was only 6.00 p.m. and perhaps Nigel would be in any minute. Whilst the meal was cooking she went back into the sitting room and put the TV on to watch the news. If there had been an accident she was sure it would be on the local news.

When Nigel had not arrived by 7.00 p.m. and her texts were unanswered she was highly anxious. The chilli was ready, but she had no appetite. Perhaps he had gone to Ellie's or Laura's. She wondered if she should ring them. She needn't say she was trying to track down Nigel. She could just say she had phoned for a chat and that Nigel was working late. They would soon tell her if he was there. She poured herself a glass of wine, remembered she should not be drinking and tipped it away before phoning Laura. There was no answer and she realised that it was Laura's bridge night. She didn't leave a message, but phoned Ellie who answered the phone sounding bright and happy.

"Hi Ellie. How are you? You are sounding much more like your old self. Or your young self I should say."

"Hi Fliss. Nice to hear from you. Yes, all is fine here. I've had a temping job and am feeling good. How are you? Anything special going on?"

"No, not really. Nigel's working late so I thought I would take the opportunity to make sure you are OK. I did try Laura too but I think it is her bridge night."

They talked about nothing of any consequence for a while and said they would see each other at the family lunch on Sunday.

Fliss sat it out until 9.00 p.m. and then was just about to call the hospital and the police when she got Nigel's text. She read it several times. If he wanted to punish her he had chosen the right way. She had been sick with worry. She called straight back but his mobile was switched off. There was no yard stick for his behaviour, it was so out of character. Good, steady Nigel who could be relied on to sort anything out and finally it was she, his loving wife, who had been the straw that broke his back. She desperately wanted to call Ellie back and confide in her, but for many reasons she knew it was the last thing she should do. She carefully locked up, checking the back door twice, and then watched TV until she could not stay awake any longer. She went up to bed and hot tears ran down her cheeks. At last she had her heart's desire. Inside her was this precious new life, whilst outside she felt as if her world had ended. She dozed intermittently during the night and was up at 6.00 a.m. There was no word from Nigel and his phone was still switched off. There was nothing to do but wait.

The roads were not busy and Nigel arrived in Clapham by 7.00 a.m. He couldn't face Fliss just yet and needed to make things right at work, so he drove to the station and caught a train to work. He was in the office before 8.00 a.m. and was busy working when Frank arrived before 9.00 a.m. Nigel went straight into his office.

"Sorry about yesterday Frank. A family emergency that I had to deal with, but I will make the time up. I know it's been a problem lately, but I think everything is clear now and we can get back to normal."

Frank looked at him quizzically, taking in the crumpled shirt and day's growth of stubble.

"Ah, yes, I decided to grow a beard. New me!" Nigel tried to smile convincingly, but his jaw felt stiff and his heart was racing.

"What is going on Nigel? I know things have been more than difficult, but you really need to get back on track now."

"Sorry Frank. Will do." Nigel turned and left, not sure if Frank believed him, but not wanting to elaborate on his dishevelled appearance. Back in his office he switched on his mobile and, ignoring the messages, sent Fliss a text.

"I have come in to work. Please do not call me here. I will be home tonight."

He was starving by lunch time and went out and bought himself some sandwiches which he ate at his desk. He admired Frank and felt a little in awe of him. Frank not only had a PhD in computer science but also an MBA. He had run his own internet strategy company once before, but had lost everything in the financial crash of the early nineties. He had picked himself up and started again from scratch. It was a small team. Nigel's title was Executive Director. Frank did the marketing himself and there were five technical guys who went in to companies to help them expand the internet side of the business. They had just picked up a big pharmaceutical contract and Nigel was in charge of managing the project, as well as three others jobs that were in the pipeline. Francesca took care of invoicing, correspondence and was a trouble shooter on the telephone. There was an accountant who took care of salaries and the budget. Nigel was behind with the pharmaceutical contract and worked flat out all day to catch up.

Frank went to visit a client around 3.00 p.m. and said he would not be back. Nigel had intended to work late but his headache had returned with a vengeance and although he was the last one out he was away by 6.00 p.m. There were no seats on the train and he stood, holding on to the rail, crammed between other commuters. Although it had not been a particularly hot day, he found himself sweating profusely and then began to have trouble with his breathing. He finally managed to get a seat at Kennington, but as he looked out of the window at the station sign he realised something strange had happened to his vision. He could make out the first two letters and the last two. As for the rest, it looked as if there was a hole in the name of the station. His breathing was increasingly shallow and he seemed unable to get enough air in his lungs. Sweat was running down his back, his heart was thumping in his chest and he felt as if he would black out at any moment. He wondered if he was having a heart attack and dug his fingernails into the back of his hand to try to keep some sense of reality. The train finally arrived at Clapham Common and as Nigel stood up he realised his legs were weak and shaking. With an effort of will he got to the car and, throwing his bag onto the passenger seat, started the engine. There was no way he was going to phone Fliss, but he felt waves of panic as he drove out of the car park. He drove straight round to the doctor's surgery and was relieved to find it was their late night. At reception he apologised for not having an appointment but said he was feeling very dizzy and could not breathe properly. The receptionist went into the doctor's room and when she returned she told Nigel he would be next.

He was glad it was his own doctor on duty. At least he would be aware of the events of the previous weeks and had seen Nigel when he had a check up after leaving hospital. Nigel was almost panting as he struggled for air. The doctor took his pulse rate and blood pressure and then listened to his chest.

"Is it my heart?"

"No. I'm pretty sure you are having a panic attack. Not surprising after everything that's happened. I need you to have a blood test to make sure your thyroid is behaving itself. In the meantime pop across to the pharmacy and I am giving you a prescription for some beta blockers. The nurse will be in from 10.00 in the morning to do the blood test."

"I can't take time off this week." Nigel realised he voice was hoarse and the whole room suddenly looked very small, the doctor seemed to be a long way away.

"I would like you to take the rest of the week off, Nigel. Have that blood test and come and see me next Monday. I would also suggest that you make an appointment to see our counsellor. You have been through a lot and your body is protesting. Look after yourself."

After Nigel had collected the prescription he got back in the car and drove home very slowly. He wished he had some of Ellie's valium but took one of the beta blockers anyway. He had no water and it seemed to stick in his throat as he tried to swallow it. He felt terrible and was highly anxious about taking more time off, especially after his talk to Frank. He would have to see how he felt in the morning, but in the meantime he had to face Fliss. He pulled up onto the drive and let himself in.

Fliss didn't get up from the armchair when he went into the

sitting room. They looked at each other for what seemed an eternity and then she said, "Bloody hell, Nigel. You look dreadful. Where were you last night? I know we had serious issues, but that was just not on. I was about to phone your mother, Ellie, the police and the hospitals when I finally got your message."

Nigel sat down heavily in the other chair and then, to both their amazement, started to cry.

Fliss stood up, nonplussed. She desperately wanted to go over to him, put her arms round him and be of some comfort, but the jibe about sperm donor had stung too deep for words. So she did what Fliss always did and went into the kitchen and put the kettle on. When she came back he was more in control. His appearance startled her. His eyes, set in black circles, were now red rimmed. He looked as if he hadn't shaved for days. He had thrown his jacket on the sofa and his shirt was wet and sticking to him. He was breathing in great gasps. She went back to the kitchen and poured him a glass of water which he drank quickly.

"What on earth is going on?"

When he didn't answer her she went and fetched a cup of tea for him into which she had put sugar, although she knew Nigel never took sugar, but thought it may be good for energy and shock.

Eventually Nigel spoke, the words coming out too fast, interspersed with great gulps of air as he struggled to get his breath. "I just had to get away and found myself driving until I got to Worthing. I thought that walking along by the sea would clear my head and thoughts. Then I had a meal in a hotel and drank too much wine to drive home. I had to go in to work as I think Frank is getting fed up with the whole Jones' saga but on the way home I felt very ill. I drove to the doctors and apparently I was having a panic attack. I have some tablets and am supposed to have a blood test in the morning and not go in to work. I can't do that Fliss. I have to go in to work and I just don't know what to say to you about our row. I know you are desperately upset but so am I. I just don't know ....." His voice broke again and this time Fliss went over and knelt by him.

"Don't let's talk about it just yet. You get yourself well and then we can talk. Let me get us both some food and not talk about anything contentious and see how you feel in the morning about work."

Nigel nodded dismally and whilst Fliss heated up the chilli, went upstairs and had a shower. He didn't shave. Somehow he felt he could hide behind a beard and also he knew Fliss hated them. They ate, making conversation about the weather, about Ellie and Laura, about what to watch on TV.

Nigel found it difficult to watch the television. His eyes were still giving him trouble, so he politely told Fliss he was going to bed. When she went up an hour or so later, he was asleep. Nigel slept through the alarm that Fliss had set for 6.30 a.m. She threw on a track suit and went downstairs and made a cooked breakfast. Knowing how stubborn Nigel was she guessed that unless he was totally incapacitated he would not heed the doctor's advice and would insist on going in to work. She woke him at 7.00 a.m. The smell of bacon was appetising and he got ready quickly and went downstairs. He still had not shaved and looked like a stranger.

"If the doctor thinks it's important to get that blood test Nigel, can't you go in to work a bit later?"

"I just can't, Fliss. I had a rather frosty encounter with Frank and need to pull my socks up. What I may do is get on the tube at lunch time and go to the Medical Express clinic in Harley Street. I am sure if I explain they will do the test and send the results to my GP. Then I can ring up on Monday and see what's what."

He didn't tell Fliss about the doctor recommending he see a counsellor. Laura of course was a trained counsellor, but talking to family was the last thing he wanted and his pride would not let him book the one at the GP surgery.

"See you later. Thanks for breakfast. Let's talk tonight." He bought a paper on the way to the station and made himself read on the train, taking deep breaths and trying to stay calm.

It took most of the morning to clear the backlog of work and at lunchtime he took the tube to Baker Street and went into Medical Express. He was seen quite quickly and explained the situation. It seemed as if it would be no problem for them to liaise with his doctor. Nigel realised that for him to have taken the step of going there he had had a pretty bad scare. He worked steadily for the rest of the afternoon. Just before Frank went home at 5.00 p.m. he went into Nigel's office.

"Can't say the beard suits you."

Nigel grinned and stroked his chin. "Guess I'll soon get fed up with it."

"Look Nigel. I realise you have been under great strain. I know you have taken what we call compassionate leave, but I think I may get more out of you if you take some annual leave. If you don't want to do that then I think this may be of help." Frank put a card on his desk. "Let me know which you decide."

The inference that it was to be one or the other was not lost on Nigel. After Frank left, Nigel picked up the card. It was the telephone number of an EAP counselling service, run by BUPA. Nigel had heard of the Employee Assistance Programme. Many companies subscribed to it, presumably in an effort to stop employees suing them for stress related illnesses. If the company could be seen to be doing something proactive, litigation was more unlikely. Nigel guessed that Frank's motivation was not quite so cynical. He just needed to get 100% from him which certainly was not happening at the moment. It would be totally confidential and Nigel wondered briefly it he would take advantage of it. He needed to think about the unexpected and sudden problem with his marriage, but also about the incubus which was still boring a hole in his brain. He knew he could not tell anyone the whole truth, but maybe unburdening some of the rest of it would defuse a little of the panic and anger which were obviously threatening to overwhelm him. On the other hand a trip abroad would not be so invasive. He put the card in his wallet and left.

He had taken his beta blockers but still had an uncomfortable ride on the train. As soon as the train got to Kennington, he once again had difficulty breathing and became very hot and anxious. He clenched his fists and once he got a seat made himself attempt the cryptic crossword in the newspaper.

"I'll expect you at the other canal…." The voice echoed clearly in his head, so he closed the page and made himself stare out of the window.

The walk from the station did him good, although he was dreading the confrontation with Fliss. They waited until after dinner and sat down in the sitting room, one in each armchair. Normally they would have been curled up together on the sofa. Fliss took a deep breath and began.

"Nigel. I am sorry I did what I did. I know it was an unforgivable thing to do, but I want you to understand I was desperate. I had tried to talk to you so many times and it suddenly seemed as if it was my turn to get what I wanted. We had Laura and the baby drama, then we had both Laura and Ellie to look after. You were away when Trevor was murdered and I had to hold the fort. I know it has been awful for you but I was desperate for some normality and for me at that moment it meant being a family. You, me and a baby. Like we had talked about when we first got married. Every time I tried to bring the subject up you blocked me. For God's sake Nigel, I will be forty in a couple of years! As I say, I am sorry, but I felt you were being unfair. I didn't think of you as a sperm donor." She began to cry at this point. "I see you as the man I fell in love with, still love and want to have children by."

Nigel sat for a while, watching her as she took a tissue from her sleeve and wiped her eyes. "I hear you Fliss, and while I was away I gave it some thought. It was a shock. Not only that you are pregnant, but that you fooled me in the way you did. I do understand things have been very difficult for you in all the family troubles and you coped so well. But, a baby! This is a bombshell. I know I was preoccupied, but what you did was just irresponsible. I wonder if you have thought it through. We'll be nearly sixty when it is through with education. Just as we finally have some money and can enjoy ourselves more, this….."

Fliss looked miserably across at the black bearded stranger who was the father of her child. "It's done, Nigel, and you will have to get used to it. I promise you that you will feel different when it is born, if not before. I know I handled it badly, but I so want this child. In a few weeks I will begin to show. Ellie and Laura will be thrilled to bits and in time you will be too. I am sure you would not really enjoy us getting old as a childless couple! Please be kind to me through these coming months. I do love you and I am sorry."

Nigel still felt angry and betrayed, but also felt guilty about the thing he was keeping from Fliss. He needed to decide what to do about that, and then perhaps the black dog would lift and he could embrace what was to come. "I promise to try," he said.

In bed that night they cuddled up together and Fliss was soon asleep. Nigel's mind was in turmoil. Not only was his world going to be turned upside down by a baby, but he had to do something about the wretched memory stick. He couldn't just leave it where it was and he also wondered whether he was still a marked man. He lay awake for a long time before making a decision. The memory stick should be destroyed.

He needed to make sure that 'they' were off his back and, knowing that the phone was tapped, he could use this to his advantage. He would call Jeff and not mention the memory stick on the phone, just say there had been nothing of any interest or any memoirs in Trevor's belongings. Then when he met up with Jeff he would tell him he intended to destroy the memory stick as there was nothing interesting on it and tell him that he intended to phone him from home to tell him he had found nothing of any consequence in Trevor's papers and that he and Fliss were going to have a holiday. If Jeff protested and said that he should at least hand it over to the police, Nigel would tell him that the whole episode was making him ill and that he just needed to move on. Hopefully that would put it to rest. An abduction and torture of either him or Jeff seemed highly unlikely – more the grist for a new John Grisham plot. He fell asleep feeling much better.

CHAPTER 18

Nigel's blood tests were clear. He went to see the doctor at one of the late night surgeries and told him that the beta blockers were working. He also him that he had decided not to pursue counselling, but if he changed his mind there were EAP facilities at work. He had not had any more panic attacks.

He had lunch with Jeff in what had become their Italian haunt and filled him in on his decision.

"You mean there's nothing much on it? What did he hide it for then. Don't you want to make sure there is no coded information before you destroy it? Hand it over to the police, Nigel." Nigel looked Jeff straight in the eye. "If there is something I missed, then it must be pretty damning for all this drama and the less I know the better."

Predictably, Jeff tried to talk him out of it, but Nigel was adamant.

"Enough. I need to draw a line under it. If any of it is important then it is obviously top secret and 'they' know what it is, but it didn't make any sense to me. I guess it was also on the hard drive they took from Dad's when he was murdered. It has all been taking its toll on me and if I don't toe the line at work I may lose my job. I'm not prepared for that to happen. I now need to concentrate on the family and the future. I can't thank you enough and I hope we will remain friends. I know that Fliss is hoping to ask you and Ann over soon for a meal."

Jeff shrugged. "Great. And if that is your final decision I will respect it. I'll wait for your call and let's hope that will be that. Just bear in mind that although there was nothing on the memory stick there must either have been something on your father's hard drive, or he was involved in something top secret and they are shit scared it will come out."

"Jeff, thanks, but I just want to leave it all alone now. I've had enough."

Nigel made the promised call a couple of days later. Jeff went along with it as ever. Nigel thought they should both be up for an Oscar. He wasn't happy knowing the phone was bugged, but realised that changing it or having the place "swept" would court trouble. He was glad he had not confided in Fliss about the incubus and now needed to allay the family concerns by saying he felt his mind had been working overtime, that he was suffering from stress himself and was taking steps to deal with it. Destroying the memory stick was another matter. Incineration would be the ideal but they only had a coal imitation gas fire at home. Setting the house alight would be another Jones disaster. The thought of it made him laugh to himself. More drama for the media.

Relations with Fliss slowly improved. She was still nauseous in the mornings and he began to feel somewhat sympathetic when he looked at her pale face. She finally persuaded him to tell the family at one of the Sunday lunches, before she started to show. She had agreed not to tell anyone else until the family knew.

"Turkey? And champagne? What's the occasion?" Laura was glad that everyone seemed in festive spirit. Nigel had not seemed well lately and since he had grown a beard looked dark and brooding. Fliss had seemed under the weather too and although Laura herself put on a brave face she still had flashbacks to the prison cell. Ellie was the most cheerful. She was enjoying work and seemed to spend a lot of time socialising with friends.

Nigel carved whilst they helped themselves to roast potatoes and vegetables. Fliss usually dished up in the kitchen, so to have the dinner service and tureens out was unusual. Nigel uncorked the champagne and filled their glasses, Fliss already having a glass of orange juice.

"I would like to propose a toast. To the family, to my wonderful wife and to our coming baby."

Laura was so shocked she managed to tip the champagne into her dinner. Ellie burst into tears.

"Oh Fliss. I am so happy for you both! When is it due? Is it a boy or a girl? How long have you known? Oh, how wonderful."

The rest of the meal passed in excited chatter and even Nigel felt happier about it all. For the first time he actually realised he was going to be a father and, to his surprise, quite liked the feeling.

After the others had gone he sat on the sofa with Fliss and began to ask her questions such as where the baby would be born. He then told her that he wanted to be there when she had her scan.

"And at the birth?"

"Probably," he said wryly. Now it was out in the open there was no stopping Fliss.

"Let's make a list of equipment, etc. and we need to talk about names."

"Steady on. Let me get used to the idea first."

A couple of weeks later Nigel presented Fliss with a holiday brochure.

"You still have a couple of weeks off school and apparently Frank thinks I need to take some leave. How do you fancy a mini cruise to Madeira? Now the sickness seems better do you think you could manage a short trip? Do you good. It will probably be the last holiday we have on our own!"

Fliss was ecstatic. Nigel booked it the following day and at the weekend Ellie and Fliss went on a shopping spree to choose some suitable clothes.

The following weekend they went shopping again and this time took Laura. As well as clothes shopping they looked at baby clothes, cribs and baby baths. It was exciting but also it all looked incredibly complicated and expensive. They gave up at the sight of breast pumps and took themselves off for lunch.

As soon as they were gone Nigel went upstairs and retrieved the memory stick. It looked so innocuous lying in his palm. It felt like a time bomb. He took it into the garage and removed the protective lid before putting it on the concrete floor and began hitting it is as hard as he could with a hammer. The coloured Perspex shell shattered, but he kept hitting, weeks of rage and frustration surging through him. He did the same with the lid. And then put the bits into the bottom of a small tin that he kept for cleaning paint brushes. He poured on some white spirit and then lit a match which he dropped into it. The height and ferocity of the flames shocked him. He put the tin he used for the paint roller on the top to cut off the air. Fumes and smoke made his eyes smart and caught at the back of his throat. He was shaking as he finally took off the makeshift lid and peered at the blackened contents of the tin. When he was sure it was cool he shook it out onto a piece of newspaper from the paper collection box. The blackened and mangled pieces bore no resemblance to the thing that had haunted him for weeks. He went indoors and came out with a piece of foil into which he wrapped the remnants tightly and put them into the pocket of his tracksuit. He then went back indoors and after a strong cup of coffee drove the car into town. He parked and then bought a newspaper, trying not to obviously look over his shoulder to see if he was followed. The Saturday papers were cumbersome and he had no trouble in letting the cellophane wrapped magazine fall to the ground, right by a storm drain. As he bent to pick it up he surreptitiously dropped the little packet into the drain. On the drive home he felt such a relief that he found himself singing along to the car radio – the first time he had felt carefree for a long time.

Finally life seemed to be getting back to normal. Nigel had a chat with Ellie and they decided to get Trevor's house ready for sale when he got back from Madeira. He was feeling good and Fliss was like a dog with two tails. She enjoyed packing her new clothes.

"I didn't go mad, Nigel. I won't be able to get into them for long, but they are mix and match. Smart casual for evenings with some sparkly things for the posh frock evenings."

Nigel groaned. Posh frock was not his scene. He packed a lightweight suit, a couple of good shirts and one tie. He already had plenty of shorts and tee shirts so did not need to shop.

A neighbour promised to pick up the post and leave a light on in the evenings and Ellie said she would pop over at the weekend.

Their cabin was spacious with a decent sized shower. They had never been on a sea cruise, although they had done a Nile cruise some years before. Nigel had not suggested Egypt again, partly because of Fliss's delicate state and the possibility of a tummy bug, but also because of the summer heat. An ocean cruise would be much more appropriate.

There were six others at their dinner table and they all got on well. They spent time together on the excursions and after dinner they wandered into one of the bars and watched some entertainment for a while. The day they spent exploring Funchal was magical. They all did a levada walk and then in the town marvelled at the fruit, vegetable and fish market. From a viewing gallery they could see how beautifully all the produce was displayed, the vegetables arranged to make colourful flower shapes. They had espada for lunch and then went for the famous tea at Reid's. Privately Nigel thought it old fashioned and over-rated, but apparently it was the thing to do. Fliss was blooming and he felt a surge of pride when the previous night she had told the other guests that she was pregnant in response to their questions about her not drinking.

Nigel was more relaxed than he had been for months. The sea air did him good and in spite of the beard, his face was tanned. He looked good and for the first time for a long time he was not looking over his shoulder. They were both reluctant for the voyage to end and promised the others to keep in touch. They all meant it at the time but Nigel knew from experience that with the best will in the world life would get in the way. Also, he had no intention of giving anyone his card. It was possible that someone would recognise the name after all the publicity and that was the last thing he wanted.

They got back looking brown and happy. Everything was in order at home. Ellie had been round and put a vase of flowers on the table and Laura had baked one of her apple pies. They sat with a piece of pie and a cup of tea, chatting about the holiday and browsing through the post. There was a letter for Nigel from a TV company offering sympathy for the loss of his father and saying that they were interested in his experience in getting his mother out of Thailand and about his subsequent return. He felt his pulse rate go up and he choked back an angry remark. He wondered if his mother had had any approaches, or Ellie. He would have to warn Ellie in such a way that she would think it was just to protect the family. He was sure

193

she would not want to get involved after everything that had happened, but these companies could be very persuasive. And who knew anyway who was on the board of directors and who were pulling their strings. No, he would reply in the morning and say he was not interested and would be grateful for no further intrusion into the family's privacy. As far as he was concerned his father was dead and he had now buried the rest of it. Buried it deep in the recesses of his mind, hopefully never to surface.

His complacency was to be short lived. Ellie telephoned to make sure they were home safely. All was well with her and she was looking forward to seeing them as usual on Sunday.

"By the way, Nigel, a friend of yours, Steve, called round on Saturday when I was watering the plants and collected your laptop. He said it wouldn't take long to fix and he would call you later in the week."

"Ellie, I don't have a friend called Steve and there was nothing wrong with the laptop." Nigel could not help the panic in his voice. He immediately regretted saying it, but had been so shocked that he had blurted it out.

"But he said it was all arranged, Nigel. He knew you were on the cruise and apologised for not being able to do it before. What do you mean, you don't know him?"

"Ellie, I'm probably in holiday mode and my memory is playing tricks. I'm sure it will come back to me." Ellie was not fooled and tried to pursue the conversation but Nigel said he had to go and hung up. He walked over to his study and sure enough the laptop was missing. His heart missed a beat and he wondered what instinct had made him clear the cache once he had read his father's words.

He carried the cases upstairs and began to unpack. Fliss unzipped her case and carefully unwrapped the few pieces of pottery they had bought in Madeira for Laura and Ellie. She then began sorting out the clothes that needed washing.

"What was all that about Nigel?"

"I expect it's something Frank organised from the office. My laptop had been playing up a bit. I guess he just forgot to tell me."

He turned and went into the bathroom and shut the door. He

didn't want Fliss alarmed any more than she was already, especially in her present condition, and he did not want an inquisition. He waited until he heard her go downstairs and then pulled the flush and went back into the bedroom to finish unpacking. He was totally at a loss. In his heart of hearts he had not really thought it had all gone away. The magnitude of the revelations were such that he should not have been surprised. The holiday had lulled him into a false sense of security and now it was starting all over again. He felt helpless and not a little afraid. There was nowhere and no-one he could turn to. He had no idea what they would have found on Trevor's computer, although they would find nothing of any importance on his. If Fliss or Ellie thought it had been stolen they would go banging on about the police and insurance. That was the last thing he wanted. He was pretty efficient about backing up his office work, but he would now have to spend time getting a new laptop and then download data from his office CD's, which was just what he didn't need after time off from work. He just wished there was someone to whom he could say "Look, I don't know anything. Just let me get on with my life."

Later he was to recall the old saying "Be careful what you wish for."

CHAPTER 19

The typed note came by first class post. "In strict confidence. Your laptop is now ready for collection. Please call the following freephone number for arrangements." There was no address, just an 0800 number. Nigel read it twice and then tried to see if there was a post mark on the envelope, but it was illegible. He put it in his briefcase and headed off to work, his mind in turmoil. There had already been one attack on him, not to mention the death of his father and the murder in Amsterdam, which he now believed implicitly was connected to the whole sinister business. How safe would it be for him to go anywhere to collect his laptop, especially as there had been nothing wrong with it in the first place? He desperately wanted to talk to Jeff about it, but as he had been less than honest with him about looking at the wretched memory stick he was loathe to involve him again. Apart from which he was sure that Jeff was heartily sick of the Jones saga.

Francesca was off sick and Frank left the office around 4.00 pm. The sales reps. were out on the road, so Nigel had some privacy. In spite of his misgivings he dialled the number. There would be no harm in calling. It did not mean he had to turn up anywhere. He was staggered when his call was answered by a man announcing himself as Inspector Crosby at Special Branch.

"Ah. Mr Jones. We were expecting your call. We have managed to track down your laptop and would like to make arrangements for you to pick it up. There is a need for secrecy which will be explained to you when we meet."

Nigel hesitated before answering, his mind racing. He was deeply suspicious but did not want to arouse any speculation that he was aware of 'forces' at work.

"Thank you Inspector. Please tell me on what grounds my computer was stolen. As I had not reported it I can only assume that the police took it upon themselves to take my property from my home without my permission."

It was as if Nigel had not spoken.

"As I said, Mr Jones, we have managed to track it down. I have some idea as to why it was taken. Please would you be at the following address tomorrow at 4.00 p.m. and please keep this information to yourself. Do you have a pen?"

"Yes, of course, I am in my office." Nigel could not keep the sarcasm from his voice.

"The address is 4 Beresford Street, W1. It is a mostly disused office block, rather colourful due to the graffiti. Please be on time as there is no doorbell. Someone will be waiting for you. This must be highly confidential of course. I will see you tomorrow."

Nigel realised that Inspector Crosby had hung up before he could reply. He sat for what seemed a long time, still holding the phone to his ear. He made himself a coffee and then got out his wallet and searched through for the card Inspector Sweeney had given him when Special Branch had interviewed his mother. As he dialled he realised he was sweating profusely and that his heart rate had soared. He took a few deep breaths, determined not to have another panic attack. He asked to be put through to Inspector Sweeney and to his immense relief was told that he was being connected. After a brief pause Sweeney came on the phone. He remembered Nigel as soon as he said his name.

"Ah, Mr Jones. What can I do for you?"

"Just something I want to check out, Inspector." He then recounted the story of how his laptop came to be missing and then told him about the surprise phone call from Special Branch.

"I can assure you Mr. Jones that we do not have an Inspector Crosby and that this office would not arrange a meeting in such a way. It is vitally important that we meet with you immediately. You may well be followed, so please remain in your office and an under cover agent will be with you within the hour. He will be dressed as a cleaner so please do not be alarmed. Please stay put and don't speak to anyone else about the matter. Is there anyone else in the office at the moment?" Nigel assured him that everyone else had gone.

Nigel put the phone down and for a moment wondered if he had heard correctly. If his life had not already been threatened he would have thought the whole thing was a farce.

The 'cleaner' arrived within the hour, carrying a mop and bucket. He pulled a card from his blue dungarees with an identifying photograph and his name. **Inspector John Smithson, Special Branch.** He was a big man, at least 6ft 5ins. with untidy hair and a grimy face. Nigel found himself thinking he would not like to upset him. He also found himself doubting that this was in fact Special Branch, although if it was then the disguise was good. On the other hand Nigel had spoken to Sweeney, so it must be genuine. He even wondered if John Smithson, Special Branch, was in fact John Smithson, SAS.

Nigel sat behind his desk and Smithson dwarfed the chair opposite. Nigel went over the whole story again, starting with the disappearance of the laptop and finishing with the phone call purporting to come from Special Branch.

Smithson listened attentively and then proceeded to tell him that they knew there were foreign forces at work who assumed that Trevor had access to privileged information which may have been disclosed in his memoirs and that he, Nigel, had been able to retrieve it. This was the first time that Nigel had had any official confirmation of his fears. At last 'they' were coming clean. Who exactly 'they' were was any one's guess. 'They' could be the British Intelligence Service or 'they' could be foreign forces of even some other dark force. Nigel was totally out of his depth.

"That's ridiculous," Nigel protested, "If I had any idea of the whereabouts of my father's memoirs I would have told you when we first discussed the telephone message. It was all mumbo jumbo to me and I just forgot about it as time went by."

Nigel could feel the sweat running down his back. He got up and poured some water from the cooler, offering a cup to Smithson who took it, sipped some and placed it on the edge of the desk. He looked at Nigel in silence for a moment and then got down to business.

"We would like you to keep the appointment tomorrow. Please be assured that you will be protected. You may not notice anything unusual but believe me there will be extensive protection for you. You do of course have the option say no, but if you do refuse then you may well be a target in the future, which we cannot protect."

Nigel drank the water slowly, playing for time whilst his brain went into overdrive. He just couldn't make sense of any of it. His mind went round in the old loop which was now too familiar. His father had been murdered, he himself had been attacked, a woman had been murdered in Amsterdam and now this. With the knowledge he already had from the memory stick he could understand that MI5 or MI6 wanted the memoirs kept quiet. They obviously knew what they were from Trevor's computer but they had no proof that Nigel knew anything. But why on earth would 'other forces' or even foreign powers be so consumed with it? If Diana had indeed been murdered by the Secret Service, MI5 or whatever they were called, would the implication be that it was because of a Muslim boyfriend and could then be linked to more terrorist attacks? And what about proving that Kelly was murdered over Weapons of Mass Destruction or, as had been hinted, because of his inside knowledge about Iraq's actual ability to deploy biological weapons. And why should he, Nigel Jones, do their dirty work. Why not send a decoy? Perhaps the whole thing was a set up and Nigel was like a lamb to the slaughter. On the other hand, and he was clutching at straws here, supposing his father had in fact got caught up in conspiracy theories and what he had written was the product of an old man's over active imagination? There was certainly a great deal of activity going on to suppress them, but even if they were untrue, publication would do a lot of damage. His mind went into overdrive.

'Nigel Jones murdered by assailant in London. There had been a tip off but police marksmen were unable to catch the perpetrator.'

Perhaps the fictitious Inspector Crosby and Special Branch were on the same side? Nigel would be silenced and the whole thing hushed up for good. His hand was clammy as he held the cup and drank some water. He realised that Smithson was waiting for an answer.

"Inspector, who are these people anyway? And why should I agree to this? Why can't you get a decoy to go in? There are no guarantees that I will be safe. I'm just an ordinary bloke who knows nothing and yet I seem caught up in the middle of someone else's drama." Nigel kept his voice as even as he could although inside he was seething. Sitting in front of him was a representative of a corrupt organisation which Nigel now believed to be pernicious and immoral, and yet he had to keep quiet.

Smithson nodded gravely. "I quite understand, Nigel, but they would see through a decoy immediately. There has already been one attack on you and there may be others if you don't play ball. All I can tell you is that these people are ruthless and that unfortunately your late father's memoirs seem to be the catalyst. There will of course be considerable compensation for you when an arrest has been made. Enough for you to be able to get away from it all if that is what you would like."

Nigel's jaw dropped. He almost blurted it out. "Bribery," but stopped himself in time. He suddenly felt as if he were teetering on the edge of a cliff. Perhaps going along with it would be the right option, or even his only option.

"What about my wife? I really don't want her worried, especially now that she is expecting our first child."

"We will need absolute secrecy. I can assure you it will be worth your while"

Nigel looked him straight in the eye. "Inspector, what on earth do you all think was in my father's memoirs to cause all this fuss?"

"Orders come from on high, Nigel. The less we know, the better it is. We work for the good of the State and so far we have been kept relatively secure. We will make sure you too are safe and of course you will be contributing to the greater good. You must trust us on this."

"Trust," Nigel thought, "not on your life. Or mine, come to that." The whole situation was ludicrous. Here he was having a life changing conversation with a dirty looking cleaner. His mind was racing. If he refused to co-operate he could spend a long time looking over his shoulder. This may just bring the whole shabby affair to a close. He finally, reluctantly agreed. Anything to get this shower, whoever they were, off his back.

They spent the next hour going over the plan. Nigel noticed that Smithson memorised the address Nigel had been given. Nothing was put in writing. He confirmed with Nigel that he was to turn up there at the appointed time, ostensibly to collect his laptop. He was to call for a taxi from work at 3.00 p.m. to take him to the rendezvous and the rest would be taken care of. Afterwards, when they met again, they would give Nigel a proposition that would ensure peace of mind for the future. He found himself wondering how much Hollywood would pay for the film rights. Smithson shook hands and got up to leave. To Nigel's amazement, on his way out he proceeded to mop the floor in the hallway and polish the letter box before striding up the road, his bucket swinging from his hand. Whether he had a van parked somewhere Nigel had no idea. If this was the level of protection, he didn't hold out much hope for his safety. He shivered. The cops and robbers he had joked about when he had set off for the canal with Jeff were now no longer at the level of a comedy film. This was real and he was scared stiff.

Fliss was preparing trout for supper. "Heads on or off?"

Nigel looked at the shiny, stiff bodies, dead eyes looking nowhere. "Off."

Throughout supper Fliss chatted about work and about maternity leave.

"Not sure if I will want to go back, Nigel. I've waited a long time for this." She patted her tummy, which was definitely growing by the day.

"You don't need to decide yet, Fliss." He helped her clear up and then while she sat on the sofa and watched TV with her feet up, he went into the study to check his life insurance policy.

He took a long time to get off to sleep that night, vaguely wondering if he could buy a bullet-proof vest anywhere, although a crash hat might be better judging by the choice of despatch of his father and the woman in Amsterdam. He desperately wanted to talk to Jeff. Perhaps he should write down what had been proposed and drive to Trevor's and hide it under the holly bush. Then leave Jeff a message. "Hi Jeff. I'll expect you at the other canal....." Sleep finally overtook him.

Next morning Fliss had an appointment at the hairdressers and then lunch with one of her work colleagues. Pregnancy suited her and she looked young and happy. Nigel gave her a long hug and kissed her as she started towards the door. "What's that for?"

"Just because I love you" he said awkwardly.

"I love you too," and she was gone, leaving that familiar waft of perfume in the air.

Nigel walked to the station and caught his usual train. Frank was already in and Francesca had left a stack of letters needing signatures on his desk. He forced himself to work, drank more water than coffee, and took two beta blockers. He went for a walk at lunchtime and took a sandwich back to his desk. The beta blockers had calmed him down but he had the signs of a stress headache. The situation seemed so unreal. He found himself wondering how terrorist martyrs felt before they blew themselves to smithereens. That thought did nothing for his confidence about what he was about to get involved in. He also felt bad that he was taking part in something dangerous and yet had not confided in Fliss. He suddenly needed the toilet.

Frank was out for the afternoon so there were no awkward questions when the taxi arrived at 3.00 p.m. He put on his jacket and left, just calling out over his shoulder, "See you later," to Francesca.

Beresford Street was in a run down part of Soho. Nigel glanced along the road, wondering where the reinforcements were. There was a builder's van parked opposite, probably filled with gun wielding cops as per drugs bust, he thought. Or rather hoped. The office block was as Crosby had described it, covered in graffiti. The building looked empty and neglected and the buildings either side were in various stages of dilapidation. His hand was shaking as he paid the taxi driver and walked up to the door. The young man who let him in couldn't have been more than twenty although perhaps his fair hair and complexion made him look younger that he actually was.

"Mr Jones? Inspector Crosby is expecting you. Please come this way."

Nigel shuffled through the junk mail that had accumulated just inside and followed the young man up a flight of dirty stairs. He noticed a rather dingy kitchen and a toilet with the lid hanging off as they made their way to another door which was slightly ajar. He was shown into an office. There were empty shelves on the walls and the floor was covered in stained and chipped tiles. The man calling himself Inspector Crosby stood up as Nigel was shown in. He had dark hair and a swarthy complexion and was probably in his fifties. He was wearing a navy suit, white shirt and red tie. He handed Nigel his card. It was similar to Inspector Smithson's although Nigel realised as he took it that the paper was much thinner. Nigel's laptop was on the cheap plywood desk. Crosby sat down on a grey swivel office chair on the far side and gestured to Nigel.

"Do sit down. I expect you are wondering what all this is about."

Nigel sat down on the plastic chair on the other side of the desk.

Crosby got straight down to business. "You already know that your late father was writing his memoirs. He was, as you are probably aware, under the Official Secrets Act and as such any disclosures that he made would be Government property."

Nigel nodded, not quite sure how to react.

"It seems that your late father left you a message as to the whereabouts of this document."

There it was. A bald statement. Nigel cleared his throat. "I did have some kind of garbled message but I could not make head nor tail of it and it certainly did not mention any document. But I have already explained this to your guys before. His computer was of course also stolen, so I would have thought whoever was responsible for that would know more than I do."

"So, Mr Jones, are you telling me that you have no idea as to what your father had hidden?"

"None whatsoever. I don't know that he hid anything. And before you ask me any more questions, on what authority did you arrange to steal my laptop."

Crosby looked at him icily and, ignoring the question, carried on as if Nigel had not spoken. "Tell me, Mr Jones, do you always clear the cache when you shut down your computer?"

"Fairly frequently, Inspector. We like to keep our clients' details confidential. Although we have a Data Protection Certificate at work, I don't have one for my home computer. I would hate to break the law."

Crosby stood up. Nigel felt at a distinct disadvantage as he was still sitting.

"I'm afraid I don't actually believe you, Mr Jones. Perhaps you can be persuaded to tell me the truth." He rapped his knuckles twice on the table and two men came in, from an adjacent room. They were well built, also with swarthy complexions, and they looked at Nigel with cold unfeeling eyes. He was momentarily reminded of the trout and regretted saying "Head off." His heart was pounding in his chest with that now familiar feeling of being unable to breathe.

"I don't know what you are talking about. Who are these people? And why are we here? What's wrong with the official office where I made my last statement? I would like to see their ID."

"Let me get them to introduce themselves." Crosby nodded and the two men grabbed Nigel, hauling him to his feet and twisting his arms backwards. He struggled wildly as his wrists were handcuffed behind him. He shouted out, but a vicious blow to his solar plexus brought him to his knees. He couldn't breathe and the last thing he heard before blacking out was the sound of splintering wood, of shouts and of gun fire.

When Nigel recovered consciousness he was standing again, although his knees were buckling under him. He was held up by the two henchmen and Crosby was standing to one side, a gun pointed at Nigel's head. The door was hanging off its hinges and a police marksman was aiming a gun at Crosby.

"Shoot and I will kill him." Crosby's voice was calm and authoritative.

Even in his befuddled state Nigel was aware that shooting him well be a good solution for MI5. That way he would never be able to reveal anything he knew. Fear gave him a metallic taste in his mouth and he was shaking violently. Crosby shouted at the police.

"Now, back off and let me talk to your commanding officer."

The policeman kept his gun trained on Crosby whilst a second armed policeman came up the stairs.

"I would advise you to let Mr Jones go before lives are lost."

"Give us safe passage and you can have your Mr Jones." Crosby's voice was still controlled with no sign of fear. "Now, leave the building or we shoot him."

"Just let him go now and come with us. You can't escape, and if you come quietly it will be better for you."

"Back off." Crosby was shouting now. The two marksmen retreated down the stairs and after what seemed an eternity the henchmen, pushing Nigel in front of them, left the room, Crosby behind them with the gun trained on the back of Nigel's head. Nigel's legs were like jelly as he practically slithered down the stairs, held upright by his shoulders. The marksmen were by the front door, their guns pointing straight at them.

"Out, or I shoot him."

The police backed out of the door but still kept the guns trained on them, Crosby sheltering behind Nigel with his gun held to Nigel's head.

Nigel was pushed roughly into one of the dilapidated offices on the ground floor. Crosby stood a few feet away with the gun still pointing at him. Through the window Nigel could see at least three marksmen with what looked like rifles pointing at the building whilst the police kept the office covered from the doorway. He was also aware of a flash from a window opposite, but there was no noise. Impasse, thought Nigel. Bloody impasse. If Crosby had a waiting vehicle, the police would have taken care of it by now. Crosby nodded at one of his henchmen who, still holding Nigel with his right hand, pulled a gun from his pocket and held it to Nigel's head. Crosby then eased himself into the vestibule, his own gun pointing at the police at the door.

"Back off, or we kill him!"

"You can't win. We can wait. Give up now. Come out with your hands up."

The police backed off into the street. Nigel guessed they would be back in force when they tired of the waiting game. He seemed to remember a similar case with a banker held hostage who was eventually killed as the police went in. He felt sick.

He was tied to a chair. The wall clock showed 6.00 p.m. It was too early for Fliss to worry. He suddenly wondered if his child would grow up with no father and as well as sickening fear he felt a surge of frustrated, impotent anger. His mobile was on silent, but he had felt it vibrate a couple of times.

"Look. I don't know anything. Just let me go and I'm sure they will go easy on you. And who the hell are you anyway?" He shouted the last sentence and realised that at any minute he could lose his temper and then probably his life.

Crosby peered out into the vestibule. Apparently there was no sign of the police because they suddenly left Nigel tied to the chair and he could hear their footsteps clumping up the stairs. Nigel was puzzled. He thought that upstairs was the last place they would want to be. What the hell were the police doing? Nigel was soon to discover when the megaphone started up.

"Come out with your hands up. Make it easy on yourselves. You have five minutes, then we come in."

The building was now silent. No voices, no footsteps upstairs. Nigel struggled with the rope that tied him to the chair. It was even more difficult as he still had on the handcuffs. At one point he thought the chair would tip over. It was futile. He didn't need another bang on the head if he went down. He watched the clock. Five minutes seemed an eternity. He thought about Fliss and the baby. He could kick himself for getting into this. With all his misgivings about MI5, how could he have been so stupid as to trust the Special Branch anyway?

After five minutes, the megaphone again. "Last chance. Come out now."

"I would if I bloody well could" Nigel yelled.

Then there were blood curdling shouts and the sound of heavy boots thundering up the stairs. A young man holding a rifle kicked open the door where Nigel was held.

"Put your hands above your head."

"Don't be so bloody stupid, and get me out of here, you corrupt cretins."

It could only be the SAS, Nigel thought, as the well built young man in some sort of body armour trained his rifle on him.

"The hostage is in the kitchen," he shouted, whilst upstairs the thuds and kicking in of doors accompanied by the shouts added to the general pandemonium.

Someone hacked Nigel free from the ropes and he stood up on shaky legs, his hands still cuffed behind him.

"Get these off!" he yelled, but apparently there was no key. Or, maybe they were being very cautious. He was led out of the house and should not have been surprised by the flash photography. Bystanders had obviously been very busy. The white van he had noticed had the back doors open, obviously concealing the 'protection' he had been promised. He was pushed into the back of a police car but the driver made no attempt to start the engine. After another five minutes six officers emerged from the house. One was talking on his radio.

"No-one there sir. Yes sir."

"Back inside, men. We need to take the place apart." Two armed police remained on guard outside the door whilst the rest went back inside. Presumably, thought Nigel, there would be a similar presence round the back. Another man materialised from the far side of the car and got into the passenger seat. He turned to Nigel.

"You OK Mr Jones?"

"What do you think?" Nigel growled.

"Where did they go?"

"Your guess is as good as mine. Now, get me somewhere to get these cuffs off so I can phone my wife. Heads are going to roll over this."

Back in Clapham Fliss had phoned Frank who had no idea where Nigel could be. He was not answering his mobile. She phoned the police who said it was too soon to make a missing person's report, and then she phoned the local hospital. This was like Worthing all over again. She switched on the evening news. If there had been an accident on the rail network no doubt it would be on the TV, but the headlines were about a terrorist attack in Soho. Then she saw him. Nigel being led out of an office block in handcuffs. No, it must be a Nigel look-alike, she thought. But it was definitely Nigel. She had ironed that blue shirt last night and there he was, her husband, presumably arrested on terrorist charges. What the hell was he doing in Soho anyway? She remembered his unexpectedly tender goodbye that morning, and her heart sank. All that rubbish about the canal and phone messages months ago, and now this. Just supposing he was indeed involved. Her Nigel, a liar and a terrorist. In spite of herself she laughed. He may have been keeping some of his concerns from her, but he was as straight as a die. The phone rang and she nearly fell over rushing to get it. "Nigel?"

It was Ellie who was predictably hysterical. "Have you seen the news, Fliss? I'm sure it was Nigel who has been arrested for terrorism. Please tell me he is in and sitting with you?"

"He didn't come home from work Ellie. I don't know what the hell is going on, but get off the line and I will find out. Don't say anything to Laura. It's her bridge night and with any luck she won't see the news tonight. I'll get back to you." She replaced the receiver and it immediately rang again.

"Nigel?"

"Good evening, Mrs Jones. This is Darren from the National Morning Mail. We helped your family when your mother-in-law was arrested in Thailand. We understand that your…" He got no further.

"Fuck off" Fliss slammed the phone down, then picked it up again and dialled 999.

"Police. Now." she said.

Nigel was taken to Special Branch division and was gratified to see that Sweeney was working late. He was probably waiting for him, Nigel thought, and once he had the handcuffs removed and been given a cup of coffee he was ready for battle.

"How dare you get me to do your dirty work? You said I would be protected. Do you know what I have been through? And where's Inspector Smithson? I assume you are privy to the dirty little deal."

Sweeney folded his arms protectively across his chest. "I'm sorry, Mr Jones. I am sure it has been quite a trauma. It is not appropriate for Inspector Smithson to be here for reasons I am sure you appreciate, but you are here, and in my book that is good protection.

Those guys were out to get you and what we hoped to do was finally get our hands on them. You would be a lot safer if we had."

"And?"

"Unfortunately they seem to have given us the slip temporarily. But we have found out a good deal of information, thanks to you."

"And no thanks to you I am sure that I have a very worried family at home. If you will excuse me I need to phone my wife," and ignoring Sweeney, Nigel pulled out his mobile and called Fliss.

To his amazement she knew a great deal more than he did.

"I've seen you on the News. What the hell is going on? How did you get involved in a terrorist bust? And then to be arrested. What is it with this bloody family?"

She paused momentarily for breath. "I am glad you are safe Nigel, but you have a lot of explaining to do. I refuse to be kept in the dark any longer." She was shouting now and Nigel tried to pacify her.

"Calm, Fliss. I'm OK. Think of the baby."

"You think of the baby Nigel. I never did ask you about the maggots, but this is totally different."

"I'll be home soon. I'm just helping the police with their enquiries."

Fliss slammed the phone down and burst into tears. Nigel stared at the phone for a moment. Maggots?

Even in his shocked state he took in what Sweeney had said, that he, Nigel, would be safer if 'they' had been caught. Was this finally an admission that terrorists were interested in Trevor's memoirs, or was it passing the buck? It seemed that Sweeney's lot knew what was in the memoirs and wanted them hushed up and that the other lot were desperate to know what was in them. Whoever these 'lots' were and whoever were pulling their strings was beyond his powers of guesswork, although one 'lot' seemed more obvious than the other.

Nigel leaned across the desk and spoke slowly and quietly. "How much money and when?"

When Nigel finally arrived home in a police car, it was mayhem.

"Déjà vu. Not again." he thought. The road was filled with vans, mopeds and the now familiar battery of flashing cameras and reporters falling over each other to get to the car. The police cleared the way and ushered Nigel into the house, following him inside.

"Someone will call to see you tomorrow, Mr Jones. Please don't go anywhere."

"Did it occur to you or your precious Inspector that I have a job to do and I would like to keep it as my wife is pregnant!" Nigel was now shouting. The policemen hurriedly said goodnight and left.

It suddenly registered with Nigel that Ellie was there too. For God's sake, that was all he needed, a hysterical sister. At least his mother was not present. Fliss was torn between giving him a hug and giving him a kick in the shins. She was only deterred from the latter when she noticed his chafed wrists and the beginning of another black eye.

"I'm up to here with all this, Nigel. If you don't tell me what is going on I am going to leave."

Ellie and Nigel looked at her in stunned silence. For once Fliss did not put the kettle on as was her wont in an emergency, but just stood glaring at him.

"OK" he said, "but not now." He went into the kitchen and put the kettle on whilst trying to gather his thoughts. On one level he could not believe he was alive and free. On another level he was furious. How dare 'they' set him up so they could track down the sinister 'other force.' As far as Nigel was concerned they were all sinister forces and he now had no doubt that he had been right all along. The whole thing was insidious, spreading like cancer from Mr Plod to the Special Branch, SAS, MI5 and probably MI6. Yes, he could understand that the British Government would do anything to stop the truth from coming out. On the other hand, why would foreign forces be so keen to get their hands on the information? Perhaps, and now Nigel stood stock still, the kettle poised above the mugs, (Mugs, he thought belligerently. Not cups. Sod the sitting room.) just perhaps his father had also worked for the other side and they, unlike MI5, had no idea what was in the memoirs. A double agent? Nigel's head ached with that now familiar throb. He would think it through in the morning. For now the enemy was within. He squared his shoulders and, holding the tea tray in front of him as some kind of psychological defence, went across to the sitting room to face Fliss.

CHAPTER 20

The press must have camped out all night. Ellie stayed over, partly because she was too upset to drive and partly because she did not want to run the gauntlet of flash photography and a barrage of questions shouted at her. The phone rang incessantly from 7.30 a.m. Frank wanted to know if Nigel was in prison.

"Just thought I'd check, Nigel. Seems to be a family trait." He laughed derisively, as if that would take the sting out of the sarcasm.

"It was a misunderstanding, Frank. I'll be in as soon as the police have finished their enquiries. In the meantime I will work from home and send copy by email. I'll explain when I see you."

Just what he could explain Nigel had no idea. He put the phone down and it rang immediately. He let it go to answerphone.

"Nigel or Fliss. This is Jeff. Call me if you need me."

Nigel had phoned Laura before 7 a.m. just in case she watched the news. He guessed she was still in bed as the answerphone was on, so he left a message.

"Good morning Mum. Nothing wrong. Just thought I would mention that the police mistook me for someone else yesterday and you may see me on TV and also there may be press intrusion. Don't worry. I'm fine. Please don't talk to the press and I'll call you later."

The headteacher at the school also rang early to speak to Fliss, who was just finishing her coffee and was dressed and ready to go when she took the call. She came off the phone white and shaken.

"Well, Nigel. You have plenty of time to tell me what the hell is going on. They have suspended me temporarily until all this has blown over. Apparently as the wife of a suspected terrorist it is not appropriate for me to be with children."

She sat down and burst into tears.

Ellie looked daggers at Nigel. "I think you owe everybody an explanation Nigel."

"It's just a case of mistaken identity. I need to clear it with the police and then I will explain. They have asked me not to say anything at the moment and I know that is hard on you, but there are good reasons." He carefully put his coffee mug on the counter, and then added, "All will be revealed."

"For God's sake, Nigel. Who do you think you are? Sherlock Holmes?" Ellie put her coat on, gave Fliss a hug and, keeping her head down, ran down the path to her car, ignoring all the shouts from the press. She practically had to run them over in order to set off up the road.

Fliss put on the TV and Nigel stood in the doorway watching in horror at a replay of him leaving the disgusting graffiti-covered building, in handcuffs and being bundled into a car. In fact he was quite shocked by his appearance. He could easily have been mistaken for a terrorist himself with his black hair and beard and his dark ringed eyes. The beard would have to come off soon, he thought. No wonder Fliss had been so distraught when she had watched the news the night before. He would have to tell her what had happened, but a sanitised version. There was no way he would ever reveal the truth about the memoirs. He would have to tell her about the memory stick, but would have to lie to her and say there was nothing on it and that the police did not know he had found it. That should allay her fears. He was about to launch into his speech when the telephone rang. He was literally saved by the bell. Inspector Sweeney was up early too and was calling to say that a car would come for Nigel at 9.00 a.m.

"They had better have ID or I won't be going anywhere."

Fliss wanted to come too. She was very nervous about letting Nigel out of her sight, but he wouldn't hear of it.

The policeman who came for Nigel had ID and was in a marked police car. Great fun for the neighbours, Nigel thought bitterly. As he came out of the house with the policeman at his side, the newsreel cameras and flash photography reminded him of the worst of the paparazzi. They were pushing and jostling for a prime place and at one time thrust a camera into Nigel's face, shouting questions at him. The policeman stood at the top of the steps and raised his hand, then shouted at the crowd.

"Please leave. Later today there will be a Press Conference when you will all be informed of the situation. Now, please leave the family in peace."

Sweeney was standing looking out of the window in his office when Nigel arrived. There was a tray on the table with a coffee pot, two mugs and a plate of biscuits. He repressed the impulse to tip the coffee over Sweeney's head. Instead he sat down and waited, not trusting himself to speak. Sweeney poured the coffee and sat down opposite Nigel, the desk between them covered in files and papers.

"You did us a great service, Nigel. It is unfortunate that they got away, but at least they showed their hand and we now have some positive ID on the man calling himself Crosby."

Nigel looked at him, his eyebrows raised in mock surprise.

"So, you use me as a pawn and when I lead you to a terrorist safe house, because that is obviously what it was, you let them go! How did that happen, Inspector? Did they vanish up the chimney?"

Sweeney managed a crooked smile.

"Almost, Nigel. They had apparently disappeared into thin air. We obviously had the back of the house covered, but when we took the first floor apart we discovered a backless cupboard with a staircase leading down into the back door of a strip club – a euphemism of course for a brothel.. We had no warrant to search the place. Our quarries could have simply sauntered out into the street, assuming they were not entertaining themselves in other ways. The good news is that there was a lot of electronic equipment in the loft which will be invaluable to us and of course one of our operatives had a hidden camera and we now have positive ID on the man calling himself Inspector Crosby."

He finished his coffee. Nigel said nothing. He had risked his life and now wanted to know what was in it for him.

Sweeney shuffled the papers on his desk and continued in a calm voice. "The press unfortunately, but inevitably, are involved.

214

This afternoon we are giving a Press Conference which will get them off your back."

Nigel stood up, placed his palms on the desk and leaned across, his eyes blazing.

"I have no idea what is going on and I doubt you are going to inform me. You know the catalogue of events since my mother got arrested in Thailand, and don't give me any waffle about a random burglary at my father's house, resulting in his murder, or the discovery of a body with my mother's passport in Amsterdam, or the subsequent attack on me when I was trying to take my father's cigarette cards to the bank. I do not know anything about my father's memoirs and refuse to play your little game any more. You either buy me off handsomely or I go to the press myself."

Smithson's eyes narrowed. "I don't think that would be a good idea, Nigel. Let's just say we are all dealing with the unknown. A powerful unknown. I told you that you would be compensated and as long as you remain silent about the whole thing the safer it will be for you. Your wife will obviously want to know where a considerable sum of money comes from and I suggest we call it compensation for wrongful arrest. There will of course be conditions attached. London is not a safe place for you and it would be a good idea for you and your family to relocate. It would probably be as well for Mrs Jones senior to relocate too, considering her high profile and the fact that she was married to Mr Jones senior."

Nigel remained standing, his eyes fixed on Sweeney. "I hear what you are saying Inspector and I take it as a threat. A threat to my safety if I do not go along with you and your monstrous idea that my family should be uprooted. That would make good reading."

"Believe me, Nigel, the threat would not come from us and would be out of our control."

Nigel felt the throb in his head and had difficulty breathing, but managed to keep his voice even. "Do tell me Inspector, why I should believe you?"

Sweeney now also stood up and confronted Nigel. "Because you have no choice if you want to keep your family safe and together."

Nigel sat down and realised he was shaking. His hands were

white-knuckled as he made a fist which he banged down on the desk in frustration.

"I would like to call my lawyer."

Sweeney looked at him pityingly. "Not a good idea Nigel. This ends now."

He sat down and took a piece of paper from the desk on which he wrote a figure, sliding it across to Nigel. Nigel was about to say that no amount of money would be adequate compensation, but then saw the figure.

"Choose your moment and then talk to your wife and mother about relocating. Tell them you are tired of the rat race and would like your child to be brought up in the country, etc. Then put all this behind you and leave the clearing up to us."

Nigel's head was swimming and he was angry to the point of hysteria. Was there no end to the corruption? He briefly wondered if Fliss would consent to a move. And what about his mother?

"I seem to have no choice but to take your blood money, Inspector."

On the way home in the police car Nigel switched on his mobile. It rang almost immediately. It was Jeff.

"What the hell now? Do you need me, or Divine Intervention?" Jeff had not lost his sense of humour, but was bursting with curiosity. Nigel said he would meet him for lunch once the paparazzi were off his back. In the meantime he had to run the gauntlet of his long suffering wife and his poor mother. Presumably she would also have had the intrusion of the press again, but was probably used to it by now.

Fliss was waiting for him when he got home, her arms folded defensively across her chest.

"Don't flannel me anymore." Her voice was even and hard. "No tea. No coffee. No tears. No tantrums. I have had enough."

Nigel squared his shoulders, but inside felt as if he were unravelling, like the knitting his mother put right when Ellie was learning to knit.

"Look," he said, "it was a case of mistaken identity. I was strolling to get some fresh air before going back to work when I stumbled on what turned out to be a police raid. The gang grabbed me as a hostage and then all hell let loose. I'm just glad to be alive."

Fliss didn't bat an eyelid. She just kept her arms folded and spoke very quietly.

"In Soho, Nigel? What were you doing in Soho?"

The inference was clear and Nigel was furious.

"If you must know, I was trying to find an exclusive Chinese Restaurant to treat my lovely family to a special lunch. Seems I can't do anything right." He was aware that he sounded pathetic but it was the best he could come up with. "I'll have a sandwich and then I'm going to work. There should be a Press Release later exonerating me and then perhaps you can get your job back. Although now may be a good time to begin that maternity leave."

"I will leave when I want to, Nigel, with a leaving party and flowers and cards. Not because my husband is a suspected terrorist. Let me know when you have made the sandwiches." Her footsteps resounded as she stomped upstairs.

Laura had been awakened by the phone ringing at 7.00 a.m. She let it go to answer, turned over and pulled the duvet over her head, but she was suddenly wide awake with her heart racing. Who would be calling her at this hour? Surely not someone telling her she had won a prize or a trip to the Bahamas. Scammers. Reluctantly she got out of bed, went into the kitchen and put the kettle on and then went into the sitting room to listen to the message. She played it through three times, then with her heart pounding, went into the kitchen and made some tea which she took through into the sitting room before putting on the TV.

Apparently the police had raided an office in Soho, looking for suspected terrorists. It took her a moment to realise that this was in fact what Nigel had warned her about because there he was, being led out of a house in handcuffs. A case of mistaken identity he had said.

"The police will be issuing a statement later today. We will have more on the story later. And now for the weather forecast."

She snatched up the phone and called Nigel. Later she would be amazed that she had not been worried, just very angry. She knew

217

there were things that were being kept from her by the glances between him and Fliss when there was any mention of Trevor or Thailand. They must think of her as a dotty old lady, not to be trusted with certain information. Well, that would change. She was about to reinvent herself.

"Nigel. Yes, I have seen the news and thank you for warning me. Do you think you could trust yourself to let me know what is going on?" She had nearly said, "Or trust me," but had managed to change it just in time.

"I was just in the wrong place at the wrong time, Mum. Nothing to worry about. The police have apologised and are going to issue a statement later."

"Nigel. I am sorry to have to say this, but I don't believe you. There has been too much going on since I supposedly stole a baby and I think it's about time you came clean. Ellie is in a state because she thinks a lot of it is her fault by talking to the press in the beginning and now this. To be frank we just want to get back to normal!"

She surprised herself by shouting the last sentence. Nigel mumbled something about there being nothing going on and not to worry herself.

"I'm not worried, Nigel. I am angry. I am not going to charge over now. I will come on Sunday as arranged and you and Fliss can tell Ellie and me what is going on. I am going to call her now in case she has not heard the news."

"Actually, she does know Mum. She saw the news last night and came straight over."

"And no-one had the decency to call me?"

"You weren't in!"

Nigel sounded irritated now, so Laura said "Take care Nigel. I will see you on Sunday."

Laura immediately called Ellie who had just arrived home and was dashing about getting ready for work. "Ellie, I understand you knew about this latest fiasco? Could you not have called me?"

"Sorry Mum. They did try, but you were out and then it got really late, so Nigel said he would call you first thing. Apparently it has been sorted out and it was a mistake. The police are going to issue a statement later exonerating Nigel and then, hopefully, it will all blow over. I just hope it's not linked to whatever else is going on. I think we all need an explanation."

Laura switched the TV off and got herself some breakfast. Soon after 9.00 a.m. she had three phone calls, two of them from the ladies she played bridge with. She told them quite curtly that it was a case of mistaken identity and they soon rang off. Laura knew they just wanted to gossip. Safely married, or rich widowed women who wanted to dine out on the latest exploits of Laura Jones, divorced. A couple of them were in fact quite nice, but the others made it quite clear that Laura was not one of them. Then Jane rang and Laura had a chat with her about it all.

It was after the telephone calls that she began the reinvention plan. Thailand had been a disaster, but it had opened her mind to a whole new world and she was not going to let what had happened defeat her. She had a hot bath and then, wrapped up in her bathrobe, turned on her computer.

Back in Clapham, Nigel was making cheese and tomato sandwiches for his lunch. He usually bought something out, but knew he needed to put in a full day at the office. Nothing seemed real. It was the end of life as they knew it, and yet the family had no idea. Nothing would ever be the same again - this house, their friends and neighbours, in addition to a great upheaval for Laura. He could feel bile rising in his throat as he thought of his father. He slammed down the knife and sliced a deep cut in his finger. He found some plasters and then finished the sandwiches. As Fliss came down the stairs he gave her a hug, and putting his sandwich in a plastic bag left for work before she could ask any more questions. Glaring at the photographers he walked to the station. The weather had turned colder and it was drizzling. He was dreading the long winter ahead and all the upheaval. He felt impotently angry and at the same time despondent.

Nigel had just placed his briefcase on his desk when Frank walked in.

"So glad you could join us today, Nigel. Do you think you may be staying long this time? Any forays to Soho? Any appointments with Her Majesty's Government?"

"Wrong place, wrong time, wrong guy, Frank. There will be a Press Release later and all will be revealed."

Frank did not reply. The look said it all as he went back to his office and slammed the door.

Francesca brought in the post. "What is it with you Nigel? Death wish or something? I have an awful feeling that Frank is getting to the end of his tether."

"Lucky he is not in my shoes then." Nigel picked up the phone so that Francesca would get the message that this was not up for discussion. He really wanted to phone Jeff, but needed to be seen to be proactive with what he was paid to do. He found that by forcing himself to concentrate solely on work, and to do so with almost feverish actions, the morning passed quickly. He ate his sandwich at his desk and worked through the lunch time.

"His mobile rang at 2.00 p.m. "Nigel, you free to talk?"

"Hi Jeff. Thanks for your message. Divine Intervention may come in the guise of a Press Conference this afternoon."

"Couldn't believe my eyes last night, Nigel. Do you need any legal help? And of course, I want to know what is going on. There seems to be no end to it old boy."

"No legal help needed, thanks, Jeff. A case of mistaken identity. Are you free for lunch tomorrow? Italian?"

Nigel left at 5.00 p.m. determined to be at home for the Six O'clock News. The Press Conference was brief and to the point, even if it was a total fabrication. Basically there had been a tip off about terrorist activity, there had been a raid and unfortunately a passerby had got caught up in the drama. Nigel Jones was not implicated in any way and due to security issues to protect the public, there would be no further enquiry. In other words, a gagging order on the Press in the cause of public safety. He looked across at Fliss. "Satisfied now?" He could not keep the sarcasm out of his voice.

"After supper I want you to tell me everything. There seems to have been a cascade of events and in spite of what you say I do not believe that there is no link between them. No more cover ups,

Nigel. I've had Laura on the phone and she sounded terribly angry. She is so upset that she actually couldn't face seeing you! That shows how badly affected she is." She went out into the kitchen and dished up fish fingers and instant mashed potatoes which she banged down on the dining room table and then burst into tears.

"Ok. Look, no tears. We'll eat our dinner and then have a chat. This looks good. Any ketchup?"

Whilst he was eating Nigel's mind was racing. It would just not wash with Fliss to say there was nothing he was keeping from her, but he also knew that he could not be totally honest with her. He decided, however, to tell her as much as he felt he could safely say and trust the fact that she would not talk to anyone else. He loved Fliss and hated to see her so upset. It was time to come clean. Well, as clean as he could, he decided. They talked until gone 11.00 p.m. He began with the answerphone message.

"I didn't want to give you cause for concern, Fliss, but it worried me a great deal. It was so unlike Dad to call me at all. And as you know the message was so weird. At first I thought it might be something to do with the canal where Dad and I fished when I was a kid. That's where the maggots came in! Jeff and I went on the pretext of fishing, found nothing, but realised we had been followed."

Fliss put down her coffee and Nigel saw she was trembling.

"Don't worry. It's all sorted. Hear me out."

"Do you mean Jeff knew all along but you kept it from me?"

"I needed Jeff on board. He is our legal representative. You must understand that. I didn't want you worried. Jeff said the message seemed pretty cryptic and that's when I realised it could be like a cryptic crossword clue."

Nigel went on to explain about the holly tree and the root canal theory. He knew Fliss would be upset when she realised that the 'garden party' had been a ruse, and he was correct. She was furious and it took Nigel a while to calm her down so he could continue.

"Well, I was right and I found a memory stick under the holly bush. I didn't look at it for a while, basically because there was the little matter of my being attacked and in hospital, but eventually I did and it was a rather boring account of Trevor's life in the Civil

Service with absolutely no reference to anything that could be of any interest to the government or anyone else."

Nigel had rehearsed this so often in his mind that the lie tripped off his tongue easily.

"I did suspect that the phone was tapped, so set a trap by phoning the bank about taking the security box in. Of course the rest is history and I realised just how dangerous the whole thing had become."

"Nigel, you could have been killed. Why didn't you go to the police with your fears?"

Nigel took a deep breath. "Because," he said evenly, "I was pretty sure there was an involvement by the Secret Service." He decided not to mention foreign forces. Fliss had enough to take in.

"How on earth did they get to know anything about it in the first place?" Nigel shrugged and raised his eyebrows in a 'think about it' look.

"Oh God. Not Ellie blabbing on about memoirs!"

"Precisely. But for heaven's sake don't ever breathe a word."

"No wonder they gave Laura a grilling. Why didn't you just give them the tape if there was nothing on it?"

Nigel had been expecting this and was prepared. "I guess I panicked. I felt caught up in something I did not understand and just wanted shot of it, so I destroyed it. As far as they are concerned I didn't understand the message and found nothing. Fliss, this is vitally important. This is just between us. Understand?"

His tone frightened Fliss and she nodded. After a few minutes she regained her composure and continued. "So, what about this latest drama, Nigel?"

"Special Branch still believed that Dad had left some incriminating documentation in his memoirs and this was reinforced when my laptop was stolen."

"Stolen? I thought it had gone for repair."

"I know, sorry about that. Ellie would have had a breakdown if she felt she had handed it over to anyone involved in any of this. It was best left as a robbery. Well, the police realised that someone else was very interested to know if I had found anything and, although I don't know any details, set me up to visit a house in Soho where they thought there was a cell who were involved. I was to try to get my laptop back and see what was going on. Unfortunately it all went wrong as you now know."

Fliss banged her coffee cup down, spilling coffee on the table. "How dare they set you up? Why can't you go public?"

"Two reasons, Fliss. One, these people are ruthless. Think about Dad being murdered, about the woman in Amsterdam, about the attack on me."

Fliss folded her arms protectively across her body. Her voice was high and afraid.

"Are we safe now? All of us?"

Nigel waited a moment before continuing. "It seems so. The second reason I cannot go public is that someone in a high place has paid me off. Hush money if you like."

"But that's evil! People have a right to know!"

"And we have a right to live in peace."

"What on earth was Trevor working on that frightened them all so much?"

"No idea. Now, I know this is a lot to take in all in one go, Fliss, but they are paying me compensation and it is a considerable amount of money. With the money from Trevor's estate it is enough for us to move away from all this." As he said this, Nigel could feel the pain start in his head and the anxiety beginning to affect his breathing. "Excuse me. I just need some water." He went into the kitchen and took a beta blocker.

When he returned Fliss was pacing up and down the room. "Move? Why should we? What for? Where to? What about Laura and Ellie? What about our jobs?" The questions came thick and fast and Nigel waited quietly for the storm to abate.

"There is a lot going on that we do not understand and to be honest I don't want to know. It will be better if we get away. What happened to me in Soho, coupled with the attack by the car has, quite frankly, scared the shit out of me. I don't want to go there again and I don't want you, or any of the family, to be at risk either."

Fliss sat down and, taking a deep breath, looked his straight in the eye. "Are these the terms of your blood money?"

"Look, I know it is a lot to take in. Let's try to get some sleep and talk more in the morning. And Fliss, you must never breathe a word of it to anyone – even family."

Fliss lay awake for hours, her mind going round in circles. Presumably if there had not been the latest disaster in Soho, Nigel would still be keeping all this to himself.

What pressure he had been under. No wonder he had nearly cracked up. With everything else going on the baby must have been the last straw. Thank God he had come round to the idea and was really looking forward to it. They had not decided whether they wanted to know whether it was a boy or girl although Laura kept threatening to knit things in blue, saying that girls could wear blue but boys not pink.

Fliss wondered if the phone was still tapped and if they were being followed. Nigel had made her promise not to talk to a soul and she was glad he had trusted her enough to confide in her. At least they had each other. It must have been hell for Nigel, although she now knew that Jeff had been privy to much of it. She couldn't even ask what he thought of it all. Moving away would be such a big step but after their talk she suddenly didn't feel safe in her own home. Perhaps a new start would be the right thing to do. She knew that Nigel would worry about the impact on Laura and Ellie. Whether they would move too would be anyone's guess. Fliss had often dreamed about moving to Devon or Cornwall when they retired, but it was so far off that she had never really given it serious thought. She finally drifted off to sleep imagining the sound of the sea.

She was awake again at 3.00 a.m. and made herself some hot chocolate. For the first time she wondered about Trevor's job. No wonder he had seemed so remote. Poor Laura. She had been married to a shadow. A man who had really been married to his career. What on earth had he been involved in to cause such interest now that he was dead? No wonder the Special Branch had put Laura through so much questioning. Then there was Ellie who had always feared that her talking to the press had caused a problem. If only she knew! She was fragile at the best of times, but to know the truth would just about finish her off. And when would she and Laura be told about a move? The more Fliss thought about it the more it seemed the most feasible option was to move away. Away from the rotten world of spies and lies. A place where they could breathe clean air and where Nigel could feel safe himself and keep his family safe.

She finished her chocolate and got back into bed and as Nigel turned over she took his hand and placed it on her tummy.

"What?"

"Our baby is in there."

"Good show," he said before drifting back to sleep.

Nigel was unusually apprehensive on the Sunday morning. Fliss put the joint in the oven whilst Nigel went out to do some tidying up in the garden. He did not want to think about the impending inquisition. He had no idea what to say and as he trimmed the edges of the lawn he realised he felt sick. He went in to have a shower and get changed. He looked in the mirror and, seeing a threatening terrorist lookalike staring back at him, decided that the beard had to go. It took ages to shave it off. After his shower he cleared the steam off the mirror and quite liked what he saw. He thought he looked younger and somehow the black rings under his eyes were not so noticeable.

When he went down into the kitchen Fliss turned to ask him if he would set the table. "Oh wow! Thank God for that. I've got my handsome husband back!" She went over and gave him a kiss, the first for a long time without feeling his hairy face against hers. God, she hated beards! "New life, new Nigel," she said happily.

Ellie arrived first, which was unusual as she and Laura usually came together.

"Nigel! That's better! You don't look like a terrorist any more! Perhaps everyone will leave you alone now!" She laughed, missing entirely the sharp intake of breath from Fliss.

"Thanks for that Ellie! Where's Mum?"

"She said she would come a bit later as she had some things to do first."

"What sort of things?"

"I have no idea. I haven't spoken to her since the Soho episode, apart from a brief chat about it when she found out. We have texted each other, but she has not been available on the phone."

"I tried her during the week too, but although I left a message she didn't call back."

Nigel was carving the meat when Laura finally arrived. She usually let herself in with her key, but had changed her handbag and left the key at home, so she rang the bell. Fliss wondered who it could be, knowing that Laura had a key. She opened the door a little and there was a strange woman standing there. She was about to ask her what she wanted when she realised it was Laura. The whole scene was surreal, rather like trying to look at one of those jumbled hologram type pictures by holding it at a certain angle until suddenly there is a clear picture.

"Well, don't just stand there Fliss. Open the door properly and let me in."

She walked past Fliss, who stood open mouthed by the door. Ellie was sitting at the table with a glass of wine and Nigel was still carving. They glanced up and froze in mid tracks. Laura's dark blonde hair, greying at the temples, had been cut and highlighted into a modern geometric style. Her eyebrows had been plucked into neat, surprised semi circles and her face glowed with a warm bronzed tan and shimmering blusher. Her eyes were enhanced by grey eyeshadow and cleverly administered eyeliner and mascara. She was wearing a red designer suit, the skirt knee length, and black patent high heeled shoes. The old handbag, which usually pulled the shoulder of her coat down with its worn strap, was replaced by a shiny black number with a large buckle. She was also wearing new earrings, large silver studs with a small diamond droplet. She looked stunning.

"Well. Don't just stare at me! Let's have dinner and then you can tell me what is going on." She put her bag on a chair and they noticed her red designer shaped nails. Probably acrylic, Ellie thought.

"Laura. You look fantastic! I am so sorry, I just didn't recognise you. Not that you don't always look good, of course."

"Well, it's about time I found myself. Nigel! It looks as if you've had a shave. That's better. I have my son back at last! This is the right sort of shave – I am fed up with your 'close shaves.' She laughed at her own witticism whilst Fliss and Nigel did their best to manage a smile.

They sat down to dinner and Laura took over the conversation. "As I said, after dinner I want to know what is going on. This last adventure is almost farcical. I am fed up to the back teeth with it all. Arrests in Thailand, robberies, murders, accidents in the car. I was not born yesterday. And you, Ellie, were falling apart even before all this. Look at the state you were in when you got back from France. Well, you can all tell me what's going on without all this cloak and dagger stuff, and if you don't then I really don't care."

Nigel coughed nervously. "Of course we will talk to you. Let's enjoy our meal and then we can all have a cosy chat."

Fliss glared at him and he shrugged his shoulders as if to say "Well, you do better then."

Ellie said through gritted teeth, "I'll look forward to it."

In between mouthfuls Laura continued, "I'll get my news out of the way, then you can proceed uninterrupted when you are ready."

Nigel was reminded of the tone of the police officers. "When you are ready, Mr Jones. In your own words." He had no idea what he was going to say, especially now there was compensation involved which would obviously change their lives.

Laura had a sip of wine and putting down her fork looked at them all in turn. They still could not get over the change in appearance. Before she could start Ellie turned to her. "Mum. I don't want to sound rude, but have you had a makeover or something? And can we have the number?"

Everyone laughed and the mood was lightened. Fliss looked at Nigel and smiled conspiratorially.

"Well now," Laura continued, "as you have already noticed I have decided to make some changes. Thailand was the first step in my doing something for myself, but unfortunately it did not quite work out as I had hoped."

Nigel grimaced. "You can say that again."

"Well, I could either go into a depression and give up any ideas of adventure, or do something about it. During the past week I have

227

realised that I have been totally bound up with all of you and the events of the past months. Don't get me wrong. I do value your looking after me and I am thrilled about becoming a grandmother, but if I'm not careful I will slip into my dotage without even noticing. There is more to life than playing bridge, worrying incessantly about others, being surrounded by problems and depression in my working life and watching soaps."

She paused for breath, holding her glass up to Nigel for some more wine.

"No, I got a taxi here and am being picked up at 5.00 p.m." She had some more wine whilst the others waited apprehensively for the next instalment.

"I have joined a dating site and have had an interesting correspondence this week with a retired architect. I had coffee with him yesterday morning and we got on very well. He is going to pick me up from here and we are going to a quiet country pub for a chat and a drink. If it works out then perhaps next year we will go to Glasgow so he can show me the architecture of Charles Rennie Mackintosh. I have always liked the design although it is a shame it is stuck on tea towels and carrier bags. I want to see the School of Art and apparently there is a house he designed for Walter Blackie."

"You've learned a lot in two days!" Nigel could not believe his ears. His mother! Dating!

"It will all be above board. Separate rooms of course. For now." Nigel could have sworn that she blushed. "But if we get on then he hopes to take me to Barcelona to see the Gaudi. I know it is a bit sudden, but at our age we have to get a move on. I'll give you his contact details of course." Before they could digest this information she continued. "I have also joined an organisation called Women Welcome Women Worldwide. It is an international organisation for promoting friendship between women in different countries. I don't want to put all my eggs in one basket with Arthur, so I intend to explore friendships with women in other countries and travel with some of them, or stay with some of them. I also have enough room to host some of the women myself. That way I can travel safely and not get into the pickle I got myself into in Thailand."

"Sounds like a lesbian club to me" Nigel muttered.

Laura raised an immaculate eyebrow. "Don't be ridiculous Nigel. You don't understand or know what you are talking about. Look it up. 5W. I have also been in touch with the Embassy in Thailand."

At this point Nigel banged his glass down with such force Laura thought it would shatter. "You did WHAT?"

"I called Jennifer to ask her to let me know the name of the orphanage where she found Nitnoy because I want to know the arrangements for adoption."

Nigel literally choked on his wine. "You're not thinking of *adopting* her?" he spluttered.

"Don't be silly dear. Apparently many Thai orphans are adopted by Americans. If that is the case then eventually I want them to put me in touch with the adoptive parents and I want to go and see her. I am after all almost her surrogate mother. I know the paperwork takes ages, but at least I have expressed an interest."

"Well, you have been a busy bee Laura, and it seems to be doing you good." Fliss was not sure what else she should say, so she began to gather up the plates which she and Ellie took out into the kitchen.

"Well," Ellie said, whilst Fliss was dishing up rhubarb crumble and custard, "who would have thought it! And presumably after dessert we'll all retire to the sitting room and hear what Nigel has to say, although it may be a case of 'follow that!'"

"I doubt it," Fliss replied.

After they had finished eating the girls cleared up. Laura sat in the sitting room waiting for her coffee as she did not want to chip her nail polish by doing any of the pans. Nigel finished clearing the table and made the coffee. When everyone was seated with their coffees in the bone china cups she looked up and spoke directly to Nigel.

"Are we all sitting comfortably? Then you may begin. And it had better be good! I think we all feel we have been kept in the dark about a lot of things, Nigel."

Nigel had already primed Fliss about how much he would tell Ellie and Laura. She knew that she must never breathe a word about Nigel actually having found the memory stick but was nevertheless impressed at how clever he was at the evasion.

They both knew things would be particularly difficult for Ellie, who had always maintained that she had contributed in some way to the murder of her father, but it had become increasingly apparent that both she and Laura deserved to know what was going on, or as much as Nigel felt he could disclose. He certainly couldn't just tell them that he and Fliss were moving away and that perhaps Laura should come too without some sort of explanation.

He began by telling them about his shock on his return from Thailand to the bizarre message from Trevor.

"Why weren't we told? I suppose you knew about it Fliss? And what about you Ellie?" Laura's voice had an acrimonious tone.

"Nigel didn't tell me for ages. When he tells you everything you will understand why he couldn't say much." Fliss didn't dare look at Nigel when she said "when he tells you everything."

Nigel went on to explain that he had suspected someone, and he did not know precisely who, was very worried about the contents of Trevor's memoirs being made public, but that he thought he could handle it himself. He said he had tried to interpret the message and had even gone with Jeff to the Grand Union Canal on the pretext of a fishing trip. He told them how his fears had been confirmed when they realised they had been followed and also told them about the tree.

Ellie interrupted, near to tears. "See. I told you it was all my fault."

Fliss took charge. "Ellie, this is not about you. Just pull yourself together and listen."

Ellie hated it when Fliss criticised her and bit her lip in anger, but managed to keep quiet. Nigel had decided not to tell them about the true reason for the garden party, but he did tell them about the ruse with the cigarette cards and the subsequent attack and about the removal of his laptop.

"My fault again" Ellie muttered, whilst Laura was clearly shaken.

"Luckily I had backed up all my work, so it was not crucial, but it did tell me that 'they', whoever 'they' are, were still trying to find how much I knew. I had by then been to the police and told them about the phone message. I think they were pretty twitchy which is why Special Branch got involved. I would hazard a guess that whoever murdered Trevor and took his computer knew what he had written and needed to make quite sure that a) he had never talked to Mum about it and b) I had not been able to make sense of the phone message or access any memoirs." He paused, finishing off his coffee, and asked them to leave any questions until he had told them everything. He went on to explain about being in Soho and his wrongful arrest. The lies tripped off his tongue smoothly and Fliss couldn't help but feel admiration for the way he was handling it all. He then told them that he thought the phone was tapped.

"Oh my God. What is going on?" Laura was sitting bolt upright, her newly arched eyebrows almost disappearing under her fringe.

Ellie, with a burst of sarcasm of her own, put up her hand. "Permission to speak?

Presumably if I had not told the Press about Nigel's memoirs, none of this would have happened. I fail to see why it is not my fault."

Laura, sitting next to her daughter, put a comforting hand on her arm. "You may as well say, Ellie, that if I had not gone to Thailand none of this would have happened. If I had not found a baby none of it would have happened. We cannot put the clock back. We all did what we thought was right at the time." She turned to Nigel. "Obviously we had no idea what you have been through and I understand why you kept it to yourself. No wonder you have been looking so dreadful. And I am glad that you have shaved off that preposterous beard, especially before the baby is born. You don't want to frighten it to death." They all managed a laugh which lightened the tone.

Ellie was like a dog with a bone. "And I suppose it was not my fault that your laptop was taken? Don't flannel me with that nonsense about you had forgotten that guy was coming round. I guess that is part of this drama as well?"

Before Nigel could reply Laura was asking questions about the reporters in Thailand. The questions came thick and fast. Had Nigel any idea of who 'they' were, was the telephone still tapped, was

Nigel's life now safe, had he told the police he knew nothing about any memoirs? Nigel had rehearsed the scene so often in his mind that more lies, or bending of truth as he preferred to see it, came easily.

He stood up, went to the dresser and poured himself a brandy. Ellie was driving, Fliss not drinking, but he raised the glass to Laura who declined. He sat down and listened to them asking Fliss how much she had known and how awful it must have been when Nigel was attacked on the way to the bank.

"I did suspect, but didn't actually know until later."

When Nigel had finished his brandy he continued. "Look. It is not all doom and gloom. Apparently wrongful arrest in such dangerous circumstances is pretty serious and as the police want it all kept as quiet as possible I have been offered and accepted compensation."

Ellie instinctively sat further forward on the sofa, as if she were watching a film which had reached its climax. "How much?" She looked at Nigel expectantly.

"The final figure has not yet been confirmed, but what has been agreed is that none of what we have talked about ever gets out. I need an undertaking from each of you. As you will now appreciate, this is of the utmost importance."

Laura and Ellie nodded their heads in agreement and Fliss said "Of course, Nigel. It goes without saying."

"Thanks, Fliss, but it needs to be said."

After a moment he continued. "Fliss and I have agreed that the best course of action is to take the money and move away."

Ellie and Laura sat staring at Nigel. Laura finally spoke. "Are you sure it is not a bribe for silence, Nigel?"

He ignored his mother. "Ellie, you and I have already come to an agreement to sell Dad's house and I suggest we do that soon, and then Fliss and I will sell this house. You will of course get half the proceeds from Dad's house which will be quite a decent sum. You and Mum may both feel that you want to get away too." He did not actually say that it might be safer but guessed that after all the revelations they would probably work that out for themselves. "Fliss and I have decided to move to the West Country and, if we can find it, we would like a farmhouse with a cottage in the grounds. Mum, if you want to be near us, the cottage will be for you. You will have no financial worries any more and of course will be on hand for babysitting duties! No pressure of course!" He managed a laugh as he said this. "Ellie, depending on where you want to go, if you decide to move, I will help you in any way I can and will of course meet the difference if you need more for a property. You can come to the West Country of course, but I don't exactly see you mucking out horses and growing beets."

If Nigel had expected excitement he was to be disappointed. Ellie and Laura just sat in stunned silence. Fliss wished she could have a brandy.

"When is this likely to happen Nigel?" Laura spoke very calmly and was almost businesslike. Nigel felt that Laura was reinventing herself in more ways than one.

"Well, we would like to put the houses on the market soon with a view to moving if possible before Christmas. There may still be a bit of red tape about selling Dad's but we can certainly get everything underway. We would really like to be settled well before the baby is born, which will be around Easter."

Ellie turned to her mother. "What are you thinking Mum?"

"Well, there is so much to take in that I need to go away and think about it. Don't worry, Nigel, I do understand the gravity of what happened and will not discuss it with any one else."

Ellie was in agreement. "No, nor me. I need to think too. Fliss, do you mind if I go and make some tea? And then maybe Mum would like to hear Trevor's phone message. I know I would like to hear it again."

They took their cups of tea into Nigel's study and stood around the phone whilst Nigel rewound it and played his father's message. Ellie began to sob and Fliss actually put an arm round her instead of berating her.

Laura said nothing, but returned to her seat on the sofa in the sitting room. Presently she looked at her watch. "Heavens! Is that the time! I can stay for another half hour or so, but then will need to go. In one way I feel I am abandoning you all, but on the other I really need a distraction, so I think it will be a good thing. Don't worry! After all the excitement I am sure you needn't worry about my being abducted by an old aged pensioner."

The discussion continued and Nigel parried questions as they asked him who he thought was behind it all. Laura talked about Positive Vetting and mused about Trevor's actual role during the time he was abroad and also his latter years in London.

"He never talked about work" she said. "In fact he never talked much anyway in the latter years. Now I wonder what he really did."

Refusing more tea Laura eventually said she should go, and sent a text to the mysterious Arthur to ask him to pick her up. "I don't know his other name yet, but this is his mobile number." She handed Nigel a scrap of paper with the number on then excusing herself went up to the bathroom, coming down as immaculate as when she had arrived, her lipstick freshly applied and an obvious dab of perfume behind her ears.

"Thank you for lunch. Quite an experience. I am so glad you finally told us what is going on, Nigel. What an ordeal it has been right from my little trip to Thailand. Let's hope the move will see an end to it. I'll give you a call tomorrow. Bye Ellie. Give me a ring if you want to talk."

She turned to Nigel "I don't suppose my phone is tapped too?" Nigel grinned at her. "I very much doubt it Mum, but just to be on the safe side, please, neither of you ever talk to each other about today on the phone and certainly don't mention anything when you telephone here. If you have any questions about it all, give me a call and say you want to talk about the house move."

Nigel showed her to the door and watched whilst she walked elegantly down the path and into a waiting silver Mercedes. Automatically he noted the registration number as they drove away, and wrote it on the shopping pad on the hall table before joining the others.

They talked for another half hour and then Ellie said she too would go.

"Won't you stay for tea? Are you OK? You can stay the night if you like."

"I'm fine, thanks, Fliss. I have a lot of thinking to do and if Laura can reinvent herself, then I am sure I can too!" She picked up her bag. "Let's talk soon, Nigel. I would like some figures. I assume we should soon go through the house together and see if it wants a lick of paint. Luckily the garden is done. What a great day we had there in the summer." She turned towards the hall, missing the wry looks exchanged between Nigel and Fliss.

As she was showing Ellie out, Fliss caught sight of herself in the hall mirror and realised how tired she looked. She ran her fingers through her hair and smiled at her reflection in an attempt to look better. She went back into the sitting room and began gathering up the cups. "Didn't Laura look amazing? I wonder what she will decide to do. She didn't look as if she was about to resume a life of counselling and bridge! And what about her dating? Even if the friendship with this chap doesn't come to anything I rather think she has opened a Pandora's Box. I don't like not knowing his surname."

Nigel said "Don't worry. I got the number of his car."

CHAPTER 21

Ellie had arranged to go out with Liz and Izzy for a drink, but after the afternoon's revelations she thought it better to cancel. She knew she would never say anything about the situation, but with so much going round in her mind she needed to let things settle before she could socialise and make small talk. After she arrived home she phoned Izzy and apologised, saying she thought she was going down with something as she had a bad headache and was going to go to bed. She then lit a scented candle which she placed on the coffee table and settled down on the sofa with her feet up.

Poor Nigel. And although Fliss had not known everything she must have been through a lot, what with the attack and theft of the security box coming after all the trauma of Laura's arrest and then Trevor's murder. No wonder she had bitten her head off. To actually want to move away must mean that Nigel was under extreme pressure and probably not a little scared. She desperately wished she could put the clock back and have taken Nigel's advice and not called the newspaper. Suddenly the picture of Trevor in his study after the murder came into her mind and then the tears came. She knew from experience that once her mind got on to the murder she would not be able to stop crying, so she made herself get up and put on the TV. Thank goodness there was no threat of her seeing her mother or her brother on the news.

She watched the programmes mindlessly, her thoughts still churning. She refused to think about her Dad and only to focus on her mother. She hoped Laura knew what she was doing, that it was in fact "moving on" and not a rebound reaction to all that she had endured. She certainly looked great and she had been on her own a long time. Perhaps the events of the past months had been the catalyst to help her find her own identity. And what about she, herself, Ellie, daughter of Trevor Jones, deceased? What had she done with her life since running away from France? She had never addressed the issue of what had happened, just got on as best she could and confided in no-one. Her mother had gone through a trauma and was now coming out of it, whilst Ellie had coasted, making sure she would not be hurt again by just not putting herself out there. She didn't want to confide in her mother, although she had been tempted at one point and she certainly did not want to talk to a stranger. Although Steph was her best friend and she trusted her implicitly, she had never been able to bring herself to talk to her about the rape. She needed, she realised with sudden clarity, to take charge of the rest of her life.

She turned the TV off, went to her bedroom and made herself go through her wardrobe, putting in a pile for the charity shop everything she had kept 'just in case it would come in handy,' plus everything she had not worn the previous winter. She would go shopping for a new wardrobe before the cold weather set in. The winter stocks were appearing in the shops and Ellie felt it was time to reinvent herself too.

As she sifted through things she remembered how she had taken the dress she had worn to the club the night she had met Louis and cut it into pieces in her apartment in Paris. She would treat herself to something special for the coming party season. Party season? When Nigel and Fliss moved, and perhaps Laura too, did Ellie want to stay where she was, temping and going out with the girls. She had given thought to doing an interior design course, but apathy had taken hold of her once she realised how much work would be involved. She went out into the kitchen and brought back a black bin bag into which she put the clothes for the charity shop. Then she followed this with shoes and bags. It was amazing how liberated she felt when she had finally finished and had colour coded what was left, making sure there were no wire hangers and that every hanger had the hook facing the same way. She felt better.

Back on the settee with a glass of white wine and a sandwich she wrote a list of the things that interested her and the hopes and ideas she had had before Paris. She quickly realised that the impact of the attack actually helped her now to see that many of the things she had thought important before now seemed facile, such as massage or nail technology courses. She realised that dreadful events were happening to people, like rapes that went unreported, Laura's stories of the young girls sold for sex by their parents in Thailand so that the boys could be educated; wrongful arrests and the incarceration in prison of innocent people. She went to the computer and googled VSO. She vaguely wondered if she were looking for a hair shirt to compensate for what she believed to be her part in Trevor's murder, or whether the rape and miscarriage had given her a new perspective on life. What really mattered, she realised, was what she felt now, and looking at the information online made her feel better than she had for a very long time.

Reading it helped her focus 'outside the box'. There was so much to take in, but the two things that interested her most were the countries that needed help with planting crops and self sufficiency, and those with needs for education, particularly in teaching English. She was fascinated by the information on the various countries helped by VSO and could feel a stirring within her to do some good in the world.

She then went onto the website for courses on teaching English as a foreign language. There were many courses online and Ellie spent another hour researching the various options and then requested a prospectus. She realised she felt much better. The thought of staying where she was depressed her, but the thought of moving to the West Country with its slower pace of life, distance from the buzz of London and Nigel's plan for a smallholding, did nothing for her either. She had been to Plymouth once and although the area near the yacht club was attractive she felt that the city itself with its shops and car parks looked as if chunks of concrete had been dropped from a great height. Cornwall was even further away. A little thrill sent a tingle down her spine as she found herself thinking that India or Honduras or Eritrea sounded much more interesting.

Just as she was about to log off she came across a site for Womankind Worldwide, an organisation that helps women in East Africa who have been victims of rape, forced marriage and genital mutilation. As she read the information she found herself in tears. What she had suffered in France was nothing compared to the suffering of these young girls. She felt enraged that this should be happening and at the same time she felt compelled to find out more and see if there was something she could do. She sent them an email immediately, requesting more information and for the first time she felt she had taken a step towards the rest of her life.

It was 9.00 p.m. by the time she switched off the computer and poured herself another glass of wine. Her mind went back to her brother's revelations and she found herself mulling over the whole catalogue of disasters, right from the moment of Laura's arrest. She wondered again about Trevor's work. The whole thing was beginning to look more like a spy novel than the life of her family. None of them had mentioned the murder of the woman in Amsterdam, but presumably there had to be a link as she was carrying Laura's passport. No wonder Nigel wanted to get away, although in fact it seemed as if he were being forced to leave. She was not sure how much she now believed about the so-called wrongful arrest in Soho, but decided that it was all out of her league and, like her mother, this was a time for a radical change.

She watched TV for a while and then went to bed and slept surprisingly well. In the morning whilst she got ready for work she found herself thinking about the TEFL course and the email she had sent to Womankind. She wondered how Laura had enjoyed her evening with Arthur.

In fact Laura had enjoyed her evening very much. She had joined the internet dating site under the pseudonym of Miriam and for the moment had decided to let that stay. She just hoped that Arthur would not realise she was the woman who had been arrested in Thailand and the subsequent family problems. She guessed that Arthur had used his real name. He took her to a quiet pub and they sat at a table near a log fire. She drank a glass of red wine whilst Arthur had a beer. He told her about his career, about how he had lost his wife to cancer three years earlier and only now felt ready to move on. He had two sons, one lived in Scotland, married with two children and the other lived in Boston with his American wife and two daughters. He asked her about her family and Laura told him that Nigel worked in the City, was married to Fliss and that they were expecting their first child. Ellie had worked in Paris for a while but was now temping in London whilst deciding what she wanted to do with her life. The wine could have loosened her tongue but she decided not to say anything about Thailand and the high profile murder of her ex-husband. That could wait until they knew each other better. Conversation was easy and she felt very comfortable with him. He dropped her off outside her house and she resisted the temptation to invite him in for coffee. In the old days, coffee meant coffee, but these days she knew there could be other implications. He got out of the car and opened her door for her, then, giving her a brief kiss on the cheek, said he would give her a call during the week. She went indoors feeling happy, having managed to put the revelations of the afternoon behind her for a while.

She also slept well, but awoke in the morning with the Jones saga very much on her mind. She made herself some tea and went back to bed with her journal. It took her more than half an hour to document the order in which she now knew things had happened, starting with her arrest in Bangkok. Hearing Trevor's voice on the answer phone message had been a shock and she carefully noted exactly what she had said to the press when they visited her in the cell and what she now knew of Ellie's part in the press coverage. She then went through the grilling she had received from the police on her return and the intrusive questions about Trevor. She was not sure of the exact date the poor woman in Amsterdam had been murdered, but certainly it was before the police questioned her. She continued with what she knew about Nigel's foray to the Grand Union Canal, the attack on him and the theft of the cigarette cards, and then the seemingly unrelated arrest in Soho. No, Nigel knew more than he was saying and the fact that he now felt forced to move away made her deeply suspicious of everything. How much more Fliss knew she had no idea, but she was not taken in by Nigel's explanation.

When she had finished her list she had a shower and got dressed in her new black trousers, winter white jumper and pearls. It would have been easy to stay in her dressing gown or put on an old track suit, but she enjoyed the new Laura and wanted to stay that way. Whilst eating her breakfast her mind went back to the years she had been with Trevor and the fact that she knew so little about his work. On one occasion she had been surprised when he came home from work and opened his briefcase, emblazoned with the Crown, to see that it contained an apple and a sandwich box. There were no computers at home in those days so he obviously kept the paper trail very much at the office.

If the fact that he had written his memoirs was engendering such dramatic interest, she wondered what on earth it was that he actually did. The more she thought about it the more she determined to let it go. Nigel was obviously spooked about something and the less she knew the better. She picked the phone up and arranged to meet Jane for lunch. She may even tell her about Arthur, but that would be the extent of the disclosure.

Back in Clapham, Nigel had left for work and Fliss got herself busy phoning Estate Agents to have the house valued. In one way she felt scared but in another way she felt relieved. There had been too much happening that filled her with fear and the sooner they got away the better. She just hoped that moving would put an end to it, whatever 'it' was. She believed in her heart that Nigel was keeping things from her, but knew him well enough to realise that if this was the case then he would have good reason. She had no intention of sitting him down and giving him the third degree. For one thing she had the baby to consider and needed to stay as calm as possible, and then she was aware that Nigel had been under unprecedented strain and was afraid that pushing him may result in another panic episode. No, if Nigel said the deal was that they had to move, then so be it. There would be upheaval certainly, but nothing could compare to the upheaval of the past months. In fact the thought of a property in the West Country seemed quite attractive and if Laura moved as well Nigel would not worry about his mother as she got older. Fliss smiled to herself at this thought. The way Laura had looked and her obvious determination to start dating and going out meant that 'old age' was quite a way off.

Appointments were made for both properties to be viewed, their own house on Wednesday and Trevor's on Thursday. They would have to start spending weekends clearing out Trevor's things. Most of the paperwork had been removed, but there were still some legal matters to be finalised and at least they would have some idea of valuation. It should not take too long to deal with his clothes and to make the house look homely again. After lunch she drove over to Trevor's and polished the furniture, vacuumed the carpets and put a couple of vases of flowers on the tables. She also made herself some strong coffee and left the percolator on the side, hoping the smell would permeate through the kitchen until Thursday. She had read how this helped to give the right ambiance, but baking bread was not an option. Thank goodness the garden still looked stunning after all the hard work.

Summer slipped into autumn, although there was an interlude of a couple of weeks of Indian summer. Fliss and Nigel worked hard at Trevor's. Fliss insisted on polishing their own house from top to bottom and Nigel was dispatched to wash down the front door and garage.

Fliss had enjoyed a good final send off from the school and everyone tactfully let it be known they assumed she was leaving due to her pregnancy. No mention was made of the suspension and Fliss decided not to make a fuss. She had been reinstated after the holidays, once the police had issued their public statement.

The regular family Sunday lunches were ostensibly on hold, although they all guessed it was the end of an era. Ellie seemed to have recovered her old exuberance and was going out with friends at weekends. She did go round to Trevor's a couple of times to see if she could be of any help, but the offer was somewhat half-hearted and Fliss and Nigel seemed to have everything pretty much under control. She found that the only way she could deal with Nigel's disclosures and the imminent departure of her family to the West Country was not to discuss it, but to get on with her own plans, which she kept pretty much to her chest as far as family was concerned.

As for Laura, she absented herself from Trevor's house. She said she would be available if any help was needed, but felt it had been his private domain and would have been uncomfortable looking through his things. Her relationship with Arthur was going well and they spent most weekends together. It was a very easy friendship and it seemed inevitable that at some point they would go away together for a few days. She didn't discuss it with the family and they didn't pry, although they made sure she was well and happy. She had eventually told Arthur who she was, but only spoke of the Thailand ordeal, changing the subject when he asked about Trevor, which made it apparent she did not want to talk about it.

One Saturday afternoon Fliss had decided she wanted to go shopping with Nigel, to look at duvets and throws to smarten up Trevor's decidedly bachelor bedroom. Once they got into Kingston, Nigel realised that she was also very keen to look at nursery furniture, cots, sterilising equipment, and much more. He smiled dutifully but his heart sank. They were going to move, for goodness sake, and it was far too early to buy a lot of 'stuff.' There was nowhere to keep it at Clapham and he hoped they would be settled in the West Country before they actually decorated a nursery. He wisely said nothing, just looked and smiled. He still smiled, a little more ruefully when Fliss settled on buying two new tops and a pair of stretch trousers, although he thought it was better than ordering cots and buying nappies. He just remembered Laura talking about "layettes" although no doubt these days everything was covered by something called a 'baby shower.' There were even things called babygrows. He assumed you didn't just put the baby in it in the hope that it grew, rather like the grow bags he used for his tomatoes.

When Fliss had finally exhausted herself, they wandered over to a restaurant overlooking the river. Fliss ordered fishcakes and a glass of orange juice and Nigel had sausage and chips and a beer, not only because he fancied it, but because he would not be allowed to have such unhealthy food at home. With their coats on it was just about warm enough to eat outside. They ate in companionable silence, enjoying their meal and the wonderful sun with the light reflecting on the water.

"I'll miss all this. I wish you could tell me why you are so scared, Nigel, and what hold the police have over you. It seems so extreme that we have to move."

"Just wait until you sit in a restaurant by the sea, Fliss. We'll wonder why we didn't do it before. It will be great to be out of the rat race. For the first time in our lives we will have no money worries and our children will be raised in a healthy environment with none of the stresses they would have if we stayed here and were both working."

Fliss ignored his clever deflection. "Presumably you will have to work too, Nigel. The money will not last for ever."

"I can easily get contract work, especially it we live within commuter distance of somewhere like Plymouth. I know Plymouth is not the prettiest of cities, but I seem to remember there are some lovely parts. It also has good facilities including a hospital with a good maternity unit. Yes, I checked! Tell you what, I'll take a few days off and we'll go down and have a look round. Sorry. I've been so tied up with all the bureaucracy of the paperwork, solicitors, probate, etc. as well as keeping Frank sweet, not to mention the houses, that I just haven't had a moment. Let's see if we can go next week. I am sure Frank will understand if I take a couple of days off."

Fliss finished her meal and sat back with her eyes closed, enjoying the sun. She now had a definite bulge under her skirt and Nigel realised he had been so tied up with everything else that apart from trailing rather half-heartedly round the stores he had not really taken much notice of the forthcoming event. "Aren't you supposed to have a scan or something to check everything is all right? And do we get to know if it is a boy or a girl, assuming that we want to know."

Fliss opened one eye, squinting against the light. "Two weeks' time, at the clinic, 2.00 p.m. It's a Tuesday and you'd better be there. No arrests or fishing trips or you and I are finished. OK?" She grinned at him and told him that the date was pencilled on the kitchen calendar and he had better put it in his agenda. "We may get to know the sex, although it is not guaranteed so early. The next one will be at 20 weeks and that should confirm it. Personally I do want to know. I should feel it move in a few more weeks. Then we can buy a baby name book and have a few arguments!"

Nigel ordered a coffee and a decaf. for Fliss who had resumed her impromptu siesta in the sun. Whilst waiting for the coffee Nigel felt the beginnings of one of his tension headaches. Why it should happen when they were relaxing he had no idea until he realised that the talk of the baby coupled with a move in the not too distant future was stressful in itself. Then there was the history of the past months plus the pressure from the police to move, however much he prettied it up for Fliss. Instead of the usual internal railing against his father and the memoirs, he found himself seething at the hypocrisy of the system that had given rise to everything that had happened, and was about to happen. The revelations plus the behaviour of those who were supposed to protect him made him feel physically sick. Thank God he had had the presence of mind not to tell the police, and the nodding dogs in this game, that he had actually found something. Even now, with the blood money in the bank, he himself still did not feel safe. Suppose one of 'them' decided he was too much of a loose canon to let him live anyway. He shivered in spite of the sun and his coat.

The coffees arrived, but before he nudged Fliss awake, he sat for a moment with a vague plan floating about in his mind. He would think about it later. They finished their coffee and then returned home.

Fliss was relaxed and happy when they got back, but rather tired so she went upstairs to have a rest.

It was still sunny in the garden, so Nigel took a cup of tea outside and allowed his mind to wander. He would set aside time later to think about his idea, but for the moment immediate matters seemed more pressing. Although he had been reassuring to Fliss, he had begun to wonder if the time scale he had set for moving was a little unrealistic. He had been so alarmed by recent events that if it had been possible he would have gone immediately, even rented a place in Devon and put everything in the hands of the Estate Agents. Sweeney had called twice to see how things were progressing and each time he heard his voice Nigel felt his heart rate increase. With regard to the money, he needed to have easy access to funds until the houses were sold and then they would know just how much he could invest. He did not want a local financial advisor to know the full extent of the windfall so had already hired a city investment manager to make sure he was getting the best interest available on a large chunk of it. He secretly dreamed of a red Maserati and told himself that he deserved it after all he had gone through, but could just imagine Fliss's face. Enough to quash that dream, at least for the time being.

He had not thought that probate would be so complicated, but there were issues with Land Registry and Title Deeds to be amended and although Philip Blasey seemed very efficient it was all taking longer than Nigel thought. The Estate Agents had rather jumped the gun and there had been a viewing on Trevor's house, but the couple were not in a chain and wanted to move quickly. The Estate Agent had been co-operative but realistically he and Ellie needed to hold the Title Deeds in their hands before the house could actually be sold.

Nigel realised he was getting chilly again, so went back indoors and into his study where he began to search the internet for hotels in Devon. He found one at a place called Hope Cove. "Hope," he thought, "that's the place!" The pictures of the hotel were delightful, on a hillside overlooking the sea. He picked the phone up and made a reservation for a long weekend in a couple of weeks' time. He printed out the picture and put it on the counter in the kitchen.

Fliss came down suitably refreshed. "What's this?"

"Hope springs eternal, darling. I've booked it for our little break next weekend. I think Devon may be the best place to start looking, especially now that Frank says he may be able to get me some contract work if we are near Plymouth. Cornwall seems a little too rural! Maybe when we are old and grey!"

Whilst Fliss watched TV that evening Nigel went into his study and spent an hour typing. He was not sure whether it was therapeutic, but felt better to be doing something which had been needling him for weeks. When he went back into the sitting room Fliss was sitting with a map of Devon spread out in front of her.

"Looks like M5 and then A38 is the quickest route. See what you think Nigel. I think we should leave early. There seems a lot to see and if we are seriously looking round we will need as much time as possible. It looks as if Salcombe, Kingsbridge and Dartmouth are all fairly near. If I don't think about the actual idea of the upheaval, I could get quite excited."

Nigel had chosen his moment carefully to let Frank know that he would be leaving. Frank appeared neither surprised nor regretful, although he made all the right noises. "Sorry to lose you, Nigel. When will this take place? I think your contract says six months' notice. That should give us time to find a replacement. Where are you hoping to go?"

246

"Probably the West Country, Frank. This year has been rather difficult to say the least and it will be good to make a fresh start. Anyway, I can't thank you enough for being so patient through all these Jones catastrophes. You've been great."

Frank looked thoughtful. "You are a good worker and before all this were a great asset. If you will be living within commuter distance of say Plymouth, perhaps we can find you some contract work, if that is what you would like."

Nigel looked at him astounded. After all the chaos he had caused he would have thought Frank would have liked to see the back of him entirely. He tried not to sound as if he would bite Frank's hand off. "Thanks for that, Frank. I will do a bit of research. Thanks again."

From there he had gone to tell Sebastian the latest and to thank him for the professional way he had helped with the Thailand/Laura/Baby episode.

"No problem, Nigel. Glad to have been of help. Jeff's a good bloke. I think he still thinks he is a private eye, so this was right up his street."

Nigel had told Jeff as much as was necessary about moving away, sticking to the story of compensation for wrongful arrest having given them the opportunity to start a new life by the sea. They had met up for lunch in their Italian restaurant soon after what he now thought of as 'The Family Disclosure Meeting.'

"Bit sudden, Nigel? Any pressure from anywhere?" Jeff said this in such a way that Nigel found it difficult to be totally evasive. Jeff, after all, already knew about the attacks, the phone tapping and the so-called wrongful arrest. With his training as a lawyer and his experience as a private investigator, Nigel knew that Jeff realised a lot more than he was letting on. He probably had surmised that whatever Nigel was withholding was for the right reasons and knew better than to pry. Nevertheless he was obviously intensely curious.

Nigel hesitated for a moment and then answered in an equally measured tone "I think you already know as much as I can tell you, Jeff."

Jeff raised his glass. "Point taken, old boy. You know where I am if you need me. As I said before, Divine Intervention is a bit more difficult!"

They chatted over lunch about how life might be in Devon or

Cornwall. Nigel tried to sound enthusiastic, but Jeff thought him a little subdued. "It will be great to raise a child by the sea. Fliss has warmed to the idea. We are not sure what Laura will do yet. Did I tell you she was courting?"

"Did you say courting? Laura? When did this happen?"

"She's being doing some internet dating"

"Internet dating? Your mother? Well, good for her." Jeff tried to keep the amusement out of his voice, but his expression said it all.

"It's OK, Jeff. We were all amazed at first, but you haven't seen her for a while. That thin, elderly woman in prison has been replaced by a Helen Mirren wannabe! Look, why don't you and Ann come round for lunch on the Sunday following our weekend in Devon. The family Sunday lunch routine seems to have gone by the wayside for the time being. It will be great to see Ann again. We've been spending too much time working on the houses at weekends. This will give us a good excuse to unwind. Let me just give Fliss a quick ring to confirm."

Whilst Nigel was dialling Jeff poured them both another glass. Neither was driving and, although Nigel had a backlog of work at the office, he was enjoying seeing Jeff again. He could stay late at the office to catch up.

It was good to see Ann the following Sunday and after lunch they spent the afternoon looking at maps of Devon and Cornwall and reminiscing on places they had visited. Ann and Jeff knew the area pretty well and talked about one holiday they had had in Dartmouth. "Lovely place. You can get the ferry across the Dart and it's not far to Brixham. You'll just love it there."

"You must come and stay once we are settled. It will be lovely to have friends from the buzzy city. Bring wellies and we'll get you mucking out the farmyard!"

At one point Ann did ask a few questions about their seemingly hasty decision to move, especially as Fliss was pregnant, but Nigel explained that the difficulties of the previous months had made them take a life inventory and they had decided to get away from the rat race. Jeff privately admired Nigel's verbal dexterity and wondered just how much he had kept to himself during the summer.

Nigel got into the office very early the following Tuesday and cleared a backlog of work before setting off to the hospital to meet Fliss for the scan. She was both excited and nervous. "If they see something wrong I expect they'll tell us."

Nigel squeezed her hand in the waiting area. "It will be fine I'm sure."

"Felicity Jones?" They followed the nurse into a small cubicle and Fliss lay on the couch with her tummy exposed.

"This will feel a bit cold."

The nurse spread some gel over Fliss's bump and then as she did the scan they could see the first pictures of their baby on the monitor. That first glimpse was amazing. They could see it moving about and hear the heart beat. They found they were both very emotional. "Is it OK?" Fliss had a tremor in her voice as she asked the question.

"Looks fine. Everything seems to be progressing as it should. I am afraid it is too early to see if it is a boy or a girl. Occasionally we can tell at 14 weeks, but it is not always accurate and with this little one I really can't tell."

They left the hospital with a couple of pictures of their baby which Fliss kept looking at in the café where they stopped for tea before Nigel went back to work. They celebrated by having a hot jam doughnut which was usually forbidden food as far as Fliss was concerned.

"See you later, little mother!" Nigel kissed her before setting off back to work.

Frank came into his office mid afternoon and was intrigued to see a new picture pinned up on Nigel's wall. "Amazing," he said and judging by his expression he meant it. "Didn't have that in our day. Do you know if it's a boy or a girl?"

"Not yet. Another six weeks. I'll stay on a bit tonight, Frank. I'll be away from Thursday night to Tuesday morning. Doing some preliminary property search in Devon. We're hoping to look at several towns and villages not too far from Plymouth."

"Good show. Good luck. Good hunting," and with that he was gone.

CHAPTER 22

Both Ellie and Laura wanted to see Fliss and Nigel before they set off to Devon. Ellie insisted on bringing in pizzas as she knew they would be busy packing and didn't want Fliss to have to cook. They hadn't seen Laura for a couple of weeks. She looked well and happy and although her hair had begun to grow out of the chiselled style that had been part of her makeover, she had brushed it behind her ears exposing large silver earrings. She still looked great.

"You must bring Arthur round to meet us when we get back. He is certainly doing you good. Perhaps you could both come for lunch one Sunday?"

Laura smiled as she accepted the invitation.

"Then I'm coming too! I can't wait to meet this mysterious lothario!" Ellie spoke whilst examining a map of Devon. She too was looking much better. There was an energy and enthusiasm about her that they had not seen for a long time. She still had not told them about her long term plans because nothing was decided and she did not want either any negative feed back, or the possibility of having to back down if she changed her mind. She had nearly finished a TEFL course online and was in touch with a couple of charities who seemed quite interested in her CV.

Laura had a dreamy look as she gazed at the map. "Brixham. I went there when I was a teenager. Gosh, that's nearly half a century ago. My parents hired a chalet on a hillside above a wonderful cove called Churston. I made friends with some other youngsters on the site and we had a midnight picnic on the beach. There was a raft moored a little way off the shore and we would swim out there during the day. In my memory it seems that it was always hot and sunny. I had my first kiss one night on the beach. He was about twenty and smelled of tobacco. It was all so innocent in those days. Even a kiss was daring"

"Well, when we are settled you must come down and we will take you to Churston Cove."

"I'm not sure I could climb down those rocks nowadays."

"Then Nigel will carry you! There's no way we will let you miss a visit back in time."

"And there's no way I will let Nigel carry me! I just need walking shoes and grit. I can do anything!"

Ellie looked up at her. "I really think you can!"

After they had gone Fliss finished her packing and got ready for bed. Nigel couldn't believe she needed such a large case for a weekend, but wisely said nothing.

He threw a couple of tops and a spare pair of trousers, some socks and his toiletries into his sports bag and was done, apart from his toothbrush in the morning. He then spent another hour typing on his laptop. Fliss was asleep when he finally climbed into bed. They set the alarm for 6.00 a.m. and were on the road before 7.00 a.m. stopping for breakfast at Bristol. Once they were on the A38 Fliss got out the map.

"It seems there's still a way to go. Off at the Kingsbridge turn, but then we have go through Dartington and then through Totnes."

"We've made good time. I think we'll take a look at the Estate Agents in Kingsbridge to get a feel for properties. I have looked online but there's nothing like actually being here, in Devon! We can have a look round before setting off for Hope Cove this afternoon. I don't think there's much there – probably no Estate Agents. I just felt the name of the place appropriate after all we have been through. And it looked charming."

They parked by the creek in Kingsbridge. The tide was in and there were boats moored alongside with sea gulls perched on the masts. They sat outside The Creek Inn with a sandwich and a beer before crossing the road to the Estate Agents.

"I am not sure Kingsbridge itself would be right for Laura. It looks as if the shops are up the Himalayas." Fliss was looking up the steep hill lined by shops. They went into three Estate Agents who could not have been more helpful, especially when they gave them a rough idea of the price of property they would be looking for.

"We know it is very premature as our houses are not sold yet, but if we found the right property we could easily get a bridging loan." Nigel had no intention of telling them about the fortunate financial position they found themselves in. Certainly their own house could be sold even if there were still probate problems on Trevor's, and with a lump sum in the bank things looked good.

The third Agent they found was keen to show them a property in one of the outlying villages. It was a large farmhouse which had been modernised. There was also a refurbished farm cottage on the considerable land and there were stables. They made an appointment to view the following day and made their way back down the Himalayas to the car. Fliss was impressed that there was a real butcher, a fishmonger, several coffee shops and even a small cinema.

They consulted the map again and set off for Hope Cove. The roads were very narrow with lots of bends.

"I wouldn't fancy having to back up along here on an icy road."

Nigel laughed. "They rarely get snow here darling. Only on the moors."

Hope Cove was more than they had hoped for. The hotel was perched on a cliff top overlooking the sea. Their room was delightful with a view of the cove and they spoiled themselves by having afternoon tea in a drawing room with a wonderful view. They even had cream scones. Nigel felt the weight of the past months begin to lift and for the first time for a long time felt safe. He realised that subconsciously he had been looking over his shoulder since the attack with the car and the trauma in Soho.

Fliss looked across at him. "I like it here."

They sat for a long time just gazing out to sea and watching the changing colours as the sun began to slip further towards the horizon. They had dinner in the hotel and both felt they were on holiday instead of house hunting just for the weekend.

After breakfast they wandered down to the beach. The waves were making dramatic spray over the rocks and a few surfers were wading out to sea in their wet suits. The village had a little gift shop and post office, but apart from a pub and a couple of restaurants there was really nothing much there, just the wonderful sound of the sea and seagulls. They pottered about for a while, picking up shells and pebbles, before making their way back up to the hotel. Fliss was out of breath by the time they arrived. "Himalayas everywhere," she said. "This will keep us fit."

They had coffee back in Kingsbridge before going across to the Estate Agent for the visit to the farm. The agent they had seen was not available so a young woman called Kate took them on the viewing. She drove out of Kingsbridge and down a narrow road signposted to Sherford. There were a couple of farms along the way and then the road went through some pretty woods before they turned down a track, and there it was: "Woods End Farm."

Fliss was surprised that the owner was not an apple cheeked, rotund farmer's wife, busily making pies or plucking chickens in the large farmhouse kitchen. In fact she was about Fliss's age, an attractive blonde woman who introduced herself as Syliva, with two small children playing out in the yard. The expected collie cross made a fuss of them, jumping up and making muddy prints on Fliss's smart pressed trousers.

Nigel laughed. "You'll have to get used to that my dear!"

Both Kate and Sylvia showed them round. The farmhouse was delightful. A large kitchen with an Aga and a huge table surrounded by six chairs. There was a large sitting room with a fireplace set back in grey stone. The dining room was spacious and there was a playroom for the children, plus a toilet and shower room.

"Ideal when the kids come in muddy from the fields. When is your baby due?"

It was the first time any one had commented on Fliss's condition and she found herself blushing. "Around Easter time."

"Lovely time to have a baby. We love it here, but my husband's mother has died and we have decided to move to Cornwall to help run their farm and look after my father-in-law."

"How soon do you want to move?"

"As soon as possible. We have friends in Mullion and they will put us up if the farm is sold before we have found somewhere."

There were five bedrooms, two of which had en suite bathrooms which had obviously been added fairly recently because they were bright and modern with lovely tiling. The view across the fields from the master bedroom was stunning. Sylvia made them all some coffee whilst they went outside. There were two barns, a stable and various outhouses with farm implements. Built in one of the nearby fields was a charming cottage.

Kate took them across. Apparently it had been with a view to Sylvia's parents coming down, but in the end they could not be persuaded to leave Northamptonshire, which is where Syliva was born.

The cottage had two bedrooms and two reception rooms plus a small study. It had a pretty garden which had been well looked after.

"I think Mum would love it here, but whether she wants to be in Devon after all her adventures, and now with her new life, is anybody's guess. But if she doesn't, and if Ellie doesn't want to come down permanently, it will make a lovely holiday retreat for them and of course for friends." Nigel sounded enthusiastic and Fliss too thought it would be perfect for Laura.

They went back into the house and had their coffee whilst Sylvia phoned Max, her husband, to tell him they had arrived and could he show them round the land. He joined them shortly afterwards, a tall, well-built man who seemed very fit and muscular. He was easy to talk to and he filled them in on some aspects of the farm. "We rent out some of the fields and just keep two for vegetables. I teach Biological Diversity at Plymouth University. We have help in the fields of course. We keep a couple of pigs and a few chickens, but that's about the sum total of our animal husbandry! Not enough hours in the day."

On the way back to Kingsbridge, Kate asked them what their thoughts were.

"It was delightful and ticks lots of boxes, but of course we really need to talk this over! Thanks so much Kate."

There was a little market in the square and they pottered around for a while before collecting the car and driving to Slapton Sands. They were amazed at the expanse of beach and fascinated by the history about the Second World War and the armoured tank which was displayed at the end of the car park. They found a pub along the front which did wonderful fish and chips and then they walked along the beach in an effort to compensate from yesterday's cream tea, the cooked breakfast and the fish and chips.

Behind the car park was Slapton Lea which they learned had a variety of birds. There was even a bird hide in the car park. Fliss was enchanted. "I do so like it here," she said, peering through their binoculars across the water.

Fliss chatted happily on the way back to Hope Cove. She thought Nigel was more relaxed than he had been since the dreadful news from Thailand all those months ago and although she knew there were things he was keeping from her she trusted him implicitly. If Nigel thought it important that he kept some things to himself she was sure he had a very good reason. She also did not believe that his frantic typing away until the early hours in his study at home was just catching up with paperwork and insurance issues, but did not pry. For her part, she was getting increasingly more tired and rather enjoyed going to bed very early with a good book. Sometimes Nigel would tiptoe into the bedroom and find her fast asleep, propped up with her book in her hand and the bedside light still on. She did not awake when he gently guided her down into the bed. Lovemaking was out of the question at night but at weekends they usually made love in the mornings. Nigel was particularly gentle, always aware about the baby. They both enjoyed this closeness and afterwards he would bring her tea in bed and they would talk about the changes coming up in their lives.

They left the hotel soon after breakfast on the Sunday and had a leisurely drive home. Nigel decided to take the A303 to avoid the madness of the motorway and they stopped half way home for coffee. He felt much better about the whole thing now that they had actually seen the possibilities of a new life. He felt much less pressured and angry and realised that not only would they be in a beautiful part of the world, but for the first time in their lives they would have no money worries. There was just his little project to get finished and then he would feel as free as possible in the circumstances.

There was an apple pie on the kitchen table and a note from Laura. "Hope it all went well. Hope to speak to you tomorrow (Monday). I was wondering if I could introduce you to Arthur next Sunday? I think lunch may be a bit much for a first meeting, but maybe for a cup of tea in the afternoon? I would of course like to speak to you first about your weekend and long term plans. Any chance of you popping over one evening? Love Mum."

"Well now. This is a serious step if she wants to bring him to meet us." Fliss put the kettle on and cut two wedges out of the pie.

"About time if you ask me! She's right of course. We really need to bring her up to speed about Devon and what her plans are and find out whether she wants to move down too. And of course we need to speak to Ellie. It's obviously not appropriate to have a pow wow on Sunday with Mr Romance present! Perhaps we could have an early supper one evening and then pop over to see her, and maybe Ellie would like to come too. I'll give Mum a ring tomorrow. She's obviously out today judging by the note. I'll give Ellie a call in a while to update her."

Ellie had been out for lunch to a Lebanese restaurant in Holland Park with Steph. She had been working all Saturday on her TEFL homework and enjoyed time out with Steph. She was dozing on the sofa listening to some music when Nigel rang.

"How was it? Did you like it? Did you look at any properties?" The questions came thick and fast.

Nigel told her they had made some progress and told her a little about the farm.

"Let me talk to Fliss. Men are not good at the detail, dear brother."

They were on the phone for half an hour. Nigel wondered what Ellie would make of it all. He took the Sunday papers into the sitting room and switched off from the giggles and chatter from the kitchen. He was doing the cryptic crossword when Fliss came back in.

"Sorry about that, Nigel. She would love to talk about our plans and also apparently some of her own. She would like to meet up at Laura's either Tuesday or Thursday evening, whichever suits Laura of course." She went upstairs to unpack.

"What are we going to eat? Do you want me to start something?" Nigel called up the stairs.

"Pasta and a glass of red ha ha! I can't wait to have a drink again. Pasta and a glass of orange juice. Yes, you do it if you like. There's some garlic bread in the freezer."

They had supper and then Fliss was suddenly felt exhausted after all the excitement of the weekend and the long drive home, so she kissed Nigel on the cheek and went to bed. Nigel cleared up and then went into his study and spent a couple of hours on the computer before finally giving up as his eyes were beginning to close.

The following Tuesday they went round to Laura's, who had insisted on preparing supper. Ellie had brought a bottle of wine and some grape juice for Fliss. After supper Fliss took out from her bag a postcard of the hotel at Hope Cove, a couple of photos of the farm and the Estate agent's details of the house, cottage and land. "Of course you would need to see it, Laura, but what do you think of the idea of moving into the cottage? No need to make a decision now, but just the general feeling you have about making the move?"

"Well, I do need to see it of course, but from the Estate Agent's details it does look a bit cut off. I assume there is no village shop within walking distance and it doesn't look as if it is on a bus route. Fine for now, but as I get older I do need to think about the practicalities such as access to the doctors and hospital. I don't want to sound negative, but I do need to consider these things."

Nigel tried to reassure her. "We'll be on hand, Mum. You won't need to worry about things like that."

"I know, dear, but I do like my independence. It sounds idyllic to be living near the sea and with my family at hand, not to mention watching a grandchild grow up. And babysitting too of course. Yes, I would love to take a look, but at the moment have my doubts as to whether it is right for me. It just seems a little too remote."

"Good points, Mum, but do take a look. We could all go down for a weekend, perhaps at the end of the month?"

Nigel looked at Fliss for approval and she smiled and nodded before turning to Ellie. "What about you, Ellie? How would you feel if we all moved away? Any thoughts of becoming a West Country girl yourself? With the sale of your flat and the money from your Dad you could probably afford something very nice. If we do buy the farm then you could certainly live in the cottage to get the feel of the place until you make up your mind."

"I think it looks gorgeous and sounds idyllic, but like Mum I do think it is a bit cut off. Have you thought how you will get to schools and doctors etc.?"

"I'm sure people who live on farms have kids too! In fact the couple who own the farm have two children. He commutes to Plymouth. They don't run it as a farm, but lease out the fields. It seems to work for them."

"That's a relief. I couldn't quite see us any of us on a working farm." As she spoke Laura was regarding a chipped nail with some concern. Fliss and Ellie looked at each other, raising eyebrows conspiratorially. So far, Laura was still reinvented.

They chatted about the pros and cons for a while and then Ellie produced some papers and literature from a briefcase she had beside her. "I have something I would like to show you too. After all the drama began to die down, and especially after Mum made some changes, I felt it was time for me to rethink what I am going to do. I didn't want to tell you before, partly because you were still going through some difficulties and partly because I didn't want to be talked out of it. I am about to take a TEFL exam. That's Teaching English as a Foreign Language. Once I have that under my belt I am going to apply to work abroad with a charity. I am hoping to work with one that helps women who have been repressed, abused or raped, possibly in Africa. Some of the women are not much more than children. This is the literature from a couple of the agencies and copies of some correspondence."

"Africa?" Laura almost shouted, and then repeated "Africa?" before turning to Nigel as if he could put a stop to this nonsense.

Nigel and Fliss said nothing as they glanced through the papers. The ensuing silence seemed to last for ages whilst Ellie sat quietly waiting. Finally Nigel looked up at her. "Well. This is a surprise Ellie, but if it's what you want to do, good luck. You seem to have researched it well and you have no ties here, so go for it."

Laura glared at him whilst Fliss nodded in agreement with Nigel. "Good for you Ellie. Do it while you can."

Laura said nothing more, her mouth betraying her thoughts with her lips pursed as if they had been stitched together.

"Thanks for bringing all that, Ellie." Nigel was gathering up the papers and photos Fliss had brought and suddenly the evening was at an end.

Ellie's cheeks were flushed and her eyes bright, but if Laura had expected tears and capitulation she was to be disappointed. "After what happened to you I am sure you are just worried on my behalf, Mum, but I need to do this for me. This family has had its share of dramas abroad and nothing is going to happen, so don't worry!"

They all stood up to go. Fliss gave Laura a hug. "We are so looking forward to meeting Arthur on Sunday. Say about 3.30? By the way, I assume he does know about your Thailand notoriety and all the subsequent drama?"

"He didn't for a while. When you date via the internet you don't give your real name. He called me Miriam at first, but I have been Laura for a few weeks now. He did say he felt he had seen me before, but once I told him my name and where I live, it all fell into place. Don't worry. I just told him about Thailand, but said I didn't want to discuss the subsequent events and he has never pried. I am sure we all know how serious this is and will never disclose anything."

Nigel looked visibly relieved. "Thanks for that Mum. We will look forward to seeing you both on Sunday. It seems we all have exciting things happening. Take care. Bye Ellie."

Ellie kissed her Mum on the cheek and left at the same time as Nigel and Fliss. She didn't want the third degree which would inevitably have happened if she had stayed behind.

On the way home Fliss asked Nigel how he thought the evening had gone.

"Well, a bit of a bombshell from Ellie, but coming back to the farm, I think Mum has a point. It is a bit cut off and we need to think about that, but I certainly don't want to give up the idea. Let's see how this relationship with Arthur is going. Perhaps they will get together somewhere and we can keep the cottage for holidays for them and for Ellie, if she ever leaves Africa of course. I hear it is pretty addictive. The call of Africa and all that."

Fliss made some hot chocolate, taking hers up to bed. Nigel took his into his study and typed away for a couple of hours before going finally going to bed. He didn't sleep very well. Thoughts that he had pushed away began to surface in that strange time between being awake and sleeping. There were too many unanswered questions, but he could not go back to the police and ask them without arousing suspicion about his actual knowledge of Trevor's disclosures. He needed to see Sweeney one more time, but also needed to think through very carefully what he would say. He finally drifted off to sleep in the middle of an imaginary conversation he would have at the police station. Unfortunately Sweeney would not have the script that Nigel had written for him.

The rest of the week passed uneventfully. On the Saturday Fliss and Nigel went through a major clear out, taking books to a local second hand book shop and several bin bags of bric-a-brac and clothes to the local charity shop. They then called in to the Estate Agent to ask them to push forward with the sale. They knew it was more difficult to sell a house once winter set in and neither of them was keen to have a scenario in the spring where Fliss went into labour on moving day.

"I think we need to take Laura down to the farm very soon, and of course have a second look ourselves. Perhaps Ellie would like to come too. Let's talk about it tomorrow and put a firm date in the diary. Maybe we could take a trip down the weekend after next?" Nigel sounded enthusiastic and decisive. It made Fliss feel more confident when Nigel took charge, especially when something of this magnitude was involved.

Ellie arrived early on the Sunday so that they could have lunch at midday. That way everything would be cleared away ready for the big introduction to Arthur. Ellie talked about the course she was doing and about her plans. She was more animated than they had seen her for a long time and took great interest in Fliss and Nigel's plans for Devon.

After lunch Nigel loaded the dishwasher whilst Fliss set out cups on a tray ready for tea when Laura and Arthur arrived. Ellie cut slices of a date and walnut cake that Fliss had bought from the supermarket. "No time for baking these days," she said. "What do you think Arthur will be like?"

"Tall and thin with wispy greying hair. Probably wears a deaf aid and stoops a bit."

Fliss laughed. "You are unkind, Ellie. I think he will be rotund with red cheeks. A bit like a Toby Jug."

"Now who's being unkind? What do you think Nigel?"

Nigel had already had the paranoid thought that Arthur was an undercover Secret Service Agent who was trying to find out how much Laura knew about Trevor's work. He decided not to share that with the girls, realising just how ludicrous it was anyway. "I don't know. Perhaps a retired sergeant major type with a handlebar moustache."

After they had stopped laughing Ellie said that she thought they should stop trying to imagine what he was like because if any of them was right they would not be able to keep straight faces. "It is a bit odd," she said, "all those years when Mum was vetting our dates and now we are vetting hers!"

In the event, Arthur was none of these things. He was tall and rather distinguished looking with a full head of wavy silver hair. He was wearing an open necked shirt and blazer and as Laura introduced him he shook hands confidently with them. "I've heard a lot about you. All good things of course."

He was easy to talk to and asked about their plans for moving to the West Country. "I was brought up in Dartmouth and still have some relatives there. I left to study architecture and lived in Scotland for a few years before getting married. My work took us to Richmond and I have kept the family home since my wife died a few years ago. One son lives in Scotland with his wife and two kids and my other son lives in Boston with his American wife and two kids. I'm not sure what he does. Something incomprehensible in I.T. No grandchildren yet. Oh yes. Congratulations to you two on the forthcoming event."

They went on to discuss the anticipated move and Nigel asked

Ellie and Laura if they would be free to come down to Devon the following week to look at the farm. Ellie said she would let them know as she had rather a lot to do before her exam. Laura looked across at Arthur.

"Arthur had invited me to Glasgow next weekend, to look at the Charles Rennie Mackintosh buildings."

"No worries. We can do that another time. It's important that you get this resolved," Arthur said.

When they had left there was the inevitable post mortem and the general consensus was that he seemed a very nice man and they felt much happier about Laura now they had met him.

"If he has links in Dartmouth, I wonder if Laura would like him to come down too. After all, they were going to go away together anyway. I'll give her a ring tomorrow and see how the land lies."

Ellie left an hour or so after Laura and Arthur. Fliss spent the evening sorting through old papers and Nigel did some work in the study.

The For Sale board went up the following day whilst Nigel was at work. Fliss was surprised that she felt rather tearful. She had resigned herself to a new life, but they had so many memories in the area and their lives had changed so quickly that she had not really had enough time to adjust to such a major upheaval. By the time Nigel returned from work she had recovered her composure. After dinner Nigel phoned Laura and asked her how she would feel about Arthur coming to see the farm too.

"It's certainly an idea. We were going to go away next weekend anyway. Let me discuss it with him. I'll get back to you by Wednesday.

When Fliss had gone to bed Nigel went into the study to do some more on his project. He had explained to Fliss that he was sorting out insurances. There was certainly a lot to do and it took him a while each night to save his work to a memory stick which he hid in the binocular box, and to clear the cache.

CHAPTER 23

The weekend in Devon was a resounding success. Fliss had thought it could have been rather awkward, but Arthur had shown himself to be both sensitive to the situation and considerate. They took two cars so that they would not be in each others' pockets and whilst Nigel and Fliss stayed again at The Cottage Hotel in Hope Cove, Arthur had booked the Dart Marina in Dartmouth. He realised that Laura may feel embarrassed if they shared a room in the same hotel as Nigel and Fliss, and also he knew the area well. Laura had also told him about her love affair with Brixham and her girlhood memories of Churston Cove. He knew there was a ferry from Dartmouth to Kingswear, and then a short drive into Brixham.

They met up for dinner in Hope Cove the first night and then had dinner in Dartmouth on the Saturday. Arthur regaled them with stories about his travels. He had been involved with building projects in many countries and some of the stories about foreign labour and customs had them all laughing. Laura did talk a little about Thailand, but drew the line about talking about her arrest and her subsequent experiences. She was obviously concerned about the lot of young girls involved in prostitution and the unfair way that many of them had to support the education of their brothers. Fliss told Arthur that Ellie wanted to get involved in charity work helping disadvantaged and abused women and although the subject was serious, somehow the conversation flowed and there was no atmosphere of despair. The talk then turned to the farm and their plans.

Laura had fallen in love with the farm and the cottage and many of her misgivings had vanished when she saw the delightful location. She would still be able to go off on trips and according to Nigel all her financial worries would be taken care of. She had no idea just how much compensation he had received, but coupled with his inheritance from Trevor's estate and the money from the sale of the house in Clapham, he and Fliss would be pretty well off. He had made it clear that he considered he had a moral duty to help Laura from the money from Trevor's estate. "After all, you stayed and looked after us all those years, even though things were rather difficult. Of course you should not have to struggle now."

Laura thought the cottage had a happy feel to it and she loved the way the early autumn sun lit up the sitting room. There was also a real fireplace and she could just picture herself sitting round a fire on a winter evening. She smiled to herself as she realised she was already choosing a colour scheme and where she would put her pictures. Her relationship with Arthur was very recent and it would have been premature to put him into the equation of where she should live. All she knew was that she felt excited at the prospect of being in such a lovely place and with the added bonus of being near her first grandchild. Nigel could tell by her face that she was very interested but realised that she was not saying too much because of Arthur's presence.

They drove home via the coast road, admiring the views as they went through Strete and Blackpool Sands.

"This will be our back garden." It took Nigel a moment to realise that Fliss was not talking to him, but to their baby.

Laura phoned them on the Monday evening and spoke first to Nigel. "What a great weekend. What do you think of Arthur?"

"He seems a good bloke. And what did you think of the cottage? Any thoughts?"

"To tell you the truth, Nigel, since Thailand I have been feeling very restless, as I am sure you noticed, and I think I would like to test the water, so to speak. When you are down there and the cottage is ready, I'd like to move in for a trial period. I will keep this house, just while I decide if I could make a life there. If not, I can come back and will not have burned any bridges. I'll obviously come down to help get the cottage ready. I'm sure you will have your hands full getting straight and of course Fliss will be rather cumbersome by then! What timing, Nigel!"

Nigel was smiling as he handed the phone over to Fliss. He guessed she would be on the phone for ages, and then would probably phone Ellie to update her, so he went to his study to work on his project, his 'insurance.'

Fliss felt the baby move a couple of weeks later. It was like the fluttering of a butterfly, deep down in her belly. She couldn't wait for Nigel to get home from work and made him spend what seemed like hours with his hand on her belly, waiting for a kick.

"I know it's just the first flutter and the football team will follow in time, but Nigel, I felt it! Our little baby. By the way, don't forget the scan on Tuesday. Then we'll know if it will be football or dollies."

"How sexist is that! Of course I won't forget!"

The nurse moved the scanning instrument across Fliss's tummy, which was slippery with gel. They were amazed to be able to see clearly now the head, body and limbs of their baby moving inside the womb, although try as they might they could not see if there was an appendage or not!

"Do you want to know the sex of your baby?"

"Yes please!"

"Well, it is definitely a boy." As she spoke the nurse pointed to a tiny button between the baby's legs.

Fliss promptly burst into tears. Between sobs she said, "It's not because I want a girl. It's because I can see our son!"

Nigel squeezed her hand, not wanting to admit that he also had a lump in his throat.

Back in the waiting room Fliss texted both Laura and Ellie. She wrote 'Knit blue' to Laura and 'Footballs' to Ellie.

Nigel put his arm round her. "You were right. That was amazing!"

"I won't say 'I told you so' but will take that as an apology! I think that coffee and doughnuts are in order."

In the coffee shop they spread the scan print out on the table, admiring the little person who was their son. Nigel had taken the day off, which was just as well because when they arrived home there was a note through the door from the Estate Agent saying could they do a viewing that afternoon. Twenty-four hours later their house was sold. Nigel agreed the details with the Agent on the phone from work and then called Fliss, who was both delighted and scared. She put the phone down and stroked her tummy. "Well, little one, what an adventure we will have. Looks like you will be born a Devonian! We just have to get a name for you now."

Nigel left work a month later. Frank took him out for lunch and reiterated his offer of some consultancy work with a couple of his clients in Plymouth. When they got back the office was decorated with balloons and there was a bottle of champagne and a set of art nouveau pewter wine mats and a matching wine holder. Nigel shook hands with Frank, thanking him for all he had done, and then gave Francesca a hug. He wondered if they should ask Frank to the farewell party that he and Fliss had decided to put on, but decided against it. The end of an era. He was very pleased that Frank thought enough of him to offer him a consultancy and that there would be a continuation in their working relationship. When the dust had settled they would have to talk about contracts and terms, but for now he was satisfied.

Probate, death duties and inheritance tax were so complicated that Nigel left it all to his solicitor. It seemed that Trevor's house could finally be put on the market in the near future. Nigel decided to leave it until they were settled in Devon, then come back to sort things out at Trevor's. He still had difficulty thinking of it as belonging to him and Ellie. He could stay at Laura's. He had enough on his plate at the moment.

Now that the house was sold they decided to have a leaving party. It was very different from the garden party at Trevor's in the summer. This time there was an air of finality and as the weather had turned cold, instead of the Sangria they had mulled wine. They had invited Jeff and Ann, and Ellie had invited her best friends, including Steph who had held her hand through the worst of the dark days after Trevor's murder. Fliss had asked a couple of the friends she still kept up with from school and of course Laura came with Arthur. Fliss and Nigel had thought of inviting the neighbours, but decided not to as they did not really see much of them and also

266

did not want any questions about the dramas of the summer and the seemingly endless array of police cars and photographers.

Fliss looked radiant. Her skin was glowing and the red top she wore over black trousers suited her dark hair, which she had let grow. "You are all invited to Devon as soon as we are straight."

"Probably after our son is born," Nigel interjected with a huge smile on his face.

Everyone drank a toast. "Best wishes to you both and welcome to Jones Junior!"

Jeff went into the kitchen to pour himself another glass of wine. Ann was driving so he was off the hook. "Any chance of you coming up to town for a last Italian before you depart?"

"You bet! We've had some pretty odd conversations in there over the summer, Jeff. Only right we should have one more before I go. And of course you and Ann have an open invitation to Devon. Come into the study a minute and I'll show you photos of the place."

When they had all gone and they had cleared up the plates and glasses, Fliss put her arms round Nigel. "What a wonderful send off," she said. "Whatever the future holds I am so grateful to have you by my side."

The week of the move Nigel had hired help with the packing, carefully removing his memory stick from its hiding place. He had taken the precaution of making a copy, so the day he went to London he had one in a small package in his jacket pocket and the other in a sealed package in his briefcase. He had used his mobile phone when he made an appointment with the manager of a bank in town, and that was where he set up the safety deposit box, having gone through the terms of anonymity before placing the package in the box and taking his numbered receipt. His second visit was to the solicitor who was holding his Will. He had gone to a different solicitor to make his will after the monies were finalised and now added a codicil. "In the event of my untimely or premature death either by accident, or where there are suspicious circumstances, my safety deposit box, details and number herewith, is to be opened and the sealed envelope handed over personally to the National Morning Mail." He then met Jeff for lunch.

They had a bottle of red and pasta with garlic bread. Nigel thanked Jeff again for all his help and insisted that he and Ann come down for a holiday in the summer. "May be a bit noisy with Junior on board, but I am sure you will love it there."

He then leaned across and talked to Jeff in the low tones he had used in the days when he had felt it necessary to inspect the soles of his shoes at the table.

"Do you remember the gardening party?"

Jeff nodded, a sudden feeling of apprehension making him choke on his wine.

"Well, I am going to plant up my new garden, in memory of that little party. I noticed a holly bush quite near the cottage. If ever, and I am not anticipating that it will, but if ever anything untoward happens to me I'll expect you at the other canal. Is that OK with you Jeff? You'll know what to do."

Jeff nodded without saying as word although he really wanted to grab Nigel by the shoulders and shake him.

After a few minutes he said, "Did Fliss ever find out about the maggots?" The moment had passed and they both laughed before Nigel set off for his last appointment of the day.

Sweeney stood up as Nigel entered his office. "Nigel. Nice to see you. How are things going?"

Nigel nearly said "Well, I expect you already know that the house is sold and that we are moving to Devon," but he managed to bite his tongue. "Fine thanks, Inspector. The money has allowed us to buy a very nice farm in Devon, with a cottage for my mother. We will be moving very shortly."

"That's good news. I'm glad you found the compensation so useful."

Nigel looked at him in silence for a moment, just enough time to make his next statement more meaningful. Then he leaned forward and spoke very quietly. "Inspector, we both know that there was more to the circumstances surrounding my father's death than a random murder. The police seem to have given up trying to find the perpetrators. We also know that there is a price for my silence about what happened in Soho. We have an agreement and I will honour

268

that." Nigel suddenly wanted to say 'Honour among thieves,' but once again held his tongue. "My family thinks the compensation is for wrongful arrest and my wife does not know just how much money is involved." Once again he hesitated before continuing. "I just wanted you to know that I have taken out a Life Insurance Policy."

"Very sensible. Is that what you wanted to tell me?"

"Yes, it is. I was very confused about everything that happened after my mother's arrest and the subsequent events. I have therefore set down *everything* I know and the document is now inaccessible and not traceable unless I meet a premature or accidental death, in which case it will be made public. I am sure you will make certain I'm well protected. I sincerely hope that *The Other Canal* will never be published."

Without giving Sweeney a chance to reply Nigel stood up, turned on his heel and left.

Epilogue

James Nigel Jones arrived safely in Derriford Hospital, Plymouth on Easter Sunday. Nigel was present at the birth which he found the most emotional and amazing experience imaginable. He drove his family back to the farm the following day where Ellie and Laura had decorated the house with vases of daffodils in every room.

Laura decided to move to the cottage that summer. She has a trip planned for the autumn with Arthur to visit his family in Boston, and then go to Tennessee to meet the prospective adoptive parents for Nitnoy, who should be in the USA by the end of the year.

Ellie left for Africa that September and loves not only her work, but the handsome Canadian doctor she works for. They plan to get married the following spring.

Fliss enjoys living on the farm and has created a beautiful nursery for James, who she thinks is the most adorable child in the whole world. She sells the eggs from their own farm in Kingsbridge market. Jeff and Ann have been down a couple of times.

Nigel goes into Plymouth a couple of days a week to work with clients from the South West branch of Frank's business. He has bought a boat and enjoys days out on the Dart and the new friends he has made at the yacht club. He still looks over his shoulder when walking on his own and realises he is apprehensive about the two new members in the yacht club, especially as they don't seem to know much about boats.

To date *The Other Canal* has not been published.